The thought of n̶e̶v̶e̶r̶ ̶t̶a̶l̶k̶i̶n̶g̶ was messing with her head.

With the last sip of her margarita, she spotted a gorgeous beast of a man. He was six foot two was an inch, all packed nicely into cowboy du , boots and hat.

M̶ e exactly what she needed was to bring one of se hunky cowboys home tonight. Preferably, t̶ andsome beast making direct eye contact w er.

H credible eyes never wavered. They stayed on he . And she returned his scrutiny, finding not a flaw n the sharp angles of his face, the set of his ch ed jaw or the deep ocean blue of his eyes.

"̶ ade her breath catch. He made her hot.

silent communication between them was re to combust.

* * *

The Texan Takes a Wife

part of the series Texas Cattleman's Club:
Blackmail—No secret—
or heart—is safe in Royal, Texas…

000002145138

THE TEXAN TAKES A WIFE

BY
CHARLENE SANDS

First Published in Great Britain 2017
By Mills & Boon, an imprint of HarperCollins*Publishers*
1 London Bridge Street, London, SE1 9GF

© 2017 Harlequin Books S.A.

Special thanks and acknowledgement are given to Charlene Sands for her contribution to the Texas Cattleman's Club: Blackmail series.

ISBN: 978-0-263-92843-3

51-11

Our products are natural, renewable and recyclable products made from wood grown in sustainable forests. The logging and manufacturing processes conform to the legal environmental regulations of the country of origin.

Printed and bound in Great Britain
by CPI

Charlene Sands is a *USA TODAY* bestselling author of more than forty romance novels. She writes sensual contemporary romances and stories of the Old West. When not writing, Charlene enjoys sunny Pacific beaches, great coffee, reading books from her favorite authors and spending time with her family. You can find her on Facebook and Twitter, write her at PO Box 4883, West Hills, CA 91308, USA, or sign up for her newsletter for fun blogs and ongoing contests at www.charlenesands.com.

This story is dedicated to the little munchkins
in my life who make every holiday
wonderful and exciting.

With love to my special girls—
Everley, Kyra, Madyson and Lila Dawn.

One

Some of her friends had bucket lists, things they wanted to do before they kicked it, but Erin Sinclair had a list of Never Do's and riding a mechanical bull in an arena of highly capable-to-the-bone Texans was one of them. The legless, leather-clad metal bull scared her silly as it jerked around, keeping only the most proficient on its back.

Yet as she sipped her second Cadillac margarita in the Dark Horse Saloon outside the Royal city limits the thought of never doing it, never taking a risk, was messing with her head.

She'd broken from the pack of women she'd come here with, half a dozen welcoming ladies from the Texas Cattleman's Club who'd befriended her and invited her to a birthday party at the Dark Horse. Now the party was over and all of those women had gone home to their boyfriends or husbands. Erin had neither. It was November and she'd be heading back to her hometown in Seattle the first of the year, without having done anything Texan, anything remotely wild.

"Ready for another, blondie?" the bartender asked, his gaze on the near-empty glass in her hand, yet it was the dubious look in his eyes that brought her five-foot-four frame to attention. "Or maybe you've had enough?"

"I haven't had nearly enough," she said. "One more." She offered him a sweet smile. "Thank you."

The bartender walked away shaking his head and she focused back on the bull that seemed to be calling to her. Was she being an idiot, or was that bull looking straight at her, tempting her to take a chance, teasing her with his grotesque fake horns to come get him?

With the last sip of her margarita at her lips, she spotted a tall, gorgeous beast of a man. He was six foot two if he was an inch, all packed nicely into cowboy duds, boots and hat, his shoulders wide enough to carry that longhorn over his shoulders without breaking a sweat.

Speaking of Never Do's: in all her twenty-six years, she'd never done a Texan before. She burst into a fit of giggles. Good thing no one around her noticed or she'd really look like an idiot. But the sad fact was, there were also forty-eight other states' worth of men she hadn't been with. Her home state of Washington housed her ex, Rex Talbot. Now, he was a piece of work. And she was glad she was staying in Royal, Texas, at least for the holidays. Rex had nearly ruined her reputation in Seattle, but she wasn't going to dwell. Not tonight.

Maybe exactly what she needed was to bring one of these hunky cowboys home tonight. Preferably, that chunk of handsome beast making direct eye contact with her. He had perfected the art of smolder, had it down to a science and she was loving all the attention and the fact that he'd picked her out of a sea of stunning women.

His incredible eyes never wavered. They stayed on her. And she returned his scrutiny, finding not a flaw on the sharp angle of his face, the set of his chiseled jaw or the deep ocean blue of his eyes.

He made her breath catch. He made her yearn. He made her hot. The silent communication between them was ready to combust.

Sheesh, maybe she shouldn't have another margarita. She was really thinking outside the box tonight. She turned to the bartender to tell him to forget that last one. She didn't need it.

And when she turned back around, ready for another round of eye contact with her handsome broad-shouldered Texan, he had disappeared. She searched for him, desperate to find him, scanning the entire saloon with eyes peeled, but it was no use. She'd lost him in the swarm of the crowd. He may have gotten bored and left the saloon.

Disappointed, her stomach clenched. Story of her life. So much for taking a risk.

But then, there was always the mechanical bull.

Yes, that's exactly what she'd do. She'd ride the darn thing. Why not? She needed one lasting memory to take back with her to Seattle. One thing she could say she'd conquered while in Texas. The ex-nanny, a woman who also knew her way around a music room filled with children, might just need this bit of excitement to cling to once she left the lone star state.

Ha!

And suddenly, that bull didn't look so intimidating anymore. Suddenly, the challenge bolstered her courage. She could do this. She could ride that silly-looking contraption. And her bravado didn't waver while she stood in line to take her turn. It didn't waver when one rider after another eventually got tossed off. Just a few seconds, was all she was asking. Five. Five seconds on that bull, and she'd be satisfied, and thrilled and proud.

"You can do this," she muttered under her breath.

And when it was her turn, the arena host whose booming voice rose above the patrons of the saloon announced, "This little lady is Erin from Seattle, and she's gonna give Destroyer a go."

She gulped and a crewman helped her up onto the leather back of the bull. "We'll take it slow," he said. "Use your thighs as a grip and try to keep yourself centered as the bull begins to move."

Once he moved back, she took a big breath and nodded to the crewman to start up the robot.

And the bull began to jerk.

Erin looked up into the dazzling blue eyes of the beast. He was kneeling over her, staring at her face, a frown pulling his very kissable mouth down. Had she slept through her very best fantasy? What was going on? She moved and the cushioned padding at her back rebelled with a squeak. "What the…"

"You took a fall," he said in a deep baritone voice. With a nod of his head, he gestured to the metal bull.

She realized where she was instantly. And that the crowd circling the arena was watching her. "How long did I ride?"

That brought a smile to his lips. Oh, and it was a killer. "About three seconds."

She grimaced.

"Your head?" he asked.

When a crewman approached, the beast gave him a glare that would have sent the Hulk cowering away.

"I feel fine," she answered. She did. She'd been tossed

off the bull and landed hard on the padding, but nothing hurt, nothing seemed fuzzy. *Anymore.*

Except that her handsome beast was at her side, helping her to her feet. She was met with a round of applause and cheers. She chuckled out of sheer embarrassment and then her body tilted, swaying sideways and everybody else seemed to be leaning. "Uh-oh."

"I've got ya," he said, catching her before she lost her balance and lifting her into his arms. "You need air."

She stared up at him again, amazed at his strength. From this angle, he was even more appealing. His size, the sexy base of his throat, the scruff on his face and those blue eyes, locked him into a category all his own. He carried her as if she was a handful of marshmallows, instead of a twenty-six-year-old woman. And before they got too far, she pointed toward the bar. "My purse."

He nodded and changed directions, carrying her over to swoop up her purse off the bar stool with the grace of a panther. He glanced down for a second. "I'm Dan."

She smiled. What an odd way to meet. But she was not complaining. "I'm Erin. Nice to meet you."

He grunted a reply.

The contrast of the dimly lit smoke-filled noisy saloon to the cool crisp fall Texas air outside helped to wake her up out of this steamy sort of dream she was in. She didn't want Dan to put her down, but it was awkward and she didn't know where to put her arms, so she'd looped them around his neck. Now that they were outside, touched by moonlight and facing the parking lot where it was quieter, the reality of the situation was starting to dawn on her. "I, uh, I'm fine now," she said. "You can put me down."

He gave her another glance, nodded and then took great care to allow her to slide down his body. For safety's sake, she assumed, but oh, the brush of his body with hers sent all the right signals and she shivered.

"Cold?" he asked.

"No," she answered. "I'm, uh, this is silly. I hardly know you, but…"

She couldn't finish her thought. Was she about to tell this gorgeous cowboy that just a brush of his body to hers made her tingle from head to toe? No, she couldn't do that.

"Got it," he said, and without any discussion at all, he seemed to know. Oh God. How embarrassing. Did women fall at his feet like this all the time?

"So why the bull?" he asked.

"Because it was there," she answered immediately.

His brows furrowed. He didn't get her little joke.

She tried to explain, "It's just that, I'm from Seattle, staying in Texas for the holidays and I wanted to do something Texan. You know," she added quickly, remembering her thought a while ago about doing *him*. "I mean we don't have a lot of mechanical bulls in Washington."

"I don't suppose." Still, the furrow.

"And I… Well, you see my nanny job brought me here. And then a few friends I'd made invited me to a birthday party tonight at the Dark Horse, so I tagged along with them, but they all went home, and I wanted…"

He was a good listener, but he wasn't adding much to the conversation. And she wasn't going to babble on anymore. "Never mind."

Talk about the strong silent type. He was that and so much more.

"You sober enough to drive home?" he asked.

"Oh, uh, yes. I stopped drinking a while ago. I'm feeling fine now, aside from the humiliation."

He stared at her for what seemed like a minute, his

eyes flickering over her mouth and in that heated moment, she wanted nothing more but to lock lips with him, to taste his whisky breath and feel the absolute thrill of kissing him. Almost as if he heard her thoughts, his mouth cocked up and he drew a long breath.

And then he said, "I'll walk you to your car."

Disappointment that the stranger who'd just rescued her didn't want to kiss her into oblivion, she said, "Okay."

In a few minutes she'd be headed back to her guest cabin at the Flying E, with no job, no prospects, and trying to find a productive way to spend the next month or so. Her job being little Faye's nanny had ended when her employer Will Brady had found love here in Texas. And apparently, scandal-plagued grade school music teachers were not in hot demand, apparently in Seattle or anywhere else for that matter.

She pointed to her car. "It's just over there."

She could dream of a goodbye kiss from the stranger. Or she could give him one herself. It was risky, but she was warming to the idea. Executing it would be a different—

A car came to a screeching halt, right in front of them on the street. Then a loud yelp rang out and something hit the pavement with a thud. And a dog began to whimper. The sound of his pained cries curled her stomach and she glanced at Dan. He didn't waste a second. He grabbed her hand and took off running toward the downed animal. The car sped off, the driver not even giving the poor animal a glance. Dan was at the dog's side immediately, kneeling beside him, cradling his head. "You'll be alright, boy," he said, whispering confidently near the dog's face as he began a thorough scan over his body. His big hands were gentle as he probed. He found a few gashes on the dog's backside where blood was beginning to pool. "You need some patching up, is all."

"Are you a vet?" she asked, noting the care he took with the animal.

"No, but he needs one. He's scared, probably in shock. That A-hole just drove off after hitting him."

Erin couldn't believe it, either. It was heartless and cold. She wished she could've gotten a look at the license plate.

The dog looked to be a mix of collie and German shepherd with big round brown eyes. He watched Dan carefully, giving him blind trust. "Will you stay with him?" Dan asked, sparing her a brief glance. "I have a blanket in my car."

"Sure, of course."

Dan rose and Erin took over his position. "You're gonna be just fine, pretty boy," she said, carefully stroking the dog just above the eyes. She made massage circles and the dog's whimpers stopped as his eyes drifted closed. He wore no collar and there was no way to contact his owner, if he even had one. Why had he been wandering out so late at night?

"That's it, boy. Rest. We're going to get you all fixed up."

Dan was back in an instant, and immediately tucked the blanket under the dog, careful not to cause him injury. The blanket was thick enough to absorb the little bit of blood at the wound site. "Bleeding isn't too bad."

"That's good, right?"

He nodded.

"What can I do to help?"

"You mind watching him in the backseat of my SUV? My vet is gonna meet me at my house. It's closer than his office."

"Sure," she said, stroking the dog's golden coat gently. "Of course I will."

And once Dan got her situated in the backseat of his car, the big blanketed dog scooted next to her and planted his sweet mug on her lap. Thatta boy. She smiled and continued to massage the dog's head, just over the eyes and occasionally stroking over his ears.

Dan didn't say much as he drove, but he kept glancing in the rearview mirror to see how the dog was doing. She was touched by his concern, the kindness in his eyes.

"Pretty nice vet to come out in the middle of the night for this sweet guy," she said.

Dan nodded, and she didn't think he'd say anything but seconds later, he admitted, "I do business with him at my ranch. He's a neighbor."

So Dan really was a cowboy. "Is it far?"

"Five more minutes."

And a short time later, Dan pulled into one of the garages of a beautifully appointed two-story estate. It was dark; she couldn't see more than what the ground lights surrounding the property gave away, but her instincts told her this ranch was massive and successful.

"I'll set up a bed in the kitchen and then come get him," Dan said.

Lights flicked on in the garage as he entered his home and Erin waited patiently. The dog was breathing heavily, but other than that, his whimpers from earlier were all gone. Thank goodness. Erin had never owned a dog, but back in her college days she used to walk dogs to pick up extra spending cash, and she'd grown fond of the species, even as she was also picking up their poop. She was sure this big guy would've stolen her heart too. He had those kind of eyes that seemed to touch her deep inside.

Once Dan came back, he removed the dog from the

backseat, lifting him with as much care as he'd lifted her from the mat after her mechanical bull fiasco. Erin followed him inside to a kitchen a chef would envy. Despite the ivory cabinets, black granite countertops trailing with gold vein, contemporary appliances and stone fireplace, the room looked cozy and lived-in.

Dan set the dog down and stroked him lovingly a few times. Then he grabbed a towel he'd soaked with warm water and began dabbing at the animal's wounds.

"You came up with that bed really fast," she said, kneeling beside Dan, curious about this man. "I'm impressed."

He shrugged. "I sorta rescue animals."

"You do?"

"Not deliberately."

"How does that work?"

"If strays come by, they end up staying. One I found stranded by the side of the road, another was left behind after the family moved out of Texas. The cats are all freeloaders. They kept coming around searching for food and I fed them."

"How many pets do you have?"

"Four dogs, three cats, a string of horses."

"Is this a horse farm?"

He shook his head. "Cattle ranch."

"Lots and lots of cattle, I assume."

His lips quirked up a bit. "Something like that."

Erin could easily imagine Dan surrounded by animals. He was one of those men that appeared tough on the outside, but she didn't doubt he was a total softie on the inside. When the dog was hit, Dan went into action mode, seeing to the injured animal's needs immediately.

Sort of like how he'd come to her rescue with the bull.

A few minutes later, Dan's neighbor, a man he introduced as Doug Bristol, walked into the kitchen armed with his medical bag. He quickly went to work on the dog, giving him a thorough visual examination along with poking and prodding him gently in a few places. "He's lucky," he said after his exam. "He got pretty banged up, but nothing seems broken."

They watched the vet administer pain meds to the dog and then bandage his wounds. When he'd done all he could for him, Dr. Bristol told Dan to bring him by his office in the morning. "I want to examine him again. What's his name?"

Dan shrugged, then said, "How about we call him Lucky?"

Dan gave his neighbor a nod. "Lucky."

"Okay, I'll see Lucky, then, tomorrow. Nice to meet you, Erin."

"Thanks for stopping by, Doc," Dan said, and the two men shook hands.

After seeing his neighbor to the door, Dan walked back into the kitchen and there was stony silence. Now that the dog was sleeping and seemed fine, there was no reason for her stay any longer. Awkward moments passed as both of them stared at each other. "I should go," she whispered. "You managed two rescues in one night. You must be tired."

"Not tired, are you?"

She shook her head. She couldn't believe how easily she'd done that, knowing full well if she'd said she was tired, Dan would've driven her back to the Dark Horse to pick up her car. "No, I'm not tired. Kinda keyed up after what happened tonight."

Perhaps admitting that to Dan was the riskiest thing she'd done all night.

"Yeah, me too. Cup of coffee? Something stronger?"

No more alcohol for her tonight. She wasn't quite sure if it was the mechanical bull or the two Cadillac margaritas she'd had earlier that landed her flat on her ass at the saloon. "Coffee sounds perfect."

And the man of few words set about making coffee.

Erin sipped Dan's coffee and nibbled on a warm giant chocolate-chip cookie oozing with melted chocolate. Warming the cookies before gobbling them down was her mother's trick, and tonight Erin put it to the test. A few seconds in the microwave made even a stale cookie speak to the senses.

"Aren't they good warm?" Erin asked Dan.

He nodded. "Good."

Instead of Gorgeous Beast, maybe she should call him Caveman. The man seemed to have perfected the art of grunting, nodding and giving one-word answers. But his eyes spoke volumes and right now she was the object of his intense smolder. Not that she was complaining. He was almost as delicious as the cookie that was coating the interior of her mouth with chocolate goodness.

"So how long have you lived here?"

"In Texas? All my life," he said.

"I'm from Seattle."

He sipped coffee. "So you said."

"I did? When?"

"After the bull tossed you off."

"Oh yeah. That bull thing was a dumb idea."

He nodded, a smile lifting the corners of his mouth. "Kinda courageous."

"Really?" She perked up. Had he just complimented her?

"But not real smart." He tossed the last of his cookie in his mouth.

She rolled her eyes and he laughed, a big hearty he-man sound that did things to her sanity. "I really should go. Would you mind calling me a cab?"

He stood. "I'll drive you."

"But you shouldn't leave Lucky alone."

Dan gave the sleeping dog a glance. "He's getting the rest he needs. I doubt he'll wake up before morning."

But she suspected it was more than that. Dan was the kind of Texan bred with incredible manners and he wasn't about to send her off alone in the dead of night. He'd see her safely back to her car. "Only if you're sure."

"I'm not sure I want you to leave," he said quite candidly. "But I am sure about driving you."

Wow. Not only did he surprise her by speaking in full sentences, but he admitted he wanted her to stay longer. "Thank you. I'll take you up on that ride."

Dan nodded, appearing neither relieved nor disappointed.

She really wanted to stay, but her risk-taking skills were momentarily disabled. "You know, I don't think I ever thanked you for saving my pride and my hide this evening. It was really kind of you." She reached up and planted a kiss to his scruffy, super sexy cheek.

Just as she was backing away, a strong arm wrapped about her waist, drawing her against the wall of his chest. He was massive, in a very good sort of way, and an image of him shirtless muscled its way into her head.

"I need to thank you too," he said.

"For?" Trapped against him, her breath hitched. This was different from before when he'd carried her out of the Dark Horse Saloon. This was more intimate. They were alone in Dan's big ranch house. Two consenting adults.

"Helping with Lucky." Using his thumb, he tilted her

chin up until she met his striking blue eyes. Oh boy. He was going to kiss her and she gave him a nonverbal okay. He took his time, inching closer to her mouth. And he was taking forever. The anticipation was killing her.

Then his mouth came down on hers and her lids lowered. She fell into the delicious, fiery, heaven-help-her, hot, hot kiss. The taste of chocolate and coffee mixed with sheer raw passion. Having his lips on hers blew her away. It was like a force of nature, something powerful and inspiring. She roped her arms around his neck and he circled her waist, connecting them, freeing them to continue whatever this was.

Dan's mouth became more demanding and little throaty sounds pressed from her lips as she indulged. Their tongues mated and Dan let out a grunt of approval that made her smile inside. Her hands threaded through his dark blond hair, the strands curling up at the collar of his shirt. She stood incredibly close to his rock hard body and it was difficult not to notice the state of his arousal. She found herself in the same situation—*wanting*.

Wanting to stay.

Wanting more time with him.

Wanting to take a risk with this tall Texan.

And just as those thoughts were cementing in her head, Dan ended the kiss and backed away. "Sorry." He shrugged. "I got carried away."

She smiled, missing his lips on her, missing his warmth and heat. "That's my line. I got carried away. By you, back at the saloon."

"I didn't plan on bringing you here."

"I know. It was just Lucky, I guess." She giggled at her own joke and even the big man smiled.

"You think so?" He pulled her back into his arms. "'Cause I was feelin' lucky just a minute ago."

She stared at his mouth. "It's been a long time since I felt this lucky," she said softly. He furrowed his brows again, something he did often. She found that trait incredibly appealing.

"Same here, Erin. Will you stay the night?"

She nodded, murmuring a soft, "Yes."

Then without another word, Dan took her shaky hand and led her out of the kitchen.

He liked Erin. If he was being honest, probably too damn much, and it had been a long while since he met a woman who sparked his interest. He'd spotted her at the Dark Horse, and almost instantly there was a connection. And also almost instantly, he knew she didn't belong in the saloon. When she'd climbed up on that mechanical bull, he figured she was in for the ride of her life. For a few seconds, that is. But as soon as the bull tossed her off, he'd come running to her rescue, shielding her embarrassment, making eye contact with the crowd, daring anyone to laugh as he carried her off.

What was it about him? He rescued animals and damsels in distress, or so it seemed. Bringing her to his cattle ranch at Hunt Acres had never been his plan, but then the dog was hit by a car and all of a sudden, they were here together in the middle of the night and now she was on his bed, reaching for him.

It was damn hard to think straight *or at all*.

He lowered onto the bed, taking her into his arms and kissed her again, careful not to crush her small frame. She was sweet and sexy and willing. Was he the risk she'd decided to take tonight too? He had to make certain this was what she wanted, had to give her a way out. "Are you sure, Erin?"

Her pretty blue-green eyes darkened. It was heady

stuff seeing her nod and murmur, "Yes, I'm sure." Then she chewed her lower lip and added, "Aren't you?"

Her question caught him off guard. He nearly laughed, but held back. Didn't she know how much he wanted this? He'd picked her out of a crowd at the Dark Horse, hadn't been able to take his eyes off the sweet blonde in tight jeans and a gold blouse the exact shade of her pretty hair. A woman who'd appeared completely out of her element. She'd intrigued him from the get-go.

Now she was in his bed. "Absolutely."

Relieved, her expression softened.

"You didn't really doubt that, did you?"

She smiled, a stunner that made his body go completely rigid. He was through talking and ready to give Erin a much better ride than she'd had on that bull.

Erin was taking a risk, making a memory she'd bring back to Seattle when her time in Texas was up. She wasn't going to dwell. She wasn't going to admonish herself. She was all in. Dan's size thrilled her. He towered over her, all brawn and muscle, solid and sure, yet his touch was tender. She placed incredible trust in this man already. She loved his hands on her, his fingertips caressing her face as he kissed her. She responded to him carnally, soft murmurs of approval and pleasure parting her lips.

Dan kissed a path down her throat, his hot breath searing the slope of her breasts. In just a second, he had her blouse unbuttoned and his mouth moved over her, teasing her nipples to rosy points. She moaned, relishing the laps of his tongue on her skin. Her bra disappeared magically, Dan's talent making her head spin. She loved this feeling of being loose, unbridled and unaware of anything but the man spreading heat and excitement through her body.

Her zipper was down, her jeans pulled off and Dan

was there, cupping her panties in his large palm. The warmth seared through her, the pressure unbelievably perfect. He lay beside her on the bed, making her dreams come true. And just then, she stopped, a coherent thought pressing through the pleasure. His shirt was still on. He was fully clothed and that just wasn't fair. She needed to touch him, to make him lose all thought the way he was doing to her. She needed her hands on him and pulled at the snaps of his shirt. They opened easily, and with his help wrestled him out of his shirt.

Oh wow. His shoulders, squared and broad, were massive in size. There was just so much of him to touch and she didn't hesitate. She laid her palms on him and his eyes shuttered closed. "Sweetness," he rasped.

She explored eagerly, sinking her hands over his taut muscles, the ripped cords of his skin and lower still until she met with the fine hairs below his torso.

His erection pulsed against her.

"Dan," she murmured, and pressed over the bulge.

"Hang on, woman." He gritted.

Instantly, she was on her back again, his one hand tying her wrists above her head, while the other worked her panties down her legs. When he touched her folds, her eyes squeezed shut and her hips arched. The strokes of his fingers were like music, each one bringing her to sighs and moans and desperate whimpers. He played her sweetly and then the strokes came stronger, harder and her breaths hitched higher and higher.

She was ready. So ready.

She cried out, her release overpowering. And Dan was there, kissing her, stroking her hair and making it all so much better. She came down slowly and dared to look in his eyes.

They were dazzling, gleaming and hungry.

"That was a beautiful thing," he whispered.

She had to agree.

She'd poked the bear and he wouldn't be denied.

Thank goodness.

He kicked off his boots and she reached for his belt buckle. He was all too willing to help her divest him of his clothes.

Naked now, Dan's raw power excited her all over again. His beauty lay in his solid strength, his massive frame, the tenderness in how he made love and as she gazed below his waist for the first time, she took a big gulp of air.

Dan caught her eyeing him and concern wrinkled the corners of his eyes. He said so much in his expression and she heard him loud and clear in the nonverbal way he seemed to like to communicate. Relieving him of any worry, she rained kisses on him again and tucked her body under him.

Her explanation went a long way in making him understand and he wasted no time in searching through his jeans to pluck out a condom. Then he rose onto his knees, this beautiful man towering above her and the image seared her brain, not to ever be forgotten. Ready now, she pulled him down and dipped her tongue into his mouth. It was heady to be the aggressor, to show him how much she wanted him, to hear him groan and whisper her name.

Dan took over from there and she followed his lead as he feather-touched her breasts until she was ready to scream, nudged her legs apart, grabbed on to her hips and guided himself home.

Two

Erin opened her eyes thirty minutes later and found herself alone in Dan's king-size bed. Her entire body was one sweetly serene sigh. If only she could bottle that feeling and keep it close, she'd be satisfied forever. It was truly luck and her clumsy attempt at the bull that brought her here, to Dan. She smiled and rolled over and came face-to-face with a gray-and-white fur-ball of fluff. "Hello," she said to the cat sitting in a regal pose on the nightstand beside the bed. "Who are you?"

The cat blinked several times.

She chuckled. "A big talker, I see. Just like your owner. So where do you suppose he is?"

She didn't wait for the cat's reply. She grabbed Dan's shirt from the floor, laced her arms through the sleeves and fastened a few snaps.

She rose to check out her appearance in the mirror and was happy she didn't find a bad case of bed head.

Considering how often Dan had run his hands through her hair, she took it as a good sign and strode out of the room. As she made her way down the hallway, she was met with a cocker spaniel mix of some sort with short stubby legs who was doing his best to keep up with her. The dog was much too animated for this time of night. As she reached the top of the stairs, she looked into the soulful eyes of a friendly black Lab. Friendly, she assumed, because his tail had started wagging as soon as he spotted her.

"You're a pretty one," she said, giving the dog a pat on the head. Then she made her way down the stairs with her entourage following behind.

She entered the kitchen and found Lucky sound asleep on his cozy bed. He was just as they'd left him, dozing calmly, and it did her heart good to see him resting. Then her gaze drifted to the other end of the room, where she noticed Dan by the counter, filling a bowl of fresh water for the dog. His concern for Lucky was touching and incredibly sweet, but nothing, and she meant *nothing*, compared to how her breath caught at the sight of him.

The dim kitchen light illuminated his very tanned, very bare chest, the dip of his low-slung black jeans and the sharp, almost too rugged planes on his face. Handsome to a fault, she thought. She wrapped her arms around her middle, suddenly a bit shy. "Hi."

He strode over to her, his eyes narrowed on the shirt she wore that touched her midthigh. His brows lifted in an approving way. "Hi."

Then his hands came to her waist and he gave a little tug, drawing her closer, and kissed her softly on the lips. Her shyness disappeared and she smiled. "Checking on Lucky?"

"Yep."

"How's he doing?"

"Seems fine," he answered, never taking his eyes off her. "I like you in my shirt."

"Oh, um, I hope you don't mind."

"Hell no, I don't mind." He dipped his head to meet her eyes and gave her waist a squeeze. "Everything okay?"

"Mmm, everything's fine," she assured him. "I met some of your friends." She pointed to the two dogs sniffing around Lucky's bed. The cat began rubbing her cheek up against the edge of the bed tentatively, wary of the sleeping animal she had yet to meet.

"That small cocker spaniel lapping around is Buggy. This big guy is Rio," and just as he offered that, the black Labrador sat down beside him and nuzzled Dan's leg.

"What about the cat?" she asked.

"That'd be Juliet."

"Juliet?"

"Yep, Romeo is probably sawing logs right now with the others."

"You have quite a family here."

"I suppose I'm the Pied Piper of stray animals."

"And of stray women?"

Dan blinked. "No, never have gathered stray women, Erin. I don't think of you that way."

She set her palms flat on his chest and his gasp filled the silent room. "I'm very glad about that."

"Are you?" His eyes flickered and moved over her body lazily, as if physically touching her again, as if thinking of new ways to please her.

Goodness, she was asking for trouble.

He bunched the material of her shirt in his hand and slowly tugged her closer. "I like you touching me," he rasped, his voice deep and low.

She gulped down a big noisy breath. Her body immediately transformed from sated and relaxed to crazy tingling bouts of tremors. She moved her hands on him, her fingertips grazing over his pecs, and her breathing sped up.

He let her shirt drop and reached up to cup her face in his hands, his eyes two dark pools of deep blue. "You want this?"

He didn't have to say it, again. She knew what he was asking. "Yes. I want you. Do y—"

"Just for the record, sweetness," he interrupted. "The answer is hell yes."

She barely had time to smile before his mouth came down on hers and she was being lifted off her feet, his big hands holding her cheeks from behind. Automatically her legs came around his waist and she clung on to him. Her core pressed against the rigid length of his erection. The impact had her moaning and Dan too was affected. A guttural groan coming from somewhere deep in his gut, sounded in her ears. They were lost in each other, mouths wet and hot and devouring.

He strode forward until her back was against the wall. "Like this?" he asked.

"I've never... Yes."

He crushed another kiss to her mouth and as soon as she opened to take a much-needed breath, he dipped his tongue inside and a hot spiraling fire erupted, melting her bones. Sensation after sensation ripped through her body. She was so ready for him, she could hardly stand it. It was amazing how much she craved being with Dan. He couldn't have done anything more, said anything better to her, than he wanted her again and again and again.

An awkward second passed as Dan maneuvered his jeans down and sheathed himself and then, he was nudging her entrance, his large hands driving her body closer, into him, until he was there again. Thrusting into her, silky hot tension grew stronger and stronger. He fit her and she fit him and it was the very best. She matched his pace, absorbing the bulk and feel of him as he gave her his heat.

She opened her eyes to see the gritty determination on his face, the carnal lust that belied his tender lovemaking from before. She relished each move, each explosive thrust of their joining. His hair was slicked back, curling at his nape, his eyes nearly closed, his mouth grinding out curse words she could barely hear, words that normally would shock her, but now only served to heighten her pleasure.

Her body seized tight, sensitized by each potent thrust. Each calculated move shot her closer and closer to the brink. "Dan," she called out.

"I'm right here, sweetness." He gritted out the words. "Don't hold back."

And it was the pleasured pain in his voice and not the words themselves that caused her to shatter, pulsing out a release so strong her body began to tremble. Dan held her tight and joined her, squeezing out every last ounce of power he possessed.

They stayed joined for a long moment, clinging to each other, holding on to something that would never be equaled. At least it was the case for her.

And finally, once their breathing slowed and their bodies cooled, Dan whispered, "Let's go to bed." He kissed her lightly on the mouth and carried her up the stairs.

Erin woke up before dawn. She'd gotten very little sleep during the night and as the big man beside her rolled over to spoon her, she smiled at his light snoring. She could stay in his arms all day, naked as she was, and drift peacefully in and out of sleep. But she wouldn't be the woman he couldn't get rid of in the morning. She knew how these things worked. She'd stay through morning coffee and then take off. Dan obviously had a ranch to run, and she had…well, she didn't have her job as nanny anymore, since Will Brady had fallen deeply in love and little Faye soon would have a loving stepmother in Amberley Holbrook. She couldn't fault them their new future.

She'd been hired in Seattle and when Will was summoned to Royal to find Maverick—the creep who'd been harming good upstanding members of the Texas Cattleman's Club by spreading their secrets and blackmailing them via the internet—Erin had taken the trip with him to help out with Faye. Caring for the baby had been a blessing and being her nanny had helped Erin heal, or at the very least distracted her from the pain of Rex's betrayal. Sweet, busy little Faye had kept Erin on her toes. In the very best way.

Erin didn't know too much regarding the facts in the case Will was working on, but this Maverick guy seemed to be wrecking people's lives. Will's help here in Texas had been essential.

Her boss had been generous in paying her salary until the end of the year so she could stay on at the guest quarters of the Flying E Ranch until the time she'd have to return to her studio apartment in Seattle. And recently, her thoughtful employer had had a keyboard delivered to the cabin too, so Erin could continue playing music when she felt like it. Up until this point, she hadn't the heart to play again.

She was hoping the scandal with Rex Talbot that nearly ruined her reputation would've blown over by now and she had vowed to never put herself in such a vulnerable position again.

And if that meant saying goodbye this morning to Dan she-didn't-even-know-his-last-name, she'd do it. If he was interested in her, he'd have to make the first move.

Erin gently unclamped Dan's arm from about her waist and slowly sat up in bed. Last night, Dan had been adept in popping each of the snaps on the shirt she wore, insisting they both sleep in the buff, promising her he'd keep her warm. She had no doubt he would and sure enough all during the night he'd kept her cradled in the heat of his big beautiful body.

Giving the sleeping man another glance, she sighed and plucked up her clothes from the floor and then tiptoed into the master bathroom to shower.

She was sore in all the right places and the warm spray eased some of the aches. She hadn't had such a vigorous night of sex in forever. Once she was cleaned up and dressed in her street clothes, she ambled down the hallway with Buggy and another little runt of a dog—this one looked more like a poodle mix than anything else—following behind. She entered the kitchen, finding Lucky awake. She went to him and crouched down. "Hey, boy. How're you doing this morning?"

The dog's tail began to wag. Relieved he was looking much better, she stroked his coat a few times and the dog's wet tongue came out to lap at her hand. Sweet. Lucky was truly lucky he'd been rescued and taken care of by Dan.

After petting the dog, she set about making coffee. She'd watched Dan last night and was pretty sure where to find things in the massive kitchen. Seemed everything about Dan was large. She grinned, thinking oh, how much that really was true.

The dogs huddled around her feet as she measured out the coffee. And when she turned to grab two mugs, she jumped and gasped. A middle-aged woman, dressed in black and wearing a white apron, entered the kitchen.

"Good morning," the woman said, giving Erin a pleasant smile.

She was obviously Dan's housekeeper. Oh Lord. Had she been in the house last night? Had she heard them going at it in the kitchen in the middle of the night? Heat rose up Erin's neck and her cheeks burned. "Hello. I'm, uh, Erin."

"Erin, glad to meet you. I'm Darla White. What would you like for breakfast? Dan always eats eggs, bacon and toast. If you'd like anything else, I'm happy to make it for you."

"Oh, no, thanks. Coffee is just fine. I, uh, got it started."

Mortified, Erin wanted to fall into a sinkhole.

The woman didn't take exception to her. She went about her business, pulling out frying pans, getting eggs out of the fridge. Was she used to having strange women show up in Dan's kitchen? Or was she just unusually tactful?

Dan walked into the kitchen then, his hair wet and combed back and the scent of freshly showered man and musky shampoo wafted in the air. He hadn't bothered to shave and the facial scruff today was darker, more pirate-like, sending chills up and down Erin's body. "Mornin'," he said.

Despite the effect he had on her, she wanted to bop him over the head for not warning her that aside from his menagerie, they hadn't been alone last night.

Dan scoped out the scene and arched a brow at Erin's state of embarrassment. "Darla, I'd like you to meet, Erin. Erin, this is Darla. She lives in the guesthouse on the property with her husband, Ted. Ted is foreman on the ranch."

Darla did her best to hide a smile, yet the silent communication going on between the two didn't fool her. And Dan's expression was bordering a grin. The rat. He'd known all along what she'd been thinking, but he'd also been quick to relieve her embarrassment.

Erin's cheeks began to cool as she sat quietly at the kitchen table while the housekeeper served the coffee. Dan walked over to the dog's bed in the corner of the room, crouched down and gave the animal a once-over. Lucky was already terribly in love. As Dan gave his head a pat, the dog scooted closer, licking Dan's hand, arm and face. Dan ate it up, displaying a killer smile. "Hey, boy, looks like you filled your belly a bit."

The water in his bowl was almost gone too. And when Dan straightened his body and stood, Lucky was right there, curling his body around his legs. He shot Erin a quick look. "Excuse me. I've got to take him out to deal with nature."

"Of course."

Dan walked out the back door leading to a beautifully sculptured garden. Lucky had limped behind him to relieve himself in the tall grass and then follow Dan back inside the house. As he took his seat facing her, Lucky camped out beside Dan at the table. Maybe they should've named him Shadow.

Dan seemed totally at ease, while Erin was at a loss, wondering if they should discuss what had happened between them. She didn't know what to make of a one-night stand. She'd never done anything like this before. The few men she'd been with sexually she'd dated and had a relationship with. She'd never gone home with a guy she'd picked up in a bar.

Well, that wasn't exactly how it had happened with Dan. There were extenuating circumstances that had brought her to Dan's ranch. But that didn't diminish the fact they barely knew anything about each other. They'd had carnal sex last night, and emotions shouldn't get in the way. But Erin truly liked Dan. Sheesh, after last night, how could she not?

Darla served the food and then disappeared into another room of the house.

"Have some breakfast, Erin," Dan said. "You should eat."

"I'm not much of a breakfast person. Coffee and toast is fine."

She made a production of lathering butter on her toast and then stared at it on her plate. Dan was so not a talker, so where did that leave her? She didn't want to be the cliché woman clinging to a man. She didn't want to ask, where did they go from here?

Dan sipped coffee and then cleared his throat. "I'll drive you to your car after breakfast."

"That's not necessary. I called a cab."

"Already?" He seemed truly surprised.

"Yes, a bit earlier this morning. The ranch is quite a ways out. I figured it might take a while for a taxi to get here."

Dan pursed his lips and leaned in, bracing his folded arms on the table. "I like you, Erin."

"I like you too, Dan."

"I, uh, don't want to be a jerk about this because last night was incredible, but I don't do long-term commitments and I don't think you're the kind of woman—"

"I get it. You don't have to say anything more." Oh man. He was about to hit her with the I'm-not-good-with-relationships speech. She didn't want to hear it. She knew the drill. But somehow she was gravely hurt and disappointed because, for her, last night had been about more than sex. It had been about relating to another human being. It had been about opening up and, yes, taking a risk. But Dan had laid down the rules. And she wasn't going to break a one of them. "Last night was amazing but that's where we'll leave it. Okay, Dan?"

He blinked a few times. For a second, he seemed uncertain and that was a small triumph.

"Yep," he said finally.

She took a bite of her toast and prayed the taxi wouldn't take too long to arrive.

Dan hated putting Erin in a cab. It seemed so impersonal. So doggone harsh. But she'd insisted and in the end, he'd thought maybe it was better that way. He gave her an awkward kiss and stood on the porch at Hunt Acres, surrounded by Rio, Buggy, Juliet and the rest, watching the yellow car drive off his property.

Once she was gone, he was struck by a deep sense of loss. Had he made a colossal mistake letting her go? Not even asking for her phone number.

"Fool," he said. She must think him an entitled rich bastard for sending her off that way. Hell, he would agree. Thirty-one years old and he was still pushing people away. Or rather, he pushed *women* away. He wasn't one to get caught up in a relationship that would eventually go awry. He liked his life the way it was. Risk-free. With no chance of getting injured. With no chance of being abandoned. Again.

Erin seemed different. Special. She was the first woman in a long time that he'd truly liked. It wasn't wise liking her so much. Dan was a loner and he wanted to keep his life simple. It was the standard he lived by these days. Don't get too close, don't allow anyone in. He kept his scars hidden, where they belonged. His dogs and cats filled the void that could otherwise consume him. And so he'd made up his mind after an incredible night together, that's where it had to end. He wasn't going to get involved with her. They'd met by chance, not by design.

Yet the look in her aquamarine eyes as she'd climbed into the back of that taxi popped into his head and hinted at disappointment and regret, hidden by a healthy dose of pride.

Dan strode into his study and sat at his desk. His computer counted some thirty-odd emails for him to go through. Hunt and Company, the family business that supplied beef to restaurants nationwide and ran its own chain of steak houses, chunked out a big portion of his life and he had a heavy workload to get through today. He opened the first email, narrowing his eyes, trying to make heads or tails of the message on the screen. The words didn't make a lick of sense because his mind was elsewhere.

"Is she gone?" Darla's voice broke into his scattered thoughts.

Grateful for the intrusion, he mentally thanked her for saving him from twenty-nine more daunting emails. Swiveling around in his chair, he faced his housekeeper. These days, she tended to keep more than his house, and some part of him appreciated that. "Yes. Erin is gone."

"You didn't drive her?"

Dan shook his head. "She was stubborn about it."

"She out-stubborned you?" Her voice reached a pitch of incredibility. It was not a compliment.

A chuckle rose from his throat, but with a hefty dose of guilt too. He hadn't fought Erin hard enough on that battle. "Yeah, guess so."

"Too bad. I liked her."

"You *liked* her?" Dan's brows gathered. "Is that some secret woman perception thing? You only just met her, how do you know you liked her?"

"Because, you liked her." She sighed and gave her head a shake. She was twenty years his senior and at times took to mothering him. "And let's face it, this house has been lacking female attention for a long time. Erin was very nice. She colored up redder than a greenhouse tomato when I walked into the room. That says something about a gal."

Dan noticed too and he'd tried to remedy her discomfort. "She helped me with the dog last night."

"I have no doubt." His housekeeper's smile was a little too bright.

"Hey Darla, give a guy a break, okay?"

She laughed. "I'm only saying you're gonna die an old lonely man if you don't step up your game."

"I don't have game."

"I'm beginning to think that's true, Dan. A pity."

She whirled out of the room as fast as she'd entered, and Dan turned back to his computer and stared at the screen. "Ah, hell." He was in no mood for work this morning.

He planted his feet, lifted from his seat and left the study, taking Darla White's words along with him.

Lucky's prognosis was good. Doc Bristol's exam determined the dog had no internal damage and Dan was given a dose of antibiotics to administer for a week. The dog should heal in time, with no residual problems. It was good news and Dan returned to the house by early afternoon.

He set to work in the study, reluctantly getting back to

answering emails, checking over his accounts with the Cattleman's Club to make sure everything was set for the next few months of inventory. His company's steaks were a big draw at the club.

He forced himself to sit there until his work was done. Well, almost done. By four o'clock, he'd had enough of numbers and computer screens. He was restless, antsy. He didn't want to get into his head about why that was. He only knew he had to get outside.

The front door slammed shut behind him as he exited the house and fresh brisk November air hit him. He loved the fall, when the summer air cooled and the humidity vanished. Ah, a man could really breathe again. He stood on the veranda of the house, his sanctuary, and filled his lungs. He'd gotten used to the smells around him, until beeves and earth and leather all seemed to blend into one solid Hunt Acres scent. It tended to calm him down, to keep him leveled.

He strode down the stairs and followed the path to the corral. His mares, all three of them, trotted over as soon as they spotted him, hanging their heads over the top of the fence. "Hey, girls." He gave each one attention, stroking their manes and patting their shiny coats.

"How's your day going?" Ted asked, coming out of the stable, holding a handful of carrots.

"Hey, Ted. Fine. Just fine."

Ted handed him half the bunch of carrots and he gave two of his mares a treat, while Ted fed the other horse. All three mares chomped eagerly and waited for more.

"I hear you brought someone home with you last night."

Dan stilled. It wasn't anybody's damn business and it was uncanny how fiercely he wanted to protect Erin from any scrutiny. "You hear that from your wife?"

"Nope, not Darla. I saw the dog with my own eyes this mornin'. What happened this time, and is he stayin'?"

Dan choked back his relief. He should've known Ted would be more discreet. Even if he had seen Erin, he wouldn't have said anything. "Hit and run. I witnessed it and brought him to Doc Bristol. He's stayin' unless someone comes to claim him."

"Does the dog have a name?"

"Lucky."

"Fittin'. Him gettin' hit in front of you might've saved his life, that's for damn sure," Ted said, slapping him once on the back. "You never could resist a body in need."

Dan smiled at Ted's comment because it was so true.

And a little while later, he suited up in a pair of new denim jeans and a solid royal blue shirt. With his belly full thanks to Darla's fried chicken dinner, Dan gunned the engine in his four-wheel drive SUV and headed off the ranch. He knew where he was going and he told himself it was only to see if anyone at the Dark Horse was missing a half shepherd, half collie mix.

And once he arrived, he scanned the parking lot, finding clusters of people milling about by their cars, but no one looked familiar. No one was asking about a lost dog. A damn chuckle rose from his throat. He was such a fool. He'd blown it big-time and now was hoping to see Erin again. To find her, and then to do what? Hell, he didn't know.

He continued on until he was inside the saloon, standing at the bar. "Scotch. Double. Straight up," he told the bartender. The barkeep set a tumbler down in front of him and poured from a bottle two inches high. Dan took a healthy sip.

"Have you seen anybody come in here looking for

their dog? Medium-sized collie-shepherd mix?" Dan asked the barkeep.

The guy shook his head. "Can't say as I have."

Just as well, Dan thought. He was growing fond of Lucky. He turned his back to the bar to look out into the crowded dance floor. A leggy brunette came out of nowhere and batted her eyes at him. She was put together, wearing a low-cut eye-popping blouse.

"Are you looking for your dog?" she asked.

"Something like that. I found a dog."

"Oh, um. Well, I can help you ask around if you'd like."

"No, thanks." He sipped his Scotch. "I'm good."

"I think so too," she said. Her eyes gleamed darkly, a flicker in them that would have most men paying the check and escorting her home. She leaned in closer. "I'm Yvonne."

Yep, ripe for the pickin', his buddies would say, but Dan wasn't interested.

"Yvonne, I was just about to call it a night. Thanks for the offer, but no thanks."

Her eyes snapped in surprise. "Sure," she said, her chin up as she pivoted on her three-inch heels and walked away.

Dan turned back to the bar and polished off his drink.

"Oh, man," the barkeep said.

Dan gave him a look. "What?"

"You're looking for that chick who rode the bull last night? You, uh, helped her out, right?"

Dan didn't respond.

The bartender shook his head. "She doesn't come in here. She's not a regular. Doubtful she'll be back. You can always tell, you know. This place didn't suit her, if you ask me."

"I didn't."

"There's always the internet. Look her up."

"What?"

The bartender grinned as if he knew all the truths in the world. What a dumbass. But Dan had to agree. Erin didn't fit in a place like the Dark Horse.

He was wasting his time. She wouldn't be back.

Three

"Thanks for inviting me to lunch, Chelsea," Erin said as she sat across from Chelsea Hunt in Royal's number one new resort, The Bellamy. "This place is amazing."

Erin didn't know Chelsea well, but she'd heard that Chelsea had been the latest of Maverick's victims. She'd been secretly photographed in the TCC locker room and those images had emerged on a popular internet site causing quite a splash. It had been a bold move on Maverick's part, to hack a hacker, Chelsea being the CTO of Hunt and Company. Her friendship with Max St. Cloud and Will Brady culminated in their being tasked to investigate the crimes. Erin's heart went out to Chelsea. It must have been so awful being violated like that.

"Yeah, I thought the two of us could use a break and I've heard The Glass House has incredible food."

The entire resort was something out of a modern tech dream and this restaurant, made of more windows than walls, looked out upon beautiful lush greenery mingled with colorful fall flowers. Inside the restaurant, everything from the napkin rings to the delicate chandeliers over each table was made of the finest handblown glass.

She and Chelsea had bonded one day over tall lemonades while playing with little Faye Brady on the Flying E Ranch. Erin missed her little eleven-month-old charge.

She was out of a job, too. With a ton of time on her hands and no prospects. Will had insisted on keeping her on his payroll until the end of the year and so she figured why not go to a five-star resort and splurge a little?

The little buggy voice in her head hollered, *Remember the last time you splurged?*

She'd splurged alright, on adventure at the Dark Horse Saloon and ended up having a one-night stand with a man that had topped her list as a forever kind of guy. A guy who took great care with animals. A man who didn't say much, but allowed his actions to speak volumes. A man who had treated her with the utmost respect.

Dan.

She sighed. It had been two weeks since their night together. And though she felt the loss of him all the way down to her bones, she didn't plan on splurging like that anytime soon. She'd stick to splurges like hot fudge sundaes at the Royal diner, or fifty-dollar lunches at a swanky resort.

Opening the menu, she glanced at all the choices. "Wow. I can't decide. It all sounds delish."

"If you like seafood, I recommend the scallops in lobster sauce."

The thought of it made her stomach clench. "I'm not really a fish person."

She was, sometimes, but today a meal doused in all

that sauce didn't sound appealing. "I think I'll stick to something basic, like chicken."

They ordered their meals and sipped iced tea through colorful straws. While they were chatting, she caught Chelsea sighing and staring out the window a few times.

"And so the cat howled at the moon and the dog turned green."

Chelsea turned to face her, shaking off whatever it was in her head. "What? I'm sorry, I didn't hear you."

She smiled. "You went somewhere."

"Yeah, I did. Forgive me."

"It's okay. I think I know what it's about."

Chelsea stared into her eyes for a second and then shook her head. "I still can't believe some creep actually snapped nude photos of me in the club's locker room and posted them on *Skinterest* of all places. I'm no wilting willow, but I'm floored by his or her audacity. This Maverick has been causing havoc at TCC for months now and we're no closer to finding out who it is than the day it all began."

Erin sympathized with her. She hadn't had nude photos displayed to the world, but she had been involved in a scandal in Seattle, and she knew how violated she'd felt when it all came down. She softened her voice. "Will shared some of that with me. Gosh, I'm so sorry. For a while, didn't they think they'd found the jerk doing this?"

"Yeah, there was some evidence pointing to Adam Haskell, even though the man hadn't any keen knowledge of computers, certainly not enough to cyber attack the residents of Royal. But it became obvious after Mr. Haskell died in a car crash that it wasn't him. Evidence had been planted in his car, making him a victim of Maverick too."

"Poor man."

"Yes, that's why I seem so distracted today. Those photos that surfaced are proof that the cyberbully is alive and well, and who knows what else he'll do."

"Chelsea, I've got nothing but time on my hands right now. I would love to pitch in and help in any way I can to help you find this guy. I'm not as tech oriented as you or Will, but I can come at it from a fresh perspective. Maybe find something hiding in plain sight."

"I think that's a great idea. I've been splitting my time between the investigation and working at the family business. I could really use the extra help. But are you sure?"

"Believe me, I'm sure. I know a little of what you're going through. That feeling of being betrayed and the helplessness that settles around your heart."

"Oh, wow, Erin. Sounds like you've had man trouble. Recently?"

Well, Chelsea was perceptive. And Erin wasn't going to hold back any longer. She didn't really have anyone here in Texas to talk to, and Chelsea had already shared so much with her. Fair was fair. Besides, Erin could use a friend and her inner voice was telling her she could trust Chelsea Hunt. "Yes, back in Seattle. It was an awful situation. I was involved with a man named Rex Talbot. Have you heard of him?"

"Vaguely, but I don't know much other than he runs a megacorporation. He keeps a low profile."

"Yes, well, when I met him, it was at a private school's music program. I'm a musical director and teacher by profession and initially I thought he was the father of one of the students. He was charming and lovely. My interest in him had nothing to do with money. It was the furthest thing from my mind, and I truly liked him. After our first date, he confessed that he was the school's anonymous benefactor. I was over the moon thinking I'd met such a kind and generous man. He told me he wasn't married and had no children and I had no reason not to believe him. He wasn't over-the-top, we did low-key things that didn't warrant any sort of glamorous news. I fell for him and we had an intimate relationship for months."

"And don't tell me, then his wife showed up?"

"Yes. Cliché, isn't it? I never thought it would happen to me. I was blinded by his charm and had no clue he was lying to me. But his wife, who had been out of the country the entire time, returned with a vengeance and found out about our relationship. As low-key as Rex was, his wife, a socialite from birth, made all kinds of noise in the local school district, thinking nothing about scandalizing my good name, blaming me, of course, for home-wrecking. It was humiliating and the situation brought the school undue negative attention."

"Oh, wow. I'm so sorry, Erin."

"Thanks. But if there was a silver lining, it was that the school administration was wonderful, sticking up for me and defending my reputation. They asked me not to resign my position, but at that time, I was distraught and embarrassed for myself as well as the school. I appreciated their support more than they'll ever know, but I just couldn't stay on.

"The worst of it was that Rex didn't stick up for me. He crawled back to his wife and threw me under the proverbial bus. My judgment was way off and I made a big mistake."

"Honey, don't you dare put the blame on yourself. He lied to you. He led you on. He was a jerk. That's a fact."

A chuckle escaped her mouth and she grinned. "You're right. I am so over Rex Talbot now. I figure the two of them deserve each other."

"For sure," Chelsea said. "I take it Will's job offer came at a good time for you?"

"It did. I needed change. Will's a good friend who went through a terrible loss when his wife died. We were both at loose ends, and so because he believed in me, he hired me as Faye's nanny. Oh, I loved taking care of that little doll. When Will's job brought him here to Royal, I came along as her nanny."

"Well, I'm glad you're here. I'm glad we've met. And if you're available to help with the investigation, I'm actually going to the club's main office tonight. My big brother was supposed to meet me, but something came up and he had to cancel. I plan on diving into some files. If you're free, you could help me. I know it's short notice and—"

"Of course. I would love to. What time?"

"Can you meet me at nine?"

"I'll be there."

That evening with a renewed sense of purpose, Erin entered the main entrance of the Texas Cattleman's Club, and showed her guest pass to the attendant at the front desk. It was late at night and the place, normally bustling with both men and *women*, now that the club allowed both sexes in equally, was nearly empty but for a few people walking out of the facility as she was walking in.

She strode past the dining area and secondary lobby, and walked down a long corridor of offices until she came to the door at the end of the hallway marked Texas Cattleman's Club and underneath, Staff Only.

She was ten minutes early and anxious to get started. She didn't mind the wait. This was the most exciting thing going on in her life since her ride on that bull and her encore ride—showing much more endurance with cowboy Dan—later that night.

She'd giggle and think it funny, but it wasn't a laughing matter. Not only did she miss the cowboy, not being able to get him off her mind, she'd also missed her period two days ago and she was normally right on schedule, month after month. Stress could mess up a woman's schedule, and it had only been two days, after all. She filled her lungs and steadied her breathing.

At least she could assist Chelsea in finding the sleaze who'd posted those pictures of her. Erin was glad she'd asked for her help. She'd been just about ready to throw in the towel and scurry back to her studio apartment in Seattle with her tail between her legs, as discouraging as that notion was.

On habit, she pulled out her cell and studied her phone messages, checking to see if Chelsea had texted. Then she heard the definite sound of footsteps on the floor, getting louder and heading her way.

She dumped her phone back into her purse and turned to face Chelsea.

Only, it wasn't Chelsea, it was a big tall handsome beast of a man, wearing a black Stetson, jeans and a tails-out white shirt. The sleeves were rolled up, hugging his biceps to distraction.

She blinked.

"Erin?"

The low timbre of his voice did crazy things to her, reminding her how he'd whispered her name over and over while making love to her.

"What are you doing here?" he asked.

His eyes were so blue, so amazingly bright right now, she wanted to throw her arms around him, but she also wanted to thrash his hide for not pursuing her, even a little.

"I'm, uh, meeting a friend," she said. "What are you…?" Then it dawned on her like some insanely wicked twist that maybe this wasn't a coincidence. Oh no. "You're not Chelsea's brother, are you?" she squeaked.

"You know my sister?"

Erin's eyes blinked shut. She couldn't believe this. She leaned her back against the door so it could hold her upright, rather than having her limbs crumble to the floor. She managed a nod.

"How?"

She opened her eyes. "We have mutual friends."

Dan moved in on her, his presence surrounding her like a fortress, his lime scent reaching her nostrils. He wasn't smiling, but his eyes blazed with some sort of relief. He put his hand up to touch her face, but then let his arm drop down before making contact. His gaze stayed on her and she didn't know which emotion to cling to, which emotion to believe: the one that wanted to invite Dan to touch her, because oh how she craved it; or the one that poured acid into her stomach, warning her not to go near him again.

"I went back to the Dark Horse the next night looking for you," he confessed.

"You don't have to say that."

"I say very little, but what I say means something." He spoke with enough authority to sway any nonbelievers.

She stared into his eyes, captivated by the honesty she saw in them. "Why?"

"Why?" He smiled then, an apologetic smile that touched something deep in her heart. "I wanted to see you again."

"Because?"

She wasn't letting him off the hook that easily. Even

if she had to pry the words out of his mouth, she wanted to know what he was feeling.

"Because… Well, hell. I just did, Erin. We weren't through."

She gulped. "What does that mean?"

"I don't recall you asking me a ton of questions before."

"Yes, well… I never thought I'd see you again."

"Are you glad?"

"Are you?" she asked.

"Damn glad. I should've never let you go that morning. Not that way."

Those were words she'd been dying to hear. Words she never thought she would hear, because she didn't think she'd ever see Dan again. "Are you apologizing?"

"For the best night of my life? No. Can't apologize for that. Don't think you'd want me to, either."

Her face flushed from his blatant admission. Dan wasn't holding back. And somewhere deep inside she knew that this cowboy wasn't smooth or polished. But he was real. And he'd just paid her a compliment.

"I am sorry I didn't get your full name and number, Erin."

"Why didn't you?" After what they'd shared that night, she'd been baffled at his noncommittal attitude in the morning. She hadn't pegged Dan for a love-'em-and-leave-'em kind of man. Sure, Dan said he hadn't thought it smart for her to ride that bull, and then she'd blathered on and on about being from Seattle, losing her job and wanting to do something Texan. "Did you think I was a…" God she hated to say it. "A bimbo or something?"

Dan's smile only lifted half his mouth. "Exactly the opposite."

She shook her head. "I don't get it?"

The sound of footsteps rushing forward stopped Erin up short.

"I am *so* sorry I'm late." Chelsea reached the two of them at the door. She wore a fitted trench coat and an apologetic expression. "Erin, thanks for coming. I see you've met my brother Dan already. Good." Then she faced Dan. "Why are you here? I thought you weren't coming tonight, big guy. You had a date you couldn't get out of or something."

"I got out of it."

"You broke your date?"

Erin put her head down. This was awkward. Was that why Dan hadn't pursued her? He was dating someone. Her stomach squeezed at the slice of jealousy wedging tight inside.

"It wasn't a date, Chels," he said, slightly irritated. "You needed me, and I'm here."

"Thanks, bro. I appreciate it."

Then she turned and punched five numbers into the keypad on the wall and pressed a button. "Here we go." She opened the door before Dan could get to it and breezed into the room. Dan held the door for Erin and they followed inside, the door shutting closed behind them.

Erin immediately felt his big presence engulf them in the twelve-by-twelve room.

There were a few chairs and one good-sized desk in the middle of the room, while a dozen tall metal file cabinets lined three of the walls. The usual decor at the Cattleman's Club was spacious and generous with tall ceilings and an air of openness now, especially since the remodel after a tornado had swept through causing some destruction, but this out-of-the-way room reminded her of something she'd seen in an old detective movie, small, stuffy and dingy.

"This is where all the paper files are kept for the Cattleman's Club members," Chelsea said, removing her sleuthing coat. "Most records are digitally input now, but the club makes a habit of keeping all the original files. Some date back since the club's founding."

"So, what are we looking for exactly?" Dan asked, his brows doing that adorable bunching again.

Erin took a hard swallow and turned away, pretending interest in a file drawer labeled A-C. Dan hadn't mentioned that he knew Erin and she'd been too taken by surprise to correct Chelsea's assumption that they had never met each other. She was feeling guilty about that, but she couldn't very well blurt out now that she and Dan had hooked up for one wild night and then hadn't spoken again.

"Since all of Maverick's victims are members of the club, we've been given special permission to check into these files. The board and all the members don't like the negative publicity. It's hurting the club's reputation and we all want to catch the creep, sooner rather than later. We don't want him hurting anyone else, that's for sure.

"We're looking for anything that strikes you as odd. Something that would spark this guy's rage. Formal complaints registered against the club or a member. Anything that doesn't add up. Marriages, divorces, births. The computer files have been scoured already, but maybe something important didn't get input. We can't afford to skip over anything.

"The files reflect parties given at the club, including any violations or disturbances, tennis and golf lessons taken, holiday stuff. There's a lot to go through. And if we get anything substantial, we'll take what we find to the authorities to follow up on. I know it's a lot of work and I appreciate your help."

"Chels, you know I have your back," Dan said.

"I'm happy to lend a hand too, Chelsea."

"We're going to catch that asshole," Dan said forcefully.

Chelsea smiled. "I hope so. Either way, I appreciate you both for helping. Erin, my brother runs Hunt and Company, our family business and he also has a poor man's version of an animal rescue on his ranch at Hunt Acres. The man has a heart of gold and picks up strays faster than—"

Dan cleared his throat, loudly.

"Okay," Chelsea said, getting the hint. "My big bro is too humble. He doesn't like me expounding his virtues. So I won't. But, Dan, you should know that Erin is in between jobs right now," Chelsea seemed compelled to explain. "And she insisted on helping. She, well, she knows a little about what I've been going through from past experience."

Dan turned to look at Erin. One brow arched, his expression deeply curious. "Yeah?"

A cold shiver ran up and down her body.

Don't go there, Chelsea. I don't want to explain to Dan.

"None of your beeswax, big bro," she said, giving Erin a big smile, letting her know she wouldn't betray her.

Dan shot a mock frown at his sister. But Erin could see the determination in his eyes. He was ready to protect his sister, no matter what.

"Let's get down to business," Dan said.

"Sounds good," Chelsea said. "Dan, why don't you and Erin look at the files together? You can double-check each other, since we're not sure what we're fishing around for."

She turned to pull out the very same A-C drawer that Erin had focused on before. A stack of manila folders ten inches high landed on the desk in front of her. "Here you go."

Erin batted her eyes a few times and slowly lowered into a chair. Dan took the seat next to her at the desk, grinning at her behind Chelsea's back. She did a mental eye roll.

She was trapped in this tiny room with a man who made her pulse race.

"I'll take on the next batch," Chelsea said, reaching into the file cabinet again and didn't miss a beat, taking the chair opposite them and opening the first file in her huge stack.

Erin tried to concentrate on the words on the page. There were dates and information about spouses—very detailed records. In a way, she felt like a Peeping Tom, privy to strangers' lives, reading about things that were highly personal. Yet, she had to remember that somewhere in these files they could find clues to Maverick. Chelsea's ordeal made it more personal for her, as a woman. No one had the right to violate a woman's privacy that way. No one had a right to secretly stow away to take nude photos and then publicly humiliate someone.

Just thinking about it, ticked her off all over again.

"It just isn't fair," she whispered.

Dan's head snapped up. She couldn't believe she just blurted that out. "If I catch the guy—" he started to say.

"Dan," Chelsea said. "Thank you, big brother. But I don't want you getting thrown into jail for assault."

"More like murder." A tick worked at Dan's jaw and the set of his chin made him look dangerous.

"Dan!"

He shook his head. "Kiddin'."

He gave Erin a quick glance and winked. She'd bet her entire bank account, tiny as it was, that although Dan would love to give the jerk more than a piece of his mind, he wouldn't resort to any sort of violence.

"You better be kidding," Chelsea said, "and believe me, I appreciate the support."

After going over dozens of files, Erin's eyeballs burned and she glanced at her watch. It was almost midnight and immediately as if her body clock was rebelling, she yawned. Chelsea caught her in the act and yawned, as well. "You know what? We should call it a night. Dan gets up at dawn and it's later than I realized."

They'd made a bit of progress, piling up a stack of member files that they could rule out. The initial process of elimination was a good start, but it wasn't near enough.

"I can come back again anytime," Erin offered. She liked being a part of something and having a purpose again.

"Count me in too," Dan said.

Of course Dan wanted to help, but didn't he have a big mega ranch to run? It baffled her how she hadn't put two and two together when she'd first met Dan. Hunt Acres. Hunt, as in Chelsea Hunt. Hello.

"That's great," Chelsea was saying, "but I have that darn convention in Houston tomorrow. I'll be gone for a few days. Unless," she said, narrowing her eyes at her brother, "you step in for me and represent the ranch."

Dan shook his head. "Not a chance in hell," he said. "I'm no good at that stuff."

"Kidding," Chelsea said. "But that means we can't get together again until the weekend."

"Give me the key code to this room, Chels. I'll come back as often as it takes."

"Really?"

"Yeah."

"I shouldn't. But you are a long-standing member and you'd be under my authority," she teased.

Dan snorted, and the sound echoed in the boxy room.

Erin giggled, a nervous little laugh that she sometimes couldn't control. Both sets of eyes turned her way. She gulped air. In for a penny, in for a freaking pound. "I'm available too."

She couldn't look Dan in the eye after that comment, yet she sensed his gaze piercing her. All that blue heading her way could make a girl dizzy, so she ignored him and nodded to Chelsea. "There's a lot to still go through."

"True. Thank you. I'll leave the details to Dan and you can work it out with him. If that's okay?"

"It's…fine," she said, finally looking at him and relaying in unspoken words that this didn't mean anything. She would work alongside him to help Chelsea with her investigation. Period.

"Fine by me too," he said in a clipped tone.

And then gave her a solid look that said something much different.

After saying good-night to Chelsea, Erin headed across the parking lot toward her car. Dan walked beside her, and no amount of arguing could convince him he didn't need to escort her. The parking lot was lit like the Fourth of July, but Dan wouldn't take no for an answer and rather than make a scene in front of Chelsea, she shrugged her shoulders, aware of the big man slowing his strides to keep pace with her shorter steps.

"It's a good thing you're doing, helping my sis," he said, breaking the ice. But with Dan it wasn't idle small talk. Dan meant it. She could give him that. He was loyal to his sister and obviously loved her very much.

"It was horrible, what Chelsea went through. I'm happy to do what I can."

"She appreciates it. And so do I."

They took a few more steps together before Erin asked, "How's Lucky?"

The dog had been on her mind lately and she couldn't very well ask Dan about him while they were in the office with Chelsea. Caught off guard and with bad timing, neither one of them had volunteered to Chelsea that Erin and Dan had already met. Looking back on it, it was a mistake. They could've made something up quickly to keep the deception to a minimum. Erin liked Chelsea too much to hide the truth from her, but it was sort of too late now.

"He's doin' well," Dan said.

"That's good to hear. He's such a sweet boy. I've been thinking about him a lot. Are you keeping him?"

"Unless someone comes to claim him. I've put out word."

Erin kept on walking. Only ten more feet until she reached the little Toyota that Clay Everett had generously provided to let her drive while staying in Texas. Not only had he and Sophie put a roof over her head in an adorable cabin in their ranch, they'd given her wheels too. The Everetts had been gracious hosts to Will and now to her too. They'd taken southern generosity to a whole new level.

When they reached her car, she finally gazed up at Dan. "Well, this is me. Thanks for walking me."

A small acknowledging grunt pulled from his throat. There was more in his eyes, something he wanted to say, but until he made up his mind to say it, wild horses couldn't drag it out of him.

"Good night," she said, turning to unlock the door.

"Erin." The way he ground out her name and the

slightly desperate tone of his voice had her turning back around.

"Yes?"

"I'm no good with—"

"I get it, Dan. You're forgiven for whatever you think you need to explain to me. You and I had one night. It was pretty terrific," she said, granting him a small smile. For a minute there, she thought he was going to say something different, something she secretly wanted to hear. "But it ended and—"

He cut her off by stepping close and cupping her face in his hands. Taken by surprise, she sucked in oxygen and the next thing she knew, Dan's lips were all over hers, firm and demanding and oh wow, almost desperate. She didn't even try to stop him. It would be futile. He was a man of action, not words, and right now he was telling her things she wanted to hear.

He was sorry he hadn't called her.

He really liked her.

He didn't want this to end.

She heard all that in his kiss. In the way he pressed her body up against the car and roped his arms around her shoulders, closing the gap between them as he moved in. She heard it in the relieved breath he took between kisses and the small but convincing things he was revealing to her. "I'm no good with words, sweetness," he whispered. "That's what I wanted to say."

As his kisses deepened, she broke out in goose bumps, her entire body standing on end. It was the same ridiculous magnetic pull they'd had the other night.

When she couldn't stand it another second, little tiny whimpers rose from her throat. Those sounds hopefully relayed to him that she understood, that she wanted more also, that she really liked him too. Because she couldn't say those words aloud yet. She couldn't trust in what she was feeling. But she wanted to, and that was progress against Rex's ultimate betrayal and the scars he'd left her with.

It was obvious they had something going. Maybe it was simply lust. Maybe it was real chemistry. But maybe it was something more. They could barely keep their hands off each other. Here they were in a deserted parking lot, kissing like two teenagers who had snuck out without their parents' permission.

She was taken by surprise when Dan broke off the kiss, took hold of her shoulders, gave a squeeze and backed away from her. She already missed the comfort of his body, felt the cool midnight November air hit her like a pack of ice.

"I think we should call it a night," he said on a big sigh. "Get a little breathing room."

She blinked. Was he backing off again? What kind of game was he playing with her, kissing like his life depended on it and then shutting her down? Her engines were running hot and she was ready to unleash her fury.

Then Dan spoke again. "I want two things. To find whoever did this vile thing to my sis, and to get to know you better. I don't want to meet you in some stuffy office tomorrow night."

"What do you want?" she asked, truly curious and not sure where he was going with this.

"Dinner, with you. And then work at either my place or yours. Are you interested?"

"Dinner, as in a date?"

He nodded.

"Are you asking me out?"

Amused, he smiled. "What's your last name?"

"Sinclair."

"Erin Sinclair," he said, as if tasting her name on his lips. "Yes, I am asking you out on a date. Would you like to have dinner with me?"

"Well, now that you put it that way, Dan Hunt. Yes I would."

His next smile was of relief. "Thank you."

"And work at my place, afterward," she added.

She wanted to be on her own turf, in case things went sour. She wasn't sure where Dan's head was at, but she had a feeling their kiss tonight was as good an indicator as she was going to get from him. "But how will you get the files?"

"I have the pass code and permission, remember? I'll double back and grab the next batch of files and we'll look them over after we have dinner."

"Are you sure?"

"You might not know this about me, but I eat dinner all...the...time." He grinned.

She laughed, her mood lightening up considerably. Dan had a sense of humor, after all. And she wondered what a real date with Dan Hunt would be like.

Four

Sunlight cut through the white shutters cracked slightly open in Erin's bedroom, lending brightness without any real heat. The morning air brisk and cool, she cuddled down into her covers, her head cushioned by a fluffy pillow. Her guest quarters at the Flying E Ranch were like a dream. More cottage than ranch cabin, she was surrounded by a picturesque garden that kept on giving, regardless of season, thanks in part to the groundskeeper, who always had a smile and wave for her.

Tapestries covered the walls in flowery settings, and she focused her gaze on one of them. But the artwork, a cobblestone path leading to a birdbath pond, soon obscured in her mind as an image of Dan entered, popping into her head, just like that.

She smiled. Her discovery that he was Chelsea Hunt's brother had shocked her, but seeing her hadn't shocked Dan. He'd seemed glad, although she shouldn't make too much of his apparent relief at seeing her again. Because, according to her latest tally, most men didn't live up to the hype, *and* their meeting again had been purely accidental.

Yet, it had been torture sitting beside Dan during the night, trying to concentrate on files when her mind was going to the secret places Dan had taken her. And then, before she could escape the parking lot unscathed, he'd kissed her, landing a knockout blow that had left her shaking.

Suddenly restless, Erin tossed off her covers and sat up in bed. She had a date with Dan tonight. She hadn't been on a date since Rex. But he no longer counted. She was removing him from any importance in her life. The floor felt cool to her feet as she rose and padded over to her closet. It wasn't what she'd call brimming with clothes, she'd left much of her stuff back in Seattle, but after a quick scan, she gave her head a bob. She could work with what she had and put together an outfit for her date tonight.

That settled, she slipped on her robe and ambled into the kitchen to set a pot of coffee to brew. She had approximately ten hours before Dan would pick her up for dinner and she created a schedule to keep herself busy. She'd take her daily jog around the ranch, tidy up the cottage, bake a cake, and continue her job search for a position back in Seattle. Her present situation ended on December 31. After that, she'd have to head home, jobless.

Working on the investigation made her feel useful. She looked forward to solving the mystery of Maverick or at least, lending a hand in tracking the cyberbully down. From what she'd gathered, he'd attacked one member of TCC after another over the months and it was why Will Brady, her ex-employer, had been called to Royal in the first place.

After a breakfast of raisin toast and coffee, she dressed in a pair of faded comfy workout pants and a deep purple sweatshirt marked by the Washington Huskies logo, and went outside. She jogged the ranch grounds stretching her legs and breathing in the crisp cool air. It was warmer than winters in Seattle, and there was sunshine, something you didn't see in Seattle too often.

Half an hour later, she had her hand on the cabin doorknob, ready to head inside and face her computer, when a familiar voice rang out. "Morning, Erin. Wait up."

She turned to find Will Brady coming up the path, holding little Faye in his arms. The little one recognized her and bounced in her daddy's arms. Erin's heart melted. "Will, good morning to you too."

When Will reached her, Faye was holding her arms out and Erin immediately grabbed her. "Hello, my little princess. How are you this morning?" Every time she spoke to Faye, her voice rose an octave and today was no different. She gave Faye a big fat kiss on her rosy cheek and set her on her hip. It was as natural as breathing, holding this baby.

"I hope we're not disturbing you. Are you busy?" Will asked.

"Yes, I'm busy holding your adorable little girl, and offering you a cup of coffee. Come inside."

Will laughed and entered the house behind her. "Have a seat," she said. Using her free hand to open the pantry door, she pulled out a box of teething crackers, leftover from when she was Faye's nanny. "Can she have one?"

The baby spotted the box and was reaching for it.

"Of course," Will said.

Erin handed Faye a cracker and the baby immediately went to town on it.

"Sit. I'll pour you a cup of coffee," she said. She

knew how Will liked his coffee, black with two spoon-fuls of sugar.

"No, thanks, Erin. But I'll sit with you."

He pulled out a chair for her and she took a seat, plant-ing Faye comfortably on her lap. "How are you?" she asked.

"We're all great." It did Erin's heart good seeing how happy Will was now. He'd been closed off before, a wid-ower grieving the loss of his wife, and now that he'd found love with Amberley, vibrancy had come back into his life.

"Wonderful."

"How are you, Erin?"

"Me? I'm doing fine. Enjoying my time here."

Will glanced at the papers she had strewn about the other end of the long table, along with her computer ready to be fired up. "I have good news. At least I hope you'll think it's good news for you."

Erin flashed him a look. "For me? What kind of news?"

"A job in Seattle. How would you like to interview for a full-time music teacher position? It's at a private elementary school in Seattle."

"Really? That would be perfect. I've been doing a job search every day and I haven't seen this come up."

"I know a guy who knows a guy," Will said.

"You pulled some strings for me?" Erin was touched.

"You helped me raise Faye, Erin. I trusted you with my child and you did a great job. So, I owe you. Besides, it's not all that nefarious. My friend told me the music teacher at his school is going to have a baby. She's work-ing until the end of the year and then plans on being a stay-at-home mom afterward. I simply put in a few good words for you."

"Thank you."

Will nodded. "They will set up a phone interview soon. The rest is up to you. And you can stay on here through the holidays. There's no rush to go back to Seattle. We want you to have Thanksgiving with us."

"Oh, uh...this is good news. I've been trying to figure out where to go from here. Your faith in me means a lot."

"Do you need time to think it over?"

She gave her head a shake. "I don't think so. It seems perfect. I need a job and you know I've wanted to get back to teaching kids about music." She came partly out of her chair, baby and all, to give Will a kiss on the cheek. "Thanks again for the opportunity. I don't know what else to say."

"Say you'll always be in our lives. I want Faye to know you too."

"Of course. You won't be able to get rid of me. We'll always stay friends."

"Yep," he said. "I have no doubt."

"And now," she said, giving Faye her full attention, "my little princess is about to meet the tickle monster."

Erin carried Faye to the sofa and the baby gave her a five-toothed grin, knowing exactly what was to come. She tickled Faye under her chin, a sensitive spot that never failed, and the giggles began. They were the softest, sweetest sounds Erin had ever heard. One day she hoped to have a child of her own as sweet and adorable as Faye.

And that day may come sooner than she expected.

She was still late.

And she didn't want to start thinking about what that could mean.

Dan knocked on Erin's door at precisely six o'clock. Erin opened it and her eyes immediately flew to the yellow roses he held in his hands. Her mouth gaped a little and she gave her pretty head a tilt. He didn't date much, but he knew how to treat a lady. The pleased look she granted him was well worth his effort. He loved how her eyes brightened when something made her happy.

"Hello, Dan." Her voice was sultry, soft, inviting. A force of nature couldn't hold back his smile at that greeting. "Come in."

He stepped inside and offered up the roses, his fingers brushing over hers gently, igniting a spark that traveled the length of him. "For you."

"Thank you." She admired the roses and hugged them to her chest. "They're lovely."

"So are you," he said, without skipping a beat. Erin looked dazzling tonight in a pretty sky blue dress that heightened the unusual aqua hue in her eyes and allowed a view of creamy shoulders and nice legs. The dress fit her form, showing off her tiny waist and shapely curves.

Dan removed his Stetson and kept it pressed to his side.

"Thank you again," she said. "Would you like a drink before we go?"

"Hold that thought until later," he said.

Her chin rose in question. "We'll need coffee to keep us awake. I've got a huge stack of files to go over after dinner. But first, I must feed you."

Erin laughed. "Let me get my jacket," she said. "I'll just be a sec."

While she was out of the room, Dan sauntered around the cabin, making note of her view out the parlor window, the stone fireplace and the homey feel of the place. Entering the kitchen area, the only thing not tidied up was a small mound of papers left out at the edge of the table beside her computer. He walked over and gave it a glance, scanning the top paper for a second, feeling guilty for doing so, but curious enough not to let that stop him. Apparently she was looking for work as a music teacher. In Seattle.

The thought of Erin leaving town left him with two thoughts. One was relief, because he knew her departure would guarantee nothing of permanence between them and that steadied his nerves some. His mother's abandonment when he was a kid had never really healed. He'd been injured more than anyone would ever know because Dan didn't show his feelings. He didn't talk about them. He only felt them, down to his bones. As a boy, he'd learned to hide his emotions from his dad, his sister, Chelsea, and his brother, Bradley. They'd been raised motherless by a father so heartsick over losing the woman he loved, he'd died early in life. Dan's mother was out there somewhere, but she'd never contacted the family again. It was as if they didn't exist.

Erin was leaving town. But Erin Sinclair was also getting under his skin. Quickly. He'd had no intention of asking her on a date, yet here he was, like a lovesick pup, waiting for her to enter the room so his heart could turn those somersaults again.

Dan was back in the parlor when Erin returned. "I'm ready," she said, wearing a pretty waist-length leather jacket over her dress.

Looking at her vanquished the darkness inside him and he lit up again.

Erin sipped Pinot Noir in a cozy corner booth of a restaurant called The Oak House. Dark wood beams above caught the flicker of candlelight from an array of twinkling votives placed around the room. Their table was topped with a textured cream tablecloth and a bowl of deep red roses. Across the room a live band played soft music on a stage and a few couples sashayed to country music on the polished wooden dance floor.

Dan sat next to her, looking over the menu, giving her time to study his profile, the deep angles on his face, the contours defining his masculinity and the scruff on his jaw that always cast him in a dangerously sexy light. His hair curled at the bottom of his collar and she wanted to wrap her fingers around them and give them a hard tug.

She giggled.

Dan's eyes snapped. "What?"

"Nothing. I'm just thinking."

He stared at her with those blue eyes. Over the flicker of the candles his gaze was mesmerizing. "Of?"

"You don't want to know."

"Maybe I do." He gave her a killer smile.

"On second thought, I don't want to tell you. But it's a good thing."

He closed the menu and set it down, giving her his full attention. "A good thing, huh?"

Then he turned to her and gave her a perfect kiss on the mouth. Enough to shock her, but not enough to cause a scene in the fancy restaurant. "That's what I was thinking."

"I didn't ask."

"Imagine what you'd get if you did."

Her eyes opened wider, the comment suggestive enough to make her melt. Heat burned her cheeks and she blushed. As if that wasn't embarrassing enough, she let out a tiny gasp.

Dan grinned, very happy with himself, and took a sip of wine.

She buried her face in the menu, her momentary hideout, until the color faded from her cheeks.

"See anything you like?" he asked.

She put down the menu and met his eyes. "I see a few things I'd like to set my fork into."

He laughed wholeheartedly and so did she. Then he rose from his chair and offered his hand. "Dance with me."

This she didn't expect. She didn't peg Dan for a dancer. But then, Dan did express himself more with actions than words. Oh boy, did he. She didn't make him wait. She placed her hand in his and as he closed over her fingers, a sensation spread across her body like warm honey. She followed him to the middle of the room.

The band played a sweet country ballad, the lead singer crooning mellow lyrics and the soft sounds drifted to her ears. Dan took hold of her waist and she set her hands on his shoulders. Underneath her fingertips she felt his strength and power, but as he began to move, she marveled at how graceful he was. "You're a good dancer," she said.

"Surprised?"

"A little."

He nodded his head, a smile curving his lips.

"When did you learn?"

"A while back."

"That's not really an answer, Dan," she said softly. The more time she spent with him, the more he intrigued her. And the more she wanted to learn about him. But he wasn't a man who spoke more than he had to and yet she continued to press. "I would love to know how you came to dance so beautifully."

"Beautifully? No one's ever said that to me before."

He moved her around the dance floor, gliding easily and she gazed up at him, waiting.

"My best friend's mom taught me."

"What?" she blurted.

He grinned at her reaction. "That's why I don't tell people."

"Please, tell me. I want to hear this."

He debated a few seconds. "I was big and clumsy in high school, towering over everybody. Couldn't get a date to save my life."

She found that hard to believe, but didn't question him. She didn't want to distract him from telling this story.

"Peter's mom had been a professional dancer before she came to live in Texas. She overheard me complaining about how clumsy I was. I mean to say, she could see it with her own eyes. It wasn't a huge revelation that I was a clod, I tripped over my own feet daily. At that rate, I'd never get a girl to date me, much less go to the prom. I think she took pity on me."

"So she offered to teach you how to dance?"

"She did. Mrs. Brewer was very kind. She told me, once I felt confident on the dance floor, I wouldn't be so clumsy at school and that would solve two problems. At first, I declined her offer. I mean, it seemed so weird and all. But Peter egged me on and I finally agreed."

"Wow, well you can tell her she did a fine job."

"I think she knows."

"So what happened to Peter and his mom?"

"Peter is a colonel in the army. He comes home from time to time."

"And his mom? Does she still live here?"

"She does. She runs a dance studio for underprivileged children."

"Really? That's wonderful. What's it called?"

"I don't recall, actually," he said, with a shake of his head.

And then she was pulled close, so that Dan's big body brushed intimately with hers and she could feel his heat.

Her arms automatically roped around his neck and she laid her head on his chest. Rapid beats of his heart pulsed in her ear. "Dan?"

"Hmm?"

"Mrs. Brewer's place, it isn't called Dan-cing Dreams, is it?"

He didn't say a word.

"I remember passing it in Royal. I thought it odd, the way it was spelled. She named it after you, didn't she?"

Silence.

And then she knew, as sure as she knew her own name. "You had something to do with financing the studio, didn't you? I bet you gave Mrs. Brewer a place to teach dance."

She moved her head off his chest to look up at him. But his eyes rested somewhere over her head, refusing to connect with hers. "I'm right, aren't I?"

"You talk too much, sweetness. Anybody ever tell you that?" Then he cupped the back of her head, guiding it back to his chest and began taking long sweeping strides across the dance floor that required her utmost concentration to keep pace.

Which quite effectively shut her up.

"My folks live in a retirement village in Arizona," Erin said to Dan. She was taking the finishing bites of her quinoa salad. Dan had arched a brow when she'd ordered butternut soup and salad for dinner. The place was known for their cuisine he'd told her, but he didn't press the issue at her simple meal. Instead, he'd asked her about her life. And she'd started in the easiest place, telling him about her parents. "They're blissfully happy and lead a very active life there."

He nodded, polishing off a tenderloin steak. Of course.

Dan was a cattleman. He was probably a connoisseur and knew what a good steak should taste like.

"We're close, in that we talk all the time. And we try to make time to see each other. But they're gone a lot. They travel with a group and love every minute of it. They've earned it. They worked hard all their lives."

"What did they do for a living?" he asked, seeming genuinely interested. As far as dates went, this one rose above all her others. Dan was attentive, mannerly, sweet, funny and humble. He'd seemed to get truly disconcerted when she'd guessed, by her skills of brilliant deduction, that he'd built that dance studio for his friend's mother. Clearly, he didn't want to talk about it. He didn't want to take credit for doing something so incredibly generous.

Finally, she'd met a man with integrity.

"Dad was an attorney for most of the thirty-five years they've been married. My mom worked as a school administrator. After I came along, Mom took a few years off, but went right back to work as soon as I was in school full-time. They were both workaholics and now, I have to say, they're playaholics."

Dan chuckled at her made-up word. He was doing a lot of smiling tonight. It looked good on him. As if the man needed anything else in his favor, now he was granting her luscious smiles.

"And what about you?" he asked. "Have you always been a nanny?"

"Not at all. I'm a music teacher by profession. I learned how to play piano early on. I took to it naturally, according to one of my instructors, and I really did love it. If asked to practice for half an hour every day, I'd practice for an hour or longer. It kind of shocked my folks, pleasantly, I should say. They encouraged my love of music and it's always been a part of my life in one way or another. I would sing in live productions in high school and college. Sometimes, I'd accompany the orchestra. I haven't a clue where my musical abilities come from, really, since my folks both are analytical."

"I would love to hear you play some time," he said.

"Me? It's been a while." She shrugged. "I'm afraid I'm rusty. Haven't played for a while."

"But you play when you teach school, right?"

"I did. But I, um... I had to resign my last teaching position." She didn't want to discuss Rex. First dates, even if they were doing this all backward since they'd already broken the ice *in bed*, shouldn't involve talk of your past heartaches.

Dan's brow furrowed and before he could ask about her resignation, she quickly moved on. "I was lucky enough to land the position of nanny for little Faye Brady, back in Seattle. She was motherless and poor Will had his hands full. I love kids, and he needed a nanny, so it all worked out for those months I took care of Faye." She heard her voice softening. "She's a little sweetheart."

Dan's gaze flicked over her, blinking rapidly as if he'd just learned something else new about her. "I hope to meet her one day."

"I hope you do."

The conversation died then and the silence was sort of nice. As far as she was concerned, she could stare into his blue eyes all night. But then the real reason for this date popped into her mind. To feed her before they dove into the investigation again.

They'd had drinks, danced, eaten and now she was gawking at him which was pretty darn unsettling because Dan was gawking back. "We should probably get to those files," she whispered.

Dan's forehead crinkled, as if he too had lost sight of

their main purpose tonight. "Would you like to have dessert before we go?"

"Dessert is waiting at my house. It's a surprise." She gathered up her jacket and purse. "You won't be disappointed."

Dan cleared his throat. "You're full of surprises, sweetness."

As soon as they arrived at her cottage, Erin set out the coffeemaker and reached into the cupboard for a pair of rose-patterned china coffee cups rimmed in gold that matched the dessert plates. The cabin came equipped. There was nothing she found lacking when she'd set about creating her grandmother's recipe. The dessert was a family favorite and it was waiting in the refrigerator to make a grand entrance. But they'd both agreed to let the dinner settle a bit before indulging.

Dan set out the TCC files on the table and began flipping through one folder. Deeply engrossed in his work, his head didn't come up once as he scoured over the pages. She sat down next to him, grabbed a file and immersed herself in the papers.

They'd just had a great dinner date and learned some things about each other. Well, Dan had learned about her life, since he'd asked and she'd answered. But Dan didn't seem to like answering questions about himself and she'd had to pry and guess her way through some of the conversation tonight. Even with that, it was one of the best dates of her life. Mainly because Dan was a what-you-see-is-what-you-get kind of man. How refreshing. He didn't mince words and didn't try to charm her. But his charm came through anyway.

She half feared that they wouldn't get any work done tonight, repeating the last time she'd been alone with

Dan. Hot kisses, soft caresses and then mind-blowing sex. But to his credit, and hers, if she was being honest, they'd gotten down to work immediately, both wanting to help Chelsea more than give in to temptation.

A while later, Dan's chair scraped back and he got up and walked over to the coffeemaker. Holy crap, she'd forgotten about the coffee.

"Sorry, Dan. I got lost in this file," she said, standing up.

"Sit," he ordered her pleasantly. "I can serve you a cup of coffee. Black with one sugar, right?"

He remembered. "Yes. Uh, thanks." She sank down into her seat and watched Dan move around in the kitchen.

"No problem. You finding anything worthwhile?" he asked.

"No, are you?"

"Nothing yet. Nothing even close." Dan let go a frustrated sigh as he set the delicate cup down in front of her and took his seat again. "This may be a big waste of time," he mumbled.

"I hope not. There's got to be something in these files that might point to Maverick."

Dan ran his hand down his jaw. "The thought of that guy getting away with what he did to Chels doesn't sit right with me."

"I agree." She shrugged and gave him a sympathetic smile.

His eyes flickered for a second and he leaned over her chair and touched his mouth to her cheek, pressing a kiss there. Then he took his seat, cleared his throat, avoiding her gaze, and opened a new folder.

She did the same, putting her head down to concentrate on a file. Every so often, she would lift her head to stretch the kinks out of her neck or sip coffee and their eyes would meet.

A flash of something hot would stream through her body and she'd force her head down to peer at the file again. They were fully aware of each other, an electric spark that ignited with every glance, stolen or otherwise. Dan, in his dark slacks and blue button-down shirt he nearly muscled out of, looked good enough to eat.

Then she remembered. "Dessert," she blurted.

"What?" His head was just coming out of the file.

"I promised you dessert and it's almost midnight. I'm so sorry."

He turned his wrist to look at his watch. "It's a little after eleven. And there's no rule that says we can't indulge in a midnight snack. Is there?"

"No, of course not."

"I'm game. If you are." He patted his flat stomach and her gaze flew there, remembering what that taut skin felt like under her palms. Remembering too many things about being naked with Dan.

"Let me get it," she said, retrieving the pretty plates and putting them on the table while Dan pushed aside the folders.

"Need help?"

She shook her head. "I'm good."

She brought out the cake plate and placed her rather beautiful creation in front of him. This time, thank goodness, the cake had come out perfect. She'd had her share of mishaps over the years, but she'd taken more time and care and made a big deal about getting everything just right. For Dan. "Have you ever had hummingbird cake?"

He eyed the tall two-layer tower covered in buttercream frosting and chopped pecans. "Wow. Nope. I think I'd remember if I had. What's inside?"

She smiled, relieved and it unnerved her how much she wanted to please this man. "Cake."

His brows lifted and the next thing she knew her hand was snatched and she was tugged down. She landed with a plop onto Dan's lap. "Don't be cute," he said. Then he thought about it and said, "Never mind, you can't help it."

"I'm *cute*?"

Dan nodded, not giving her anything else to go on.

Was it a good thing that a gorgeous man with whom she'd had earth pounding sex just called her cute? Shouldn't he be saying she was alluring, tempting, stunning? Okay, not stunning, but maybe something along those lines.

Sitting on his lap this way, she peered down into his eyes. They were smiling, so blue and clear.

"Bananas and pineapple and stuff…is inside the cake."

Dan did that adorable thing with his brows and shook his head.

"It's my grandmother's recipe and not all that easy to make, I might add, so I hope you enjoy it. I mean, it's really good but it's not everyone's cup of tea, not that you drink tea, b—"

"Erin?"

"What?"

His hand splayed the back of her head and she caught sight of the ceiling tiles as she was lowered down in his arms. His eyes reached hers first, and then his mouth came dangerously close to hers, speeding up her heartbeat. "You went to a lot of trouble for me," he rasped. "I appreciate it." Then his mouth was on hers, tasting her, licking at her, as if she was the dessert. As if he couldn't get enough.

Dan had her at his mercy. She was in a vulnerable position, lying across him this way, his strength and power evident in the way he held her in his lap. He could easily shed her clothes, touch her until touching wasn't enough, and she would let him and relish every single second. But as soon as that thought struck, her world was up-ended again, literally. Dan brought her up quickly to a sitting position.

He brushed a kiss to her mouth, tightened his hold on her and gave her a wobbly smile. "Feed me cake."

She blinked and then a chuckle broke from her chest. "From here?" From her perch on his lap?

He nodded. "Do it, Erin. I'm having trouble being a gentleman here."

He didn't need to be a gentleman. Not after that display. He could've taken her right on the kitchen table and he had to know that, but there was a look in his eyes, and a tone to his voice that didn't warrant an argument. "Okay," she whispered softly.

She turned slightly to pick up the knife. The piece she cut separated nicely and the cake was firm and moist as she carefully held it and swiveled her body back to him. Their eyes met then, his gleaming in anticipation, and she knew then that Dan was wrecking her from enjoying cake in the customary way, ever again. His mouth opened and she pushed the frosting-topped cake into his mouth.

He chewed and groaned and his eyes shuttered closed. "Real good. Too good for me not to share," he said, reaching out for another piece. He offered it to her and slowly, keeping her eyes trained on his, she opened her mouth. Sugary banana scents wafted to her nose, just as Dan guided the piece inside.

"Mmm," she muttered and chewed. Just the right texture, just the right taste.

She fed him and he fed her and it was like something

out of an erotic fairytale, without the sex. It was wildly arousing sitting on Dan's lap, feeding him a lush dessert by hand.

Dan was equally aroused; he had no hope of hiding it with her on his lap. Her breaths grew heavy and her heartbeat raced, and just when she thought this night wasn't going to end with cake, Dan lifted her off him, stood up and brushed crumbs from his shirt. "Thank you," he said. "It was delicious."

She stood facing him, wondering what the heck was going on. Dan brought that curious notion out in her more than she'd like to admit. "I'm glad you enjoyed it," she said more harshly than she intended.

"I, uh, it's late. I should go." His face contorted a bit, as if he couldn't believe he'd just said that. She could gain some comfort in knowing it wasn't easy for him to leave.

"Okay." What else could she say? *I wish you wouldn't go.* "Thank you for dinner."

"Thank you for dessert. I don't think I'll... Never mind."

"What?" Anger bubbled up. "Can't you finish a thought?"

"Hell, yeah, I can finish a thought," he barked back.

"Then just say it, Dan. Say what you want to say and be done with it." Her voice rose way above her normal pitch.

"Okay, I'll say it, damn it. It was the best first date I've ever been on. I don't want to leave, but I'm going, because I want to take you out again. I don't want you to think I'm just here to—"

God, the man of few words was giving her an encyclopedia of his thoughts. She wouldn't stop him now. "To...?"

"To take you to bed. Although I want that, more than

you can ever imagine. So, I'm leaving now and asking you out again for tomorrow night."

"What time?" she asked, her voice nearly shrill.

"Six."

"Fine," she said and walked to the front door, not entirely sure why she was so darn ticked off.

"Okay, I'll see you then." He grabbed the files up in his arms, walked to the door, leaned over on his way out, giving her a peck on the cheek, and then exited.

She slammed the door behind him and then glanced over to the half-eaten cake on the table and the scattering of crumbs on the floor.

Her face cracked into an unwelcome and uninvited smile.

She couldn't hold on to her anger any longer.

She had another date with Dan.

Five

Dan knocked on Erin's front door at exactly six o'clock, holding a box of the best darn fried chicken and mashed potatoes in the county, and the dog by his side.

The door opened seconds later, and Dan was hit by how lovely Erin looked tonight dressed in jeans and a ruffled white blouse, her hair clipped back as blond waves touched her shoulders. Looking into her pretty aqua eyes made it hard for him to breathe, and that scared him silly, but not enough to stop seeing her. He wanted her in his life for as long as she was staying in Texas.

"Hi," she said. And then her gaze immediately shifted down to Lucky. "Oh, Dan. You brought him." She bent to pet the dog, and was greeted by eager wet licks on the chin. Her giggles touched something deep inside. She was obviously glad to see the pup.

"I hope it's okay."

She roped her arms around Lucky's neck. "More than

okay. I'm good with staying in. What did you bring?" She was nuzzling the dog's face, catching up, giving him love. Her affection, aimed at the dog, was a heady thing to see. He could never fall for a woman who didn't like animals.

But was that what he was doing with Erin? Falling for her? "Fried chicken from The Royal Diner," he said. "I think you'll like it."

"Smells yummy. Come in. Did you bring files too?"

He had texted her that morning and she'd been in full agreement they should continue work on the case. He gave her a nod and walked into the cabin, Lucky staying back, waiting for Erin. "In my car. I'll get them later."

He hated having to combine his dates with Erin with work on the investigation, but it was necessary to catch the jerk and put his sister's mind at ease. No one knew when Maverick was going to strike again or who would be his next target.

"That's fine. We need to keep working," she said, closing the door and entering the great room.

She reached for the box in his hand. "I'll take that," she said, and their fingers brushed as she relieved him of the food. Her touch was like a match igniting, the sparks causing an electric reaction to his system. Damn. He was supposed to play it cool tonight. Dinner, work and then see where things would lead.

Dan had kicked himself a dozen times today for leaving Erin wanting last night. It had taken all of his will-power to stop their erotic cake buffet and shift her off his lap, halting a trip to the bedroom. And because of it, he'd been in a sour mood all day, anxious to get here and make up for lost time.

He followed Erin to the kitchen. Lucky was close on his heels and took to sniffing out the place. She set the food down on the counter and when she turned around he was right behind her. He'd shocked her, coming up so close, looking into her pretty blue-green eyes, breathing in her scent, which was a cross between fresh rain and roses and uniquely hers. "You're beautiful, Erin," he said, unable to hold back.

He took her face in his hands and stroked down her cheeks and as he leaned in close, her lips parted, inviting him in. "Dan," she whispered.

The plea in her voice put Dan at a loss. A man could only take so much, and when Erin looked at him like that, sweetly sultry and so damn arousing, he made a decision. He brought his mouth down on hers and kissed her and kept on kissing her, until she was laboring hard for breaths. He was in no better shape. He inched away, giving her room to breathe, brushing a stray blond tendril off her cheek. She peered up at him, her gaze connected to his without so much as a blink of the eye. "Are you hungry?" he asked.

"Not for food."

Air exited his chest. Oh man. She was a temptation. And he was grateful for that. "Where to, sweetness?"

She folded his hand in hers and led him out of the kitchen.

There wasn't much Erin could do to stop the hurricane force connecting her to Dan. She held his hand— her heart rate clocking a new record for speed—and made her way into her bedroom. Rays of the moon sliced through the curtains, giving off light amid the shadows, the illumination enough for her to see the color of Dan's eyes.

"Here we are," she announced, keeping her voice low.

"Nice," he said, squeezing her hand. His gaze never

touched upon the room, his eyes were solely on her. And oh, how *nice* and thrilling it was.

"Sweetness," he rasped, bringing her into the fold of his arms. Lucky intervened, sliding between their legs and she let a little chuckle escape. Dan didn't think it too funny. "Go," he told the dog, pointing to the corner of the room.

Lucky trotted off with his tail between his legs.

Dan kissed her then, impatiently as if he'd been starving for her. She felt the same way, the lightness of the moment vanishing into a fiery explosion of hands reaching for each other, clothes being shed and moans reverberating in the room. Dan slipped behind her, kissed the back of her throat and used one hand to cup her breast and gently massage the peak until heat stoked like wildfire between her legs. She whimpered and made a move to turn around, but Dan held her firm, his body fierce and protective, as he slid his hand down past her navel to sink into the oblivion of her folds. She fell back against him, the sound of her soft cries and his kisses echoing in her ears.

"Hold on," he whispered, but it was too late for holding on. She was in his grasp and he was making her crazy. Her body gave way, releasing quickly and forcefully, her cries amplified as she shuddered and splintered. It was the best and quickest she'd ever experienced and when it was over, she slumped in Dan's arms, her knees going weak from pleasure.

"Sweetness," he muttered, awed. His body rigid, his erection pressing her, he turned her around and kissed her deeply on the mouth. Then he lowered her onto the bed and came up beside her. It was only a minute before he was sheathed and inside her, holding her cheeks tight in his hands from underneath, raising her up easily and thrusting into her inch by inch.

Her teeth clamped down, the sensations so ripe, so raw. When she opened her eyes to look at him his desire burned hot and steamy, his thrusts harder now, more powerful. But his gaze never left hers, as if he was gauging her, making sure she could handle his size, his weight, his power.

"Yes," she cooed, accepting all he had to offer. Had it been this good the first time they'd made love at Hunt Acres? The sex, yes, but the feelings behind it didn't even come close.

"Erin," Dan whispered, and she wasn't sure he knew he called her name, he appeared that lost, that fully immersed in her.

The bed shook as he moved faster, his thrusts going deeper. His face contorted. She felt the same pressure build again within her. How could it not? Dan was her elixir, the catalyst to her wildest fantasies. Their joining was hot and amazing. Just looking at Dan, having his big body joined with hers was all she needed, to climb, to seek, to let go.

"Sweetness." His body surged, pushing her toward release again.

She gripped his shoulders, her fingertips going deep into his skin. "Dan."

And then his body broke apart, just as hers did. The mating timed perfectly, they rocked back and forth, huffing out each other's names.

"Oh man," he breathed out noisily. "That was eff-ing great, sweetness."

"Yeah." It was the understatement of the year.

"You okay, baby?"

She looked into the clearest, most amazing blue eyes

and found something there she hadn't seen before. Something, she was afraid to name. "I'm more than okay."

Dan laughed and folded her into his arms.

Lucky took that second to jump onto the mattress and make himself comfortable at the foot of the bed.

This time, Dan didn't seem to mind.

A short while later after dinner, Erin sat cross-legged on the bed and Lucky scooted close to her, laying his head on her lap. She scratched him under the ears and the dog rewarded her by wagging his tail and licking her hand. "You sweet boy," she said, kissing the top of his head.

"Not sure if I should be jealous," Dan said, coming into the bedroom with a stack of files. They were both semidressed, Erin wore Dan's super soft flannel shirt and he'd put his jeans back on along with his white undershirt.

"Of him or me?"

"Both of you. You're gettin' pretty darn cozy together."

"Yeah, well, Lucky's special." She stroked the dog's coat.

"He must think you're pretty special too. You tossed him chicken under the table."

"Guilty as charged," Erin replied. Dan hadn't been wrong, Royal Diner's chicken was the best she'd ever had and she had no qualms about sharing with the dog. Those big brown eyes had gotten to her.

The mattress dipped as Dan set a knee on the bed and then climbed in next to her. "Is he gonna help us find the culprit in all these files?"

"He'll be our mascot."

"Yeah, well, I hated this creep Maverick before. But

now that we've got to delve into these files tonight, when we could be—"

"Cuddling?"

Dan stopped to smile and wink. "Yeah, sweetness. That's what I was gonna say."

A rumble of laughter forced through her mouth. "You're a terrible liar."

"I know," he said, horse-collaring her closer and kissing the very top of her hair.

"It has to be done, Dan."

"True, but I don't usually end a date by breaking out folders."

"How do you end a date?"

He rubbed at the whiskers along his jawline and shook his head. "It's been so long, I can't recall."

Erin didn't really believe that. Dan was too handsome, too great a guy not to have females dropping at his feet. "You're lying again."

"I'm not. Chelsea says I'm picky when it comes to women."

"Oh." If that was a compliment, she was happy to take it.

"What about you?"

"What about me?" Erin asked right back at him. Her antennae were up. She didn't like talking about her love life. It was hard and awfully discouraging.

"You know what I'm asking." Dan's eyes went to a deeper shade of blue, the way they did when he got serious. He held her gaze firm and she couldn't look away.

"I do. It's…hard to talk about."

"You got your heart broken," he stated.

"I…did. You really don't want to know."

"Maybe I do."

She put her head down. "It's embarrassing."

"More embarrassing than getting dumped on your ass by a fake bull?"

"Yes," she said, a smile pulling her lips apart. "Okay. There was a bit of a scandal in Seattle and I was in the center of it."

This did not seem to shock Dan. She wasn't sure if that was a good thing or not, but he didn't blink or laugh or curse. He just stared at her, waiting.

His patience and willingness to listen encouraged her to speak. She went on to tell him about Rex Talbot and how they'd dated, how he'd led her to believe he was single and how, after a few months when his socialite wife came back into the picture and found out about their love affair, scandalized Erin's good name.

It was hard revealing this to Dan. She didn't really want him to know how stupid and gullible she'd been, but at the same time, it was freeing getting that off her chest. By revealing her secret to him, somehow she felt closer to him, giving him her bond of trust.

"So you never suspected he was married?"

"No. Maybe I didn't want to see the signs. Maybe I just wanted to believe him, no matter what I might have suspected."

"Why would you do that?"

She shrugged. "My folks have this amazing marriage. They respect each other and are honest about things. I grew up believing it was all possible."

"And now you don't?"

"I don't know what I think anymore."

Dan sighed and studied her face. Did he believe her? Was he thinking her a fool for not being more intuitive or questioning Rex's motives? In hindsight she saw some telling signs, but didn't pursue them at the time because she'd had faith in mankind. And then that faith had been shattered.

"I appreciate you telling me," he said quietly.

"I am not proud of it."

He blinked then and a question came into his eyes. He had something on his mind, but he wasn't going to ask. "I am over him completely."

He let air out of his lungs. "Okay."

The files he held landed with a thump on the night-stand and he turned to her. She looked at him carefully and felt his gentle force as he lowered her down onto the bed, tucking her into the curve of his body and holding her tight. Her eyes closed and she waited for him to move, to take her to places that made her forget the bad things. And when nothing happened, she whispered, "Dan, what are we doing?"

He kissed the base of her neck and whispered back, "Cuddling."

Tears immediately welled in her eyes and her throat constricted. She could only nod and press herself more solidly into the safety of his arms.

Dan took the shirt off her back, literally, since it was his shirt she'd worn as they'd made their way through a batch of TCC files tonight, after they'd made love and cuddled sufficiently.

"I've got an early appointment in the morning." He sighed and brought his mouth to her bare shoulders, planting tiny kisses there. "Or I'd love to stay and make you blush again."

"I don't blush," she said softly.

"You sure about that? 'Cause from this end, it's pretty damn thrillin' seeing your skin color up that way when we come together."

"Dan," she whispered, her body beginning to flush again, hearing his deep velvety smooth voice caress her with sexy talk.

He slid his arms through the sleeves of his shirt and let it hang off his shoulders. "God, I hate to leave you."

She grabbed his shirt with both hands and went on her tiptoes, giving him a brush of her lips. He dug in for more, deepening the kiss and when he was through her quiet sigh was more like a purr of absolute contentment. "I hate for you to leave too."

Naked but for a pair of silky panties, she was totally comfortable standing before Dan, allowing his eyes to roam over her and yes, see her flush of color again. See the want her body couldn't conceal. She was getting in too deep with Dan and on a self-defending note, backed away and put on her warm pink robe. "I'll walk you out," she managed.

He gave the keyboard a glance. "Do me a favor before I go?"

Anything. "Depends."

Dan's brow went up and she smiled coyly. She could be a tease when she wanted to be.

"Play for me. Just once, sweetness."

She wanted to say no. She was rusty and it was late and she wasn't ready. But the excuses in her head didn't play out. She couldn't deny Dan, not when he hadn't denied her anything tonight, except his heart. That, he seemed to keep under lock and key.

"Okay."

Dan picked up a ladder-back chair with one hand and scooted it over to the keyboard. With a flare of his arm, he gestured for her to sit down.

She took her seat and set her hands on the keys, getting familiar again. She hadn't played since she'd given her resignation at the school. It had been too difficult and she'd put that part of her life on hold for the time being. But now, she found that she really did want to share this with Dan. "What would you like to hear?"

"Your favorite. Whatever you enjoy playing."

She nodded and immediately knew what piece she would play for Dan. "This is called 'Kiss the Sky,'" she said quietly, getting her bearings on her seat, splaying her fingers out in front of her, giving them a good stretch. And as soon as her fingers touched the keys, she was off, flowing as the notes poured out and a sense of calm, not panic as she'd thought, seized her. She knew the song by heart. She'd written it.

Dan sat on the bed and out of the corner of her eye, she saw him resting on his elbows, watching her. She thought having an audience would make her nervous. She thought all of her bad memories would come rushing back, but playing this song for Dan boosted her up, giving her a much-needed shot in the arm. She closed her eyes as the notes swayed her and yes, she was rusty to her critical ear, but the song still held its spirit and came through as a shining testament to her skills as a musician with each touch of the keys.

When silence once again filled the room, Dan was there, lifting her out of her seat and into his arms. She was bulky in her robe, but Dan brought her close and she looked into the solid blue sea of his eyes. "That was something," he said, his voice gravelly. "I didn't expect… to be dazzled."

She smiled. "I dazzled you?"

"From the second I saw you. But yeah, tonight, you dazzled me. You're very talented, Erin. And clearly, you love what you do."

"I guess. I forget how much I do love it."

"Well, now you know." He smiled with his eyes. "I've got to go. I'll call you tomorrow."

"Sounds good. I'll walk you to the door."

"Not necessary. You stay. Keep playing. You should always play."

And with that, and a kiss on the cheek, Dan was gone.

In the morning, Dan hummed the tune Erin had played for him as he drove to the Cattleman's Club. His body was sated, filled with thoughts of the stunning woman he'd left some hours ago.

It was early, just after dawn, the rising sunlight blocked by big gray clouds forming overhead. The November air took on a bite, a foreshadowing of the winter days to come. He reached the club early enough not to be noticed and returned the files to their original cabinets straightaway. As far as finding any clues about Maverick, they'd come up with a big fat zero and it was disappointing.

But nothing about meeting Erin had disappointed. She continued to surprise him, each time they were together. She was a talented pianist and it was a shame she didn't play more. It was also a damn shame she'd had to resign her position at the school in Seattle too. It just confirmed his belief that life wasn't always fair. That sometimes, life could be cruel.

It had been cruel for his family when they'd lost their dad, even though it was many years after their mother had abandoned them. They'd taken some hard knocks along the way even after that, but he, Chelsea and Bradley had managed to survive. Still, they'd grown up motherless, robbed of a family life that could've been better, happier, on solid ground.

He'd learned a hard lesson then, ingrained in him since

childhood. Don't get involved. Don't get suckered in. And you won't get hurt. It's the way he'd run his life up until this point.

Not that he wasn't glad he'd met Erin Sinclair. But she was going back to Seattle to live. He had known going in that their involvement was temporary. She had to know it too. She was gun-shy about commitment after what she'd gone through and probably had trust issues similar to his. Not that he blamed her about what happened in Seattle, but he wasn't sure she was over it entirely.

Dan exited the file room and drove into Royal for a breakfast meeting with some of the local managers of Hunt and Company. It was a routine meeting at the Royal Diner, but everyone from the waitresses to his most trusted employees had one thing on their mind, the upcoming storm.

"They say it could be a big one," the waitress said, serving plates of hotcakes.

"That so? I didn't hear." He hadn't. He'd been humming Erin's tunes on the drive into Royal this morning, not listening to weather reports.

"Yep, it's all over the news now. They're issuing warnings to the entire county. Could be as big as the storm that plowed through Royal a few years back," Jeb McNamara, his Dallas manager, said.

"They're warning about a tornado?" Dan asked.

"Yep, that's what the news reports are saying," Jeb added. "Could happen as early as this afternoon. They're closing the schools, just in case."

"Okay, then. We'll make this meeting quick, and then you folks all go on home. You don't need to be on the road when it hits. Keep your families safe."

The men and women around the table thanked him and they got on with the essential items on the agenda. Dan had a few key issues to discuss with the managers about Human Resources and the new rollout of his employee-of-the-month program. Dan was a believer in keeping the morale high at the company and worked with his family to see that his employees' needs were well cared for. After that discussion, he hastened his employees out of the diner, wishing them safe travel home.

Then he reached for his phone and speed dialed Chelsea's number.

"Hi, big brother," she answered. Caller ID had its merits. "I take it you heard about the storm?"

"Yep, just now. Where are you?"

"I'm at Bullseye Ranch with Brandee and Shane, so you don't have to worry. Shane's got everything under control. They have a shelter here, in case the storm gets out of control."

"Okay. I'm glad you're not alone. Stay safe." How well his sister knew him. He'd taken it upon himself to watch out for her over the years. Even though she was an independent woman, strong and fierce when necessary, she was still his baby sis. "How did your trip go?"

"It went well. I'll tell you about it when I see you. But it's all good. What about Bradley? Is the middle child still out of town?"

"Yeah, as far as I know. Last I heard from him, he wasn't coming home for a few weeks. Crescent Moon might be in the path of the storm." He needed to check out his family home. Crescent Moon was where they were all raised and it was Bradley's home now. "I've got to see to the animals, and let the staff go home."

"That's a good idea. Be careful, okay?"

"Always."

"Uh, Dan. Have you had much luck…with those files?" He pictured his little sis biting her nails like she did when she was kid and something bothered her. Like not having a mother to help her do her hair. Like not having a mom explain about touchy female things. Dan had tried, but hell, what did he know about pigtails and braids? He hadn't been the greatest at explaining the birds and the bees either.

"I wish I had better news for you, but Erin and I didn't find a thing that looked suspicious. We've been going over the files for two nights."

"You have, have you?"

"Yeah."

"I like Erin. It's awfully nice of her to do this for me."

"Yeah."

"Dan? What are you not telling me?"

"Nothin'."

"Nothin'? As in, 'None of your business, Chels'? That kind of nothin'?"

"Maybe."

"Maybe is good. I approve. Are you dating her?"

Air blew from his chest. Hell, he liked keeping things private but as sure as anything, his sis would probe him about Erin endlessly if he didn't shoot straight with her. And if he continued to see Erin, it'd be too hard to hide anyway in a small town like Royal. "Alright, yeah. I'm seeing her, but it's a casual kind of thing."

"Casual? *With Erin*?" Chelsea laughed. As if she had some secret knowledge that *casual* and *Erin* didn't go in the same breath. "Dan, that's good. You've been alone too long."

"I'm not alone."

"Sure, sure, big brother. I know the drill. You have a company to run, a cattle ranch and your animals. You have it all."

She was poking fun at him. He should give her grief,

but the storm was looming and he was glad enough that she was safe with her best friend Brandee. "Can't argue those facts. You called it, baby sis. Talk soon," he said, and after the phone call he jumped into his SUV, and instead of heading toward his family home, Crescent Moon, he sped toward the Flying E Ranch.

To Erin.

Six

As Erin took her morning jog along one of the Flying E's paths, she pounded out a pace that would clear her head. She'd woken up feeling restless, missing Dan. Running had always brought clarity and a new perspective, and today she needed that, more than anything. She'd just had a phone interview with the administrator at Lincoln Elementary. The call had gone exceedingly well, with no mention of the Rex Talbot thing. Apparently it had all blown over, and her old school had even given her an excellent reference. Her instincts told her she would love this job. It was everything she wanted; kids, music, a place to belong. She was a teacher and a musician, and when those two paths met, it was where dreams were made.

A Seattle Mariners sweatshirt and her adrenaline keeping her warm, she breathed in the cool crisp air. Clouds gathered above, gray and threatening. This wasn't new to her. Back in Seattle, cloudy days were the norm and never stopped her from jogging.

It was great having the wind at her back. She waved to ranch employees in the distance as she thundered past the guesthouses on the property, picking up speed, her legs aching in a good way. It was time to put her life back in order and not allow what happened with Rex tear her down anymore. Coming to Texas had been the best thing to happen to her. She needed this time to find her confidence, to find her pride and learn how to let go of the past.

As she rounded the corner leading to her cottage, she spotted Dan's SUV parked in front. Immediately a smile cracked at the corners of her mouth. A few more steps and yes, there he was standing on the porch.

He turned when he heard her footsteps and gave her an up and down perusal. The grim look on his face surprised her. Before she got close enough to meet his eyes, he said, "Where have you been?"

"Jogging," she replied. Wasn't it obvious?

"You don't take your phone when you jog?"

"I do, usually. Back in Seattle I always did. But since I wasn't going off the ranch I didn't think I'd need it. What's wrong, Dan?"

"I've been trying to call you for half an hour," he said, furrowing his brows in that adorable way, yet there was a serious something in his voice.

"I'm sorry you couldn't reach me." She wasn't sure why she was apologizing. "What's going on?"

"There's a storm coming, a big one."

She glanced at the sky. "I figured. Can we go inside?" As she unlocked the door and gave a little push, a sudden cold gust blew it open the rest of the way. She looked over her shoulder at Dan standing right behind her. "After you," he said.

She entered and led him into the parlor area of the great room. "I didn't think I'd see you this morning. Didn't you have a meeting?"

"I did," he said, "I sent my employees home."

"Wow, because of the storm?"

He nodded. "They needed to be home with their families."

She kept her eyes locked to his, wondering what was up. Was he here to warn her? "Dan, it's very sweet of you to come by. I'll be sure to stay inside until the storm is over."

He shook his head, and suddenly her hand was enveloped in his, his large palm wrapping around her smaller one. His eyes intense, his expression cast in worry, the look on his face completely drew her in. "Erin, this storm could be monstrous. It's happened once before in Royal, and there was devastation. I'd like you to come with me to Crescent Moon, my family home. I need to see to the animals and make sure the staff went home. There's an underground shelter there, in case it comes to that. I promise you'll be safer with me."

She blinked a few times, absorbing his words, totally touched by his concern. "You came here to get me?"

He nodded, as if the idea was as natural as breathing. Did he think her a stray that needed rescuing? In some cases that was so true, he must look at her as a lost soul, a woman without direction at this point in her life. She hadn't told him about her job offer because it hadn't come through officially yet. And something else hadn't come through, as well. She had the pregnancy test to check out her symptoms, but hadn't the nerve to take it yet. Shelving that thought for the moment, she stared at Dan, rubbing at his jaw, waiting for her answer. He'd come here, guns blazing, ready to bring her to safety. What woman would refuse such a sweet and generous offer? The way she saw it, she had two options. She could sit alone in this cabin and wait out the storm, or spend her time with Dan at his family home and experience whatever adventure might await them.

When she thought in those terms, there really wasn't any option.

"Give me a few minutes to shower and change?"

"Just a few, Erin. And you might want to pack a bag, in case we have to spend the night."

"Okay and I'll call Will and let him know I'm going with you so he doesn't worry."

Fifteen minutes later, Erin was seated beside Dan in his black Escalade and as they headed off the Flying E, powerful bolts of rain began to pour down, slashing across the windshield. There was no preamble, no foreplay. One second the land was dry, the next the roads were slick and wet. Windshield wipers fought hard to clear Dan's vision as he drove with an expertise and caution she appreciated.

"Wow, you were right," she said, breaking the silence. "It's torrential."

"It will be, once the winds kick up. They estimate forty mile an hour winds. Did you bring your power umbrella?"

"I'm from Seattle, of course I did."

He laughed a little while concentrating hard on the road.

"How much longer?" she asked, after another long silence.

"Just another five miles and we'll be there."

The roads were relatively empty. Everyone from around here seemed to know how to brace for the storm. She huddled up tighter in her flannel jacket lined in lambswool.

"Oh damn," Dan said, staring out the windshield to his right. They passed a car on the side of the road, a woman in the driver's side with a phone to her ear. Dan immediately slowed the car and pulled over to the embankment. "Looks like she's stuck."

Erin strained to look into the car. "Dan, there's a car seat in the back. There might be a child in there too."

"Yeah, I see that. Stay put. I'll go check it out." Dan shoved the door open and climbed out, ducking his head and hanging on to his hat as he ran to the woman in distress.

Erin waited, strumming her fingers over the seat cushion and after sixty seconds of not knowing, jumped down from the car and made a dash for it. When she reached the car, Dan gave her a look and then resumed working on the windshield wipers.

She waved to the woman who indeed had a toddler in a car seat behind her. Erin reached her driver's side window, rain pelting her. "Are you okay?"

"Yes, just a little frazzled," she said. "You're getting soaked. You want to get in?"

Erin didn't hesitate to get into the passenger side and introduce herself. "I'm Erin Sinclair."

"Judy Roberts. My wipers are on the blink. They're old, I should've had them replaced. I couldn't see a darn thing and I didn't want to take a chance with my son in the car."

"That's a smart move. How old is he?"

The little blond-haired boy seemed oblivious to his surroundings. He held his juice bottle and was busy staring out the window at the downpour. "Donny's two and a half. We were at the doctor's office. He's been sick and I thought I could outrun the rain."

Dan knocked on the woman's window and she lowered

it. "Looks like I might've got them working again," Dan shouted over the rain. "Wanna give it a try?"

"Okay," she said. She turned on the ignition and the wipers cleared the windshield as they were intended. Relieved, the woman nodded to Dan. "Looks like they're working now."

"For now, anyway. If you want to try driving home, we'll follow you."

When the woman hesitated, Erin nodded. "We'll see you and Donny safely home."

"That's very kind of you. It's not far, just a couple of miles from here. Thank you both so very much."

"Glad to help," Dan told her. Then he gave her a nod. "Erin, let's go."

"We'll be right behind you," she assured Judy and then opened the car door. Her boots sunk into muddy gravel and angry drops of rain bombarded her face as she made a quick dash to Dan's car.

"Whew," she said, plunking in her seat and slashing her hand over her brow, drying her face the best she could.

Dan tossed his hat into the backseat. He was drenched and staring at her. Her hair plastered to the top of her head, her teeth chattering and her boots mud-soaked, she wasn't exactly female eye candy at the moment. But Dan's eyes were warm on her anyway. "It was nice of you to get out and help."

She pushed wet tendrils off her cheeks, finger-combing her hair. Hopefully it was an improvement. "I figured the woman might need a bit of moral support. Kinda scary getting stuck on the road in the middle of a storm, and with a child no less. But you're the one who stopped to help her, despite your need to get home."

He shrugged it off. "I couldn't just drive by. By the

time someone got to her, the storm could've been deadly. Anyway, let's see if my fix-it job worked."

Judy pulled her car slowly onto the road and Dan followed behind her.

Thunder boomed overhead, the storm's rage a threat of what was to come.

"Is this where you grew up?" Erin asked Dan, getting small glimpses of Crescent Moon Ranch between intermittent swipes of the windshield wipers.

"It is," he said.

Even though big thick drops of rain obscured some of her vision, his family home still looked magnificent. A long winding ranch house stood out on a vast green meadow. As they drove in, a path of arching trees with intersecting branches meeting like linked fingers overhead led them to the home's entrance. "It's beautiful."

He nodded. "Home to me when I'm staying in Royal, although I spend most of my time at Hunt Acres."

Where he could be alone with his animals.

But wow, this place was a far cry from the humble little studio apartment Erin called home in Seattle, but home was home. And for the most part Erin liked her place. It was just the memories of Seattle that she didn't like so much.

Dan pulled into one of the five garages on the premises and parked the car. "I've got to check on the animals straightaway," he said. "After I get you inside and warm."

He was such a protector. He'd already done a good deed today in helping Judy and her son get home safely. And if she were being honest, Dan coming to get her at the Flying E could be added to his list of good deeds. She was safe with him, making the thrill of being with him that much more intense.

"Don't worry about me. I'll go inside and change into dry clothes."

"That'll work," he said. Dan grabbed both their bags and they got out of the car. He led her past the mudroom and a marvelous kitchen, to a room, she might guess by the floral feel to the space, that was once Chelsea's bedroom. "You can change in here. There's a shower too, if you want to warm up."

"Thanks, maybe I will. Where will you be?"

"I've got to make sure the horses are secure in the stable. Should be back in half an hour or so."

"Do I come looking for you, if you don't?" She smiled, but it wasn't a joke. She had a protective streak in her too.

"Not on your life. You stay put inside. This time, Erin, I need you to heed my warning. Don't go outside. As soon as I get back, I'll show you where the bunker is."

The tone of his voice brought chills. "You really think it'll come to that?"

"It might. Like I said before, the tornado that whipped through Royal a few years back did a lot of destruction."

He waited patiently, watching her closely. "You don't come outside, got that?"

Thunder boomed again, the weighty clouds crashing together in the near distance. Another chill ran through her and she couldn't let him go without lifting on tiptoes and giving him a wet kiss on the cheek. "Got it, but please don't take any chances out there."

"Never."

Telling Dan not to risk himself for the sake of his horses was like telling a papa bear not to protect his cub. She got that, and it scared her a bit but thank goodness he was a big strong beast of a man. "Hurry back," she whispered.

She followed him to the back door and after he exited, strode to the kitchen window, catching a glimpse of him heading to a structure some distance away, his head down, his steps rapid, trying to outrun the weather. When he was completely out of sight, she returned to the bedroom.

Chilled to the bone, she stepped out of her clothes quickly, grabbed her bag and entered the bathroom. Setting the shower to medium hot, she got in quickly and the spray hit her in warm bursts. Immediately, her frigid insides began to thaw. In a perfect world, Dan would strip naked and join her there, but that wasn't going to happen today. He was out in the cold bitter storm and she only prayed that he would return shortly. She'd make hot cocoa or coffee or whatever he wanted to warm himself up.

In such a short time, Dan Hunt had become an important part of her life. In all her crazy dreams, she would never have believed this would happen to her again. Especially while in Texas, of all places. She'd come with the firm resolve to give up on men, at least in the short term. But it was happening and she couldn't do much to stop it.

After her shower, she dressed in a warm black knit sweater and jeans and covered her feet with fuzzy socks. She strolled around the room, restless, trying to ease her nerves by concentrating on an oil painting on the wall of majestic horses racing through a canyon, their manes lifting, their hooves pounding earth. It was beautiful in its simplicity.

Her phone buzzed and she was grateful for the distraction. Dan had only been gone a few minutes, but it seemed like hours. She took a seat on the bed and picked up on the second ring, smiling. "Hi, Mom."

"Hi, honey." Her mother's calm voice was just what she needed at the moment. "How are you?"

"I'm doing fine," she answered.

"Dad and I just got your message. We were out on the golf course this morning. You know your dad, if he doesn't get thirty-six holes in every week, he gets grouchy."

A chuckle rumbled from her throat. Her father had to keep ultra busy, even in his retirement. "I figured as much."

"So, you have good news, I hear?"

"Well, like I said in the message, I think so. Will recommended me for a music director job at an elementary school in Seattle."

"That Will, he's such a wonderful man."

"Yes, he's been great. Anyway, they liked my résumé and I had a phone interview with them a little while ago. Just thought I'd give you a heads-up. I know you were worried about me. *I* was worried about me, but now it looks like things might straighten out."

"So if you get the position, you'll be moving back to Seattle soon?"

"Well, yes. But the job doesn't start until the first of the year."

"That's wonderful. Dad and I were planning on taking a few weeks to visit you. You just tell us when it's convenient and we'll be there. We can do one of those duck tours. I hear they're fun."

"Yeah, they are. And I'd love seeing you and Dad."

"Wonderful. So, are you still enjoying Texas?"

Thunder clapped overhead, an insanely loud smack that shook the house. Her thoughts immediately flashed to Dan out there somewhere, in this awful weather.

"My goodness, what was that?"

"Thunder. It's raining pretty hard here, but don't worry, I'm inside."

"Well, I hope so, Erin." It was her mom's way of giving a warning, using her name in that particular tone.

After a few minutes of catching up, Erin ended the call and glanced at her watch. Dan, whom she didn't mention to her mother, still wasn't back and it had been nearly thirty minutes. Erin's heart began to race. Every second that ticked by gnawed at her gut. Where was he?

Inside the stable, Dan grabbed his left arm and applied pressure to the thick slash as blood seeped through his fingers. He looked at the wound and decided he'd live. He'd sustained much worse in his time on the ranch. That last bout of thunder scared Suzette silly and the mare reared back, slamming him into the pronged side of the gate latch. The latch cut through the thick cloth of his coat and ripped his skin.

His arm burning like a son of a bitch, he gave the area one last glance around. He'd done all he could to secure the horses in their paddocks, making sure they had enough feed and water to sustain them through the storm, and then exited the stable. Instantly, rain pelted him in large hard drops. He kept pressure on his arm and made a run for it, heading for the house. The distant sound of sirens reached his ears and he stopped midstride to make sure it wasn't just the bellowing of the wind causing the ruckus. Nope, he hadn't been wrong. It was a tornado siren.

Dan continued on, making his way into the house. He found Erin there, at the back door with her jacket and boots on, looking guilty. He'd caught her red-handed, ready to come looking for him. He was too damn glad to see her to get mad at her. There was no time for anger, just action.

"Get your bag, Erin. We have to get into the bunker. The tornado siren is going off."

"I hear it but, Dan, your arm? You're hurt."

"It's nothing. Do as I say. We need to get going."

Within a few seconds, they were heading outside to the back end of the house and going down a flight of steps into the darkness illuminated only by his flashlight.

"Hang on a minute," Dan said, ignoring the pain in his arm. He scurried around and found two battery-powered lanterns. A flip of the switch and they were lighting the space about the size of his parlor.

"Dan," Erin said, her voice a little wobbly. "This place is fully equipped, right?"

"Yep, you'll be safe here. We've got everything from food to first aid kits."

"Well, then, sit down," she said, pointing to one of three cots along the wall. "And show me where the first aid kit is?"

"Over there, in that tall cabinet against the wall." He plunked down on a cot.

It was frigid down here, something Dan could soon remedy with a battery-operated room heater and thermal blankets.

Erin found what she needed and came to sit beside him, setting the supplies down on the cot. Nimbly and with care, she helped him remove his jacket and gasped aloud as soon as she caught sight of the wound from beneath his ripped shirtsleeve.

"Sweetness, it's not that bad."

Her eyes lifted to his, sympathy and worry marring her pretty face. Clearly, she didn't believe him. "I'm so sorry you got hurt."

"It's just a cut."

"It's more than a cut." She sorted through her ammo of bandages, antiseptic and creams and suddenly her breath caught. "I think this is going to sting."

She soaked the cotton balls in antiseptic. "I have to clean this up. I hope you're up on your tetanus shots."

"I am, and have at it. I'm a big boy."

She didn't look amused. Her face contorted as she dabbed at his wound. "You okay?" She looked deep into his eyes.

"Fine."

"You know it doesn't reflect on your manliness if you admit it hurts."

"It hurts." He smiled through the gut-wrenching stinging. Erin always delved deeper. She always wanted to bring out more of him. He didn't like to show the vulnerable side of himself. But lately...

"Sorry about this," she said, continuing to cleanse the wound.

"There's a butterfly bandage in there. When you're finished, put that on and that should do it."

She nodded. "I could've never gone into nursing."

Dan disagreed. "You would've made a good one. You're compassionate."

"I'm a wimp when it comes to someone I care about."

Dan let that sink in. He was already in too deep with Erin, but that wasn't stopping him any. No, she was like a pleasant addiction and if he was being honest, it wasn't just about sex anymore. He was constantly reminding himself that this thing with Erin had to be temporary.

"You're doin' just fine," he told her.

Gently, Erin put the butterfly bandage in place and then began wrapping his arm with a long piece of gauze.

"There," she said, staring at her handiwork. But every so often, her eyes would dip down to his bare chest and he tried like hell not to smile.

"Feels better already. Thank you."

"You're welcome."

"I'm goin' to be fine, Erin." He got up from the cot and walked over to one of the three cabinets lining the wall. In one, he found a white T-shirt and walked it back to the cot. "Help me put this on?" he asked.

"Of course."

He put the shirt over his head and she helped ease the sleeve over his sore arm. "You know I'm injured when I'm asking you to help me put my clothes back on."

She laughed. "I think I do. Why don't you lie down and get comfortable?"

"Don't mind if I do." He grabbed a thermal blanket out of a cabinet and sank down onto the cot. "Join me and I'll keep you warm."

"I have no doubt," she said.

He took up most of the narrow cot, but he opened his good arm and she curled up next to him. He breathed in the scent of her hair, rain fresh with a hint of something flowery and while a violent storm raged outside, all seemed peaceful in their little nook of the world.

Erin woke to her stomach growling. Embarrassed, she grasped her belly, hoping to quiet down the noise. Dan had dozed beside her, his face tranquil now, as she watched him sleep. It felt eerie in the dimly lit shelter. She wouldn't want to be in there alone, that was for sure. Having Dan next to her kept her calm. Outside the winds still howled, but the storm pounding the earth earlier seemed to have let up.

Her tummy rumbled again. Dang it. She didn't want to disturb Dan's rest. Untangling herself from Dan's good arm, and easing off her part of the blanket, she sat up on the cot. Cool air struck her skin and goose bumps rose up on her arms. But it wasn't enough of a deterrent to make her curl back under the blanket and risk waking Dan with her very loud hunger pangs.

She planted her feet on solid ground and then tiptoed

toward the cabinets and quietly opened each door until she found the mother lode of survival foods. Scanning over the well-equipped stash, she noted most Mylar food packages required boiling water. Delving farther inside, she came up with a box filled with packets of banana chips. Ugh, not a fan. All she wanted was a snack, something to quiet her noisy stomach pains. And then she remembered she'd brought her purse down there.

She scrambled to the floor and sifted through all the items in her bag, finally coming up with two foil packages of vanilla-flavored teething biscuits. She had kept a supply for Faye tucked in the bowels of her purse, never knowing when the baby would need them. Often, Erin would eat them along with her. They were actually pretty tasty.

She sat on the floor, unpeeled the foil wrapper and dug in, remembering her times with Faye. It was just a month ago that she'd been her nanny, happy to have a job and a little one to watch over. It could very well be that Erin would have a little one of her own to care for. She wouldn't know until she got up the nerve to take the pregnancy test she'd brought home the other day. She just wanted to give it a little more time. She didn't want her relationship with Dan to be defined by what she found out in that test.

She had time. There was no sense in panicking or getting ahead of herself.

"You hogging that cookie all for yourself?" Dan's voice shattered the silence.

"Dan!" She hadn't heard him get up. He scooted next to her on the floor. "You're awake. How's your arm?"

"Better."

She gazed into his deep blue eyes and couldn't tell if he was telling the truth. "Really?"

"Yep."

Okay, she'd have to take him at his word.

"You didn't answer my question," he said, a teasing glint in his eyes. "You're holding out on me. Got any more of those cookies?"

She lifted the cookie to his face. "Yes. One more package."

"You sharing?"

"These are baby teething cookies, Dan."

"*You're* eating them," he said. "They must be good."

"They are, and of course I'll share them with you. On one condition."

Dan's brows rose in question.

"You tell me three things about your childhood that I don't already know."

He pulled back. "That's three conditions."

"True, but that's the deal." She waved the cookie by his nose again and he eyed it as if it was the most delicious melted chocolate-chip cookie in the world.

"I don't like to talk. Never did. Ever since I was a kid, I found myself relating more to animals than humans."

"That's one, although I really did figure that out about you already. Two more to go."

"My favorite color is aqua, a combination of blue and green that's rare and brilliant," he said, staring straight into her eyes.

"Um, that doesn't count," she whispered, melting a little bit inside. Dan was paying her a compliment. "Favorites aren't part of the deal."

He smiled and the warmth of his palm touched her face. "You making up the rules as you go, sweetness?"

"Maybe I am."

"Then maybe after all this, you're gonna owe me."

"What? A cookie?"

A gleam entered his eyes and suddenly they weren't talking about food anymore. "That too." As thrilling as that prospect was, she really did want him to share more with her about his life.

"Tell me," she whispered.

He put his head down, shaking it, and then lifted his lids to hers, his incredible blue eyes meeting hers, and in that exact moment, she knew he was ready to speak about his past. He cleared his throat and began, "My mother left us a week before Christmas. I was ten. It was hardest on me, because I was the oldest and really understood what that meant to our family. I spent a lot of time in the stables with the horses. But then I would come into the house and see my dad sitting in his chair, staring into space, and I knew we hadn't just lost our mom, but our father too. He was never the same after my mother left. He didn't rally. He didn't hug us and tell us it was all going to be okay. He was shell-shocked and broken. I helped raise Chelsea and Bradley. Dad sort of let me do it, giving me reign over them, because he couldn't cope with three children. He couldn't deal with the ranch, the family and the heartache."

"Do you know why your mother left?" she asked softly. She couldn't imagine it. And she didn't know if Dan would give her an answer, but every revelation helped her understand him better. His retreat into himself, the solace he found in animals.

"I didn't know why for a long time. But years later, before my father passed, he admitted that our mother had never really loved him. She'd never wanted a family. She was too free a spirit to be tied down. Dad said despite knowing that about her, he thought he could make her happy. They married young and he thought he had all the time in the world. That didn't ever happen. The old

memories I had of my mom are tarnished by what I've
learned about her from my father. She's off somewhere,
traveling the world on her own terms. She never remar-
ried, but has a cluster of friends she moves with."

Erin saw through the shield he put up to hide his pain.
It was real. It was potent and very sad. "Have you spoken
to her since she left?"

"No."

Erin took his hand and squeezed, connecting them,
trying to absorb some of his pain. She was extremely
close to her parents. They had a great relationship and
even though Erin didn't see them on a regular basis, they
were always there for her, whenever she needed them.
There was something to be said about knowing deep
down in your heart that your folks had your back, always.
And Dan never had that. Her heart broke for that little
boy, carrying the weight of his family on his shoulders.

"Dan, come with me. I have something better to give
you than a cookie."

She rose, tugged him up and led him over to the cot.
Rain drizzled now, and from what she could hear outside, the major part of the storm had passed. But there
was something else this shelter could give them, besides
safety. And she was bound and determined to show Dan
exactly what that was.

Seven

Two days later, Erin glanced out her bedroom window to a deep blue sky. The dark clouds that had hovered overhead for days were gone, and now beautiful white cloud puffs let the sunshine through. Everything outside had dried, the grass christened by rain grew greener, the leaves on the oak trees wavered in the breeze and the dark pounded earth was that rich deep red-brown again.

The storm that raged had left flooded streets especially in the flatlands and that included most of Royal, but there were no deaths and no major structural damage to the buildings and schools and roadways. Yes, there were more potholes on the streets, and some windows got blown out and a small section of town lost power for a short time, but for the most part, Royal weathered the storm pretty well.

We got lucky this time, Dan had said, after the storm had passed.

It touched her deeply that Dan had sought her out

and made sure she was safe during the storm. He had a protective streak a mile long. She saw it in the way he'd wanted to find Maverick and make the guy pay for his crimes, and she saw it in the way he gathered up stray animals, bringing them into the safety of his home. What she didn't know was, how he felt about her. Did he lump her into his "stray" category, consider her someone who needed protection from fake bulls and torrential storms? Or did he care for her more deeply?

He hadn't shared any of his feelings with her. And it was beginning to really bug her. So much so, she was through trying to hide behind her fears. She had to confront her situation head-on. There were too many unknowns in her life.

Did she have a job? She'd had a phone interview with an administrator of Lincoln Elementary, but hadn't heard a word yet about the outcome.

Was she leaving Texas after the holidays? One way or another, she pretty much had to, didn't she?

And most important of all, was she going to have a baby? Dan's baby.

She hadn't gotten up the nerve to take a pregnancy test yet.

She trembled at the thought of being pregnant. What would Dan's reaction be? He made no bones about how he spent his life as a loner, a man who didn't make relationship commitments. A man who while in the quiet shell of the bunker yesterday, spoke sobering words of honesty, revealing the terrible pain of his childhood. She couldn't imagine growing up without a mom and dad supporting her, guiding her, loving her. No child should go through that instability and heartache.

"Oh, Dan," she whispered against the windowpane.

Her phone buzzed and she walked to her nightstand to

pick it up. It wasn't Dan as she'd hoped, but it was someone she'd wanted to speak with, someone she was expecting. "Hello, Mrs. Lawrence. Yes, this is Erin Sinclair."

"Well, I hope I have good news for you. You are our first choice to be Lincoln Elementary School's new musical director. We'd love to have you on board."

Erin slid her eyes closed. This was what she wanted, it really was, but accepting this position meant leaving Texas. It meant leaving Dan. She had always planned on leaving, but now it was official and she needed a job. This job would allow her to do the two things she loved doing most, playing music and teaching children. It was a win-win.

"Thank you. I'm very happy to accept the position."

"Well, then, welcome to the staff of Lincoln Elementary."

"Thank you, Mrs. Lawrence."

"It's Shelly. We're not formal here at Lincoln."

"That's, well, it's perfect."

"We'll see you after the first of the year for a day of orientation. I'll be sure to send you all the necessary papers in the meantime. Just send them back in the mail when you're through."

"Will do."

After she hung up the phone, Erin floated around the cottage in a daze. This was great news. One month ago, she wouldn't have believed she'd ever get a chance to go back to teaching in Seattle and now the perfect job had landed in her lap. She was so thankful to Will for getting her foot in the door.

Erin still had a little more than a month here in Texas. A little more time with Dan. She wasn't ready to give him up. And just as that thought struck, a brisk knock resounded on her door and she jumped. Her surprise was instantly replaced by excitement. She knew who was on the other end of that knock.

She opened the door and there he was, her beast of a man looking stunningly handsome in a black snap-down shirt and weathered blue jeans. Everything about him lit her up and she matched his wide smile when their eyes locked. "Dan."

He strode inside, sweeping her into his arms. "Sweetness," he said, and nothing more. But Erin knew it was Dan's way of saying he'd missed her. He'd been busy after the storm and they hadn't seen each other since.

He took her face in his hands and touched his mouth to hers, claiming her in a soul-melting kiss. A tiny whimper rose from her throat and all seemed incredibly right in her world. How could that be, when there were so many questions? More questions than answers, but when she was with him everything seemed to fall by the wayside and all she could think about, all she could feel, was how wonderful it was to be kissed by him. His raw powerful scent, his unbelievably firm lips and the taste of him were unequalled by anything she'd ever experienced.

The kiss lasted a good long while, and she relished being in his arms, having him tilt her face from side to side to devour her lips impartially and when it was time to come up for air, he used his teeth to take tiny nips of her mouth.

"Hi," she said with a hiccup of a giggle.

Dan smiled, staring into her eyes. "Sorry to barge in."

Was he kidding? "You're welcome to barge in anytime."

"Yeah?"

"Yeah," she said softly. "How's your arm?"

He rubbed the area that had been gashed. "Healing."

"I'm glad. It looked pretty bad in the shelter."

"It's not," he said. "It's been looked at."

Good. He didn't need her nagging him about it. Dan was smart enough to know his own body and to take care of it.

"Listen, I had an idea," he said. "It's a killer of a day, lots of sunshine left and I wanted to take you riding with me."

"*Horseback* riding?"

He grinned at the note of fear in her voice. "Ever been?"

She shook her head.

"Wanna learn?"

"Sure. Of course. Now?"

"Yeah, we've come up empty on our search for this Maverick guy. From what Chelsea tells me Sheriff Battle and his team aren't having much luck either. We're at a dead end at the moment. Chelsea suggested that we try to clear our heads. Maybe gain a different perspective. Riding always does it for me."

"Really? Will Chelsea be coming?"

"Nope. She's busy. It'll be just you and me. If you're willing."

"Sure, I'll do anything to help clear your noggin." She tapped her fist onto his forehead several times.

He grabbed her wrist, a light beaming in his eyes. "Careful, or I might not catch you if the horse decides to dump you on your pretty ass."

Her eyes popped wide-open. "Dan?"

"Kidding, Erin. I've got the gentlest mare for you and you'll never be far from my side. Nothing's gonna happen to you. That's a promise."

She gave him a wary look, just to mess with his head. But she did believe that he would keep her safe. "Let me

change clothes. Give me ten minutes. And just for the record, nothing much clears my head when I'm with you."

Dan let out a rolling belly laugh and winked. "See
you in ten."

Dan's menagerie came rushing toward them as soon
as they climbed down from the SUV, Lucky leading
the pack and heading straight for her. Once he got close
enough, he flew through the air, nearly knocking her
down. She laughed as her knees hit Hunt Acres earth
and her arms wrapped around his neck. "Hey, boy. I
missed you too."

He did a number with his tongue, soaking her face
with doggy kisses. Normally, that was not something
Erin enjoyed, a slobbering dog, but Lucky was special
and they had a mutual admiration society going for each
other. So she let the dog lap at her cheeks and chin before
Dan pulled the dog off her. "Hey, buddy. I don't need the
competition."

Erin giggled and stood up, surrounded by the other
hounds. All were vying for attention. Dan picked up the
terrier and gave her a hug, while Erin shared her attention between the other dogs as Romeo and Juliet looked
on from their perches atop the porch railings.

Clearly the cats couldn't be bothered.

Dan came down on one knee beside her to pet all of
his crew. They were equal opportunity lickers, and Dan
came away just as doggy loved.

"They've missed you," she said.

"It's your fault. Keeping me away from home so
much."

"Ah, so I'm the culprit."

"Yes, Miss Sinclair, you are." He gave her a dazzling
look that warmed her up inside. Then Dan took her hand

and led her into the house. He tossed her a towel and they washed their hands and face. He was a businessman, smart and efficient, but it was hard to remember that when Dan looked every bit the cowboy in jeans and Western shirts, a black Stetson pushed back from his forehead. He dazzled her with his raw appeal, and made her go soft and gushy inside with his obvious love of animals.

"Have a drink before we head out." He grabbed a pitcher from the fridge. "Ever had sun tea?"

"I don't think so." She wasn't so sure what it was. The only tea she drank came from a kettle and tea bags.

"It's rare in November, because we usually don't get warm days, but Ted and I love it so much, Darla puts it outside on sunny days and hopes for the best. The tea is brewed by the heat of the sun over a day or two. Makes the taste more clean and sweet." He poured her a glass. "Here, try it."

He brushed his hand over hers making the transfer, and Erin loved how Dan found every opportunity he could to touch her. She put the glass to her lips, the lighter scent wafting up to her nostrils and then she sipped, letting the flavor slide down her throat. "Hmm, I like it."

He nodded and downed half a glass in one gulp. "Satisfies."

It was such a Dan thing to say, she had to tease him.

"I'll say." She eyed him up and down, her lids at half-mast as she gave him a coy smile. Heat rushed up his face. She'd never made Dan blush before.

"Oh no you don't," he said, grabbing the tea from her hand and setting both glasses down. "You're not gonna tempt me outta that ride."

"I'm proposing a different kind of ride." She couldn't hold back the smile cracking at the corners of her mouth.

He pointed his finger in her direction. "Hold that thought," he said. "And come with me."

He took her hand and marched her toward the stables, where a young ranch hand was waiting outside with two horses. "Thanks, Toby."

"Sure thing, Mr. Hunt."

He took hold of both the reins. "I'll take it from here."

"Have a nice ride," Toby said.

"Thank you."

The young man tipped his hat. Texans had such nice manners.

"This is Trudy," Dan explained after Toby sauntered off. "She's a sweetheart. She won't give you a bit of trouble."

"I hope not." Suddenly, staring up at the mare Erin's bravado waned. "She's tall."

"She's average size. My horse, Titan, he's tall." Erin couldn't argue. Titan was a giant of a horse. "Are you ready?"

She looked at her pretty mare marked with gray and white and nodded.

Dan rattled off a bunch of instructions but the main takeaway was for her not to panic, to show the horse who was boss and to keep her butt in the center of the saddle and her boots in the stirrups. She could do that. She really could.

With Dan's help, namely his hands on her butt, she was mounted and settled in the saddle, holding the reins.

Dan mounted Titan with the grace of a ballerina. Sitting at least two feet taller than her, he gave her a reassuring smile. "You ready?"

She inhaled a breath. "As I'll ever be."

This made him laugh. "You're gonna do fine." He gave Titan a command and he took off at a slow walk.

Erin really didn't have to do a thing, Trudy began following behind.

"You okay?" Dan said after a quiet minute.

"Yep."

He turned around to look at her white-knuckling the reins, her face probably the same colorful hue. *Don't panic*, he'd said, so she made a big effort to calm her nerves and placed her trust in him.

"That's it," he said in his gentle animal voice. There were so many tones to Dan she was still learning. "We won't go far."

"How far is not far?"

"Two or three miles. There's someplace I'd like to show you."

Erin got the hang of it after fifteen minutes. Well, maybe getting the hang of it was not exactly right, but blood was beginning to flow back into her hands again, so that was progress. They left cattle and feed shacks behind and continued to go deeper onto Hunt Acres land where wildflowers and tall grass grew in abundance. The recent storms greened everything up Dan had said, and the combination of blue sky and colorful earth, fresh air and solitude did bring a measure of peace.

Dan pulled up when they reached a creek, flowing hard with rushing waters. Large rocks banked the creek on one side and the sound of the rush filled her ears.

Dan dismounted and came over to help her down. "Swing your leg over the saddle. I've got you," he said.

She slipped down from the saddle right into his arms. "Yes, you've got me," she whispered as she turned around to face him and stare into his eyes.

He stared back, blinking several times, and then kissed her quick and hard on the lips. "You did pretty darn good on Trudy."

"Thanks. I'm learning."

"Yes, you are."

He grinned, hooked his finger into her belt loop and tugged her along. "Let's go sit."

She followed him to a boulder, one of the few on this side of the creek and took a seat beside him. "Are we still on Hunt Acres land?"

"We are." Dan's gaze roamed over the water, the trees dotting the area and the meadow beyond. "I used to come here as a boy. Would play in the water, or just come sit and stare out."

"By yourself?"

"Sometimes Bradley and Chels would come, but mostly I came by myself. Me and my horse."

"No dogs?"

He let out a chuckle. "Them too. Had this one mutt, half beagle, half something else, named Joey. He was my BFF. He passed on shortly after my mother left."

"You must've taken that hard. All those losses for a young boy." She took his hand and squeezed and stared down at their entwined hands.

"I…did, I guess." He shrugged, clearly uncomfortable with the subject.

"Is that why you don't let people get too close to you?"

His eyes snapped to hers, a denial on his lips, but then he nodded. "I suppose. Just doesn't seem worth it, you know? I mean, you had your heart ripped out too, back in Seattle. Do you think it's worth it?"

"I, um." What could she say? That *he* was worth it. He was worth the gamble, because she knew something that he didn't know. She could see into his heart. He was one of the good guys, but he wasn't willing to take another chance. He obviously didn't think *she* was worth it.

Chelsea was right. Riding out to the far reaches of

Hunt Acres, with the blue sky overhead and the air fresh from recent rains, did clear her head. "Dan, I have something to tell you."

Her somber tone had Dan lifting his gaze to hers quickly, a note of fear in his eyes. She'd never really seen that look on his face before. Did he think she was going to declare her undying love? No, she knew better. But she did care for Dan. Very much. She could no longer deny her feelings. She'd fallen hard for her Texan.

"What is it, sweetness?" he asked quietly.

"I was offered a job as musical director for a school in Seattle."

Dan waited a beat, his expression unreadable.

"I start the first of the year."

He nodded. "Congratulations. You'll be doing what you love to do."

"Yeah, that's true. So, I'll be leaving after the Christmas break."

"With a job waiting for you," he added.

"Yes."

"It's what you wanted, Erin."

Dan made it seem so logical, so absolutely clear, when right now gazing into his incredible eyes, nothing seemed clear at all.

"Let me take you out to dinner tonight to celebrate."

Sure, why not? She wasn't going to delude herself into thinking this little fling she was having with Dan, meant anything more to him than having a good time together. "That would be nice."

The wind kicked up, the afternoon sunlight beginning to wane and she shivered.

"Here, put this on," he said, removing his suede jacket. He helped to put it on over her bulky sweater. "It gets chilly this time of day out on the range."

She cuddled into his jacket, putting her nose to his collar, breathing in his scent and wanting to cry. But she didn't dare. She held her tears in check. "Thanks."

She couldn't fault Dan. He'd always been honest with her. She'd known from the beginning that he wasn't a staying kind of man. He'd practically told her so on the first night they'd met and Erin had too much pride to be one of those clingy women who wouldn't let go.

"Let's head back," he said. "Get you warmed up."

"Sounds good," she said. "I sure could use some warming up."

Dinner had been fantastic, champagne flowed and Dan couldn't have been more attentive, toasting her new position at Lincoln Elementary. But as he wound around the car to open her door, Erin wondered, what now?

Dan didn't seem to have any such qualms. He helped her out into the chilly night air, wrapped his arm around her waist, cradling her close, and walked her to the door. "Would you like to come in?" she said, not sure if she should be asking. It wasn't as if they had any future, but then, there was always right now.

"Would love to."

One look in his eyes and she was a goner. She nodded and inserted the key into the lock and entered the darkened room. Dan removed his coat and walked over to snap on a lamp in the parlor area. "It's a great night for a fire."

She hadn't used the fireplace since she'd been there. "Sounds perfect."

Dan moved to the wall-to-ceiling stone fireplace and set about lighting a fire, while Erin took their coats and hung them in the entryway closet. They looked so settled there, the two coats brushing up against one another, side by side. She shouldn't get used to seeing them that way...just a few more weeks and all this would seem like a dream, a perfect, sweet, sensual dream.

"I'll make coffee," she said and headed to the kitchen.

Minutes later, the fire was snapping, casting the room in a golden haze and the scent of coffee flavored the air. "Here you go," she said, handing Dan a steaming mug.

"Mmm." He took a seat on the rug in front of the hearth and gestured for her to sit next to him. Together they stared at the new flames erupting, sipping coffee quietly.

"There's a Thanksgiving dinner at the Cattleman's Club this week. Chels will probably be there along with some of the friends you've already made here in Royal. Would you like to join me?"

"You're too late, Daniel Hunt. I've already been asked to go."

Dan put his mug down, a look of confusion marring his chiseled face. "What? Who? Do I need to beat up the guy?"

She chuckled softly. She loved being in the position to surprise Dan and she had the feeling it wasn't all teasing on his end. Her ego could stand seeing him being a tiny bit jealous. "Maybe. Will Brady's already asked me to go."

"Will? He already has a girl."

"He does. One I like very much."

"But, you'll be my date, right?"

"If you insist," she said, smiling.

"I do." He took up his mug again and sipped as if to say the subject was closed. Erin did the same, keeping both hands wrapped around the mug to keep warm. But in reality, sitting next to Dan was enough to make her sizzle inside.

He turned his attention to her, brushing her hair aside and nuzzling the back of her neck, planting moist delicious kisses there, and her arms broke out in goose bumps.

"Erin," he murmured.

"Hmm?"

"You're beautiful in firelight."

She smiled, and a moment later he wiped it away with a breathtaking kiss. She was in deep and didn't want to get out. She was totally ready for whatever the night would bring.

On a labored groan, Dan pulled her into his lap and turned her so she straddled him. Heat from the fire scorched her face as his kisses continued to flame her body. They were all hands, reaching to pull off each other's clothes. Garments flew through the air and landed who knew where. Bodies brushed, the initial contact so mesmerizing, so intensely beautiful, that it felt new, as if it was their first time.

Dan began touching her naked skin, lapping at her breasts, stroking her thighs, making love to her whole body with his hands, with his mouth. She touched him too, running her hand up and down his firm, ripped torso. He was broad and tough, there was so much of him to touch and the flat of her palms explored every inch of him.

The fire blazed and crackled, the only other sound heard above their gritted moans. Erin gave Dan her all, openly loving him with a freedom she'd once kept hidden and reserved. Her love for him was different than what she'd felt for Rex. Now she knew what real love felt like. Even though it wasn't returned, it still hummed in her heart and gave her a tiny shred of hope. In the moment. While her rational side was put on hold.

Don't think, Erin. Just feel.

And that's what she did. She felt every tingle, every jolt, every earth-shattering second of his lovemaking. The threads of the rug tickled her back as he laid her down beside the hearth. He came over her, a tower of a man silhouetted in shadows, so handsome and powerful, and she watched as he sheathed himself. She kept her focus on him as he nudged her legs apart, caressing her core, making sure she was ready and she held her breath as he sank inside, joining their bodies.

"Ah, sweetness," Dan murmured reverently, as if it was the best feeling in the world.

"Dan," she whispered softly, reaching up to touch the gruff stubble on his face. Firelight reflected off his ocean-blue eyes, making them gleam and in the next moment, he was moving inside her, filling her up and touching the sensitive layers welcoming him deeper.

Dan's body encompassed her and she began touching him, grazing his shoulders, sinking her fingers into his back, roaming, seeking, owning. He was hers right now, fully and completely and she relished every second with him.

And when they climaxed, reaching a solemn, soul-pounding peak, cries poured out of their mouths in unison, beautifully sweet, sensual sounds that echoed against the walls.

"Erin," he said, brushing hair from her cheeks and dotting her face with quick loving kisses. "You are incredible."

"Ditto," she said and giggled at her use of that dated term.

"Ditto?" He laughed too and grabbed her around the waist and rolled her on top of him. They lay there skin to skin, body to body, smiling and staring into each other's eyes.

She knew she was more to Dan than his bed buddy. She could see it in his eyes, but Dan had been wounded, maybe beyond repair, and that made her sad suddenly.

"Hey, what's wrong?" he asked, picking up on her mood.

I'm going to miss you. "Nothing." She put on a smile. "Everything's good."

"You sure?"

She nodded and just like that, the fire that had blazed so hot died out, the embers lending zero heat, and she trembled.

"You're cold. Let's get you into bed."

Dan didn't wait for her to answer, he simply picked her up and carried her to the bedroom.

Dan woke before Erin, his eyes opening to a stream of new dawn light working its way through the shutters. She was cuddled up beside him, her citrus clean scent mingling with his body heat, creating a unique blend of sated sex and sweet woman. Her passion was addictive and something he never wanted to let go.

He'd never craved a woman like this. Hell, he had to admit that being with Erin meant more than physical satisfaction. She was fun, and good and smart and all those traits made something as simple as a ride on horseback into a monumental memory.

Watching her sleep, her breaths steady and slow and peaceful gave him a sense of belonging that he'd not experienced before. He wanted this woman in his life. He could deal with that, because she was leaving in a month's time and though it would be hard, he would have let her go.

Wanting was one thing.

Needing was another.

He didn't do need. Not ever again.

He closed his eyes to squeeze away the pain he'd felt after his mother left. She couldn't cope with having kids and a family life. She needed something different and often Dan wondered if he was cut from the same cloth. Had he inherited her inability to commit or had her leaving molded him into that kind of man?

Erin stirred, turning away from him, and he unlatched his arms from her waist. "Sleep, baby," he whispered and rose quietly, tucking her in tight to keep her warm.

He padded softly to the bathroom and closed the door. Without hesitation and trying to make as little noise as possible, Dan ran the water in the shower and stepped inside to a brisk morning wake up. He deliberately ran a lukewarm shower in the mornings to keep his wits sharp and focused at the start of the day.

After he dried off, Dan wrapped the towel around his waist and went in search of a toothbrush Erin recently kept handy for him. He couldn't find the dang thing, and as he shuffled things out of the way, he noticed a long rectangular box sticking out behind several bottles of lotion.

Pregnancy test.

He blinked several times and ten questions raced into his head. His chest pounded and his breaths became short labored bursts. What was going on? Was Erin hiding something from him? They'd been cautious, hadn't they?

He couldn't let this go. This had a direct effect on both of them. As he exited the bathroom, he held the test in his hand, and then sat down on the bed beside her. The mattress dipped and she stirred again. She seemed to sense him sitting there and her eyes opened slowly. Adjusting to the light, she squinted a bit and as she focused on him, she gave him a sweet smile.

"Morning."

"Mornin', sweetness."

"You're up early."

He nodded. "I am. Took a shower."

"Without me?"

He let that comment go. "How are you feeling this morning?"

"I'm perfectly fine. What's up?"

"Uh, is there something else you want to tell me?"

She blinked and stared at his somber face. "What do you mean?" She scooted up in the bed, rested her back to the headboard and covered her bare skin with the sheet.

She was fully awake now, her eyes wide and questioning.

He held up the pregnancy test. "I found this in the cabinet while I was looking for a toothbrush."

Her cheeks flamed, color rising rapidly on her face. "Oh, Dan."

"What's going on? Do you think you're pregnant?"

"No. Yes. I don't know."

"You don't know?"

She ran her hands down her face, pulling at the skin, and began shaking her head. "The truth is, I'm late. And I bought that as a precaution, but I've been waiting for the right time to take the test. I, uh… Oh, Dan. I wasn't hiding anything from you. I'm just not sure. My life has been kind of crazy lately, you know?"

"I do know," he said, sympathizing with her. "I get that you've been in turmoil, but don't you want to find out, and erase one more unknown in your life?"

"You want me to take the test now?"

"We need to know, Erin, but I won't pressure you. Too much," he said, unbelievably calm considering his gut was churning at breakneck speed. He could become a father. He could have a child. Something he'd never considered for himself. Something that should scare him silly, but Erin was the one who needed comfort, not him, so he kept his cool and became the voice of reason. "Whatever the outcome, you're not in this alone."

"Thank you for that. I think you're right. We should find out."

"Together?"

"Yeah, together." She sighed and gave her head a nod, a sudden determined look beaming in her eyes. She offered up her palm and he laid the box in her hand. "Give me a few minutes."

Minutes, which seemed like hours later, the bathroom door opened and Erin walked out, holding the pregnancy stick. He stared at her, her face giving nothing away. "Take a look," she said. "I think you'll be relieved."

He gave it a glance. "It's a negative reading."

"I'm not pregnant."

There was no such relief in her voice. Instead she'd spoken softly, her tone resigned.

He had to tread lightly here, her emotions were important to him, and hurting her was never something he wanted to do. He wasn't about to jump for joy. It surprised him how the relief he felt mingled with a measure of disappointment. How, if he had been the right kind of man for her, he would've been happy to have a baby. Erin's baby. It would mean that she'd stay, that they'd build a life together for the sake of the child. But now, they could go on the way they'd been going, enjoying their time together until she had to leave.

He wasn't heartless. He'd miss her terribly, but now he knew what his future held, and that was something he needed to know at all times. "At least we know now."

She nodded. "Yes, at least we know."

There was a touch of sorrow in her voice, and Dan realized something. Erin loved children. He knew how much she'd loved being nanny to little Faye Brady. She was a natural, and she would've made an amazing mother to their child. But she'd be a mom one day, he was sure, and she'd be happy in the role of wife and mother.

That disappointment he experienced a moment ago came rushing back stronger now. How had he gotten in so deep so fast? "Come back to bed. Let me hold you."

"You want to cuddle?"

A damn chuckle escaped, not that any of this was funny. "Don't sound so surprised. We've cuddled before."

"True, and I think you're an expert at it. But I think I need some time alone right now."

"Are you sure, sweetness?"

"Yes, I'm sure. I'll take a rain check on that cuddling."

"Anytime."

Dan dressed quietly, gave Erin a long reassuring kiss and walked out the door, a hollow feeling eating at his gut as he started his car and drove away.

Eight

"Just break off little chunks of butter, and squeeze the flour and butter between your fingers. It's a trick I learned from the Baking Channel and it works every time," Chelsea said to Erin as they stood next to each other in Chelsea's kitchen. It was the day before Thanksgiving and Erin was here to help bake the pies for the Cattleman's Club dinner. "The pie crust always comes out really tender that way."

"For you, maybe," Erin said. "I've never baked a pie from scratch before. My expertise is sticking a frozen pie in the oven and hoping the crust doesn't burn."

Chelsea laughed. "You're doing great, Erin. And I'll show you a trick later and you'll never burn another crust."

"From your lips to God's ears."

"I'm glad you decided to come over this morning and help me make these pies. It's more fun doing this with a friend."

Erin blew a wayward strand of hair off her face. "Just how many are we making?"

"Six."

"Six? Oh my goodness. That's enough to feed the entire town."

"Yeah, something like that. I was elected to bake the pies for TCC's Thanksgiving dinner. And we're making cookies too. I hope you didn't have hot and heavy plans with my brother today."

"Nope. Not a one. Today is a good day to wrangle me into baking with you."

"Is that so? So what's my brother up to today?"

"He texted he had a pile of work to catch up on today. I probably won't be seeing him."

"Really? Hmm."

"What?"

"It's just that you two are sorta perfect together."

"Sorta perfect? What does that mean, Chelsea?"

"It's just that Dan's been happy lately. Happier than I've seen him in a long time. He doesn't tell me much, but I can hear it in his voice. And when he mentions your name, his voice goes gooey soft."

"Nothing on Dan is gooey soft," she blurted, then slapped her hand to her mouth. "I didn't mean..."

Chelsea threw her head back and laughed. "TMI, Erin."

"I know, I'm sorry. I keep forgetting he's your brother."

"But you do like him?"

"Yeah, I do. He's an amazing man. But—"

"I know. He can be attentive and aloof all at the same time."

"You got that right, sister." Erin put both hands into the bowl and squeezed and molded the pie dough. "So what kind of pies are we making?"

"Cherry, apple, pumpkin, of course. And pecan. It isn't Texas if we don't have pecan pie. It's Dan's favorite."

"I didn't know that."

"We grew up on pecan pie. Of course, ours were store-bought. We didn't have a mother around to do any baking for us. But Dad tried his best. And we managed okay."

"So now you're making up for it, right, Chels?"

"Yep, six pies for our TCC family. But you're gonna make Dan his favorite."

"No way. What if I screw it up?"

"You won't. I'll be instructing you all the way. And Dan will enjoy it all the more knowing you made it for him."

She didn't have the heart to refuse Chelsea. She'd been such a good friend to her and she loved being included in the Thanksgiving festivities.

"Trust me, you'll do fine," Chelsea added. "Look at that dough you just made. It's perfect. Now gather it all up and roll it out."

Erin wielded the rolling pin, getting better and better at smoothing out the dough to an eighth of an inch thickness, all the while copying what Chelsea was doing beside her. They made a good team, cutting up apples, making cherry filling, opening a can of pumpkin and finally lightly roasting pecans. When they were through, hours had passed and both of them were dotted in flour and slightly exhausted.

"That's hard work," Erin said, slashing her arm across her brow.

"Yes, but look at the gorgeousness of our pies."

"I have to admit, they are pretty, all golden brown and sweet smelling."

"We done good."

"Yes, and it was fun," Erin admitted.

"It's past time for lunch. I'm starving," Chelsea said.

"I wish I was. I taste-tested all the pie fillings."

"You need to eat, my friend. Don't forget, we have cookies to bake this afternoon."

"Okay, nourish me," she said. "I should eat something that's not full of sugar."

"I've got chicken salad in the fridge."

"Sounds good to me. So what kind of cookies are we baking later?"

"Chocolate chip, oatmeal raisin and snickerdoodles."

"Is that all? Piece of cake," Erin said.

Chelsea grinned at her snarky comment. "Oh, and I almost forgot, chocolate fudge macadamia nut."

"I know, Dan's favorite, right?"

"Well, honestly that guy can pack it in. He loves them all."

"Well, at least he loves something," Erin muttered under her breath and slanted Chelsea a look, hoping she hadn't heard her comment.

"I hear you. Dan's a bit of a hard case. But I know he cares deeply for you."

Erin dropped the pretense. Chelsea was fast becoming one of her best friends and she couldn't stand not being open with her. "Sure, he cares for me, Chels, but that doesn't make my world go round."

"What would?" she asked, softness entering her eyes.

"I've fallen for him."

"Oh, I didn't realize it's gone that far."

"He pretty much told me from the beginning he's not into permanent relationships. So doesn't that make me a dope for not listening to him?"

"No, it makes you human." Chelsea took her hand and squeezed gently. "Dan's a great guy and I love my brother dearly, but he has hang-ups. Rightfully so, since after my mom left and Dad died, Dan took the reins and practically raised us. It was a lot for him, and he never faltered on his duties at Hunt and Company, either."

"He's got all he needs," Erin said, wistfully.

"I don't think so. He needs more in his life. Like I told you earlier, you two are perfect together."

Chelsea gave her a hug she sorely needed. Chelsea didn't know about the non-pregnancy, but Erin was still smarting about it. A part of her would've loved having Dan's child. The realization of how disappointed she was had dawned on her the second Dan walked out her door yesterday. She'd shed tears, her heart breaking at what could have been. An unwanted pregnancy wasn't ideal in any case, but that was the thing. She would've welcomed the news, had she been carrying his child. "Obviously we're not."

"*Obviously*, my brother needs a swift kick in the ass. As do others."

"You're talking about Maverick."

Chelsea nodded, a somber look on her face. "Yeah, him."

"A kick in the ass is way too easy for him," Erin said. "I'd like to see him with a permanent place in prison."

"It's hard to get over, isn't it, Chels?" Erin asked. Though she'd been violated too, by a man who lied and betrayed her, Chelsea's ordeal seemed more painful. To have her privacy invaded like that for all the world to see?

"I can't even begin to tell you what goes through my mind sometimes. I feel like I've been personally assaulted. It's almost physical. Even though I put up a brave front, it still hurts. But you know, it's Thanksgiving and I don't want to let him ruin my holiday."

"You're absolutely right. Let's not give him another thought. Besides, you mentioned you were going to feed me."

"I most certainly am. I need to fuel you up for cookie making." Chelsea opened the fridge and pulled out a bowl of chicken salad, her mood lightening up a bit.

"I'm only slightly better at baking cookies, than making pies. Fair warning."

"I'm so not worried." Chelsea filled two plates with chicken salad and sourdough rolls and brought them over to the table. "You're good at everything you do."

"Thanks and I mean that."

"You're welcome. Now let's have a seat, take a load off and eat our lunch."

Erin was grateful for the distraction, the friendship and the meal.

Six pies and eight dozen cookies later, Erin plunked down on Chelsea's sofa, almost too exhausted to put pizza to mouth, but the scent of garlic and pepperoni tempted her growling stomach enough for her to lift a piece out of the box and take a bite. "Oh, yum," she said.

Chelsea sat on the other end of the sofa, facing the flat screen television flashing a scene from the iconic holiday movie, *Miracle on 34th Street*. "Oh, that's good," she said, chewing her own cheesy piece of pizza. "Nothing like pizza and a Christmas movie to relax you."

"I know, right?"

"Thanks again for all your help. It's a daunting job but—"

"Somebody's got to do it."

She chuckled along with Chelsea. "I can't imagine all those desserts going after eating a big turkey meal."

"Believe me, they'll go. The club gets a big crowd

on Thanksgiving. I'm sorta wondering if we shouldn't have more."

"More what?"

She gestured with her palms up. "Everything."

"Bite your tongue, Chelsea."

"Yeah, you're right. I'll shut up now and watch the movie."

Two bites later, Chelsea's phone chimed. "I bet it's Brandee. We text wedding stuff all the time," she said. "Excuse me a sec."

Chelsea was going to be Brandee's maid of honor. She'd talked about the Christmas wedding on Brandee's Hope Springs Ranch as they'd baked this morning. According to Chelsea, Shane Delgado, the groom, was a dreamboat. It all sounded so romantic and sweet.

But as Chelsea looked at the screen, reading the text, she shook her head. "It's not Brandee, after all. It's Dan. My brother's on his way over. He says he needs to speak to me about the case."

"Really? Maybe he's on to something." Erin sat upright and grabbed her purse. "I should go."

"No way. You're a part of this too. You don't have to run off. Dan won't mind you being here."

But she did. After last night, she found she needed time to sort out her feelings. Whenever Dan was around, her thought process faltered. She stood up. "But it's getting late. I really should be going."

There was a brisk knock on her door. "That was fast," Chelsea said, glancing toward the front door. "And please don't rush off. Dan will be glad to see you."

It would look weird if she chose to leave the second Dan arrived. Not that he'd given his sister much notice. She figured siblings could do that to each other, not stand on ceremony and show up at a moment's notice. "Here, please pause the movie," she said, handing Erin the remote. Erin sank back down on the sofa, pushed the button and froze an image on the screen of a department store Santa talking to a little girl.

"Something smells good in here," Dan said, his voice carrying into the room.

"Cookies, pies and pizza. Take your pick," Chelsea said.

Erin stood up and turned to give him a smile. "Hello, Dan."

"Hey, Erin," he said in that deep baritone, and her heart did a little flip. He looked good, as always, but his eyes were rimmed with red, as if he really had worked his butt off today. "I didn't know you'd be here."

"Chelsea invited me this morning."

"You mean, she conned you into baking with her?"

"Erin helped me make every single pie and all the cookies today," Chelsea said. "She made you pecan pie, bro. But you don't get to taste it until tomorrow."

"Mean woman."

Chelsea gave her brother a grin. He made a face, and then turned to Erin, his eyes softening. "You made me pecan pie?"

"I tried."

"She did a great job. The pies are beautiful and I know they'll taste great."

"I'm sure they will," he said.

"Hey, Dan, we have plenty of pizza. Have some, if you're hungry."

"I think I will. Didn't have much time to eat today."

He walked over to a chair, and waited for Erin and Chelsea to sit down before he sat down adjacent to them.

"So what's up, big brother?"

He glanced at Erin and then focused back to Chelsea.

"I stumbled upon something today regarding the investigation I thought had merit. I was speaking to a business associate today, you know Thomas Worley, right?"

"Yes, I know him. He's an attorney and a member of TCC."

"Yep, and as we got to talking he mentioned a man from a few years ago who'd been tossed out of the club for unruly conduct. Apparently, this guy was foulmouthed and verbally abusive to some of the women workers. One waitress filed a harassment claim against him, but it turned out he was Brentley Jamison, the son of a US congressman, so he was quietly ejected from the club and his records were wiped clean. Tom doesn't know what happened to the guy and he didn't represent either party so he was free to tell me about it. It could lead somewhere, so I gave all the information I had to Royal PD and ran it by Gabe Walsh."

Dan explained to Erin that Gabe, being ex-FBI and owner of his own personal security firm, The Walsh Group, was more than capable of getting to the bottom of this.

"Chels, I thought maybe you might know something about this guy? Have you ever met Brentley Jamison?"

"No," Chelsea said. "I've heard the name, of course. His father was in Congress a long time, but I never met either one of them before. Still, it's worth a try."

Dan began nodding. "This guy's under the radar and it's worth checking into. They should know something in a day or two. He can't be hard to track down."

"Thanks, Dan," Chelsea said. "I know you both have tried hard to find the jerk."

Erin nodded. "I hope it's sooner rather than later."

"Yeah, me too," she said.

Dan reached over to pluck up a piece of pizza and took

three bites, nearly inhaling the food and chewing hard. It made her smile, seeing him enjoying the pizza so much. He polished off another piece quickly and then stood. "I should go. Let you two ladies get back to whatever you were watching on TV."

"Won't you stay?" Chelsea asked.

"I'm beat, sis."

"But you'll be missing out on *Miracle on 34th Street*."

He crinkled his nose. "Say no more, I'm outta here." He gave Chelsea a kiss on the cheek. "Thanks for pizza." Then he swung around to stare into Erin's eyes. "Walk me out?"

Erin rose from her seat. "Of course."

She followed behind him, noting his amazing backside. Dan was built solid but all his pieces were beautifully placed and she'd been privy to touching every inch of him. She wanted to do it again and again, but she couldn't think past the next month, because unless things changed drastically, which was highly unlikely, she'd be gone.

Dan took his soft suede jacket from the coat closet and put his arms through the sleeves. Straightening the collar, he walked to the front door. "You don't have to go outside. It's cold out there."

The wind howled just at the moment as if giving Dan's comment legitimacy. It was cold and late, but she wasn't planning on going home just yet. She was looking forward to watching the movie with Chelsea.

Dan wound his arms around Erin's waist, bringing her up against him, and she glanced behind her to see where Chelsea was. She was discreet enough to keep out of sight.

"I'll pick you up tomorrow at four," Dan said.

She nodded. "Thank you." She put her hands on the

lapels of his fur-lined jacket and stared into his eyes, and a moment later his mouth came down on hers. The kiss brought warmth and tingles, but it ended far too soon. Was it because his sister was in the other room? Or was Dan finally realizing that she wanted more from him than he was willing to give? She was too tired to dwell.

"Good night, sweetness," he said, and he walked out the door. She watched him saunter to his car and then turn, giving her a look of longing and maybe regret, it was hard to tell. When he put up his hand she waved back and then closed the door.

She blinked several times, noting something different in Dan tonight. A knot formed in her stomach and once again her heart ached, even though having Dan's baby would've been beyond complicated and blown up her list of Never Do's while in Texas.

"Hey, you alright in there?" Chelsea asked, coming around the corner to face her.

"Yeah, I'm fine. Are you ready to finish the movie?"

"Are you?" Chelsea pinned her with a curious look.

She put on a smile. "Sure, I'm ready for a little holiday cheer."

"Happy Thanksgiving, Mom."

"Same to you, honey. Oh, we miss you dearly." Erin loved hearing the sweet lilt in her mother's voice. It was hard being separated from her family during the holidays. "Tell me you've got wonderful plans for Thanksgiving, sweetheart."

Wonderful? She didn't know how wonderful it'd be if her instincts were right and Dan was truly backing away from her. But her mom didn't know anything about Dan yet. And she felt guilty about that. "I think it'll be a nice day. Yesterday, I helped my friend Chelsea make pies and cookies at her house. Chelsea, her brother Dan, and I are all going over to the Texas Cattleman's Club for a Thanksgiving feast later this afternoon. Will and Faye will be there, and Will's new girlfriend too. I think it's going to be a large gathering."

"That sounds lovely, but next year, I hope we'll spend the holiday together."

"I'd like that. Remember, I'm going to see you right after the first of the year."

"That's right. Your dad and I can't wait."

"So where are you having dinner tonight?"

"Sonya and Adam Marino invited us over to their house. They're marvelous cooks as you know, and we always have a pleasant time with them."

"Pleasant?" She lowered her voice. "You mean until Dad gets grumpy with all of their grandchildren running around, getting underfoot."

"I heard that," her father chimed in.

"Your father's right here listening in, and they have five little ones," her mom answered.

She smiled. "Hi, Dad."

"Hi, sweetheart. And I'll have you know I love children, but five under age five, gets a bit crazy. Even your mother admits that. Right, Eloise?"

"Well…now that you mention it, Chuck," she heard her mom say. "It's a bit chaotic at times. Not enough to stay away from our good friends though."

"You'll have a great time."

"We hope you do too," her father said. "Love you to pieces."

"Me too," she told them. "Have a great day and we'll talk soon."

After the phone call, Erin couldn't stop thinking about how much in love her parents were. Their love filtered down to her, making her feel special and honored and humbled all at the same time. She'd really been lucky having two great parents and she never begrudged them their retirement time together. It gave Erin some freedom to seek her own dreams.

At least she'd mentioned Dan to her parents, though in a way that wouldn't brook any inquisition. She didn't know what she'd tell them about Dan. She'd picked up this amazing guy one night at a saloon and they were having a month long fling?

No, that wouldn't wash.

So she'd kept them in the dark about a man she had come to love. A really great guy who'd been terribly hurt as a boy and sadly whose scars ran deep. Maybe too deep for her to break through.

Erin moved to the closet and perused her wardrobe. She hadn't done a lot of shopping in Texas, and now she was kicking herself about that. She had no clue how to dress for a Thanksgiving dinner at an elite club. Was it formal, semiformal or casual?

She made a quick call to Chelsea to get some advice on what to wear to a Cattleman's Club holiday shindig and after her conversation, Erin felt better about her choices.

She hung up the phone and showered, washed and styled her hair, leaving it down and using the curling iron to make big barrel curls. She gave her hair a fluff and looked in the mirror, satisfied with the results, and then walked to her closet and picked out the one little black dress in her closet, that worked for special occasions like this. She selected her jewelry, a single long strand of silver loops with matching earrings, and set it all out on her bed. Done.

The weather was chilly so she hadn't gone for a run this morning, but now she wished she had. She had two hours to kill before Dan picked her up, so she donned her pink chenille robe, grabbed her iPad Mini and curled up on the chair near the fireplace to finish the mystery she'd started before she'd met Dan. She hadn't been sleeping well lately and soon her eyes grew heavy and she closed them, resting her head against the back of the chair.

Loud pounding startled her right out of the nice dream she was having. Her eyes opened and it took her a few seconds to finally get her bearings. "Oh no," she said, her head coming out of a fog.

The knocking now came with Dan calling her name. "Erin?"

She rose from the chair and walked over to the door, yanking it open. "Dan, I'm so sorry. Have you been out there long?"

"A while," he said, taking in her robe and disheveled appearance.

Self-conscious, she tightened the lapels on her robe and stroked a hand through her hair. "I'm so sorry. I don't know what happened, I was reading and I must've dozed off."

"No problem," he said, stepping through the doorway. "There's no rush."

And she was finally able to gawk at him, dressed in crisp dark slacks and a silver-gray shirt covered by a black Western sports jacket, a black felt hat on his head and polished-to-a-shine snakeskin boots. "You look… yummy."

He grinned, eyeing the ties on her robe. "Get dressed, before I make us really late."

"Aye, aye," she said, saluting. "I'll be just a few minutes." Yet, a big fat thrill ran through her system at his suggestive comment.

She rushed into her bedroom, glad she had the foresight to pick out her clothes in advance. She slipped her robe off, put her bra on and turned around to pick up her dress. Dan called from behind the door, "You need help with the zipper, I'm on it."

She chuckled and a flash of heat rose up her throat. "I'll let you know."

She shimmied into her dress and reached up, reached down, and couldn't quite get to the middle of her back. Darn it. She really did need help with the long chic zipper doubling as an embellishment for the dress.

"Uh, Dan?"

The door opened and he faced her, her hands lifting her hair up and out of the way, and she turned around to give him access to the zipper. "Guess I do need help."

He came up behind her and she sniffed the very subtle, very masculine scent of his cologne. It was unique to him, probably something only rugged manly men wore, and it did things to her immediately.

Dan took his time zipping her up, inch by inch, careful with the lacy material, but he didn't touch any other part of her body, he didn't nibble on her throat, didn't kiss her at all, instead he backed away as soon as he was through. "There you go."

A sliver of disappointment wormed into her belly. Was it because they were running late? She was getting a weird vibe from him lately and it worried her.

"Thanks."

She slipped her feet into black heels and added the silver necklace she'd picked out.

"Do you have a coat?" he asked.

"I do." She grabbed her fur-trimmed coat, and slung her purse over her shoulder. "I'm ready."

"You look beautiful," he said.

He was saying all the right things, but...

"We should head out now. After you." He gestured with a sweep of his hand and she walked out of the cabin, Dan following behind.

As soon as Erin stepped foot inside the Cattleman's Club, she was in awe of the decorations. The entire place spoke of Thanksgiving. Autumn color wreaths decked with burnt orange, gold and purple leaves hung on the walls, plump ripe pumpkins sat on hay bales, fresh herbs flavored the air and overflowing cornucopia occupied the tables in the lobby area. As they walked farther inside, the waitstaff offered tumblers of mulled wine and Dan promptly grabbed two and handed her one.

She sipped gently, enjoying the new taste. They pressed on to the dining area, which was a whole new experience, from the golden candles casting the room in beautiful light to the fireplace crackling in cozy warmth. The tables were set with fresh autumn flower centerpieces and decorated with little touches adding to the holiday ambience. Christmas music played in the background.

"Wow, if the food's half as good as the decor, I'm gonna gain weight today."

Dan smiled. "It is. The staff prides themselves on their Thanksgiving meal. It's become a tradition at the club."

There were long tables as well as round tables, and they found Chelsea seated at one of the round tables with Will and Amberley and adorable Faye. Brandee was there too with her fiancé, Shane Delgado, and all of them rose as she and Dan approached. Being a part of their Thanksgiving dinner gave her a sense of belonging, a nice way to get to know some of them better.

Amberley held Faye, the baby still wearing a little overcoat, a bubbly pink hooded jacket that made her look exceedingly warm, especially in a room with the fireplace blasting. Will, Amberley and Chelsea each gave her a welcoming kiss on the cheek and introductions were made all around. She chose to sit between Will and Dan, with Chelsea on her brother's side. It was a lively group of people and as others filed in and took their seats, the room grew a bit noisy.

The event coordinator took the microphone at the head of the room. "Welcome everyone. It's our hope here at TCC that all of you will enjoy our abundant Thanksgiving feast and the fantastic desserts made by member Chelsea Hunt and guest Erin Sinclair."

All eyes turned to their table and a round of applause broke out. Erin loved being included, although it was totally unwarranted since Chelsea did all the hard work, yet she was grateful for the acknowledgment. She flashed Chelsea a big smile which was readily returned.

"So eat up everyone and from the staff and administration here at the Cattleman's Club, we wish you a wonderful Thanksgiving."

The room quieted after the announcement and finally Amberley looked at the baby. "Will, I think she's warm enough, she doesn't need the jacket anymore."

"Fine with me," he said, shrugging a shoulder and giving Erin a quick glance.

Hmm, something was up with him.

Amberley unzipped the baby's jacket and removed it down to the onesie the baby was wearing underneath and her eyes immediately teared up, her voice cracking. "Oh, Will."

Everyone turned their attention to the scene, as Amberley's hands began to shake and Will quickly took the baby from her. As he turned the baby onto his lap, everyone was privy to the message printed on Faye's onesie. "Amberley, will you marry my daddy please and be my new mommy?"

Will handed Faye to her. "Watch her a second for me, Erin."

"Certainly," she replied, and Faye fell into her arms and cuddled her neck. Immediately Erin began bouncing the baby on her lap.

Will rose from his seat and then got down on one knee, now garnering the attention of many in the dining room. "Amberley, I love you with all my heart and will until the end of time. Please be my wife, and mother to Faye. We both love you."

He opened a box and presented Amberley with a sparkling diamond ring.

Amberley was nodding her head, tears streaming down her face. "Yes. Yes."

Will placed the ring on her left hand and then rose, taking her along with him, and kissed her for all he was worth, for all the club to see.

Erin's eyes misted up as she rocked the baby. She gave Dan a glance, her heart so open, so ready for this kind of love.

Dan could barely meet her eyes, his filling with regret and a stony resolve that almost sported a frown. He watched her holding Faye, bouncing her, snuggling her up tight and then he glanced away, staring off at some obscure point in the room.

The room exploded in oohs and aahs and a big round of applause. Everyone at the table rose to give Amberley and Will their congratulations. Dan also stood and put out his hand to Will. "Congratulations to both of you," he said. Dan always said the right thing, but Erin would never ever forget the look on his face as fear entered his eyes watching Erin's reaction to the whole scene.

The meal was served and joy abounded around the table for Amberley and Will. Despite Dan's sour mood, Erin couldn't contain her happiness. Little Faye would have a mother and father now to raise and love her, and what a wonderful thing that was. Soon talk of weddings dominated the conversation. Brandee was excited to explain the details to her own wedding plans to a very overwhelmed and thrilled Amberley. "And the reception is going to be in a converted barn on the ranch. We're doing it all up with lights and flowers."

"Sounds amazing," Erin said, finding her excitement contagious.

A moment later, Dan excused himself to get some air and Chelsea gave her a sympathetic look and shrugged.

Erin bit back sweeping sadness, vowing not to allow Dan to ruin her festive mood. But it clung to her anyway, like a spider's web that couldn't be pulled free. She had so little time left with Dan. Would she be able to go another month like this, loving him and not having it returned?

Chelsea slid over to Dan's seat. She gave her a smile and whispered, "Don't give up on him."

Had Chelsea read her thoughts?

"I…won't."

"Good," Chelsea said.

"I'm thrilled for Will and Faye. They both deserve happiness."

"So do you, Erin." Chelsea squeezed her hand.

Dan returned, his face more composed, his eyes unreadable, and Chelsea slid back to her seat and he sat down just as the trays of desserts were being brought around.

"Now you get to try some of everything," Erin said in good cheer, trying to ignore what was happening between them, the sense of dread curling her stomach right then.

Dan nodded, but his eyes were downcast, laden with regret. "I'm sorry, Erin."

She didn't ask for what. She knew why he was sorry. He couldn't, wouldn't, be making any kind of commitment to her. She shouldn't have gotten so heavily involved with him. The heartache wouldn't be worth the memories and she'd been foolish to think she could go into this situation lightly.

And when offered, neither one of them had the stomach to try any of the desserts.

Nine

Usually Dan liked being quiet. Usually he was fine being in his own head, but as he drove Erin home from the Thanksgiving meal, he was finding *her* silence a bit too much to bear. What he'd hoped would be a fun, enjoyable time for Erin at the Texas Cattleman's Club Thanksgiving feast, had turned out to be nothing of the kind.

Erin wasn't happy. He'd disappointed her and unintentionally hurt her in the process. Dan hated that. He'd never been so damn outright conflicted about a woman. He cared for Erin, a great deal, but he couldn't give her what she wanted. The delight he'd seen in her eyes at Will's unique and spontaneous way of proposing to Amberley, how lovingly she'd bounced and cuddled baby Faye in her arms, how she absorbed all talk of weddings and a hope-filled future, was like a mental slap to his face, telling him to wake up.

As he headed for her home, he gave Erin a glance just

as she turned to him with those big gorgeous aqua eyes. Her smile though was sort of sad, or was he reading too much into all of this?

He pulled up to the cottage and parked the car. Erin was already getting out and he rushed around the hood to offer his hand. "Thanks," she said sweetly.

Her hand slipped into his and joy instantly filled his heart. The profound feeling overwhelmed him for a moment and he inhaled sharp and deep. He wasn't ready to let her go, they had another month together. She meant something to him. Something important and he didn't know what to do about it. He wasn't good with commitment and that wasn't about to change. This time of year especially firmed up his feelings on the subject. His mother's walking out on her family right before Christmas and all that had transpired after that, sealed the deal for him.

Erin wasn't a damsel in distress and he certainly wasn't Prince Charming in any way, shape or form. He didn't buy into the happily-ever-after scenario. He'd been scarred, for life.

He took her arm and walked her to the door. She turned her back to him and put the key in the lock. When she spun around, something flashed in her eyes and he was struck by momentary fear. *Of her leaving. Of her staying.*

Man, was he screwed up.

"Erin," he began.

"Shush," she said, her two fingers covering his lips. "Dan, don't say anything."

And then on tiptoes, she replaced her fingers with her mouth. The kiss startled him, heated him and made him want.

"Just come inside," she whispered.

Dan was hopeless to deny her anything, to deny himself more time with this amazing woman. "Sure thing, sweetness," he said, wrapping his arms around her and kissing her until she was breathless. Taking her hand, he led her straight into the bedroom.

Where neither one of them had to say anything more. Where moans and whimpers would be their only forms of communication.

Monday morning, Erin clocked herself at jogging four and a half miles and entered her cottage somewhat exhausted and sweating. She headed for a nice warm shower, reminding herself that November was coming to a quick close. Over the weekend, Erin did some Black Friday shopping with Chelsea. What she didn't find at the stores, she found online over the past few days and took advantage of free shipping from sites that desperately wanted her business. She'd taken long morning runs around the Flying E and spent most of her nights with Dan. He wasn't the same man she'd met at the Dark Horse Saloon. He was more cautious in what he said, more polite and much more determined to keep them from growing closer, to keep a divide between them. The gap was growing larger every day, but the nights were flaming hot. She couldn't quite merge the two in her mind. Obviously, Dan could. He'd showed his passion in every kiss, every touch, every way he made love to her, but then morning would roll around and he'd go back to being aloof and distant, while still being kind and generous.

It was that kindness and generosity that gave her a bit of hope, but was she fooling herself? Was she seeking out something, anything to cling to so she wouldn't have to do what her head was telling her to do? Break it off. Say goodbye. Sooner, rather than later.

But it wasn't only about Dan. She'd promised Will she'd stay through the holidays and she didn't want to miss being with Faye for her first Christmas. The Everetts, who were away for a few weeks, had made sure she knew she could stay as long as she liked in the guest cottage. Besides she didn't have anyone to go home to in Seattle. Her friends, the people she cared about were here.

Her phone rang just as she was drying off. She wrapped herself in the towel and picked up on the fourth ring. "I was beginning to think you weren't home," Dan said, his deep voice making her bones melt.

"Nope, just finishing up a shower after a long run."

"Need some help?"

"I think I got this, Hunt," she said. Dan was an expert at drying her up and then making her wet again. "What's up?"

"Remember when I mentioned the possibility of Brentley Jamison being Maverick?"

"Yes," she said, sobering up. "The guy was a congressman's son, right?"

"I'm sorry to say he's not our guy."

"And how do you know for sure?"

"The police contacted Congressman Jamison and found out his son, Brentley, has been in a drug rehab in California for more than six months."

"But couldn't he still do some damage using a computer or something?"

"Guess not. He's pretty bad off. He doesn't have use of a computer and only approved visitors can see him. He's not our guy, Erin."

"Have you told Chelsea?"

"Yeah. She's disappointed. I guess I shouldn't have mentioned it without something more concrete to go on."

"Chelsea knows you're only trying to help her."

"Thanks for saying that."

"It's true. Chelsea knows you have her back. She appreciates everything you've been trying to do to find the pervert."

"It's frustrating."

"Yeah, life can be like that sometimes."

"So what are you doing tonight?"

"Tonight? I have a hot date with a handsome guy and his two girls."

Dan paused for a moment. "Oh yeah, that's right. You're having dinner with Will."

"And Amberley and Faye," she added.

"Have a good time."

"It should be fun. I miss that little munchkin. And, Dan, thanks for keeping me in the loop with the investigation."

"Sure thing."

She was about to ask him to come over afterward, but held back. She didn't want to seem needy or desperate. Not even the suggestive banter at the beginning of the conversation meant he'd subject her to a late night booty call. That was Dan, being decent and kind. And why she was so much in love with him.

"I'll see you tomorrow night, sweetness. I'll bring dinner."

"Can you bring Lucky too? I miss him."

"Babies and dogs, a guy could get jealous."

If only.

Just minutes later the phone rang again. Erin looked at the screen and then blinked a few times, before picking up. "Hello, Mrs. Lawrence."

"How are you, Erin?"

"I'm doing well."

"That's good to hear. I'm afraid there's a situation that

involves your upcoming job. I know this is very last-minute but we're in a bit of a predicament."

"What is it?" Her heart began to pound. Was she going to lose her job, before she'd even been given a chance? A myriad of emotions ran through her body, the most being panic that she could face unemployment again. A terrible prospect. But if she did, she could stay on in Texas and find work here.

"I'm afraid that the musical director you're replacing went into labor last night, seven weeks early."

"Oh my goodness." This, she didn't expect. "How is she doing?"

"Jody had a baby boy at four this morning. Baby and mom are fine, thankfully, although the baby will need expert care to catch him up to speed. He's a tiny one, but he's doing well under the circumstances as I understand."

"That's a relief," she said, glad for mother and baby. How scary that must've been for the family. But Erin was smart enough to know what was coming next and her stomach began to ache.

"As you might expect, this puts us in a precarious spot. We have no one here to head our winter spectacular and the kids are so looking forward to it. Jody has had them working on the songs and the parents are making costumes. So my question to you is this, would you possibly consider moving up your hire date to first thing next week? That would give you a full week to work with the kids before the performance. I realize it might be difficult or impossible for you to get away so quickly, but we're hoping for a miracle here."

A miracle? Certainly, she couldn't produce a miracle of any kind, but the more she thought about it, the more sense it began to make. She didn't want to disappoint the kids at her school for one. She didn't want to let down the staff at Lincoln Elementary, either, they'd been so generous in offering her the position, basically sight unseen. And mostly, it would solve her dilemma about Dan. She would have to leave Texas eventually and going to work earlier than expected was one kind of solution. She'd be heartbroken, but it might be smarter to leave now, than after another month of seeing him. It had to be better all around to make a swift, clean break. What reason did she have to stay in Texas anyway when she was so sorely needed in Seattle?

She didn't have a rational reason to refuse. At least this way she'd go, knowing she was needed and wanted. She couldn't disappoint the kids. "Miracles happen. At least this one will. I'll come as soon as I can get a flight out. I'll contact you when I arrive back in Seattle."

"Really?" Immense joy sounded in the older woman's voice. "You'll come to work a month early? Oh, I can't tell you what this means to me, the school and the kids. And don't be surprised if we roll out the red carpet for you, you're our hero. I can't thank you enough."

"No red carpet necessary. I'm only too glad to help. I had no real plans for the holiday anyway."

"And now you do."

"Yes," she said. It was a bittersweet situation. "Now I do."

The next day, Erin jogged past the guest cabins on the Flying E, the main house and the livestock that had become a regular sight to her on her morning runs. This was her last full day here, the last time she'd run these paths, the last time she'd breathe in crisp Texas air as she worked her body to the max, feeling the strain of her muscles, the pull of her limbs. She was exhausting

herself deliberately, so she'd think about the pain rack-
ing her body rather than the pain tormenting her heart.

It was working too, and she slowed her pace to catch
her breath. The sky overhead was crystal clear today,
not a cloud to be found. The golden sun was shining but
the air had a bite to it and she relished the cooler temps
calming her revved up body.

Last night, she said her goodbyes to Amberley, Will
and Faye. They vowed to keep in touch no matter what,
and made her promise to come to their wedding. She
was swarmed with hugs and good wishes at her new position in Seattle, one Will had a hand in helping her at-
tain, and she left them feeling better about her decision,
feeling loved.

By the time she got to her cabin, she was walking at a
snail's pace, feeling drained of energy. "You are ridiculous, Erin." Running until she was ready to drop didn't
solve anything. She still had to muster up her courage
and tell Dan her news when he stopped over tonight.
She was not looking forward to it, not looking forward
to the demise of the most wonderful month she'd ever
spent in her life.

She shed her clothes and showered. The hard beads of
hot water revitalized her somewhat, and she toweled off
and stepped into fresh clothes. She combed through her
hair and padded to the closet to pull out her suitcases.
Just the sight of them on her bed made her breath catch.
Robotically, she began to fill them up, and with each gar-
ment she placed inside the darkly lined interior, memories
flooded her mind. She folded her now-infamous outfit
she wore for the bucking bull night at the Dark Horse
Saloon and placed it inside. It was where she'd met Dan
and they'd saved Lucky. She fingered the blouse she'd
worn, smiling sadly.

Next, her horseback-riding-with-Dan pants were placed on top. Beside it she put in her luncheon-with-Chelsea outfit and then added her sexy lingerie. She didn't even want to think about those heated nights with her Texan, her heart was aching enough. Her memories would be locked inside her head for eternity. Boots and other accessories filled another small suitcase and, except for the last-minute things she'd need tomorrow morning for the flight home, she was fully packed.

Thanking Clay and Sophie Everett for letting her stay at his beautiful ranch was next on her list, but the Everetts were still out of town, so she sat down on the sofa, pen and paper in hand, crossed her legs and put a thick *Cowboys and Indians* magazine underneath the paper to compose her thank-you note.

She was very grateful to everyone associated with the Flying E Ranch. They'd welcomed her with open arms, making sure she was comfortable in the cottage/cabin she'd called home for this month. A girl could get used to...

Tears filled her eyes as she penned her letter of thanks and when she was through, she realized how very much this place meant to her. In a sense she'd become a different woman here, someone who took stock in her own capabilities, someone who'd ventured out to take risks and had grown into a stronger person for it. She'd learned to love again too, the real kind of love, not just some whimsical fascination with a man, but to feel deeply inside and know what beamed brightly inside her was true and honest.

Yes, she could look at Dan and say this time with him had been eye-popping. She'd fallen in love and also helped with an investigation. Both had given her joy, but right now, both were ending in disappointment. At least for her.

She sealed the letter to Clay, closing one more door to Texas.

She spent the rest of the afternoon, straightening out the place, putting things back in order. Her mother always told her to leave a place better than when she'd arrived. Well, the cabin was perfect in her estimation, but she did find some wildflowers growing outside and filled a vase and placed it on top of the mantel.

She lit candles in cinnamon and apple fragrances that filled the entire cabin with the spirit of the holiday season. And she baked a quick batch of ready-made cookies. The mingling of scents wafted in the air. The only thing missing was a crackling fire in the fireplace, but she didn't have the heart to go that far.

By five o'clock, the sun was falling into the sky, leaving a dim, murky coolness behind. She was dressed in her favorite outfit, a bulky cream sweater and long black skirt. She wore boots and hustled around the kitchen, until the knock came at the door.

She heard the rumblings of Lucky, his tail swishing against the door, his whimpers in anticipation of being let inside. It made her smile. In that moment, quickly and without regret, she made a decision. It was probably the hardest decision of her life, but if she'd learned one thing by being there in Texas, it was to be strong, and do what you deemed was right. She'd been hiding behind her recent bad relationship too long.

It wasn't going to be easy and if the moment wasn't right, she may very well back out, but at least she had determination on her side. And a sense of clearing the air.

She opened the door and Lucky immediately lunged

for her, nearly knocking her down. She stepped back and found her balance, the dog's front paws on her tummy.

"Lucky, down," Dan commanded.

"No, it's okay, Dan. I missed him too."

She hugged Lucky, kissing the very top of his head and ruffling his fur. "You're a good, good boy," she cooed, in her baby Faye voice.

Dan entered the house, his arms loaded with covered dishes of food, and walked into the kitchen to set everything down. "Dinner," he announced.

"Thanks," Erin said, the dog underfoot as she closed the front door. "Smells wonderful." Not that she had an appetite. She really didn't. She had a lot to say to Dan and her throat was ready to close up any second.

"It's brisket and corn soufflé and creamed spinach. From Hunt and Company Steakhouses. It's one of our signature meals. It was time you tried it."

She sidled up next to him and he turned to give her a kiss on the cheek.

She gave him a small smile, her heart heavy. "I guess it is."

"One of these days, we'll go to my best restaurant in Dallas and enjoy a quiet candlelit meal."

She was going into Dallas tomorrow. Dallas Fort Worth Airport, to be exact. Will had given her an open-ended ticket when they'd first arrived. She never thought she'd be leaving without him and Faye but fate had been on his side.

Unlike with her.

Dan began opening the covered dishes. "Are you ready to eat, sweetness? I'm kinda starving. Missed lunch today."

"Sure, we can sit down and eat."

She was rescued, given a bit of a respite from having

to tell Dan she was leaving. They went about putting plates on the table, filling glasses of iced tea and dishing up the food. It was uncanny how efficiently they worked together in the kitchen. And it was hard to think this was going to be the last time.

Once everything was set out, Dan pulled the chair out for her, always the gentleman. She took her seat and glanced at the food.

"You first," he said.

She put a sparse amount of food on her plate. Everything truly did smell delicious and to be polite, she would eat some of it. Dan filled his plate, growled about digging in and he began eating. Every so often, he would give Lucky a taste and the happy boy's tail swished back and forth like an out of control metronome. It was such a simple thing, but so sweet to see Lucky at Dan's heels.

She nibbled on her meal and sipped her iced tea.

"I made cookies," she said after the meal was finished. "Would you like dessert now?"

He leaned way back in the chair and patted his firm-as-granite belly. "Can we wait a bit? I practically inhaled the meal and can't think about eating another bite."

"Sure."

"Want a fire?" he asked.

"Uh, no." She didn't think she could sit by the fire with him tonight.

"What's up? You're pretty quiet tonight."

"Actually, can we go sit in the parlor? I have something to tell you."

His eyes pinned to hers, and he gave her a nod. "Sure thing."

He waited for her to rise and took her hand. She squeezed her eyes closed, absorbing his touch, the way he took control and led her to the sofa. Lucky wasn't far behind. She sat and Dan sat beside her. Lucky roamed the room and then after circling an area a few times, found a comfy spot on the rug and nestled down.

In typical Dan style, he didn't say a thing. He simply waited for her to speak. So this had to be it. She couldn't procrastinate, she couldn't stall any longer. All the words she'd practiced in her head didn't come when she finally opened her mouth. "I, uh, I've been called in to work earlier than expected. The woman I was replacing at the school went into premature labor. I don't have much choice. They really need me."

Dan began nodding his head, watching her carefully. "How soon?"

"My flight leaves tomorrow."

"Tomorrow? Oh man," he said, running his hands down his face. "That soon?"

"Yeah, that soon." She spoke quietly. "I didn't expect this."

"No, I didn't, either. They can't do without you for a few more weeks?"

"No, they have no one else to fill in. And since they hired me, I'm sort of obligated to go. There's this winter concert the children have been working on all semester. I can't disappoint the students."

"But you can disappoint me?" He gave her a look, his eyes pinning her down.

"I don't want to disappoint anyone, Dan. We both knew this day would eventually come. I'm just…leaving sooner than we expected. I really don't want to go."

At all. But she couldn't tell him that. She couldn't reveal how breaking up with him, was also killing her inside. That she still held a shred of hope that there'd be a

Hollywood ending, where he took her by the hand, kissed her senseless and told her not to leave him. Ever.

"So this is it." It wasn't a question, but a declaration. To his credit, he hung his head and sat immobilized in his seat. The air was still, Lucky's breathing the only sound in the room.

She hated to say the words that would end it, so she held her tongue and waited.

After a few moments, he spoke. "Erin, it's a rare thing to be able to work in a field you love. And it's a great opportunity for you. Once I heard you play, I realized music has to be in your life."

She nodded, hiding her grief. She could argue that music was always in her life. And that she could teach music anywhere, not just in Seattle.

She had to lay her cards on the line. Dan had to know her feelings, even if she didn't come right out and say those three little words. "Dan, this past month has been wonderful. I want you to know, I don't look at my time with you as a casual fling. Being w-with you, meant s-something special to me. *You* mean something special to me."

"You mean something special to me too, sweetness." Dan covered her hand and tugged her close. His lips came down on hers and his kiss drew her into a mix of mind-blowing pleasure and unfair torture. She loved him. She didn't have the courage to tell him, but he had to know, to see how she gave him everything she had to give, to feel the way she responded to him.

Unable to stand it another second, she pulled away from him. "Sorry," she said, holding back tears. "This is hard."

"For me too."

Dan pushed his hands through his hair. "Let me take you to the airport tomorrow."

"No." She didn't have to think twice about it. A tear-ful public goodbye at the airport would be too difficult and quite possibly humiliating. "But thank you for of-fering."

"You're sure?"

"Yes. I'm sure." She gulped air.

"Okay."

And they sat there on the sofa for long moments qui-etly, Dan taking her back in his arms and holding her tight. It felt so right, but obviously Dan didn't seem to think it right enough.

"I can stay a little longer, if you'd like," he whispered. "Unless you have packing to do."

She took half a second to think about it. She never wanted him to leave, but she mustered her courage, aware that the longer he stayed, the harder it would be. "I have some things to do," she said diplomatically. It was a bold-faced lie, but necessary for her sanity.

"Then I'd better go."

She gave a slight nod. Staring into his handsome face, she committed it to memory and tried not to tear up. She would probably never see Dan again. Once they parted, they would walk separate paths, as if they'd never met. As if this short time was merely a blip in their lifetimes. How terribly sad.

He rose from the sofa, a deep sigh pushing out of his chest. The sound resonated and her sorrow was almost tangible. He reached for her and arm in arm they walked to the door. "I'll miss you, sweetness," he said, turning to face her as he put his jacket on.

"Dan," she began, but the words choked in her throat.

He enveloped her into his arms, giving her a big bear hug. Her beast of a man was leaving, exiting her life. Even though, she was the one going, it felt the other way around. He hadn't asked her to stay. He hadn't declared his love. He wouldn't and it was a hard pill to swallow.

As he bent his head and claimed her mouth in another tantalizing kiss, she gripped the lapels of his jacket and gave him a kiss back that he would hopefully never forget. When they finally broke apart, she felt the loss down to her toes.

"Call me if you change your mind about the airport," he whispered.

She wouldn't. "Okay, but I don't think so."

"Safe travels, sweetness," he said.

And then with Lucky by his side, he stepped out into the cold evening and walked down the path that led to his car. Halfway there, he stopped dead in his tracks, dipping his head as if eyeballing the ground. A few seconds passed. Her heart pounded, wondering what he was thinking, what he was doing.

And then he sighed heavily, lifted his head and resumed walking to his car. It was painful seeing him go, ending it this way. Her hopes died then and as he opened the car door, he looked her way and waved, his beautiful face partly hidden in the shadows of night.

She waved back, giving him a last smile.

It was over.

She closed the door and amazingly didn't fall apart watching Dan drive away. No, she'd save that for later tonight. Right now, she had something else to do.

She picked up her cell and called her new friend. The call went straight to voice mail and Erin was once again disappointed. Maybe she shouldn't have waited to tell Chelsea her plans, but she had to tell Dan first before she told his sister about her departure. "Chelsea, hi. It's me, Erin. I'm sorry I didn't reach you. Please call me when you get in. I have something important to tell you."

She'd stop by Chelsea's first thing in the morning to say her goodbyes.

It would be her last heartbreaking order of Texas business, before she boarded the plane headed for Seattle.

Ten

Erin's fingers flew across the piano keys and she nodded her head for the fifth grade class to start singing a rendition of "Winter Wonderland." The lively sounds filled her music room, most of the children singing in the right key and, all in all, their voices blending well in a song perfect for the oldest kids in the school. These children would graduate in less than six months and head off to middle school.

When the song ended, she stood from the piano bench and applauded. "That was wonderful, class." Their singing sounded better than her piano playing. She was rusty, and had come to the school the day after she'd arrived to do some informal practice. It gave her something solid to do, and boy, she really had needed the quality time at the piano.

"Next, let's practice 'Happy to All.'"

She sat down again, gave the class their cue and began

playing. The children's eyes were beaming; they were glad to be out of regular class and spending an hour doing something fun. It was no different when she was in school, only she'd had a true love of music, so coming to music class wasn't only about getting out of academics, it was about her passion.

She wanted to say she felt fulfilled at Lincoln Elementary. She wanted to say, taking this position working with music and children, her two true loves, was her everything. She was new to the school and the faculty here. She vowed to give herself some time to adjust. But right now, the wholeness she once felt teaching music wasn't there.

Her heart was still in Texas. With Dan.

She played the final note on the piano and rose again. "That was pretty good, class. But it needs a bit of work. Some of you aren't remembering the words." She grabbed a pile of printouts of the song. "Here you go," she said, passing them out. "Take this home, study the lyrics and practice it with your parents tonight."

A series of groans followed. "Hey, it's not so bad. It's a fun kind of homework," she said. "I'll see you all tomorrow. Have a good rest of the day."

After she dismissed the class, she found Shelly at the door, smiling. "That was a great practice," she said, stepping into the room. "I came by to see if there's anything else you might need? Anything we can do for you?"

"Hi, Shelly." She glanced around the classroom, the stepped rows and the shelves of musical instruments. Later on today, the fourth graders would practice ringing the bells. "No, I can't think of anything right now."

"So, your first official day is going well?"

"I think so," she said, giving her a smile.

"Great. Well, it's lunchtime. Shall we go grab a bite?"

"Yes."

After she closed up the music room, she walked with Shelly toward the teachers' lounge. As soon as the principal opened the door, Erin was hit with a barrage of twenty staff members all smiling and waiting for her and applauding as she stepped inside. Construction paper signs on the windows exclaimed, Welcome to Lincoln! Many Thanks!

Food was set out on decorated tablecloths, an abundance of salads and sandwiches and desserts.

"I hope this isn't too overwhelming," Shelly whispered in her ear. "The staff sometimes gets carried away. You saved our butts, and we wanted to throw you a welcome party."

"Oh, this is so..." Words escaped her. She *was* overwhelmed. And grateful. "It's really lovely."

And it was. Over lunch, she spent time meeting many of the teachers and staff working at the school. It gave her a sense of balance and perspective. She got an earful about school politics, rules and which parents to watch out for. That last one made her laugh. She'd had run-ins with helicopter parents before, their hovering and over-involvement bordering on obnoxious at times. But she'd met some really amazing parents too, and so it all equaled out.

Erin made a point of thanking everyone for their gracious welcome to the school and when lunch was over, she began walking back to her music room. Her phone dinged. She stopped to read the text coming up from the screen. It was Dan.

How's your first day going? he asked.

It was his third text to her since she'd been back. The first one simply was to make sure she'd made it safely back to Seattle. It wasn't much more than a friendly gesture.

The second one was a one-liner wishing her good luck on her first day on the job. She'd answered him with a short reply.

And now today. She needed a clean break from him. He had no idea how much hearing from him like this was hurting her. No phone calls. No "I'm miserable without you"s. He was trying to be her text buddy. Well, she didn't want his friendship. Or rather, she did but only if that friendship came with more.

She tucked her phone back into her sweater pocket without texting him back. She had to get ready for the fourth graders and the bells. Dan was a distraction she didn't need right now. He'd muddled up her mind and broken her heart enough for one lifetime. She was still raw from missing him, still at odds with his unwillingness to let go of his past. Still sorta mad at him for being dense. She supposed she was going through the stages of breakup grief all at once. Whatever it was, it was painful in a way that she'd never experienced before. She hated that she'd cried herself to sleep for the past few nights.

By the end of the school day, she had chucked away her first-day jitters. That at least was a positive thing. She'd made it through and it wasn't terrible. In fact, the day went smoothly enough and the welcome party was an added surprise. She could feel good about all of that.

As she got into her car, a few of the teachers waved to her in the parking lot and she smiled and waved back. They were nothing if not really friendly and she was lucky to be a part of this school.

But, even with spending the entire day singing fun winter songs, teaching the younger ones the words and playing tunes on the piano, she wasn't in much of a festive mood.

Hours later, Erin sat on her bed in her tiny studio

apartment eating almond chicken and noodles she'd picked up from China East, her favorite restaurant. It was dark in the city, the gloomy Seattle weather casting shadows earlier than usual. She was already cozy in her jammies and ready to turn on the television when her cell phone rang.

Immediately, she conjured up an image of Dan and her heart thumped hard in her chest.

Setting her food aside, she picked up the phone and didn't immediately recognize the number. "Hello."

"Hello, Erin. This is Rex. Don't hang up the phone, please."

Her stomach churned. Just the sound of his voice brought back bad memories. "Why are you calling me?"

"I need to speak to you. It's important."

She had a mind to shut him down, turn off her phone and go about her business, but curiosity was a funny thing. "You have two minutes. Go."

"Dan's been mopey all week," Darla said to Chelsea as soon as she stepped foot inside his house at Hunt Acres.

"Have not," Dan said, in earshot range of the exchange by the front door.

"Well, I'll cheer him up." Chelsea walked farther into the house. "I brought your share of Christmas ornaments. Do you have mine?"

"Somewhere," Dan said. He had no idea where he'd stashed them from last year. Decorating the Christmas tree was the last thing on his mind. He'd been thinking about Erin 24/7 and it was affecting his work, his free time and his life in general. She wasn't always prompt in returning his texts. In fact, his last two to her had gone unanswered. Was she okay? Had she forgotten about him so quickly? No, that wasn't fair. He hadn't given her a reason not to forget about him.

"Such a nice tradition, trading your family's ornaments with each other every year," Darla said.

"We've been rotating them since Dad passed," Chelsea said. "But you're not getting these, big brother, until I get yours."

Darla shot Chelsea a smug look. "I know where they've been tucked away in the garage. I'll go grab them for you."

"Do you need any help?" Chelsea asked.

"Nope, I can manage just fine," she said. "Let me take those off your hands." Darla took the box out of Chelsea's arms. "I'll put them in the spot the tree will go. Hint. Hint. Maybe it'll get you in the holiday spirit," she said and then walked out of the room.

Chelsea followed him into the kitchen and he poured them each a cup of coffee. "Here," he said, handing her a mug. Steam rose up and the strong scent flavored the air. "There are some of Darla's biscuits in the fridge. You can heat one up."

"No, thanks, I've had breakfast, but I might take one to go."

"I hear there's been a break in the case. It couldn't have happened soon enough. What can you tell me?" Dan asked.

"Yeah, well, it is good news. The authorities have a beat on who Maverick is and they're working on it night and day. Apparently, he wasn't so clever not to leave behind a clue. They found a digital footprint on the hard drive discovered in Adam Haskell's car that has led them to break open the case. We should know soon who Maverick is."

"Amen to that," Dan said. "I'd like to see justice done to that guy, in the worst way." He leaned against the counter and took a gulp of coffee.

"Until this guy is behind bars, I won't have closure. I'll never get over the violation, but it'll help knowing the criminal got his due."

He couldn't agree more. At least that was one good thing happening in his life lately.

"Dan," Chelsea said, a sisterly pout on her lips. "You look…miserable. Like you need a giant hug or something."

He rolled his eyes. He'd been avoiding Chelsea this week. His sister's heart was in the right place, but she was also a big pain. Ever since Erin left town, Chelsea had been calling or texting him every day *to see how he was doing.*

As if he couldn't live without Erin.

As if he was in some sort of pain or something.

As if his total lack of concentration had something to do with her leaving town.

"I don't need—"

She wouldn't let get him get the words out. Soon, he found himself wrapped in her arms, and she was giving him consolatory pats on the back. "I know it's hard," she said.

His teeth gnashed. "Sis…shut the eff up, okay?"

"Wow. I didn't know it was that bad."

"Nothing's bad." She could be exasperating at times.

"You let that girl walk out of your life."

"I didn't send her packing. She got a job. A good job."

"Did you ask her to stay?"

"No, and you know why I didn't, so don't pretend innocence on this. I don't do long-term relationships."

"Because you've never met the right woman. Erin wasn't just some girl you were dating. She was your soul mate. She understood you. She made you happy."

"Yeah, the way Mom made Dad happy?"

"Dan, honestly." She chewed her lower lip and gave her head a shake. "Mom never loved Dad. Not in the way that counts. She didn't return the love he'd given her. You can't keep comparing every woman to Mom, especially Erin. You know her heart. You know she's a good person."

"You bake cookies with her one day and suddenly you're an expert on Erin Sinclair."

"We've gotten closer than that. I consider her my friend. She's confided in me and normally I wouldn't betray that confidence, but you need to hear this. She didn't want to leave Texas. Or you. She told me she'd fallen for you."

Dan winced. It was hard enough speaking about Erin with his sis, but to hear her say how much Erin cared, cut a path straight to his heart.

"When was the last time you spoke to her?"

Dan frowned. "She didn't answer my last text."

"Are you telling me you haven't spoken to her, you know, using real words over the phone, since she left? You're just texting her?"

"Yeah, that's right."

"Oh brother," she said, mocking him, saying without saying, he was a real jerk. "Okay, so then, you don't know what's going on with her."

Dan's head snapped up. "What's going on with her? Did you talk to her?"

"Yes, we actually *speak* on the phone," Chelsea said snarkily. "I talked to her last night."

"And?"

Dan's heart began to pound. *Crap.* He wasn't enjoying this conversation. If something was up with Erin, he wanted to know.

"Tell me, Chels." His voice came out more like a plea

than a command. He hated giving his little sis that much satisfaction, but he'd been grouchy ever since Erin cut him off by not returning his text. He'd never felt a loss so great as he had this past week.

"Nothing," Chelsea said, "except that her ex, that Rex guy, is sniffing around again. He's broken it off with his wife for good and wants Erin back. Big-time, from what I understand."

"She wouldn't go back to him," he snapped. "That guy's a real jerk."

Chelsea didn't say anything, only shrugged her shoulders.

"What does that mean?" he asked, his blood quickly coming to a boil.

"It means, all I know is Erin is lonely and hurt and missing you. She's vulnerable right now and when women get that way sometimes they do stupid things."

Dan started pacing the floor, shaking his head.

"But since you don't care… I mean you've pretty much written her off…"

Dan glared at Chelsea. "I do care, damn it. I love her. I love Erin, okay? Nothing's been right since she left."

Immediately, Chelsea's face softened and she smiled.

Dan too felt a softening and a heavy weight being lifted from his shoulders. He loved Erin, probably fell in love with her the second she'd bravely hoisted herself up on that mechanical bull, only he'd been so entrenched in his own resolve not to let any woman hurt him that he'd suppressed those feelings.

He'd been a fool and had pushed away someone who deserved only 100 percent from the man she loved. That man *had* to be him. He was through fighting it. His heart was open now and he vowed to give Erin Sinclair everything he had to give. He only hoped it was enough.

"Dan," Chelsea said, her voice gentle, her smile encouraging. "Don't tell me. Tell her."

"Right," he agreed. Chelsea just might've been shocked at his quick turnaround. "And thanks for not gloating."

"Me?" She pointed to herself. "I wouldn't do that. I'm happy for you, Dan. Erin's perfect for you. Don't lose her."

"I won't. I promise."

He glanced at his watch. "I gotta go. Have things to do, people to see." He gave Chelsea a quick kiss on the cheek. "Thanks, sis, you're the best."

"You might not think so after I tell you this."

"Tell me what?"

Chelsea wrinkled her nose. "Erin listened to Rex for two minutes, then told him where to go and hung up on him."

He laughed. "That's my girl."

"You're not mad at me?"

"You're a sly one, but you sure do know how to get your point across and I'm too damn relieved to be mad at anyone right now."

Dan's nerves were about to split in half as he walked up the steps of Lincoln Elementary School. Distant music and children's singing reached his ears and all he had to do was follow the sounds to find the auditorium.

To find Erin.

He wore his suit for the occasion, a dark jacket over a crisp white shirt, boots and his Stetson planted firmly on his head. He carried a dozen ruby-red roses and inside his pocket was a tiny deep crimson box housing a three-carat diamond ring he hoped Erin would accept. He'd had Raina Patterson from Priceless help him design the ring and he'd put a rush on it. If anything was *priceless* it was Erin and he could only hope he wasn't too late. He'd made a mess of things and he was there to fix it. It helped knowing she'd kicked that Rex guy to the curb, but even if she hadn't, he would fight long and hard for her.

What a dope he'd been.

He stepped into the back of the filled-to-capacity auditorium, wintry snow-laden scenes on construction paper murals decorating the place. On rows of risers, a throng of kids with happy faces and beaming eyes sang their hearts out. The winter concert was in full swing.

His gaze drifted left to the woman gracefully sweeping across the piano keys, making the performance all come together.

His heartbeat sped at the sight of her and he drew deep breaths. God, he hadn't realized until this minute how much he'd missed her. Dressed in a gray-and-snowy-white sweater with a knit cap on her head, she was the best sight he'd ever seen.

She nodded her head and gave the kids their cues, and Dan waited and watched patiently for the performance to end. Class after class came up on stage, looking to Erin for guidance. It seemed like an eternity and finally the performance was over, the risers emptied and the school principal came up to say a few words into the mike.

"Everyone, let's give a big hand to Miss Sinclair for making our Winter Wonderland Concert a huge success. She saved the day and did a fantastic job, don't you agree?"

Erin rose from the piano, waved at the crowd and was met with a round of applause.

Immediately Dan marched down the aisle to face Erin at the front of the auditorium. "She saved me too," Dan said loud enough for the entire room to hear.

Her legs nearly buckled when she saw him and her face registered surprise. "Dan?"

"Hi, sweetness," he said and then bounded up the few steps to the stage. He walked over to her and laid the bouquet into her arms. "For you."

She glanced at the audience—who were now kind of mesmerized by the scene—and then she turned her pretty blue-green eyes to him. "What're you doing here?"

"I came to take my girl home, to Texas."

He removed his hat, dug into his pocket and there before the entire room of children and parents and staff of Lincoln Elementary, took a knee and presented her the custom-made, only for her, glittering diamond ring.

The room erupted in oohs and aahs, and he got the feeling everyone was glued to their seats.

Erin's eyes misted and he hoped that was a good sign. "Oh, Dan."

"Erin Sinclair, I've missed you like crazy. I love you beyond any words I could ever say, beyond any lyrics ever written. I'm here, humbled and honored to ask you to marry me. To be my wife. To take a place beside me at Hunt Acres."

Tears streamed down Erin's face now, and she began nodding her head, her body shaking, almost as much as his was. She reached for him and he rose to look at her beautiful face. "Yes, yes, I'll marry you."

Loud applause broke out around the room. Dan was oblivious to the crowd now, Erin said yes and he quickly took the ring and placed it on her left ring finger.

She stared at it and grinned, her tears flowing freely. Happy tears.

Then she faced the people who witnessed it all, lifting her left hand and wiggling her fingers. "I'm engaged," she said, awe in her voice.

Dan used his Stetson to shield wandering eyes and kissed her silly, grinning and giddy, showing her how much she meant to him. Then he tugged her off stage, the show over, but his life finally beginning.

"I still can't believe you did that," Erin said, hours later. Dan, her dreamboat guy sat next to her on the edge of her bed in her apartment. "You, Mr. Quiet, who doesn't like to draw attention to himself, brought down the house."

"I did, didn't I?" Dan had a perpetual grin on his face and Erin wasn't too far from that, either.

"You laid out your heart to me, Dan. It was…the best proposal ever."

"I love you. I wanted to show you how much."

"You did," she said. "And I love you too."

"The rescuer became the rescued," he said, taking her hand and stroking over her fingers.

"How did I rescue you?"

"Don't you know?" he asked.

She shook her head, not sure what he was getting out.

"You taught me that it's okay to take a risk. To go for it. To do something out of your comfort zone. I was so set in my way of thinking, sure I'd never truly love anyone. I wouldn't allow myself to. And then you came along and I couldn't wrap my head around how much I not only wanted to be with you, but needed to be with you."

"Would've been nice if you'd told me all that."

"I know, and I'm sorry. I should've realized what you meant to me before you left. I should have stopped you from going. I took the coward's way out and I'm beating myself up about that now. But I'm also through with it, all of it. I want you. I love you and I'm at peace, sweetness."

"And why is that?"

"Because I've let it go. Because now I have you. I'm through dwelling in the past. And if I'm being totally honest with you, when you took that pregnancy test, yes, I was scared about it but there was a part of me that was really disappointed. I couldn't find my way to ask you to stay with me but if you were carrying my child..."

"You wouldn't have had a choice. We would've been permanently tied to each other."

"Yeah, and I think I wanted that. I was just afraid to admit it. I want babies with you, sweetness. As many as you want and as quickly as you want."

"Oh, Dan. Yes, I want to have your babies. Soon, real soon."

Dan smiled warmly and claimed her lips in a beautifully sweet kiss, and she closed her eyes, envisioning a future with him, a life of fullness and love and babies.

When the kiss ended, he continued to hold her hand, giving it a squeeze. "Chelsea had something to do with all this too. She can be a devil when she wants to be."

"Oh yeah? How do you mean?"

"She let it slip, intentionally, I'm sure, that your ex was trying to get you back. I, uh, kinda saw red then, hating the thought and realizing that it wasn't just Rex that I didn't want in your life, but any man other than me."

"That's sweet." She stroked his face. "So you faced facts. You loved me."

"Yeah."

"Couldn't live without me?"

"Yeah."

"Wanted to marry me?"

"Yeah." Dan smiled "And don't forget about Lucky. He's been in a funk since you left town."

"How I love that dog. So then, I'm glad Chelsea told you, but the truth is when Rex called me, I felt absolutely nothing for him. When he told me he'd left his wife and wanted me back, I laughed. Seriously laughed at him, and told him to get a life. Without me. I hung up the phone and that was that. I guess I made my point."

"You did. I knew you'd never take him back. You have better taste than that."

She smiled, her heart overflowing. "Yeah, I do. I picked you, didn't I? And I have a confession to make to you. I pretty much knew I wasn't going to stay on at Lincoln after the holidays. They'd been wonderful to me, but that was just it. As great as everyone had been to me, making me feel wanted and welcomed, I still felt like I no longer belonged in Seattle. If I felt that way in a job I really liked, what hope was there for me? My heart was always with you, Dan. And Texas. I was going to come back as soon as I could."

"Wow, really?"

"Yes, I knew I'd never be happy here, while you were there."

"You're a wise woman."

"Glad you noticed."

He laughed and tugged her so they both fell back on the bed. Holding his hand, staring up at the ceiling, all she saw was a bright joy-filled future. Then Dan took her into his arms and kissed her solidly, reaffirming his love for her.

"I can't wait to marry you, Erin."

"And I can't wait to be your Texas bride."

* * * * *

TEMPTED BY THE WRONG TWIN
by USA TODAY *bestselling author Rachel Bailey*

TAKING HOME THE TYCOON
by USA TODAY *bestselling author Catherine Mann*

BILLIONAIRE'S BABY BIND
by USA TODAY *bestselling author*
Katherine Garbera

THE TEXAN TAKES A WIFE
by USA TODAY *bestselling author Charlene Sands*

and

December 2017:
BEST MAN UNDER THE MISTLETOE
by Jules Bennett

"Vivian, you're just asking for trouble."

"That means I don't scare you," she said in a sultry voice.

"You scare the hell out of me because I shouldn't like dancing with you. I shouldn't like flirting with you. I shouldn't want to kiss you. I shouldn't feel anything when our fingers touch, and neither should you."

"For a US Army Ranger, you're a little stuffy."

He caught her around the waist and took long steps, dancing in circles through the terrace doors and outside, where it was darker and cooler.

"Try this for stuffy, darlin'." He pulled her tightly against him and his mouth covered hers as he kissed her. He knew he shouldn't, but he was having more fun with her than he could recall having had anywhere, anytime in the past three years.

* * *

Expecting a Lone Star Heir
is part of the Texas Promises trilogy:
When three military men return to Texas
to fulfill their promises to a fallen comrade,
they find redemption…and love.

EXPECTING A
LONE STAR HEIR

BY
SARA ORWIG

First Published in Great Britain 2017
By Mills & Boon, an imprint of HarperCollins*Publishers*
1 London Bridge Street, London, SE1 9GF

© 2017 Sara Orwig

ISBN: 978-0-263-92843-3

51-1117

Our policy is to use papers that are natural, renewable and recyclable products and made from wood grown in sustainable forests. The logging and manufacturing processes conform to the legal environmental regulations of the country of origin.

Printed and bound in Spain
by CPI, Barcelona

Sara Orwig, from Oklahoma, loves family, friends, dogs, books, long walks, sunny beaches and palm trees. She is married to and in love with the guy she met in college. They have three children and six grandchildren. Sara's 100th published novel was a July 2016 release. With a master's degree in English, Sara has written historical romance, mainstream fiction and contemporary romance. Sara welcomes readers on Facebook or at www.saraorwig.com.

To senior editor Stacy Boyd
with many, many thanks.

To Maureen Walters,
as always, with thanks.

To my family,
who are all-important to me.

To my friends,
who have given me laughter and memories.

To hope, to love and to peace.

Prologue

Afghanistan, November

What else could go wrong?

In the dark, under a starless sky, they had driven their Humvee straight into an ambush, and now they were barely holding on, pinned down in a firefight with nothing but a crumbling rock wall between them and the enemy. Help couldn't arrive too soon.

Mike Moretti was one of the lucky ones—he only had cuts and bruises. His two close friends, Noah Grant and Jake Ralston, also had non-life-threatening injuries. The other member on this US Army Rangers mission, Captain Thane Warner, wasn't so lucky. Mike didn't need a doctor to tell him that Thane was hurt badly with wounds to his chest and head, an injured leg and deep gashes all over his body from flying shrapnel. Mike was trying to apply pressure to the two most serious wounds, hoping his captain and friend would hang on until help arrived. Their last communication had been cut off, but before it was he'd been told a chopper was on the way.

Thane gripped his arm and Mike leaned closer to hear him over the gunfire. His voice was raspy, his breathing shallow as he spoke through the pain that was no doubt seizing his body. "Mike, promise me you'll take the ranch job for three months at least. Promise me you'll work for Vivian. I want to know she's taken care of when I'm gone." Coughs racked his body and he grimaced. "Promise me."

"I promise," Mike said without thinking. He concentrated on trying to keep pressure on the wounds.

Thane grabbed his arm with a strength that shocked Mike as Thane pulled him closer. "Key...in my pocket... Get it."

Mike heard the desperation in the captain's voice, felt it in his grip. But he couldn't ease up the pressure on these deep wounds or the man would surely bleed out before a medic got to him. When Thane began to struggle, trying to get to his pocket himself, the bleeding worsened, oozing over Mike's hand.

"Be still. I'll get the damn key," Mike ordered.

He struggled to get the key out of Thane's back pocket—he bent closer to Thane and reassured him. "I have the key."

Thane squeezed his eyes shut and let out a shaky breath. When he reopened them, Mike saw the gratitude and the fear as clearly as if the captain had spoken the words. "Bottom of box... Packets addressed to Vivian and to you." He grimaced as the pain no doubt intensified, but he wouldn't be deterred. "Get Noah... Need him."

Mike shook his head. "If I leave you, you'll bleed to death."

As an explosion rocked the ground not twenty feet away, sending up a plume of light, Thane placed one hand over the mound of Mike's jacket pressed against his bleeding chest wound. "Get him, dammit."

Swearing, Mike turned to the man next to him and punched his shoulder to draw his attention. There was no use calling out; his voice wouldn't be heard over the gunfire.

As Noah Grant lowered his weapon, Mike told him, "Trade places. Keep pressure on his wounds. He wants to talk to you."

Without hesitation, Noah sidled up to the captain and Mike took up his weapon to keep up the barrage on the enemy, all the time hoping against hope they'd be able to get the injured man on that chopper. His eyes scanned the dark sky. Where was it?

Thane Warner wasn't only his captain; he was a good friend. Back home, Mike had dated Thane's younger sister. Though he'd gotten along with the divorcee's young child, their relationship hadn't lasted. But Mike's friendship with Thane had.

He glanced over his shoulder and saw Noah motioning him over.

"He's drifting in and out of consciousness now," Noah said, shaking his head. "But he wants Jake."

Before Mike could move to get their friend, he heard it—the unmistakable sound of a helicopter in the distance. He pointed his index finger up. "Listen. Chopper." But he still didn't have eyes on it, and Mike couldn't help but wonder if it would be able to get their captain out in time.

If not, Mike admitted with a sinking realization, he had made a promise to Captain Thane Warner and he intended to keep it.

One

April

After driving past miles of mesquite, dry creek beds and cacti, Mike turned and stopped at a pair of tall wrought iron gates. As soon as he punched in the code he had been given, the gates slid open and he drove through beneath a high ornate iron arch that claimed this to be the Tumbling T Ranch.

Eight miles from the state road, he saw fenced grounds ahead. Among the trees, ponds and white fences was what looked like a small town of houses, offices, barns and outbuildings, all dominated by a stately mansion. The grand home reminded Mike again of Thane Warner's millionaire status and his wife's family of billionaires. As if Mike needed the reminder.

He soon wound up the long drive to the front of the

sprawling three-story stone home with slate roofs and wings built on the east and west sides.

He swore quietly. He didn't want this job. It was one thing to accept Thane's offer to go to work on the Warner spread when they expected to come home and work together. It was another to return to civilian life and run a ranch for a widow he didn't know and who didn't know ranching.

It had been last year when Thane had first asked Mike to think about a job on the Tumbling T Ranch. Thane's older foreman had had back trouble and had decided to retire. The foreman had said he would wait until Thane was out of the military and had time to hire someone to take his place. Mike had planned to get a job working on a ranch once he was discharged, so why not work for a man he'd come to like and admire? Besides, the job came with a good salary.

But Thane didn't make it back home.

Mike cast his eyes on the sprawling ranch, as he recalled the days following his friend's death. He had followed Thane's request and used the key Thane had given him to open a lockbox he'd stored in their makeshift camp. Opening the box, he found an odd assortment of stuff, including Thane's cotton T-shirts, some socks, and in the bottom, three fat packets wrapped in wrinkled, torn brown paper and tied with twine. One was addressed to Mike, one to Noah and one to Jake. Mike passed them out. When he opened his envelope he read a note scribbled on a piece of torn brown paper: *Mike, please give this to Vivian.* He looked at his friends as he held up another envelope. "I'm to take this home to his wife."

Noah scratched his jaw that was covered in black stubble. "Yeah, I'm to take one to his sister."

Noah and Mike looked at Jake who held up his brown envelope. "And I'm to take this to someone who works for his dad." They all looked at each other and Mike guessed his friends were feeling the same as he was.

"Thane was the best," he said. "We've got to do what he wanted."

The others nodded and moved away to stash the envelopes safely until they could get home. Mike knew he was the only one who had another note in the box. That note informed him there was a packet for him hidden in among Thane's things. Mike rummaged through the lockbox and found it quickly. A thick packet shoved down in the toes of a well-worn army sock. Mike opened the fat brown envelope and found more brown paper tied in twine. This one had a note in Thane's handwriting: *Mike, you are the only one getting this. It is yours now. I won't ever miss it. You'll earn it. Please take the other packet to Vivian.*

Mike unwrapped the brown paper to find a stack of bills. He stared at them a moment in shock. He picked up one and looked at it closely. It was a one-thousand dollar bill. He'd never even seen one before. He thumbed through the stack of twenty-five. He read Thane's note again and shook his head. He didn't know why Thane had given him the gift. It was no secret that Thane came from a wealthy family. Along with his two brothers and sister, he was a multimillionaire, and his wife a billionaire heiress, so Thane would never have needed the money if he had lived, but it still was an odd gift. Mike shook his head again, wondering if Thane thought he was poverty-stricken since he was the only one of their group of four friends who wasn't a millionaire. No, he knew that wasn't the case because Thane was practical and Mike had never known him to throw money away. That day, and every day since, each time he looked at the bills, he thought of Thane and wanted his friend with him instead of the money.

Now with Thane gone, the foreman job didn't appeal to Mike, but a promise was a promise. Mike wasn't going back on his word.

From scuttlebutt and by piecing together things Thane had said, Mike knew Thane's artist wife was the daughter of a billionaire Dallas hotel magnate, plus now she had inherited Thane's millions from his ranch and oil interests. Vivian and Thane had only been married a few months when he'd left for Afghanistan. She knew nothing about ranching and Thane had constantly worried about her. Also, he hated to think that if something happened to him, she would sell the ranch and return home to Dallas where she had lived when she was single.

As he stepped out of the car, he pulled on his western-cut navy jacket. His gaze ran over the sprawling gray stone mansion that looked as if it should be in an exclusive Dallas suburb instead of sitting on a mesquite-covered prairie. The mansion was surrounded by beds of spring flowers. Beyond the beds was lush green grass that had to be watered constantly in the dry Texas heat. A tall black wrought iron fence with open gates circled the mansion yard.

After running his fingers through his wavy ebony hair, Mike put on his broad-brimmed black Stetson. As he strode to the front door, he realized he had felt less reluctance walking through minefields in Afghanistan. He crossed the wide porch that held steel and glass furniture with colorful cushions, pots of greenery and fresh flowers. He listened to the door chimes and in seconds, the ten-foot intricately carved wooden door swung open. He faced an actual butler.

"I'm Mike Moretti. I have an appointment with Mrs. Warner."

"Ah, yes, we're expecting you. Come in. I'm Henry, sir."

Mike stepped into a wide entryway with a huge crystal chandelier centered overhead above a small pond where a fountain splashed and deep purple and bright pink water lilies added to the ambiance. It was hard to picture the down-to-earth, tough US Army Ranger, Thane Warner as the owner of this elegant mansion.

"If you'll wait here, sir, I'll tell Mrs. Warner you've arrived."

"Thank you," Mike replied, nodding at the butler who turned and disappeared into a room off the hall. With neatly trimmed brown hair, Henry wore a white shirt and a matching black tie and trousers. Mike noticed he also wore boots and when he had shown Mike in, his hands looked rough. His shoulders were thick and broad. Mike suspected Henry might not spend all his time working inside the mansion.

He reappeared. "If you'll come with me, sir, Mrs. Warner is in the study." Mike followed him until Henry stopped at an open door. "Mrs. Warner, this is Mike Moretti."

"Come in, Mr. Moretti," she said, smiling as she walked toward him.

He entered a room filled with floor-to-ceiling shelves of leather-bound books. After the first glance, he forgot his surroundings and focused solely on the woman approaching him.

Mike had seen Thane's pictures of his wife—one in his billfold, one he carried in his duffel bag. Mike knew from those pictures that she was pretty. But those pictures hadn't done her justice, because in real life, Vivian Warner was a downright beauty. She had big blue eyes, shoulder-length blond hair, flawless peaches-and-cream complexion and full rosy lips. The bulky, conservative tan sweater and slacks she wore couldn't fully hide her womanly curves and long legs.

What had he gotten himself into? For a moment he was tempted to go back on his promise. But as always, he would remember those last hours with Thane's blood running over his hands, recall too easily Thane dying in a foreign land after fighting for his country, and Mike knew he had to keep his promise. His only hope was that Thane's widow wouldn't want him to work for her.

"Mr. Moretti, I'm glad to meet you. I've heard so much about you from Thane," she said, offering her hand.

"It's Mike," he said, smiling as he took her soft hand in his. The moment he did, he felt a tingling up his arm that shocked him.

"And I'm Vivian," she said, her eyes widening when his hand wrapped around hers. Her words came out breathlessly, making Mike feel he had walked into a major disaster. Their gazes locked and he couldn't get his breath, either. For a moment he felt a hot, intense awareness of her as a woman. A very desirable woman. And judging by her startled expression and the quick intake of her breath, he had a feeling she felt a similar reaction.

His focus shifted to her lips, a rosy temptation. Realizing they were staring at each other and standing too close, he released her hand. When he did, she stepped back, looking suddenly uncomfortable. Perhaps she labeled the attraction as unwanted as he did.

"I'm sorry for your loss," Mike said. "Your husband

was a friend I'll miss," he added, trying to get his mind back to Thane instead of on his widow.

"Thank you. Thane was special. Please have a seat," she said softly. She walked toward an arrangement of chairs and as he followed, he couldn't take his eyes off the curve of her hips.

Mike did not want this scalding awareness of his late buddy's wife. And he damn well didn't want to work for Vivian Warner.

Perhaps... He couldn't help the thought that overtook his mind. Perhaps, because she knew so little about ranching, if he took the job, she would turn running the ranch over to him and he would seldom see or talk to her. Maybe, but... Common sense told him to thank her for the job and decline the offer. But each time he thought about backing off, he knew he had to keep his promise. Thane had fought and died not only for rights, freedom and home, but for promises kept and for trusted friends. He had fought for this ranch he loved and the wife he loved. Mike also thought about that fat packet of money Thane had given him, money he'd already squirreled away and invested.

Mike would do what he felt was right, but he hoped with all his being that he rarely ever saw his new boss. This was not the woman for him and there were more than a billion reasons—each and every one of the billions she was worth. Vivian Warner was an heiress, his friend's wife, the woman Thane had entrusted to him to take care of. He couldn't give in to the fiery attraction and seduce her—and betray that trust. For all those reasons, she was off-limits, not the least of which was the fact that he could never move in her circle.

Vivian motioned him to a brown leather wingback

chair, then sat farther away than was necessary. He realized that she may have felt as trapped by this situation as he did. Thane had offered him the job and had wanted him as the foreman. Like Mike, she obviously was also following Thane's wishes now.

"Thank you for taking this job," she said, her voice lilting, soft-spoken. "Thane wrote a glowing letter about you and said I could count on you to run this place the way he would want. I appreciate that. I know you accepted the job when you were still in the military. Now that you're here, I assume that means you want the job. Is that correct?"

Her question hung in the air but he couldn't say yes. "I promised Thane I would take the job for three months to see if I fit and vice versa," he reluctantly answered.

"So you're here on a trial basis," she said, her smile vanishing, and he merely nodded. "Thane had great trust in you so I hope you like it here and stay," she continued. "Slade Jackson, our foreman, wants to retire and I can't run this ranch. Actually, Slade runs this place as if it's his ranch and that's what Thane said you would do."

"That makes my job easier," Mike answered, wondering how often he would see her once he started work. He would have to report in, let her know what was going on, but that didn't have to be a daily occurrence or even by direct contact. Email would be a salvation.

"There's a house on the ranch for the foreman. In fact, most of the men who work here live on the ranch." She crossed her legs and sat back in her chair. "I don't know what Thane told you about me. I'm an artist and I own a gallery in Dallas where I show and sell my paintings. They're also shown in three other galleries in Houston, Austin and Santa Fe, New Mexico. That takes a lot of my time and I know little about the ranch. We have an accountant and his assistant who help with the bills and payroll. There are two cowboys working here who also double, when needed, as chauffeurs. You'll see the limo in the garage. There's a landing strip and we have two planes and again, three of the cowboys are pilots. I saw on your résumé that you have a pilot's license."

"That's correct."

She nodded her approval. "We have a chef and also the wife of one of the men is a cook for the employees who live here. My cook, Francie Ellison, is here five days a week, off on the weekends unless there's something special. She has an apartment on the third floor. Heather, the woman who is in charge of the cleaning crew also has an apartment on that floor, and Waldo, her husband, is in charge of the gardening crew. I don't live alone in this house, Mr. Moretti."

"Just call me Mike."

Vivian Warner sat a little straighter and locked her fingers together. "I have a couple of problems. I think one will vanish the minute I introduce you. Since I'm isolated on the ranch and everyone in the area knows I'm a widow and alone, the issues are with two men in particular. I don't think it will ever involve you and I'm not afraid of either one because I don't feel threatened, just annoyed. Also, when Thane knew he would be away and I would be isolated, my father talked to him about a bodyguard and Thane agreed I should have one—even when other people live in the house. With my family background, I might be a tempting target. So I have a bodyguard—he and his wife live in this house, too. That way, he's close at hand."

"Henry is the bodyguard, isn't he?"

"Yes," she said, tilting her head as she gazed at him. "Thane told you there was a bodyguard?"

"No. Henry didn't look like my idea of a man who spends every working hour as a butler."

"You're observant. Henry Paine and his wife, Millie, live in this house on the third floor. I feel Henry can do a better job as my bodyguard if he's in the house."

"I agree with that."

She smiled. "His wife, Millie, is my assistant and helps with the business part of my art. As far as the problems I have, Thane knew nothing about them because he had enough to worry about where he was. I didn't want him halfway around the world and worrying about me and two men I can cope with well enough. With you taking this job, I think the least of the two problems will vanish instantly because it didn't exist when Thane was here. It concerns one of my employees." She ran a hand over her blond hair, more of a nervous gesture, Mike thought, since not one strand was out of place. Then she continued. "Thane always said Leon Major could work with horses better than any other cowboy he had known. Thane let Leon deal with the problem horses that he wanted to keep, so I don't want to let Leon go. I also haven't ever told this to Slade. Slade isn't well, plus he's older, so I didn't want to worry him. Besides, Leon isn't threatening. He's more of a nuisance. Since Thane's death, he's been by to see me a couple of times. At first, I thought it was about the ranch or business."

"And it wasn't at all," Mike said, and she nodded.

"I told him not to come to the house. He can talk to Slade, our foreman. So far, Leon has cooperated and as I said, with your taking the job, I think that will be the end of that problem."

"What's the other problem?"

"That's a bigger one, unfortunately. My neighbor, Clint Woodson, knows I'm widowed and knows I'm not a rancher. He's divorced and he wants me to go out with him. I also know he wants this ranch."

"Are you interested in selling?"

"At this point, no, I'm not. The time may come when I will be, but I don't want to do something in haste and regret it later. Also, if I don't sell to him and I won't go out with him, I keep thinking he'll stop coming by or calling me. Neither man, not Leon nor my neighbor, has stepped out of line to the extent that Henry would get involved with, so I haven't had any help from Henry about this except to make his presence known. You see, Mr. Moretti, I haven't gone out with any man since Thane, nor have I wanted to. There are other men who've called, but some are simply friends who are being nice and asking me out since I'm widowed and don't get out much. Some are a nuisance, but I can deal with that. Actually, Clint started asking me out as soon as Thane enlisted. Since Thane's death, Clint calls and drops by much more often. I don't invite him inside and Henry always makes an appearance. Occasionally, he comes by when Henry has gone to town—it's as if he knows when Henry leaves—but I don't even go to the door. I'm not afraid of Clint. He's just aggravating and I don't care to talk to him. He brings me presents, which I tell him I can't accept, so he leaves them on the porch. I give them to a charity in town and tell them to drop him a thank-you, but that hasn't stopped him. Nor have I managed to convince him that I have no interest in going out with him or selling this ranch to him."

Mike nodded. "When I'm in charge, we can keep him from setting foot on the ranch. We can stop him at the front gate and tell him you're not receiving visitors. I can also go into town and get to know the sheriff so there won't be any misunderstandings. You can think about that last one."

"I don't need to think about it. That would be excellent if it works. I've thought about changing the code but with the amount of people who live and work here, he can easily get it from one of them. And we usually have the gate open anyway."

"We can hire someone to be a gatekeeper temporarily. Or perhaps we could get several hands who are willing to do extra duty."

She nodded. "We'll see if that works." Then she added some further information about the neighboring suitor. "As soon as Thane had to deploy, Clint started being buddies with my dad. They have mutual friends, you see. My dad's business is hotels, but he does have an oil company, so he and Clint know each other in the business world, too. It won't matter. I just wanted you to know. I can take care of my dad."

"It shouldn't take long to get the message across," Mike reassured her.

Her shoulders seemed to ease and a small smile pulled back her lips. "Thane wrote a very long, detailed glowing letter about how much he trusted you and how much I can trust you."

Mike looked into her eyes and wondered how many times he would have to remind himself how much Thane had trusted him. "Thane was a buddy, a fine man, and I trusted him with my life. I'm sorry he didn't make it home."

She looked away and laced her fingers together in her lap. "I am, too. I miss him." As she stared into space he waited silently. Finally, she turned to look at him again.

"How soon can you start work? I'll tell you that we need you today, or as soon as you can start working here."

"I can start tomorrow. Because of being in the military, I travel lightly, so I can move in right away."

"That's wonderful. You can have the guesthouse as long as Slade is still here. When he goes, we'll have the foreman house done over however you'd like and you can move in there."

"Sounds good to me," he said. There was a moment of silence and she looked as if she were debating whether or not to say something so he sat quietly waiting.

"I want to ask you something. If you don't want to do this, say no."

"Sure. Ask away," he said, curious of what she had in mind.

"After you've worked here a couple of weeks, could we go out to dinner maybe a few times where people would see us?" She took a deep breath. "You don't have to agree, but I think if you went out with me where we would be seen, Clint and a couple of the other men who have called on me would back off. I think Clint would stop trying to get me to move and sell the ranch. We could go to a country club in Dallas—dinner will go on my tab, of course, because, in the first place, at the club that's automatic." Her cheeks turned pink as she talked. "You don't have to go. It is definitely not a job requirement, and if there's a woman in your life—"

"Relax, Mrs. Warner. I can easily take you to dinner," he lied, trying to sound positive and knowing that she was right about the men backing off. "There's no woman to worry about. You pick the time for dinner and you select the place because you know this neck of the woods better than I do," he said.

They would go to dinner. If it had been anyone besides Thane's wife, he probably would have politely refused, but he believed the reasons she was giving.

When she looked down at her fingers locked together, his gaze swept over her and his heartbeat sped up. Her long blond hair curled slightly where it fell on her shoulders. Mike knew she had no romantic interest in him, but with the jolt of mutual awareness when their hands had briefly touched, he suspected that any time spent with her he would be driven by two forces: the first—intense attraction; the second—the reminder that she was absolutely off-limits for him. She was Thane's wife. How many times had he already had to remind himself of that? It was easy to get lost in those big eyes and forget the world and his purpose here.

"If it looks as if we're dating, I think Clint will stop trying to buy this place. But it's merely a request and if you say no, I'll understand," she repeated.

"As I said, I don't mind taking you to dinner," he lied again politely as he smiled at her.

She looked as if a weight had lifted off her shoulders while he felt as if one had just dropped on his.

"It will help, too, if you'll call me Vivian."

"I noticed Henry calls you Mrs. Warner."

"He did that for your benefit and because you're new. He and his wife both call me Vivian, and Thane told them to call him by his first name. Thane wasn't much for formalities."

"I think it should be Mrs. Warner until we have that dinner date. I'll change to Vivian then."

She nodded. "Thank you for agreeing to dinner. And remember, it will be the weekend after this one. I have tickets for a charity ball. It's a dinner dance at a country club in Dallas. You'll need a tux."

"I can get one," he said, smiling.

"Good. Clint belongs to the same club, so there's a good chance he'll be there." She shrugged her delicate shoulders. "It's uncanny, but he seems to know most places I go and he appears there, too."

"You haven't noticed anyone following you around when you're off the ranch, have you? He could easily hire a PI."

"No, but I haven't really paid much attention." She smiled at him. "Actually, I'm not off the ranch much because I'm busy painting. I have a showing coming up this month."

"Well, I don't want you to worry about Clint. I think I can get rid of him."

"Thank you, Mike. That's a relief. He's even had real estate people call me about the ranch, as well as an attorney who represents him. It will be such a relief to have him out of my life."

"I don't think that will be difficult to accomplish," Mike replied, already suspecting his biggest problem might be keeping his distance from her.

"I can introduce you to Slade now if you'd like. He's expecting us. He'll talk to you a little and show you around."

"Thane said he has back trouble. Can he still work and get around?"

"Yes, thank goodness. He isn't able to do what he used to, but he works. He does more than he should. Thane wrote to him and told him how you know ranching. He's glad you're here. We all are." She started to rise from her chair. "I'll call him and we'll go to his office."

"Mrs. Warner, wait a minute," Mike said, wondering how the next few minutes would go. "In the last moments I was with your husband, he asked me to give something to you. He had a gift for you. He kept it with his things. Fighting like we were and on the move, we carried very little with us, but he carried your gift with him. It wasn't gift wrapped. When I brought it home, I thought about having it wrapped. Perhaps it should be, but I thought about all we went through and decided maybe it would mean something special to you to give it to you the way he carried it through fights and tough assignments. I've brought it to you like I got it from him," Mike said, standing. "It seemed more appropriate to me."

"We weren't even married a year," she said, looking at Mike's hands as he pulled the parcel from his jacket pocket. The package was wrapped in plain wrinkled brown paper that was smudged, slightly torn in a couple of spots. He held it out to her. She glanced up at him and then took it from him with icy fingers.

"Thane had this?"

"Yes, for you. I imagine he got it when we were in one of the European cities. I don't know when or where. We never talked about it, really, except when he asked me to get it to you."

She struggled with the string until he reached into his pocket. "Here, let me," he said, opening a small knife and cutting the twine. Their fingers brushed and again, Mike had that instant sizzle when there should have been nothing. Without thinking, he glanced from the package to her and saw her surprised look again as she gazed up at him. The minute he met her eyes, she hurried to unwrap the wrinkled brown paper.

When she saw the gift, she gasped. A gold chain with

a large diamond pendant glittered in the light. It looked like an antique. She closed her hand around the necklace and put her head down. To give her privacy, he walked a few feet away to a window to gaze outside without seeing anything before him. Instead, he remembered the flashes of shells and flames, the smell of blood and fire and gunpowder. He remembered Thane and hurt again over the loss of his friend.

"There's a note," she said. He didn't turn to look. He could hear her open paper and then she was quiet. And he knew she was crying because she loved her husband. "Sorry," she whispered.

"Don't be. We all miss him, including Noah and Jake, our two other friends. Thane bought that pendant for you because he loved you. He was a good man and people cry over good men."

Mike moved away, returning to his seat and looking at his phone, trying to give her a moment until she was ready to talk again.

"I always thought he would come home to me. I was sure he'd get through it," she said so softly, he could barely hear her. "I was wrong."

Mike stood. "I'll get you a drink of water," he said, leaving so she could be alone with her grief for a few minutes. He hadn't been in the hall two seconds before Henry emerged from one of the rooms.

"Can I help you, Mr. Moretti?"

"It's Mike, Henry. She told me you're a bodyguard. You're military, too, aren't you?"

"Yes, sir. Marines."

"I'm giving her a moment. I told her I'd get her a drink of water. Thane had a gift for her and a note, and asked me to give it to her. It… Well, it tore her up."

"I'll get the water. Have a seat, Mike."

Mike smiled and felt he would have a friend in Henry.

In minutes Henry returned with a tray that held two glasses and a pitcher of ice water. Cubes clinked in the pitcher as he approached Mike. "Here's one for you, sir."

"Henry, you don't need to call me 'sir.'"

"Yes, sir. Not too many people off the ranch realize I'm anything but a butler out here. It's probably better that way. As you know, she's worth a lot and this can be an isolated spot in spite of all the people who work here."

"Okay. I'll take the water to her. She should be okay now."

Henry held the door open and closed it quietly behind Mike. Vivian was at the window and turned to face him.

He crossed the room and held the tray for her. "Have a drink."

"Thanks. That caught me off guard," she said, taking the glass nearest her. "I loved him and I miss him."

"That's understandable." Mike turned away to set the tray on a table and sip his drink. He set the glass back on the tray.

"If you're ready now, I'll call Slade and see if he's ready to meet you."

"Sure, go ahead."

While she talked on her phone, he glanced around. The desk at one side of the room looked French and a sofa covered in antique blue velvet faced the fireplace. One wall was almost floor-to-ceiling glass and overlooked a fenced yard with neat beds of red roses, a flowering crab apple tree and spirea and hyacinth in bloom. His gaze flicked back to Vivian. Her clothes didn't reveal her figure or her legs, but one of the pictures Thane had carried was of both of them on a beach and Mike had total recall of her long legs and fabulous curves and a smile that could melt ice.

She turned to Mike. "Slade said he's ready, so shall we go? It's a short walk."

"Sure," he said, watching her cross the room and joining her, catching the faintest scent of an exotic perfume. He held the library door for her and then fell into step beside her as they walked down a wide hall that held potted palms and an elegant arrangement of chairs and loveseats. A splashing fountain was built into one of the walls and marble statuary and oils in gilt frames lined each side.

"Is this your art?"

She laughed, a melodic, cheerful sound that made him want to get her to laugh again. "Not all of it. Some of them. I specialize in Western art and portraits. One of the horse paintings is mine." She pointed to the nearest painting. "The black horse."

"Very nice," he said. As he commented, he thought what a pity that Thane's wife wasn't older, less attractive, less appealing and less friendly because then she would definitely be less tempting.

Outside, they followed a stone path bordered by beds of blooming yellow jonquils and purple irises to a gate that he opened and held for her.

"Thank you," she said as she walked through and he followed, closing the gate. "I really know so little about this ranch other than that we raise Hereford cattle. I do ride because we had a family farm that we went to occasionally and I had a horse, but that farm was nothing like this ranch and I didn't spend much time with my horse. And I don't here. I'm really not a ranch person. Also, I think the farm was more of a place for my father to relax."

Mike saw barns, corrals and garages for the various

cars, trucks and the one limo. In another direction there were houses and fenced yards. They approached a single-story building with lots of glass and wood.

"Here's the foreman's office. And here comes Slade," she said as a door opened and a tall, slender man came out. He was in boots, jeans and a long-sleeved denim shirt. In spite of the protection of his broad-brimmed Western hat, his skin was brown, wrinkled and weathered. His gray hair was long at the back of his neck.

"Slade, meet Mike Moretti, Thane's ranger friend. Mike, this is Slade Jackson, our foreman."

As Mike shook hands, he looked into gray eyes that stared intently at him. "I've heard about you from Thane, Mr. Jackson, and what a great job you've always done."

"Call me Slade. Hate to step down, but the time has come. This is a family ranch and it's been here through seven generations of Warners. It goes way back. I understand you've worked on a ranch."

Vivian took a step forward. "Before you answer Slade, I'll tell you two goodbye," she said to the two men. "I enjoyed meeting you, Mike, and we'll talk some more. You and Slade can come to some decisions."

He gazed into her eyes and the thought crossed his mind that he could look at her for hours. Instantly, he thought about her from a few minutes earlier, crying over Thane, the man she once loved. And still loved. Mike knew he hadn't imagined his reaction to touching her and he was equally certain that she had felt something, too. Why did they have the slightest chemistry between them when neither one wanted it? Was it really going to help for him to take her to dinner a couple of times to drive away a bothersome neighbor? Or would an evening together complicate both their lives?

Two

Vivian walked back to the house with her emotions churning. Mike Moretti was the kind of man she had expected from Thane's glowing description. What she hadn't expected was the flash of awareness whenever they made physical contact. They didn't know each other, so it wasn't because she liked him. And she missed Thane every hour of every day. She missed him, she hurt and she didn't want to go out with another man. Asking Mike to take her to dinner had been purely to get Clint to stop bothering her.

She really knew very little about Mike except what Thane had told her. She knew that her new foreman was one of Thane's best buddies. She knew he was single, dependable, trustworthy, honest, strong, intelligent and understood ranching. Thane had mentioned all of those qualities, but as for actual facts about his life, Thane had said almost nothing and she hadn't asked. She had always thought Thane would come home to her and she was still shocked over his death. She hated to ask Mike to take her out, especially on his first day here, but she wanted to be up front about it. She was becoming desperate to get Clint Woodson out of her life. He annoyed her like a fly steadily buzzing around her.

Any of her close friends would know when she went out with Mike that it didn't really mean a thing to her. Clint, however, wouldn't know that. She looked forward to the day when he was no longer bothering her and trying to get her to sell the ranch.

Her thoughts jumped back to Mike and her reaction to shaking his hand this morning. That stirring of awareness, that skitter up her spine, had shocked her and she couldn't get it out of mind. She didn't want to feel anything toward any other man. She loved her husband even if he wasn't coming home to her. Was she making a mistake by going out with Mike?

She told herself she wasn't. After all, she wasn't interested in anything romantic and he didn't act as if he was, either. She shrugged away her worries about going out with him, telling herself it would only be a polite evening with talk about the ranch and maybe good memories from Mike about Thane.

She entered her house and went to her room to change her clothes so she could paint. She didn't expect to see Mike Moretti again until he moved in and worked for the Tumbling T.

Tuesday morning, Slade was showing Mike around the ranch. Everything was in good shape, even the garages where they stopped in for a tour of the vehicles.

Mike turned when Slade held out a set of keys to him.

"Thane wanted you to have his horse and his saddle and his truck." Slade pointed out the newer vehicle to their right. "She's all yours."

"I think that'll do nicely," Mike said, shaking his head and silently thanking his friend. Leave it to Thane to have thought of everything.

After he looked over the truck, he turned to the foreman. "Looks like the Tumbling T is top notch. Is there anything this ranch needs that it doesn't have?"

Slade laughed. "Just an owner. Vivian really doesn't have her heart in this. She likes it out here, but she has no love for ranching, the horses, the land, not even that monster house he had built for her."

Mike smiled. "It is a monster house. At least some people are living in it and enjoying it."

"Yeah, they are. I think they like it more than she does."

The two men walked over to the barn for a tour.

"Wait here and I'll go get Thane's horse," Slade told him. "I can tell you that you're going to like him. He's a winner."

Slade disappeared inside and came back out leading a black horse. Mike's gaze ran over the horse and he smiled. "That is one fine horse."

"He's the best cutting horse on the place. He's fast, fast enough to race. He's the best and Thane loved him. Thane's saddle has his initials on it and it's the fanciest saddle in there. He has more than one, but you'll see the one I'm talking about and you'll like it."

Mike led the horse into a corral and turned him loose, running his hands along his neck, feeling the muscles and the smooth hide, his coarse black mane.

"I think he's waiting for something."

"He likes apples," Slade said.

"I'll remember that next time I see him."

He left, closing the gate and joining Slade on the remainder of the tour.

By the time Mike made it back to the guesthouse that night, he was ready to have a hot shower and to sit and think about all he had learned and seen of the ranch and the people he had met that day. It was dark when he finished his shower. He pulled on jeans and boots and a T-shirt, going outside to sit in a rocker and drink a beer. The guesthouse had a fenced yard and faced the back of the main house where a few lights burned on different floors. He wondered where Vivian's room was and what she was doing.

His eyes had adjusted to the dark and there was a lamp post with a light in the yard, one beyond it near the drive and one farther down along the ranch road. Houses were scattered around him and they all had yard lights. There was a big mulberry tree in the guesthouse yard with lights and there was a white picket fence around the yard. He saw something moving along the outside of the fence and realized it was a shaggy brown dog. Curious, he watched as the dog went to the gate, stood on its hind legs and opened the latch with its nose. It nudged the gate open, came inside and up to the porch, walking up to Mike with a wagging tail.

Mike had to laugh as he scratched the dog's ears. "Smart fella. That deserves a treat, but I don't have one tonight. I'll get one, though, because I suspect you'll be back. Were you Thane's dog or are you the ranch dog and get scratches from everyone?"

As he petted the dog, it raised its head and wagged its

tail faster. Out of the corner of his eye, Mike saw someone approaching. "We're going to have company."

The dog left him, trotting to the gate and wagging its tail expectantly.

"Mike?"

He stood as Vivian came through the gate. "Hey, if you wanted to see me, you could have called and I would have come by the house. Next time, send a text."

"No. I was out walking and saw your light, so I thought I'd see if the guesthouse was okay."

He smiled. "It's more than okay. It's a fully furnished house with two bedrooms, two and a half baths and a game room. And a dog must come with it because he knows how to open the gate. Come sit. Want a beer or pop or water or anything?"

"No, thanks. The dog is Sandy. He was Thane's dog, but he's friendly and likes everyone and everyone likes him, so he makes the rounds. Since Thane left, Sandy really prefers staying with Slade. Unless you object, when Slade leaves, I think you'll have a dog."

"That's fine with me. This is a smart dog. Sandy opened the gate with ease."

"Oh, yes. Sandy can open most of the gates, most of the doors. That dog really loved Thane. I think he likes you," she said, looking at the dog standing beside Mike while he scratched Sandy's back.

She sat beside him and he caught a whiff of perfume that smelled like wildflowers and he remembered her soft hand in his when he met her.

"I saw Thane's horse that Slade said is now mine. Also his truck and his saddle."

"They're yours if you want them."

"That's a magnificent horse, the best of saddles and a new truck—of course I'd like them. Thank you."

"Thane told Slade what to do with his things. He tried to take care of all of us."

Mike thought of the packet of money Thane had left him. "That he did. He left me some money, which I put in the bank."

"Whatever he gave you, he wanted you to have, so take it and enjoy it. I will treasure my diamond pendant always. I'm wearing it now."

"I understand. I saw the horses Leon is trying to gentle and I've met Leon. He looked less than happy to meet me."

"I think he's out of my life. I shouldn't have even told you about him."

"Oh, yes, you should have. Whatever happens on the ranch, I should know about. At least that kind of thing." He sipped his beer and they sat in silence. He looked at the main house with bright lights still on in a few windows. "Is your room on this side of the house?"

"Yes, as a matter of fact. It's on the second floor in the corner. I have a suite and there are windows all along the back. I have that balcony," she said, pointing up at the mansion. "I have one light on in my study there, see? I have a small studio there, too. I'll show you sometime soon."

His eyes followed in the direction she pointed "When you sit on your balcony and I sit out here, I can wave to you and you'll see me?"

"That's right."

"Interesting. Vivian, that house seems big by anyone's standards. Did Thane want a giant home or did you?"

"Thane gave it to me as a gift. Actually, it's way too

36   EXPECTING A LONE STAR HEIR

big. We wanted to have a family but… Well, at least there are employees who live in it."

"So that wasn't your idea."

"Heavens, no. I wanted a studio where I could paint. I wanted a place to hang my finished artwork. I don't know what he had in mind. He had a lot of company and thought we'd have family. Well, that didn't work out, so I've got this mansion to rattle around in." Her voice was quiet and Mike had to admit it was nice to have her there.

Sandy sat at his side while he continued to scratch his head and Mike felt a streak of guilt. Thane should be home with her, sitting beside her on a nice spring night, before going to bed with his wife. Mike pulled his thoughts from that.

"Do you walk often in the evening?" he finally asked her.

"Not really. Thane and I did, but I don't by myself. It was a pretty night and I thought I'd see if you needed anything. It's dark now and I think I'll go back."

He stood. "I'll walk with you."

She smiled. "You don't have to. There's plenty of light."

"I don't mind. I'll get to know the boss."

She nodded, accepting his company as he fell in step beside her, Sandy following them. At the porch steps he took her arm and heard her quick intake of breath and felt a tingle at the contact. As soon as she was off the steps, he released her arm.

They walked across the yard and Mike held the gate. He was aware of Vivian at his side and he wondered if she was lonesome or had simply come to see if he needed anything as she had said.

"Do you miss Dallas?" he asked her.

"Not really. I loved it here when Thane was home.

Honestly, it's empty and lonely now. I'd be just as lonely in Dallas, maybe more so. I have a condo there, but I can't see living in it all the time and I don't paint there. This has become home."

When they reached her yard, he held the gate open and they walked up to the patio where she turned to him. "Thanks for walking me home. Now you can take Sandy back with you. Sandy doesn't ever stay with me. He's a man's dog."

"If I don't see you sooner, I'll see you next Friday night at the charity dinner."

"Mike, thanks for agreeing to go with me. I really appreciate it."

"I don't think it's going to be a difficult task," he said with a grin and she laughed.

"I hope not."

"C'mon, Sandy," he said, turning, and the dog walked beside him to the gate where Mike stopped and waved to her because she still stood on the porch watching them.

When she went inside, he looked down at the dog. "What a job this is going to be, boy. You and I both have lost the anchor in our lives—the boss I thought I'd work with for years and your owner. But don't get attached to me, dog," he warned. "I'll be gone in three months."

The first Friday that Mike Moretti was in her employ, late in the afternoon, Vivian heard a motor and glanced out of her studio window to see Mike get out of a pickup, toss his hat in the window and head to the back door. He'd made an appointment to see her and she went to the door to greet him.

"Hi. You look as if you've had a hard day's work," she said, wondering what he had done because he was muddy and they hadn't had any rain. His black hair was tousled. She couldn't control the jump in her heartbeat at the sight of him and figured it was because she hadn't seen any male except Henry for the past week as she'd been holed up in the house painting.

"Sorry, I didn't stop to clean up first. We had a water leak and we'll need to replace a waterline." He glanced down at his muddy clothes and shrugged. "Didn't want to be late for our appointment. I wanted to report in about my first week."

"Want a cold drink—pop, tea, beer? Francie baked cookies, or I have some chips and salsa and we can sit on the patio."

"Only if I can clean up a little first."

"Of course you can. C'mon. I'll show you. Henry is around some place, but he's getting ready to go out tonight." She led him through the entryway and pointed to an open door. "There's a bathroom and I'll be in the kitchen. When you come out, go straight ahead and turn left at the first door."

She went to the kitchen where Francie was putting away the last of some clean dishes from the dishwasher. The tall red-haired cook smiled at Vivian. "I was finishing up before I leave. I put the last batch of cookies on that platter and the others are in the cookie jar. Your dinner is cooked and all you'll have to do is reheat it in the microwave. There's a roast that's done and in the fridge for the weekend, plus other food."

"Thank you. Mike Moretti is here. He's the man who will replace Slade. I came to get him a beer and myself a glass of water. I don't think he'll want cookies with his beer, but I'll take the platter to the patio, plus some chips and salsa."

"I have a batch of homemade salsa I can take out and—" She stopped and smiled. Vivian glanced around as Mike entered the kitchen.

"Mike, meet Francie Ellison. Francie, this is Mike Moretti."

"Call me Mike," he said. "That's easier." They smiled at each other.

"Glad to meet you, Mike. I'm leaving, but I'll take these chips and salsa to the patio."

"I'll carry them," he said, taking them from her hands. "Now you can start your weekend off."

"Thanks. Welcome to the Tumbling T. Do you need anything else before I go?" she asked Vivian, who shook her head as she opened a beer for Mike and then got a tray for everything they would take outside.

"No, thanks. You have a nice weekend and I'll see you Monday.

She was aware of her old jeans, faded red T-shirt and bare feet. She resisted the urge to smooth down her hair, which was pulled back in a thick braid, and instead, led Mike outside.

"It's been a busy week and a good one getting to know everyone," he said once they were seated and he'd taken a draft of his beer. "I'll miss Slade because he's a nice guy, but I'm happy for him to get to retire and it sounds as if he needs to."

"He definitely needs to. The last time he was home, Thane said Slade should have retired a couple of years ago. Thane thought it might have saved him so much back trouble." She took a sip of her cold water. "I hope you like the job. I'm sure Slade hopes you do, too."

Mike nodded. "It's a good job. I can see Thane's touch in things all around the ranch." He put his beer on the table and sat back on the cushioned chair. "I told you when I came that I'm muddy because we had a water pipe spring a leak. A long stretch will have to be replaced."

As they talked, she gazed into his green eyes and became so lost in them, she barely heard what he was saying. Why did she have this keen awareness of him? Was it purely the absence of a man in her life? She didn't think so. She was surrounded by men on the ranch. Henry, the staff that worked in the house and in the yard, the cowboys that she saw when she went to the garage or one of the barns. It went beyond a keen awareness and no matter how much she wanted to ignore it, she had to admit it was there. She was attracted to Mike and she knew he felt something, too. She didn't want that attraction to him and she suspected he didn't want to feel it, either.

Right now, she was acutely aware of him. Looking into his thickly lashed green eyes made her heart race. He was tall, broad-shouldered, good-looking. Maybe too good-looking, an inner voice told her. How difficult was it going to be to go to a charity ball with him next weekend? The thought of stepping into his arms to dance made her tingle from head-to-toe.

She had talked to Slade about Mike and the old foreman was as enthused about him as Thane had been, which was a relief but not a surprise. Slade was ready to step down and let Mike take over. With Slade retiring in south Texas where his son and oldest daughter lived, her life was changing again. Slade and Thane had been a big part of her life for the past year and soon they would both be gone. But Mike Moretti would not be in her life as much as Slade had been.

She didn't expect to see much of Mike when he took over. First of all, he was new to the job so she expected him to be at work most of the time when he was on the ranch. He would report during the week via emails and texts. Slade always had come by at least once a week to talk to her about the ranch and she expected him to tell Mike to do the same.

Why did the prospect of seeing him at least once a week excite her?

And why was Mike looking at her now as if he expected her to reply?

"I'm sorry," she said, forcing her thoughts back to the conversation. "What were you saying?"

"I said you're from Dallas, right? I mean, I really don't know anything about you except that you were Thane's wife and happily married."

"Happily married and married too short of a time," she said. "Sorry. I miss him. We used to sit out here and talk at night when he came in off the ranch."

"He was a really good guy."

"That's high praise. He thought you were, too. He always said he could count on you to come through."

Mike looked across the yard as if looking far away from the ranch. "I didn't come through at the last. I tried, but I couldn't save him."

"Don't take any blame there. Neither could the doctors at the hospital. A chaplain wrote to me that Thane was picked up by a helicopter and taken to a field hospital. He died when they were transferring him to the hospital."

They were both silent a moment. "You came through, Mike. You tried to save him, but they wrote he was too badly injured. You got all his last messages and what he wanted you to take home. That gave him some peace, I'm sure."

Mike turned to focus on her and another tingle tickled

her. "I don't know much about you except what I've seen in Dallas papers about your dad. I know more about him and his success in the hotel business. You have a brother-in-law who helps your dad run that business now, don't you? And your brother runs the oil business."

"Yes. My brother-in-law Sam is good at what he does. He's married to my older sister, Natalie. They have two cute kids, Holly and Fletcher. Holly is eight and Fletcher is six. I miss them, but they're in school and even if I were back in Dallas I wouldn't see them much."

"Where did you meet Thane?"

"He was good friends with Phil, my older brother. This was the Warner family ranch, but Thane's folks had a home in Dallas, too. His dad never much liked the ranch, but when Thane graduated from college, he came here to take over from his grandfather. His dad never really came back to the ranch. The oil company in Dallas was his love."

"So you knew Thane a long time," he said, looking at her. Just a glance was like a physical contact and she couldn't understand the volatile reaction she had to simply sitting with and talking to him. He was polite, even a little remote. While he was friendly, she had a feeling he had a lot bottled up inside that he didn't talk about.

"That's right. Phil and Thane were friends all through school. Thane was six years older than I am. It made a difference when I was in school. It didn't later."

"Clint Woodson wasn't around much until Thane left, right? I mean, Thane never even mentioned his neighbor."

"That's right. I barely knew who he was until Thane deployed. And like I said, I didn't let Thane know what a pest Clint has been. I didn't want to worry him when he was so far from home. He couldn't do anything about Clint."

"He could have asked some guys here to be a buffer to keep him from disturbing you."

"I was afraid he would ask Slade and Slade has all he can handle."

Mike nodded. As he sipped his beer and looked at the yard, her gaze ran over him. She guessed he was several inches over six feet. He had a narrow waist and long legs. He had one booted foot on his knee and he looked completely relaxed. With the physical awareness she had of him—she was certain it was mutual—was she asking for more trouble by going to the club with him next weekend?

He had been nothing but polite toward her, yet she knew he felt something, too. That made her doubly aware of him. At least, in Mike's case, his reactions seemed unwanted. He seemed to have no personal interest in her and she was glad. She hurt over her loss of the man she loved and she didn't want anyone else in her life yet.

"I hope we're doing the right thing by going to the club Friday night."

He misinterpreted her meaning, and she let him. "It won't hurt to let him think there's a man in your life now. Besides, it's an evening out," he said, smiling at her.

Maybe, she thought, but it wasn't an ordinary evening out. Not when her skin sizzled at his smile.

"I hope Clint is there Friday night. The tickets were bought in my name, so he can find out if I plan to attend."

"If I had to bet, from what you've told me, I'd put money on your neighbor being there Friday night." He finished off his beer then stood. "I should get going now,

Vivian." When he simply said her name, she felt another ripple of attraction.

He began to pick up the dishes but she stopped him. "Leave everything, Mike," she said. "I can carry that stuff to the kitchen."

"So can I," he said and left with everything on the tray except her glass of water. She waited until he returned.

"Thanks for coming to work at the Tumbling T Ranch."

"I promised Thane I would. I'm keeping that promise. If it's a quiet weekend, I won't even come by Monday morning. I can send you a text."

"Thanks. Be sure to make a list of what you want done to Slade's house and when he leaves, we can be ready to get a crew started making changes."

"Sure. I travel lightly, as I said before, and all I need is a bed at night, so I don't think I'll have many changes. Thanks for the beer and I'll see you next week," he said and turned to walk away in long purposeful strides.

She watched him get in his pickup and drive away without looking back.

He said he traveled light and there was no woman in his life to mind if he took her out Friday night. Thane and Slade thought he was a great guy. Other than that, she knew nothing about him. She had a feeling she would have to depend on him for a lot of things concerning the ranch. She had with Slade, but that had been different, she admitted.

She pulled the diamond pendant Thane had sent home from under her red T-shirt and rolled the diamond between her fingers while she thought about Mike. She added one more item to the list of what she knew about the man: She had an electrifying reaction to him.

"Thane, sweetie, why did you hire Mike and send him here?" she sighed. "I have a feeling he's going to complicate my life."

Mike stepped back and watched the foal stand on its wobbly legs. "She's a little beauty," he said.

"She is," Slade agreed. "Her mama's one of our best mares. The foal is perfect and you did a good, efficient delivery job here, Mike, but I knew you would. Thane really had faith in you."

Mike smiled. "I'm beginning to think Thane laid it on a little thick when he told all of you about me. And I think the mama gets credit for her baby coming easily into the world."

Slade shook his head. "Nope. Thane wouldn't exaggerate. I don't worry about leaving here now." He regarded the newborn foal more closely then turned to Mike. "You know, I worked for Thane's grandfather actually, so I've been here a long time and I can tell you, you'll like it here. This is a good place and you'll get to run it like it's your own ranch, at least until she marries again or sells the place. The hermit life she leads isn't going to get her married, though. She's had a rough time over losing Thane."

"That part about running this place the way I want sounds good," Mike said. "But in my experience, there's always something you didn't count on happening and it throws you."

"That's life, but I'm relieved you're here to handle it so I can get out of here a little sooner. I've worked hard all my life. Mike, I'm seventy-eight and I'm ready to retire and I've got a back problem that driving a pickup over rough ground or sitting in a saddle or a thousand other things around here aggravates. I want to sit under the shade of a tree with a cold beer and enjoy my grandkids."

Mike clapped the man on his shoulder. "I hope you get to do that for a long time, Slade. This is a good ranch and I'm glad to have a job here." He bent down to pick up his delivery instruments from the hay-covered floor. "Mrs. Warner doesn't seem to take much interest in it, though."

"She doesn't know anything about ranching and I don't think she cares. I doubt she'll stay. She liked it out here fine enough when her husband was alive but now... Well, I think she stays because it's peaceful for her and she can paint and she goes to Santa Fe and Houston and other places with her art. She won't interfere with you. As far as daily living, this ranch might as well belong to me and it might as well belong to you when I leave. You'll have free rein to run it the way you want. There are good weeks like this past one and then there are times when you think everything has gone to hell. Fires, bad weather, drought, but you've been in worse situations where men around you died, so this probably looks pretty good."

Mike stood up. "It looks damn good."

Slade nodded. "I figured since you were buddies with Thane and he thought you were such a great rancher that you might be more likely to want your own spread."

"Nope. I don't come from money," Mike said. "Far from it. This job is better than what I expected to begin with when I got home. If Mrs. Warner sells the place and I don't like the new boss, I can move on to another job."

"Frankly, I was glad to hear you weren't getting your own place. I was surprised, though, because I wondered how long you'd work for someone else. I thought maybe you were doing this to get some experience."

Mike shook his head. "I'm doing it because I get paid to do it." He didn't tell Slade about his promise to Thane.

"I can relate to that," Slade said, pushing off from the stall gate. "Best be going now, son. Mrs. Warner told me she asked you to take her out because of that damn Woodson. I think that will run him off fast. You go get cleaned up. This little baby looks fine and dandy." They both looked at the foal, its spindly long legs already steadier.

"She's beautiful," Mike said. "So is her mama." He finished gathering up his things and placed them in the box in the back of his pickup.

Mike climbed into the truck, waved and drove away, heading back to the guesthouse to get ready for his first date with Vivian Warner.

He only wished he was looking forward to it as much as Slade seemed to be. Mike hoped one date would be enough to divert Clint Woodson's attention from the beautiful widow.

Not to mention his own.

An hour later, Mike left the guesthouse and drove his pickup down the road to the main house. A white limo was parked in the carport at the side of the house.

He was with Slade every day and Slade sent reports to Vivian, but other than a text Monday morning and their chat last Friday afternoon, Mike hadn't talked to her since he was hired on. She seemed to have an even smaller part in the ranch than Thane had led him to believe. Slade hadn't said yet when he would hand in his resignation and Mike didn't ask questions. He liked it here, liked the work, the feel of the dirt under his boots, the people. If Thane had been able to come home, the job would have been perfect.

Mike wondered what the evening ahead would be like. Whether it'd be as awkward as he predicted, his being in a fancy club among rich folk. Mike never forgot his status in life and Vivian's: a cowboy and a billionaire heiress.

He wondered if Clint Woodson would accept that Vivian was going out with her future foreman. Mike hoped he did so this charade would end quickly.

Vivian didn't seem bothered by the monetary difference in their lives, but she knew full well that he worked for her and she was worth billions more than he was. Heck, she was buying his dinner tonight and it bothered him slightly. Even though they were a low income family, his dad had instilled a strong sense that a man should pay. He had always said to Mike and his brothers, "Never take money from a woman. It's a man's place to pay, not the woman. It doesn't work out well if a man marries a woman with way more money than he has. Look at your uncle." Mike's uncle had had a messy divorce from a wealthy woman with lots of ill feelings between the families afterward.

Growing up, Mike had heard plenty about the man paying the woman's way and it was ingrained into him to the point it didn't matter what Vivian thought. He had always agreed with his dad on the topic. It seemed right for the man to pay. He had known some low-life guys in college who let the woman always pay and that hadn't impressed him, Even when his dad died and times got really tough, he still grew up following his dad's teachings. In high school there were times he went hungry before he'd let a woman pay. There was an older teacher who knew his circumstances at home the year his dad died, and she would try to buy his lunch occasionally, He always turned her down even if it meant going hungry. When he rang the bell at the mansion, Henry opened the door. The butler/bodyguard was in a white shirt, a tan sports jacket and dark brown slacks. His collar was unbuttoned.

"Come in, Mike," Henry said, stepping back to hold the door and then closed it behind Mike. "Vivian is waiting. She told me she asked you to take her out. I'm glad. I've never trusted Clint." He held out a small slip of paper, which Mike took. "Here's my cell phone number. My wife and I are going to dinner in Dallas with your driver Ben and his wife." He explained that after Ben dropped them off at the charity ball he was meeting them at a restaurant in town. "But we won't be far should you need the limo or us for any reason," he added.

"Have you ever had trouble with Clint Woodson?"

Henry shook his head. "No, I haven't. He doesn't look the type to cause real trouble, but I promised Thane I'd watch out for Vivian and I'm keeping that promise even though you're with her."

"Thanks." Mike looked down at Henry's cell phone number and memorized it. Then he put the paper in his jacket pocket. "We won't be out late."

"Do what you want. I figure you can take care of yourself. We shouldn't have any trouble, but I'm not taking a chance. This guy has been obnoxious when he thought she was alone, but I think he'll stop trying to see her now that you're here. Slade couldn't deal with him. You can, and he'll know it the minute he sees you. And if he thinks Vivian wants to go out with you, the man should be smart enough to leave you alone. Every guy on this ranch knows you were a US Army Ranger and that means everyone in the county that has any interest in this ranch knows you were a ranger. Just like they all know I was a marine. That includes Clint. He isn't going to aggravate you."

"I don't think he will, either."

"I just want to be around if we're needed." He motioned Mike down the hall. "Vivian is in the study. I'll show you where."

"No need. I remember," Mike said, moving past Henry. He walked down the hall, turned a corner into the main hall and walked to the open study door. Knocking on the open door, he glanced around the room and saw Vivian by a window. He inhaled deeply, his gaze riveted on her as she turned and smiled at him.

She wore a sleeveless red gown of some soft material that clung to her curvy body and revealed her slender figure and tiny waist. In the low-cut V-neckline, the diamond pendant from Thane sparkled. With that one glance, all Mike's peace of mind over the past few days shattered. He thought he would remember how she looked in this moment for the rest of his life.

"You're gorgeous," he said as she walked up. He realized what he had said to her and hurried to correct himself. "I'm sorry, I know we should keep this evening impersonal."

Her melodic laugh eased the tension he felt. "Don't worry, Mike. Thane is gone and he wouldn't be angry if you complimented me, anyway. A compliment is welcome, especially from a good-looking guy, so don't apologize. We're friends, or I hope we will be, because right now we barely know each other. A compliment between friends is always welcome."

He relaxed a fraction, relieved that she had taken his admiration lightly and could laugh about it. Laughter, however, wasn't what he was feeling. He couldn't stop looking at her. She was so stunning that his heart was racing. He didn't want that kind of reaction when looking at his friend's wife. He felt an obligation to Thane to keep a distance from Vivian. It didn't matter that much that she was a widow. He felt honor bound to keep his distance. Thane didn't hire him to come home and seduce his wife.

All evening he would be with Thane's gorgeous, breathtaking wife who made his pulse pound and heated the room another ten degrees by being there. And he would have to relax and look as if he was enjoying himself or Clint Woodson would never be fooled.

Could he do that?

Before he could answer, Vivian's question broke into his thoughts. "The limo is ready, so shall we go?" she asked.

"Sure," he said, walking beside her, but taking care to leave space between them. "Your necklace is beautiful. Thane chose well," he said, thinking more about her than the necklace.

She touched it with perfectly manicured red fingernails. "I will always treasure this. I don't expect to ever marry again. Thane was the love of my life even though we didn't have much time together."

"You'll marry again," Mike said, unable to keep from smiling at her.

"I'm not going to argue that point tonight. I'm happy to go out, and I think this will stop Clint from pestering me and that's an enormous relief."

"You could have found some cowboy on the ranch to do what I'm doing."

She shook her head. "Clint would never have believed that I was doing anything except trying to avoid him. It wouldn't have stopped him. This, however, most likely will stop him. You're an unknown factor and you're good-looking and—"

"Thank you," he said, nodding at her.

"Well, that's a fact. But you have something about you that says 'don't mess with me.'"

Mike couldn't help the slight chuckle that rose from his chest. "This is going to be an interesting evening. I feel as if I'm going to get my fortune told."

"Don't be ridiculous. I have no idea about your future. I'm merely an artist and I'm observant and I've painted portraits of scores of people. I'll draw your picture if you want," she said, and he knew she was teasing him.

"Thanks. But you should use your talents on real stuff."

"You're definitely real stuff," she said while he held the door for her. She switched on the alarm and the lock clicked as he closed the door.

"I told Henry that they could ride with us in the limo, but he wanted to drive," she explained as they walked down the path.

"I think Henry half expects there might be trouble from Clint tonight. I thought you said he's never given you any physical threat."

"He hasn't. Henry's afraid he might have some guys come after you."

"I doubt that. It's our first time out and we're at a country club and we're in a limo. I don't think we'll have a problem."

"I don't think so either or I wouldn't go tonight. Clint is a pest, but I don't think he would stoop to anything violent. Or hire anyone to do something bad. I'm going to have a good time tonight. We'll convince Clint that we're attracted to each other. And while we do that, I'll enjoy the evening. Mike, I haven't been out like this in oh, so long."

"Neither have I as a matter of fact. I'm sure we can

convince Clint that you have someone in your life now. While we do that, I hope you can have a good time."

They reached the limo and Vivian greeted her driver for the evening then turned back to Mike. "Mike, you probably know Ben."

"I do," he said, looking at the tall cowboy who had changed his jeans and hat and was now wearing black slacks and a white shirt. "We were together about three hours ago. Hi, Ben," Mike said easily, offering his hand to the cowhand.

"Hi. It's going to be a nice night."

"That it is," Mike said.

In seconds they were seated in the limo and Ben went around to the front to drive. Mike sat on the long seat with a lot of space between Vivian and him. He turned slightly to face her.

"So tell me about yourself, Mike," she said. "I don't know anything except Thane trusted you totally and counted you as one of his closest friends."

"We lived in Amarillo," he said, beginning a rote description of his life that he had become so accustomed to giving, he didn't need to think about it. He was light years away from the life she'd had with limos and servants and all kinds of opportunities. "I worked on ranches and went to school on scholarships. I won some money in rodeos. My dad died when I was a teen. I have two older brothers and one younger. With four boys, my mom had a hard time making ends meet, but we all got part-time jobs, scholarships, that sort of thing." He shrugged. "That's it. Nothing exciting. I'd much rather hear about your background. You told me a little about your family. Where did you go to college?"

"The University of Texas where I majored in art. No surprise there."

"And then you came home to start painting?"

"That's about right. I opened the Dallas gallery the second year I was out of college and I did well those early years, showing my paintings and others."

Mike listened, but he paid more attention to the woman rather than the words. He could sit and look at her all evening. In the dim light of the limo he could see the antique diamond laying against her flawless creamy skin. He took a deep breath and shifted his gaze higher to look into the bluest pair of eyes ever. Vivian looked so breathtaking, that he was grateful there would be a lot of people around tonight, including some friends she had joining them. That would make it a lot easier to keep the conversation impersonal and to keep from flirting with her. The woman was head-to-toe temptation. He hoped they didn't have many of these dinners before Clint Woodson disappeared from her life. It constantly nagged at him that Thane had trusted him to come home to help her not to come home to seduce her.

Lights blazed at the country club as the limo rolled up a wide drive and stopped at the front door. Ben held the door and told Mike to call later when they were ready to be picked up.

Mike took her arm lightly as they walked inside. The minute he touched her, he had the same searing awareness that he'd had before. They weren't talking or even looking at each other, yet his skin tingled. Instantly he lowered his arm, banishing the sensation and promising himself he'd avoid further contact. He didn't want to feel that awareness around her.

In the center of the entryway, the round fruitwood

table beneath a mammoth chandelier held a large crystal vase of red anthuriums and deep purple gladiolus. Guests and members stood talking to each other while staff hurried around them. Vivian spoke to a maître d' and he looked at his chart.

"Table four, Ray," he said. A waiter in a matching black suit and bow tie with a white shirt hurried over. "Table four," the maître d' repeated as Ray gathered menus and smiled at them.

"Good evening, Mrs. Warner. Sir, if you'll please follow me, I'll show you to your table."

As they followed the waiter in single file past the tables, Mike glanced briefly at the sway of Vivian's hips. With an effort, he turned his attention to the room around him. It was an older club with polished oak floors, ornate crystal chandeliers and thick blue carpet that muffled the noise. A piano player sat in a corner playing old ballads and there was a hum of conversation. Each table was centered with a vase of fresh pink roses and daisies.

As soon as they were seated, she received a text. "My friends are about fifteen minutes away so they'll be here soon."

"This is a big crowd."

"Which means they raised a lot of money for Parkinson's disease. Oh, oh," she said. "I think you're about to meet Clint. Mike," she said, her voice lowering to a whisper, "please take my hand so it looks as if this is more than a friendly dinner."

"Vivian, look at me and forget him. He'll have to interrupt us if he wants to talk to us. Frankly, I want to meet him. It's best to know your enemy. Surprises aren't good."

As she instructed, he reached over to take her hand in his. Her fingers were cool from touching the goblet of ice water, but at the contact, heat flashed within him as quick as lightning. He gazed into her blue eyes and the dining room grew instantly warmer and he bit back several things that he would like to say but knew better not to.

Damn. He'd resolved not to touch her, yet here he was, only minutes later, holding her hand.

And now he was paying the price.

Three

"Good evening, Vivian."

At the sound of the man's voice, at first Mike was filled with trepidation at meeting Vivian's pushy neighbor, yet relieved to finally let go of her hand. He stood and held out his hand to shake the rancher's as Vivian introduced them.

"Clint, this is Mike Moretti, Thane's friend and my new foreman," she said without hesitation.

"New foreman? That's a good job," Clint remarked as he scanned Mike with a rake of his eyes. Mike felt as if he was being measured and dismissed. Clint eventually shook his hand, and Mike looked into cold hazel eyes. Broad-shouldered, Clint was as tall as Mike and handsome enough for some women to find him appealing. He had thick black hair with a few curls above his forehead. His clothes looked expensive as did the gold rings he wore on several fingers.

"I heard Thane hired you when you both were in the service," Clint said to Mike.

"That's right."

"Have you ever been a foreman before this job? That's a big job."

"Yes, it is, and the Tumbling T is a fine ranch. And yes, I was a foreman before." He wasn't about to give Clint Woodson any details of his life, but he had been a foreman on a Texas ranch for two years before he joined the Army.

"We're neighbors, in case you didn't know."

"That's what Vivian told me."

Woodson gave him another once-over, then clearly he'd seen enough. "I'll see you around." And without waiting for Mike's reply, he promptly turned his back on Mike and focused solely on Vivian. "How're you tonight?"

Mike sat down again and sipped his water while he listened to Clint talk to Vivian. "I have a new proposition I'd like to talk to you about sometime soon. I think it would be mutually beneficial to both ranches since we're in a drought."

"Maybe you can run it past Mike," Vivian replied. "Right now, I think we're doing fine, and it's April. Texas usually has spring rains."

"Yes, well, you have a good evening, Vivian," he said, leaning down slightly and speaking softly. "I'll see you around." He walked away without even glancing back at Mike.

"So now you know Clint Woodson," she said as she resumed her seat at the table.

"So I do." It occurred to him he hadn't updated Vivian on the Clint situation, so he took the opportunity. "I've already talked to Slade about keeping a man at the front gate and he's agreeable to it. Is there anywhere else Clint might enter the ranch?"

"No. There's another way in, but that gate is locked and only certain people on the ranch have keys or know the code to get in."

"Yeah, Slade showed that gate to me. I wondered if there's anywhere else you know about but Slade doesn't."

She shook her head. "But we're neighbors, so all he has to do is get over the fence that divides the two ranches. He can't drive in and Clint would never climb a fence and walk across the ranch to the house." She cast a glance over her shoulder to the rancher as he walked away, then turned back to Mike. "Thanks, Mike, for taking my hand when he approached. Clint saw that. He didn't like it and he didn't like you."

Mike looked across the room and saw Clint sit at a table. The woman sitting there turned to greet him. She was a head-turner with black hair in an elaborate up-sweep and a black dress that clung to her slim silhouette. Even from this vantage point, Mike could see the tight skirt of the dress was slit clear up to her thigh. "He's here with a friend."

"That's Dora Grayson. She has her own real estate agency in Dallas. A very successful woman." Vivian smiled, her tight voice relaxing as she said, "Here are my friends."

Mike stood and turned, looking at a couple approaching their table. The top of the woman's head barely reached her companion's shoulder and her light brown eyes sparkled with friendliness.

Vivian made the introductions. "Ashlynn and Dan, this

is Mike Moretti. Mike, meet my childhood friend Ashlynn Coleman and her husband, Dan Coleman."

Dan had a slight beard, high cheekbones and a rugged appearance that was softened when he smiled. His wife was a pretty woman with midnight tresses that fell straight over her shoulders. She wore a deep blue sleeveless gown with a straight skirt that highlighted her slender figure.

Mike received a firm handshake from Dan and Ashlynn gave him a warm smile.

Mike sat between Vivian on his right and Dan on his left. After a few minutes Dan turned to him. "Do you like the ranch?"

"Absolutely. It's up-to-date, a big operation, nice guys, it's great—all Thane said it would be."

"You get rid of Clint Woodson and you'll be the miracle man. Ashlynn and Vivian are close, so Vivian has told her about Clint. There's no love lost between Clint and me, but we stay civil to each other because we're at a lot of the same functions and know the same people due to our connections in the oil business. But I don't like Clint and he doesn't like me."

Mike knew the feeling. "Clint has already stopped to meet me and talk to Vivian. Don't worry. I'll keep him off the ranch."

"Good deal." Dan clapped him on the back. "Enough about that. Do you keep up with baseball?"

"I do since I'm home again." For the next few minutes, Mike talked to Dan about baseball, until their waiter appeared to take their drink orders.

Mike enjoyed her friends and as they went through dinner, he glanced around the room casually, each time catching Clint watching Vivian. Mike knew he should keep his attention on Vivian to convince Clint that he was interested in her. He stopped looking at Clint, focusing on Vivian and giving her his full attention, which was easy to do.

When Dan asked Ashlynn to dance, Mike asked Vivian. He took a deep breath before she stepped into his arms out on the dance floor for a ballad. He held her a discreet distance and she smiled at him, her blue eyes holding mischief.

"Scared to touch me, Mike? I don't think Thane would mind. I think we would be more convincing to Clint that we're interested in each other."

"We probably would convince Clint faster, but there are more reasons than just thinking about Thane," he said, trying to keep his voice light. "For one, you're my boss."

"Ah, the alpha male. I'll bet almost a hundred percent of the Marines, the Airbornes, the US Rangers and all their ilk are alpha males. I guess it goes with the territory."

He smiled and relaxed a fraction as he danced her around. "It does go with the territory and so does flirting with beautiful women and dancing close and hot, steamy kisses. Watch out, boss. I might forget my place."

She laughed and the twinkle was still in her eyes.

"Oh, the big strong, handsome man can be— What? Scary? No, I don't think so. Thrilling? Ah, that's the word."

This was a side to Vivian that Mike hadn't yet seen— playful, teasing. Wanting. He wasn't sure how to react to it. "Vivian, you're asking for trouble."

"That means I don't scare you," she said in a sultry voice.

"You scare the hell out of me because I shouldn't like dancing with you. I shouldn't like flirting with you. I shouldn't want to kiss you. I shouldn't feel anything when our fingers touch and neither should you."

"For a US Army Ranger, you're a little stuffy."

He had to grin. "That's a first in my life. I have never been told I'm stuffy. You're going to goad me into doing something about that." He caught her around the waist and took long steps, dancing in circles through the terrace doors and outside on to the patio where it was darker and cooler.

"Try this for stuffy, darlin'." He pulled her tightly against him and kissed her. He knew he shouldn't, but he was having more fun with her than he could recall having had anywhere, anytime in the past three years when he was in the Army.

When did his kiss change from all in fun to something deeper, he wondered. It was as if a golden chain was pulling him down into a raging fire of longing. The feel of her mouth on his was driving every thought out of his mind, burning away everything but desire. He hadn't held a woman in a long time. He hadn't held a woman like her in a lifetime. She was delectable, enticing, voluptuous, her soft curves pressing against him. She smelled wonderful and her skin was smooth, her hair silky.

And she was off-limits.

Yet he couldn't stop kissing her. Kisses to die for. Kisses that burned, scalded and made him want more. She had teased, enticed and maneuvered him into kissing her and now he was going to pay for rising to the challenge.

He swung her up and the look she gave him was serious.

"Get Ben and Henry and let's get out of here now," she whispered.

He didn't ask why they had to rush out, but grabbed his phone and typed a brief text message as they left the patio. She grabbed her purse from the table and hurried out of the ballroom with him.

Only when they were alone in the rotunda did she explain her abrupt action. "When we were...kissing, I saw Clint at the terrace door. He was looking at you and his expression was scary. His face was red and he seemed furious."

Mike let out his breath. "If that's why you're rushing out, relax. We'll leave, but Clint isn't going to do anything crazy to mess up his life. He's got too much to lose. Besides, his anger is directed at only me, not you, I'm sure. I can deal with Clint. So can Henry and Ben. Don't worry." He slipped his arm around her waist and pulled her close against his side. "We have accomplished all you wanted to accomplish tonight. That's what you set out to do—convince Clint there's a man in your life now. I think you succeeded. So smile, Vivian."

"If you say so." Yet no smile tugged at her lips. "I'll text Ashlynn that we're leaving so they don't wonder where we are."

In minutes, he heard her phone and she looked at her message. "Ashlynn and Dan are headed to the front to get their car. They're ready to go home, too."

As they walked to the front entrance, Mike looked down at her and she gazed up at him with a long, searching look. "You're really not worried about Clint, are you?"

"No, I'm not. He's not the type for violence. That would destroy what he wants. He's just angry because a guy beat him to winning you over—or so he thinks. You did exactly what you hoped to do tonight. And then some. But, Vivian, don't pressure me into doing things I shouldn't do."

Suddenly, she smiled and he thought it was like discovering a rainbow in a gray sky. Everything was bright and beautiful again.

"If you think you shouldn't have kissed me," she said softly, "you're wrong."

He dropped his arm from her waist. "You're off-limits. Totally. For a moment, I forgot that."

She stepped closer and shook her head. "I'm not 'off-limits,' cowboy. I'm a lonely widow who hasn't been out dancing in over a year. We kissed. One kiss. That's not a life-changing big deal."

"Well, thank you, darlin'," he said, unable to keep from laughing.

"Aha, see! You know you're being ridiculous. It was a fun moment and I have had damn few of them since my husband deployed."

He imagined she likely hadn't. So he smiled at her and didn't argue the point. He took her arm. "C'mon. Ben and Henry are going to come charging in here any minute now because of my terse message. They'll think I'm getting beaten to a pulp or some such."

They stepped outside where they saw Henry and Ben standing by the limo.

In seconds, they reached the limo. "We're fine," Mike said. "Just crossed signals. Hope we didn't cut the night short for all of you."

"We're here to serve," Henry said lightly. "We're fine. It's a long drive back to the ranch anyway. If you don't mind, Ben's wife will ride up front with him."

He didn't wait for Vivian's opinion. "No, we don't mind," he answered for both of them. "You'll be happy to know that I think we accomplished our purpose with Clint tonight, so it's time to go."

Henry gave him a thumbs-up as Ben held open the limo door.

Mike still left a lot of space between Vivian and him in the back seat.

"Scared to sit close to me?" she asked.

He looked up at her, able to see her clearly even in the dim interior lighting. He couldn't stop the honesty in his response. "Yes. As I said, Vivian, you are off-limits."

He heard her long sigh. "Well, for a little while there, you were fun, and I had fun," she said with a forlorn note in her voice.

It tore at him. At this moment the one thing he wanted most in the world was to take her in his arms and kiss her for the next few hours. He scooted close and drew her against his side, slipping his arm around her and holding her. "Is that better?"

"Yes, it is," she answered and her voice sounded solemn.

"I did have fun, Vivian," he said in a somber tone. "But I wouldn't be doing right by Thane if I came home and did anything to cause you harm. I also don't want to lose a very good job. Surely you can understand that." He said the words to Vivian but he wondered whether he was really trying to convince himself. One thing he was sure of—he wasn't ever going to forget kissing her tonight. That had been the hottest, most luscious, exciting kiss of his life. Could he go home tonight and forget he kissed her? A bigger question—could he resist ever doing it again?

Henry dropped them off at Vivian's where Mike had his pickup parked. As he walked across the porch seeing her to the door, she surprised him with an invitation. "Come in for a while, Mike. It's still early in the evening."

He shook his head. "It's been a fun, interesting night, Vivian, but I'm going home now before I do something I shouldn't."

"Is it because you still see me as Thane's wife?"

"That's part of it," he answered truthfully. Only a small part. He felt torn in two now because half of him wanted badly to stay, but the other half of him knew if he did, he wouldn't be able to keep from kissing her again. It was safer, smarter, better to go back to his place.

"So what's the other part?"

"I think we might complicate each other's lives."

"You don't want to come in because I'm your boss. That's it, isn't it?" she asked, sounding disapproving. "You're incredibly old-fashioned."

"I might be," he said, "but I'm not going to let you provoke me into losing my control for the second time tonight." He backed up. "I'll see you Monday morning."

He hadn't taken two steps off the porch when he heard her again.

"Mike, it was a terrific night and it was great to be able to forget heartache, loss and grief for a short time. Thanks."

He stood with his back to her, breathing deeply, torn between wanting to go back and kiss her or doing what he knew he should do and get in his pickup and go. He turned around to look at her. She stood in the light from the porch and she looked so forlorn, his heart actually ached for her. "Damn," he whispered so softly she couldn't possibly have heard him.

He walked back to her, stopping about a foot away.

"Vivian, I'm not going to come home and make love to my friend's wife."

"Thane's gone out of my life, Mike. And it was just a kiss. For a few minutes tonight, life was happy again."

He sighed and closed the distance between them, taking her in his arms and kissing her again. Once he made the decision, he threw aside his reluctance, his guilt, his good sense to keep his distance. He threw himself into another impassioned kiss, holding her tightly against him as he leaned over her while his tongue stroked hers.

She wrapped her arms around him, her fingers winding in his short hair at the back of his head. He groaned. She was soft, passionate, sensuous, and she was making him hot and hard. More than anything he wanted to carry her off to bed—but that was a line he wouldn't cross.

He ran his hand down her back, over the fullness of her bottom, down to the split in her dress to push it open and caress her warm thigh. He was on fire, yet at the same time trembling while he hung on to his control to not go any further.

He swung her up, gazing into her eyes. "You're going to get yourself into trouble, Vivian."

"I feel as if you're bringing me to life again, bringing me back into a world of passion and joy. I've had a wonderful time."

He released her and stepped back. "I'm glad, Vivian. But I have to go now."

"I'm glad you came back," she said softly.

"So am I," he said, smiling at her. With an effort he turned away to walk to his pickup. He drove back to the guesthouse. Only when he saw in the rearview mirror that she had gone inside and closed the door did he fully let out his breath. He ached and he wanted her and he wondered if he would want her for the rest of his life.

But Vivian Warner was off-limits to him. He didn't want to be dazzled, set on fire with scorching desire by a woman who was his deceased buddy's wife, a billion-dollar heiress and his boss to boot. But how was he going to resist such an incredibly sexy, desirable woman? How would he ever be able to forget her? The one thing he knew was that he better not ever fall in love with her, because they had no future and he would be miserable.

He could never ever be happy married to her. He had old-fashioned ideas and he believed in them. In the first place, he didn't want to return to Thane's ranch and have an affair with Thane's widow. That was breaking a deep, important trust that his best friend had in him. She was so off limits for him. In addition, he didn't want to marry her and work for her and have her support him. That was ingrained in him by his dad since he was a kid. And after his dad died, by his oldest brother—the man earns the money and has the money. He does not take money from women. He would never be a billionaire, not in his wildest dreams, and he couldn't cope with that.

He entered the empty guesthouse and stood in the center of the living room. He looked around, not knowing what to do next. His thoughts were on Vivian. How was he going to be able to go out with her again next Friday night? It couldn't take many times to convince Clint that she was interested in another man. But Mike couldn't take many more nights like this one. He wanted to keep his promise, do what he should regarding Thane's wife and his ranch, but temptation was monumental with Vivian.

He couldn't take kissing her again.

* * *

Vivian walked into the mansion without seeing her surroundings. Her lips still tingled and her breath still trembled. She'd had a wonderful time tonight. Mike was fun when he wasn't being stodgy. She smiled when she remembered telling him he was stuffy. She had seen the surprised look on his face and then the determined look. The alpha male had risen to the bait.

She'd wanted Mike to kiss her. Even now, the realization struck her like a lightning bolt as it had earlier tonight when they were dancing. Ever since Thane's death, she'd been closed off, isolated both physically here on the ranch and emotionally. But tonight she had felt different. Ready to have fun, to live. For six months, people had been telling her that Thane would want her to go on with her life. Tonight, for the first time, she understood them. She was certain her one true love would want her to live, just as she was certain that if it was the other way around, she would want Thane to go on.

Had Thane sent Mike to marry her?

The thought pulled her up short, but she laughed. That hardheaded...

She laughed. That hardheaded, old-fashioned man wouldn't marry her even if he was wildly in love with her. She knew he felt honor bound to come home and take care of Thane's ranch, but to keep his distance from her. And right now he wasn't in love and neither was she.

She looked around the room and her eyes lit on Thane's picture on the mantel. She picked up the silver frame. "I love you," she whispered to him, knowing he was never coming back to her. She sat down, holding the picture against her heart with one hand while the other hand wiped the tears that slid down her face. "Thane, I miss you," she said softly as she sobbed. It hurt and she wondered if she would cry the rest of her life.

After a time, she dried her tears, trying to focus on the present. For a little while tonight, she had had fun with Mike. He was exciting and his kisses made her hot, dizzy with longing. It had been exhilarating to flirt and dance and kiss him. Until she had looked up and seen Clint at the door to the patio. He'd watched Mike with such an enraged, hateful expression that in that moment she had been frightened. But Mike hadn't been frightened at all and that had reassured her.

Mike seemed so certain, so calm about Clint that it had eased her fears and actually made her forget all about her insidious neighbor.

The delightful evening had been too brief. Mike had driven away her loneliness and grief for a little while and made her laugh and enjoy life again. Her lips still tingled and she wondered whether she would sleep at all tonight. Excitement still filled her and she felt as if she had swallowed bubbles that were dancing inside her. She could have danced until they closed the place, and next Friday, she intended to make a full evening of it.

She knew she should be careful, because she didn't want to fall in love with Mike. She could tease him into kissing her, but he wasn't the man for her to fall in love with, because she had been through one giant heartache when she lost the love of her life. Mike had given her only three months and then he would possibly move on. She didn't want another heartbreak. She hurt enough now. Besides, he was an outdated alpha male through and through who would hold to his backward ideas about women and life. He would never be able to get past her income unless he won billions in the lottery that would put him on the same financial level with her inheritance.

Reality took some shine off her excitement and she sighed. She shouldn't want to go out with him as much as she did. Right now, she was too vulnerable. Mike Moretti would never be the man for her to fall in love with. He would be a heartbreaker.

She sighed and tried to stop thinking about Mike. When she couldn't sleep, she went to her studio and began to paint. The painting needed to be finished tomorrow to be shipped to Austin for a gallery showing on Thursday.

Then the day after that she would go out with Mike again. Would that be the last time or would they have to keep going out for several more weekends? Maybe it was the novelty of being social again that was so great after such a long time without having an evening out with someone exciting. She told herself the novelty might wear off.

"Right," she said out loud.

She picked up the brush and gave herself some much-needed advice as she applied the first stroke of paint.

"Forget him, Vivian." If she didn't, he could walk away in three months and take her heart with him. She didn't want to deal with another big heartbreak.

If it was only that easy to do.

On Thursday afternoon, Mike was driving across the ranch in his pickup to meet Slade who was moving some cattle from one pasture to another when his phone buzzed. Seeing the call was from Vivian who was in Austin for her showing, so he stopped and answered.

"Hi. How's the gallery show going?" he asked, curious why she had time to call.

"Mike, Clint has been in. He knew I was having a showing here and he wanted me to go to dinner with him. Of course, I'm not going."

Her pronouncement had his stomach in angry knots. The guy just didn't give up.

Vivian went on. "Ben drove me this morning, but I'm trying to get in touch with Henry. I'd like him to come to Austin and ride back with us. Clint made me nervous today. He was very persistent and I think he'll be back. Can you find Henry? Get him to drive here and get one of the guys to ride with him and drive his car back. I'd feel better if Henry rode back with us."

He could hear the tension in her voice. "Sure thing. Don't worry and get Ben to hang out with you in the gallery."

"He is. I know this is silly because Clint is simply a pest, but I don't like having him around me."

"Don't let him worry you. He's a creep, but he's harmless, only a nuisance. Ben's there. We'll get rid of Clint. Enjoy your show. And think about going out with me Friday night. You might even get a chance to goad me into kissing you again."

She laughed. "Okay, I feel better now."

"Good. You'll be home before you know it."

"Thanks, Mike."

As soon as the call ended, Mike called Slade instead of Henry. As it rang, he got into his pickup and when he ended the call, he headed back to the guesthouse.

Vivian stood with a customer who had purchased a painting, which was being packaged and wrapped for him to take home.

"I hope you enjoy your painting. Thank you," Vivian said. "I enjoyed meeting you and talking to you."

The man nodded. "My wife is going to like this picture, I'm sure."

"Have a fun time tonight at her birthday party."

"I think the painting will be the highlight of the evening."

She smiled as Ben picked up the painting to carry it to the car for the customer. As he left, she looked outside the gallery window and her heart skipped. Was it really Mike standing outside talking to the man who had just purchased her painting? Her gaze raced over his matching white hat and shirt, brown jacket, a bolo tie, jeans and boots. It was every inch Mike and then he turned toward the door.

Suddenly self-conscious, she glanced at a mirror that hung across the room and straightened her deep blue suit jacket. She shook her hair away from her face and smiled as Mike came through the door. There was no way to ignore the rush she felt when she looked into his green eyes.

He looked so handsome, strong and solid that the sight of him made her want to hug him. "How'd you get here so quickly? I talked to you only a little more than an hour ago."

"I had Jason fly me here. Henry's parking the rental car. He can ride back with Ben. You and I will fly back to the ranch."

"I feel ridiculous, but Clint bothered me. He wanted me to go to dinner tonight and stay over in Austin. I've never gone out with him once, so why would he think I'd go to dinner and stay over?"

"Don't ask me how Clint Woodson's mind works."

Henry came through the door. "Hi, Vivian, Ben."

"Thanks for coming, Henry," she said.

"Sure. Glad to. That's my job. How's it going?" he said, turning to Ben.

The cowboy shrugged. "Okay. Woodson's been in once, but I'm betting that he'll be back."

Vivian looked at Mike. "It's been quiet and peaceful other than Clint and he really didn't do anything to disturb anyone except me. Clint came in when Ben went to lunch. The morning was busy and pleasant and the gallery people were here along with some friends."

She turned and called out to the gallery owner. "Marta, come meet some people from our ranch." The tall brunette held her hand out to Mike as Vivian introduced him and then Henry.

She brought over three more women connected with the gallery, and then finally she and Mike were alone again.

"I'll look around, and Henry and me will hang out for the rest of the afternoon," he told her. "What about the paintings? Do they go home later?"

"Not now. The gallery wants to show them, so they'll be here for a couple of months."

She watched Mike walk around the room. He took his hat off and disappeared in the direction of the offices and reappeared shortly without it. While he was gone, Marta appeared to ask about a painting and Vivian had a chance to give her a brief explanation of why Mike and Henry had appeared, telling Marta Clint was harmless, but too insistent on wanting her to go out with him.

She was busy with customers and art lovers until after four o'clock when there was finally a lull. But instead of relaxing, she tensed up when she looked out the window. She walked over to Mike where he sat in a chair quietly talking to Ben and Henry. "I just saw Clint drive up and park out front."

Mike stood. "Henry, I think you two can hang where you are. At least for right now." Mike put his arm around Vivian's waist. They both turned as the bell over the door sounded.

The minute Mike touched her, Vivian stopped thinking about anyone else. She was keenly aware of his arm lightly around her as he stood close, holding her against his side.

"Mr. Woodson," Mike said, nodding.

Clint glanced around at the men, nodding and giving a cursory hello. "I see you brought help along," he said, smiling at her. "Have you had a good showing? I sent some people over."

"Yes, I have. I've been busy all day."

"Hello, again, Mr. Woodson. Do you want to see some more paintings?" Marta asked, approaching him.

"Sure. I might buy one this time." He walked off with Marta while she talked about the paintings.

"Thanks for being here," Vivian said quietly to Mike. "I don't even want him to own one of my paintings, but I can't do anything about that. Except hope he'll leave when he finishes the transaction."

"Come on. Let's go into Marta's office and wait until he's gone," Mike replied. "Henry, Ben, we'll be in the back." The men nodded and Mike put his arm around her shoulders to walk down the hall. Clint glanced at them as they passed the room where he stood listening to Marta tell him about a painting.

They stepped into Marta's office and Mike closed the door, removing his arm from Vivian's shoulders. Instantly, she felt the loss.

"Mike, I've been thinking about it. Clint pops up whenever I leave the ranch. Someone must be telling him where I'll be. It gives me the creeps for him to be around when I leave town." She felt a shudder dance over her spine. "I've also been thinking about this. Maybe you should move into the main house at the ranch. I already have Henry and Millie and Francie living in my house. There are big suites and all kinds of entrances and exits. You wouldn't have to see me and you could come and go as you please where you wouldn't see anyone else. If you moved into my house, word would get around and—"

He smiled. "Stop. That house is bigger than some hotels I've stayed in. Yes, I'll move in. If that doesn't get rid of Clint, I don't know what will. You know, he's probably paying someone who works for you to tell him where you are."

"That's annoying if it's my employee."

"He's probably paying a lot and he probably makes it sound harmless. I think he is harmless, just a creep, an annoying bully. He wants you and he wants your ranch but we'll get rid of him," he said.

"You're always so confident."

"Only when I know I'm right," he said, and she smiled.

"You sure you're okay with moving in?"

He nodded. " I'll stay for a few weeks. Word will get back to Clint and that should do it. Besides, that and seeing us today with my arm around you and the other night kissing out on the terrace, he'll get the message. He can't be that dense."

"I feel sure we'll see him this Friday night. We're going to an old downtown Dallas club. We belong and so does Clint. I can't imagine that all this won't run him off soon."

"I agree." Mike gave her a long look that made her breath catch and then he crossed the room to her. The closer he came, the faster her heart beat. He didn't pause, but wrapped his arms around her. She noticed his after-shave, an enticing woodsy scent. His green eyes had tiny gold flecks near the center, his slight stubble that showed on his jaw added to his already tough look, and his black tousled hair curled on his forehead.

"Maybe we should give him something to think about," Mike said. He wrapped his arms around her, looked at her as if to see if she agreed and then he kissed her.

Four

The minute his lips met hers, she forgot everything else. Her world became Mike, his arms, his body, his mouth and what they were doing to her. Her heart pounded and she clung to him. He wound one hand in her hair as he held her tightly. Desire heated her and for a moment she forgot where she was or why she was there. He was solid, exciting, sexy and he made her feel alive again.

When he released her, she felt dazed as she looked into green eyes that had darkened with obvious desire. He took out a handkerchief to wipe her lip gloss off his face and then touched it to the corner of her mouth, wiping gently. He unbuttoned the top button of her white silk blouse. "That adds to the effect."

"That one button is barely noticeable, but it's enough," she added hastily.

"Clint will notice. I'll see what's going on. Come join us when you want."

"We look like we've kissed."

The corner of his mouth lifted in a crooked smile. "I think we did. I must not have made an impression."

"You know you did," she said softly. "You rocked my world." She crossed the room to a mirror to look at herself.

"I thought you wanted to give Clint the impression that you and I are a couple."

"I do and I will if he sees me now." She ran her fingers through her hair and shook her head. "But we'll probably shock Henry and Ben."

"I imagine they'll both know exactly what we're trying to do. They know you're trying to run him off."

She sighed. "You're right." She joined him and he held the door, stepping out behind her and then closing it. He held her arm as they walked down the hall together.

Clint stood near the door talking to Marta. He glanced at Vivian and his eyes narrowed slightly as he looked from her to Mike and back again. "I bought one of your paintings, Vivian. I'll think of you when I look at it," he said. "Marta is having it sent to my house in Dallas."

"Thank you, Clint," she said quietly while Mike stood at her side. He was looking at a small pocket reminder book he carried and he made a note in it. She glanced back at Clint whose gaze raked insolently over her.

"Well, I'll leave you to your art show," he said. He turned and left, causing the little bell over the door to ring as the door opened then shut.

"He won't be back today," Mike said, "so I'll join the guys. Anything you want, let me know."

"Anything I want?" she asked softly in a sultry tone.

He'd been about to turn away, but he turned back to her and stepped close again. "Vivian, you're flirting and you're going to get yourself in trouble if you aren't careful," he said almost in a whisper.

"Oh, I'll be careful, Mike, but you asked me."

He shook his head and walked away while she grinned.

The bell rang and Marta stepped to the door. Three women entered and wanted to meet Vivian and see her paintings. Vivian was busy for the next two hours and then it was time to close the gallery.

It took another hour to get everything recorded, divided up and put away. Finally, she turned to look at Mike. "Are we flying home now?"

"Yes, you and I. Henry will ride back with Ben so we're set. I called a few minutes ago and told Jason to get the plane ready." He turned to face Marta who was straightening a picture on the wall. "Marta, it was nice to meet you. Thank you for what you did today."

He moved closer to Vivian. "Just let us know when you're ready and Ben will drop us off at the airport."

"I'm ready." She turned to Marta to thank her again for the showing. They talked briefly about the paintings and then left. Outside, Vivian turned to Henry. "Thanks, Henry, for flying with Mike."

"Sure. Ben will drop you two off at the plane and then we'll head back to the ranch."

"Thank you," she repeated.

"Thanks, guys," Mike said. At the small private airport, Ben drove past three hangars and stopped near the waiting Tumbling T plane. In minutes they were onboard, seated with their seat belts fastened. She watched out the window while the limo turned in a circle and left.

"From a work standpoint, this was a fun, successful day. I saw friends, showed my art, made new friends and sold some of my paintings, which is nice. Then again, there was Clint." She turned to Mike and looked him in the eyes. "Thank you, Mike, for coming to my rescue. Clint is a pest, but I feel sure he'll be gone soon."

"I haven't run him off yet."

Jason, their pilot, announced they had been cleared for takeoff and she looked out the window for a moment as the plane gained speed and then lifted and was airborne.

"Mike, I have another favor to ask you," she said, voicing what she had been thinking about all morning. She took a deep breath, hoping her question wouldn't send him running. "Mike, when we talked about you moving into my house…well, there's a lot of room and you can live where you never have to see—"

He cut her off. "I told you I don't mind. It won't be permanent and if it helps get rid of Clint, it's all worth it. If someone from the ranch is keeping him posted on where you are and what you're doing, then he's sure to get the report that I'm in the house."

"But not anywhere near me." She paused a moment, gathering her courage to voice her request. "Would you consider moving into the big suite at the end of the hall from mine? If you're there, on the same floor and not too far away, no one will know how much we go back-and-forth to each other's suites."

He didn't hesitate. "I think that would be best. I'll even come to your suite at night if you think we need to do that," he said, and she saw the sparkle in his eyes and knew he was teasing.

"Seriously, Mike, you were inconvenienced today and you'll get paid extra for it. I'll do the same for Henry. Ben gets paid to do this, but he'll get extra for this trip."

Mike looked at her a moment before he finally nodded. "Okay, thanks," he said and she felt as if he thanked her simply out of courtesy and he really didn't want her to pay him extra at all.

He was an old-fashioned guy, she thought, wondering why she had such an intense physical reaction to him when she couldn't understand his outdated ideas. "You don't like taking money from me, do you? If Thane was here with you and he made that offer, you'd say thanks and like it and never give it another thought."

"You might be right. Vivian, I grew up with a dad who died when I was thirteen. There were four kids in our family and my mom was a high school dropout. My oldest brother was like a dad to me. My two older brothers went to college, got jobs and helped put me through college. I went with their help and with scholarships and the money I made working my own jobs. And winning in rodeos. Mostly bull riding and calf roping. I graduated, got a job on a ranch and helped put my youngest brother through school. Now all of us help take care of Mom. It hasn't been easy. I got my ideas from my dad and my oldest brother after my dad wasn't around. And for some reason, they probably are old-fashioned. But, Vivian, wherever my ideas come from, surely you can see you're way out of my league," he said quietly.

"It shouldn't be such an issue. Life's more important than money."

"Well, it's a little different when you don't have any."

With his words, she felt a wall rising up between them and suspected he would never change his views. "You were friends with Thane and you didn't seem to care what he had."

"That's entirely different."

She laughed. "To someone in the last century."

He gave her a crooked smile that made her tingle. Even

arguing with him was fun and she couldn't understand her own response to him.

Mike leaned closer. "Sweetie, Clint will get out of your life. I'll go back to living in the guesthouse house and who knows, maybe I'll move on myself, someday. I'll be out of your way and you won't have to put up with me and my old-fashioned ways."

"Well, maybe," she said, gazing into his green eyes. "But right now, you like to kiss me and when you do, you forget about all those rules you have about what a man does and what a woman does."

She was slightly exasperated with him and his antiquated views of her wealth. And she couldn't stop thinking about his kiss in Marta's office. A kiss that made her want more. He had to have felt something because he'd looked as startled and as filled with desire as she'd felt.

"You, darlin', stir up trouble easier than a gnat finding fruit," he said.

"My kisses are trouble? Imagine that. I thought they were quite harmless," she said, teasing him and having fun in the process, wondering if she could goad him into another sexy kiss.

"See, you know you're doing it right now. For you, my kiss may be as harmless as watching the clouds roll by, but when I kiss you, it's as dangerous to me as jumping into a fire and you know it. And, Vivian, you're pushing right now." He unbuckled his seat belt and turned to slip an arm behind her as he leaned over.

She started to reply, but when his mouth covered hers, whatever she had been about to say was gone forever. Her heart raced as he kissed her passionately, a demanding kiss that made her forget their silly conversation and her teasing. His lips started a fire low inside her. She wanted the seat belt out of the way. She wanted her arms around him and his around her and she wanted every inch of him pressed against her. Every barrier between them gone.

His kiss was pure seduction. Her breasts tingled, her body ached for his hands, his mouth, all of him. Common sense, resistance, wisdom burned away in the first few seconds. All she knew was she wanted him to keep touching her and kissing her and to never stop. Dimly she was aware of the release of her seat belt and his hand drifting in circles over her breast. She moaned as she held him tightly, running her fingers over him, down over a bicep as hard as a rock.

She felt his fingers unbuttoning her blouse before releasing the catch on her bra and then cool air on her bare skin and then his tongue, hot, wet, trailing down over her bare breasts. "Mike," she whispered and pushed lightly against him.

Instantly, there was space between them as he rose slightly and she looked up at him. Desire, making his eyes darker, was so obvious that she trembled. "We don't have any privacy and we're about to go where each one of us knows we shouldn't."

"Vivian, you know what to do to get me going. Don't do it unless you want to deal with me and with the results."

She bit back a teasing reply because he looked pushed over a limit and she wasn't ready to go any further, and they didn't have privacy on the plane anyway.

"Okay, Mike," she said, feeling subdued even as her heart still raced and her body quivered with desire. She wanted him. She wanted his arms around her, his mouth on hers again, his tongue and fingers making her come to life and feel loved and desired once again. She had been so alone, so lonesome and now Mike was driving all that away, most of the time in fun, but not now. Now it was a blaze of hot, passionate kisses and caresses that were headed straight for a fantastic seduction.

She closed her eyes for a moment, trying to get control, to get the sexy thoughts out of her mind, to return to a normal afternoon with two employees. Knowing that wasn't going to happen, she opened her eyes to find Mike intently watching her. There were moments when his intent looks seemed to go right through her and she felt as if he could discern every thought she had.

She straightened her clothes and glanced toward the cockpit, thankful for the panel that kept her seat from Jason's view. He might see Mike, but he was back in his seat, his seat belt on.

She cast a look his way and saw he was still aroused. She too tingled all over, but wisdom had finally returned and she was hanging on to it like a lifeline in a crisis. Only that wisdom could tell her what she should do.

She had looked forward to this showing at the Austin gallery, and it had been successful, but the only part of the day she would remember was Mike. Long after she had forgotten the rest of the day and the people in it, she'd recall him and his kisses.

Once again, a familiar thought ran through her mind. Had Thane sent Mike because he knew Mike would run the ranch the way Thane wanted it ran?

Or had he sent Mike because he knew Mike would fill a lonely void in her life?

It would be just like Thane. When he was alive, all he'd wanted to do was take care of her. He had loved the fact that they were together out on the ranch, far from her father. He'd even urged Vivian to not move right away if something were to happen to him. He'd told her to take her time, let things settle and then decide. Several times he had reminded her that she couldn't go back once she moved away. Was her wonderful late husband trying to take care of her from beyond the grave?

Mike interrupted her thoughts. "Are you okay? You're quiet."

"Thanks to you. I'm on fire and you know it."

He took her hand lightly, casually holding it. "Well, we both got ourselves into a twist then. To calm things down, let's talk about what you want to do when we get in. We can have Jason change the flight plan and land in Dallas. We can go to dinner there and drive back to the ranch. Or we can fly back to the ranch," he said and released her hand.

"The ranch is fine." She turned to look out the window and settle herself. After a few minutes she thought she'd put it all in perspective. "Mike, it's been a long time since Thane was home. I stay on the ranch and paint, so I don't see a lot of friends. Maybe I've just gotten carried away with you around."

"I hope so. It's fun, Vivian, but we're both being reckless. I've been in a war zone and you've been through a loss and living isolated in a lot of ways. Maybe—" He stopped himself. "Forget it. I take things too seriously sometimes."

"Ah, good," she said, feeling better and smiling. "You've got your sense back."

"Sort of," he said. "Though if I had any sense, I'd sit across the aisle from you."

She put her chin in her hand, her elbow on the armrest and looked closely at him. "I do that to you?"

"See, dammit! You and I need to get out and circulate more. We can't keep from flirting and teasing each other when we both know where it will lead and neither one of us wants that."

"Oh, speak for yourself, cowboy," she said, laughing and sitting back, getting out a magazine from her tote bag. "I'll sit and read and leave you in peace and quiet. Hey, look at this," she said, pointing to the shout line on the bottom right of the cover.

He twisted slightly to read aloud: "'How to Keep the Man in Your Life Happy.'" He looked up at her. "Vivian—"

She smiled at him, unable to resist teasing him. "I'd say right now you're the man in my life. Don't you think? Well, I know exactly what will keep you happy. Leave you alone like an old bear in its den."

"Correct. You do that. You're finally getting on the right track."

"Watch out, Mike. You'll hurt my feelings."

"No, I won't, and we won't argue that point. I'll nap."

She laughed. "Of course, you will. I'm sure you feel so sleepy now." He gave her a look of exasperation that made her be quiet. He turned his back to her and placed his head against the seat. She knew he wasn't napping, but he was tuning her out and she suspected she needed to leave well enough alone—they'd had a passionate moment that still resounded for both of them.

She looked at the back of his head, his neat haircut that was probably due to the military influence. He was fun to tease, irresistible and sexy and exciting. And dangerous to her well-being. She knew he would never fall in love with her and if she did fall in love with him, she would have nothing but heartbreak. He would never get past her income, her inheritance and her position as his boss. How had he gotten that way? Was it from the tough times he'd had growing up when they were so short of money? Was she so accustomed to her wealthy dad that she didn't give her status and bank account a thought?

All she knew was that she should keep her distance from Mike, guard her heart and use more sense around him. But he was too appealing, too sexy and she had been too lonely after Thane's death. From the very first moment she'd met him, when they'd shaken hands, there had been a sizzling reaction that she knew he felt, too. How could she resist that?

With a sigh she turned away, looking down at the magazine cover and smiling over showing it to him. "How to Keep the Man in Your Life Happy." Well, in reality, the only man who really wanted to be in her life was a pest she was trying to get rid of. The man seated next to her was trying to ignore her and he sure wasn't in her life except to be in her employ. She did have a date with him, though, for Friday night. Granted, it was at her own request, but it was a date nonetheless. When they were out together, he couldn't resist flirting any more than she could. And he could dance and was fun in spite of trying not to be, the way he was right now. She smiled and almost reached out to run her hand over his, but she didn't.

He had come through for her this afternoon, taking her call and acting on it immediately. She was certain if there had been any way to save Thane, Mike would have found it. He kept a cool head in a crisis. Mike, Henry, Ben, Jason, Slade—Thane had done well in the men he had hired. The only one that wasn't a responsible, stand-up guy was Leon, but Thane couldn't have known that because he was all Thane had hoped when Thane had been home. Come to think of it, Leon must have gone back to that type of guy now. She hadn't heard a word about him from Mike and she hadn't seen Leon anywhere near her. Maybe Mike's presence was an influence on the horse trainer. Now she could only hope he had the same influence on Clint Woodson.

When they landed at the ranch, Mike's pickup was parked near the hangar. He held the pickup door for her and closed it, going around to get in the driver's seat.

Once they were on the road, Vivian resumed the discussion of his move. "If you can, why don't you move into the house next Saturday? I'm sure you can get some guys to help if you need it."

"All I have to move is my clothes. I'm assuming the suite in the main house is fully furnished like the guesthouse?"

"Yes, it is."

"Then I won't need help moving."

"You should still make sure some of the guys know what you're doing. After all, I want word to get back to Clint."

"It'll get back to him and the guys will know. You can't dig up dandelions around here without everyone knowing it."

She brought up the subject of the horse trainer that she'd thought about on the plane. "Mike, what about Leon? You've never mentioned him."

"No need to. He hasn't been up to the house, has he?"

"Not at all."

"He won't come around. Word is out that I was close with Thane. Slade likes me and word is also out that you and I are friends. That's enough for a man like Leon. He doesn't have the money or the clout that Clint does, so he isn't going to cause trouble. You've seen the last of him unless you hunt him down."

"That's good to hear."

They were both quiet until Mike stopped the pickup at the mansion and walked her up to the porch. At the door, Vivian turned to him. "So I'll see you Friday night. I thought we could stay at my penthouse condo in downtown Dallas. That way, Ben can go do what he wants Friday night after he drops us off. My family owns three condos near mine and near Dad's office. Ben and his wife stay in one when they're in Dallas. Henry and Millie stay in the other, so they'll be close at hand. And, my old-fashioned friend, my penthouse condo is big. You can have your own suite and I wouldn't dream of trying to seduce you," she said in a sultry voice, unable to resist flirting even though she didn't want to fall in love with him She reminded herself he would go out of her life as suddenly as he came into it.

"Vivian, you're pulling my chain again," he replied in a husky voice.

She smiled sweetly because she saw the sparkle in his eyes. "Well, the last time I did that I got a big kiss. What will happen this time?"

He stepped close and put his hands on either side of her face, turning her head so she had to look up at him. "I think you like to kiss and you want to kiss. And, darlin', I will oblige," he said, and his mouth covered hers.

A wave of desire poured over her, hot, tingling, steamy need that made her want him to hold her the rest of the night and kiss her and let her hold and kiss him. Her heart pounded and she slipped her arms around his narrow waist, holding him tightly, feeling his hard body against her, his muscles and long legs.

He broke the kiss and looked down into her eyes. In their green depths she saw blatant longing. "Mike," she whispered, all teasing forgotten.

He accepted the unspoken invitation in her word and his mouth claimed hers again. He kissed her long and passionately, making her heart drum, making her forget all the reasons she didn't want to get too close to him.

When he released her, he looked at her intently. "I need to get out of here for both our sakes. Good night, Vivian." He brushed a kiss on her cheek and hurried to his pickup, driving away without looking back.

She stood a moment, watching him drive into the darkness. His kisses had melted her and at the same time stirred a sweeping need for hours of loving in a strong man's arms. She missed her husband, missed so much about him. But there was something about Mike that drew her to him. Something she was having a hard time denying. Till she remembered... Mike was too ingrained in his old-fashioned beliefs and he'd never get past her inheritance. Ironic, she thought, because there were men out there who would want the inheritance more than they would want her.

Mike had been good to come today when she needed someone. He came and brought Henry and he would move into her house for a brief time. She should leave him alone, not get too close. He wasn't going to stay. Slade had warned her and he should know. Mike could break her heart if she fell in love with him, and she was still living with heartache over losing the only man she'd ever loved.

She missed Thane every day. He had been hell-bent on enlisting, serving his country, doing his patriotic duty. His grandfather fought in Korea. His dad fought in Vietnam. Because of family tradition, Thane had felt he owed his country some service. If only she could have gotten pregnant, she might have been able to hold him at home; but their attempts hadn't been successful before he'd left. The doctor had assured her she'd be able to conceive if she just relaxed, but that had been easier said than done when Thane was making plans to join the Rangers.

Now she was alone and vulnerable because of her loss. Too vulnerable. She needed to take care with Mike.

She had no illusions. Mike was a tough ex-ranger. He knew self-discipline and control and he didn't want to love an heiress, a woman who had more money and power than he did, and he would stick by that conviction with that iron control he had. When his promise to Thane was up, he would be gone. She didn't have a single doubt about that. Neither did Slade. She sighed. "You sent home a reliable guy, Thane. But I wish you'd sent one who could bend a little and be more like you."

She thought about Mike's kiss today. He could set her on fire with longing and need.

Tomorrow night she was going out with him. Even if he didn't like taking her out, he was fun and she'd miss that when he stopped. When Clint got out of her life, Mike would, too. Until then, she'd have a blast at the club. She had shed buckets of tears over her lost love and over being alone. Friday night, she planned to have a good time and Mike would help her do just that.

Friday night, Mike wore a charcoal suit with matching boots, his black Stetson and a black-and-gray striped tie. They were going to an old established club in downtown Dallas, a club that once had been men only. Then they would go back to Vivian's penthouse condo. He sighed and warned himself one more time to use some common sense and to avoid letting her get to him, teasing him into losing control again. It was difficult to resist her taunts. He knew she was being playful, but that made her all the more irresistible. That and knowing what it was like to kiss her.

He could kiss her all night long and it wouldn't be enough. She was incredibly sexy and her body had luscious curves. She was soft, but she had her feisty moments when he lost it and wanted to grab and kiss her.

He wanted to run Clint off and be able to stay away from Vivian before she snagged his heart, then it would hurt like hell to leave her.

In the meantime, he couldn't wait to go out with her.

Then next week he'd be moving into her mansion.

He strode up the walk, the waiting limo behind him, and looked up at the massive house. He couldn't even imagine the cost of building such a home out on this mesquite-covered prairie.

When he entered the front door, Henry held the door.

"I thought you're off on Friday night."

"I am. I leave when you two do. Millie and I are going into Dallas for the weekend. So I'll see you Monday morning unless you have an emergency. You have my number."

"We better not have an emergency. Did she tell you I'm moving into this place next week?"

"Yes, she did. Good idea. That ought to finish Clint being in her life. And it won't be any hardship to have another person live here. You could drop a hotel inside this house and still have room. I think Thane thought they would fill it with kids, friends and relatives, but life doesn't work out the exact way you plan most of the time." He shrugged. "Have a good time tonight. Millie and I've been out with her a few times, but she's been shut up alone here for too long. She'll probably wear you down."

"Yeah, well, I'm ready to party myself. There wasn't much partying where I was last year."

Henry nodded, and Mike knew the ex-marine could relate firsthand to what he was talking about. "I'll see you. And next week I can help you move."

"Sure. Have a good time, Henry. Hopefully, there won't be a peep out of us."

As he watched Henry walk down the hall, a voice from behind startled him.

"Have you been waiting long?"

He turned to see Vivian coming down the sweeping spiral staircase. She wore a pale blue dress of some soft fabric that swirled around her knees with each step she took. Thane's diamond pendant glittered in the light. Mike's heart thudded and beat twice as fast. Vivian looked like a dream. Her blond hair fell on her shoulders, turning up slightly. The sleeveless dress emphasized her tiny waist and the high-heeled sandals highlighted her long shapely legs. He wanted to take her into his arms and kiss her while he scooped her up and found the closest bedroom.

That wasn't going to happen. He needed to constantly remember Thane sent him to take care of Vivian. She was so off-limits to him. He smiled and said hello and told her Ben was outside with the limo.

She gave him a dazzling smile. "I'm ready for some excitement."

He took her arm and they left, going to the limo, and soon they were on their way to Dallas. He sat close to her and she placed her hand lightly on his knee. He wondered

how aware she was of touching him. It was a casual touch
on her part, but the result wasn't casual to him. He had
an instant reaction to her hand on his leg. He didn't want
to make an issue of it, so he kept quiet and tried to talk
about something that would take his mind off his arm
around her or how close she sat, lightly pressed against
him, her hand on his leg.

He tried, but he couldn't stop his awareness of her.
Or the trepidation that had been building in him all day.
Was he being driven in a long white limo to a destina-
tion that would change his life? He didn't think so, but
he also didn't want to get hurt badly. Falling in love with
Vivian could be disastrous. He was holding the hand of
Thane's wife and he couldn't get past that.

The club was on the top floor of one of the tallest
buildings in Dallas. Through the floor-to-ceiling windows they could look out on the glittering lights of the
city below. The band was good and the crowd already
partying.

They ordered drinks and sat at a table for two. When
the drinks came, he raised his eyes, looking over the rim
of his glass into her big blue eyes. "Here's to you, Vivian. May you get what you want in life to make up for
what you lost in the past."

"I'll drink to that," she said, holding up her glass and
touching it lightly to his crystal goblet. She watched him
as she sipped and he wanted to skip dinner, skip dancing
and go to that penthouse condo of hers and make love
to her all night long. But if he didn't want his life in a
tangled snarl, he shouldn't do any such thing. He should
stay right here, party, enjoy looking at her, flirt with
her a little, relish in her company and dance with her,

but avoid with all his being getting any more entangled with this woman.

His gaze shifted to her full red lips and he drew a deep breath, remembering how those lips felt beneath his. He looked up to meet her wide-eyed gaze that held desire, a come-hither look that set him on fire.

"Let's dance, Mike," she whispered. "I need to move around. I've looked forward to this all day long." In minutes they were on the dance floor, dancing to a lively number, and he watched her as she moved around him with abandon. The more he was with her the more he wanted her in his bed. Get through tonight, he told himself. One day at a time and soon he would be away from her.

After dinner he shed his jacket and got down to dancing in earnest, ending two fast songs with one slow ballad, finally taking her into his arms to hold her close. She smelled wonderful and was as soft as he had remembered.

Holding her, he couldn't help but anticipate the rest of the night at her penthouse. They'd be alone, just the two of them, and he envisioned doing all the things to her that had kept him up at night. But he didn't dare. He shouldn't even think about it. It would be smarter to stay here at the club until it closed, to be with people and avoid getting in a situation in the condo where he would kiss away his determination to not complicate his life.

Vivian looked as if she was having the time of her life and he felt a clutch in his heart as he thought about Thane, remembering those last moments of holding his friend and trying to stop his blood from flowing away. She and Thane had loved each other and she'd had a lot of lonesome months since his death. She was isolated on the ranch. She had Henry and Millie and Francie to talk to, but Henry was out doing things and Millie had her work, and Mike doubted if she hung out in the kitchen with Francie very much. He was surprised she had remained on the ranch this long, except that it was one last tie to Thane that hadn't been broken.

"I think it's time to move on," she finally said about the same time the band stopped playing. He nodded and walked back to the table with her to get her purse. Her condo was close and it was a nice night so they walked. As he left the club, he wondered if he was walking straight into heartbreak.

Five

Noticing her perfume again as he walked beside her, Mike wanted her in his arms and he was having a silent argument with himself. It would be best to tell her goodnight and go to his room and lock himself in there. But that wasn't what he wanted to do at all.

He tried to think of all the reasons not to get intertwined with her. First of all, she was Thane's wife. Even though Thane was no longer living, Mike felt there was some unspoken agreement that when Thane asked him to take the job of running the ranch, and he accepted, that he would not cause her heartbreak or any unhappiness. He also felt certain Thane didn't send him to the ranch to seduce her.

She was his boss. That would be bad business. She was his friend's wife, his close friend who had hired him to help her and look out for her. Any time he touched her, he felt he was breaking an honored trust. She was the daughter of a billionaire. She had inherited Thane's millions, making her wealthy beyond his wildest dreams. She was accustomed to getting what she wanted, when she wanted it. He was not accustomed to having a woman like that in his life and he didn't like it and he didn't want to get emotionally wrapped up with her. And he damn well didn't want to fall in love with her. He could never buy her a ring or a necklace or any other thing that would be as beautiful as she could buy for herself. Not only the disparity between their incomes, but also when those three months were up , he was leaving. He wasn't going to live with this arrangement for years. He would have worked the three months he promised Thane.

"You're quiet, Mike."

His mind raced for a believable reason, because he certainly couldn't tell her the truth. "I was thinking about the ranch," he lied. "I think Slade will leave soon and he should. I'm urging him to go. I feel certain that it'll be sooner than he first said. He's decided I can take over and do his job and that frees him up to go."

"Do you feel ready to take it over?"

"Yes, I suppose I do. You take each problem as it comes."

"Then when he talks to you about it, do what you feel is best. As far as the ranch goes, you're going to run it as if it's yours. That's what I need and want. I don't know anything about it and running a ranch isn't my deal. Thane said I'd never have to take charge." Her voice weakened on the last and she looked away. He knew she hurt over Thane, and Mike hurt because he couldn't do anything for her.

"Here we are," she said, stopping at a tall oil and gas

building. Lights were on in the lobby and an attendant sat at the desk. "There's the night watchman." Lights played over the front of the building, so everything was well-lit and big flower boxes were packed with multicolored blooming spring flowers. She punched a button and Mike heard a beep and clicks and then she opened a door.

He took Vivian's arm and they crossed an empty lobby. The attendant at the desk said hello and called Vivian by name. She answered and introduced Mike to the night watchman.

After leaving the front desk, they stepped into the elevator and it was a fast ride to the penthouse where it opened directly into the condo.

As the doors closed behind Mike, she tossed her purse on a table. He glanced around at an entryway that held a crystal chandelier, potted palms and Queen Anne fruitwood chairs covered in a muted design of red-and-blue damask. "Is this whole floor yours?" he asked.

She nodded. "I told you there's plenty of room for you to stay tonight."

Mike walked into the living area with floor-to-ceiling windows that gave another panoramic view of the sprawling city. It was even more breathtaking than the restaurant's view with all the twinkling lights. "This is spectacular." He turned to look at her and amended his thought. It was Vivian who was spectacular and took his breath away. The soft light spilled over her, highlighting her blond hair and creamy skin. He met her gaze and saw the desire in her eyes that he felt. It was hot, intense.

"Would you like a drink?"

"You know what I'd like," he said quietly. He couldn't look away. He was caught and held by her big blue eyes as he walked toward her. "I should get in that elevator and get the hell out of here. You and I don't belong together."

"Are you telling me you don't want to kiss me? I've seen the way you've looked at me all evening."

"I'm going to complicate my life and yours."

"You make way too big a deal out of it, but I'll tell you what, I'm not going to push you into kissing me." She raised her chin and turned to walk away. "I'll get us drinks—"

He stepped up and lightly placed his hand on her arm, turning her. She looked around with her eyes widening as surprise filled her expression. "Mike, don't kiss me if you don't—"

"You know damn good and well I want to kiss you with all my being," he said. His voice was gruff. "And you want me to kiss you. Come here, Vivian." He drew her to him, his mouth coming down on hers and coaxing her lips open as his tongue thrust inside.

Breathing heavily, he raised his head to look into her eyes. "I want you. I want to kiss you the rest of the night, to hold you, to make love to you." He framed her face with his hands, his gaze searching hers. "You want me, too, don't you?"

"Yes," she whispered. "I want you to kiss me until I melt from loving. I want kisses that for tonight will stop heartaches and emptiness. Something to wipe all that out even briefly and something I can cling to in nights to come. Hot memories that don't leave me crying. I just want to feel alive with someone. I want to feel wanted, Mike, by a sexy, desirable man and I want to make you happy in return."

"You don't have to worry about that one, darlin'. Ah, Vivian if you'll take tonight—"

"Mike, I'll take whatever I can get," she said, brushing his mouth with hers. His heart felt as if it would pound out of his chest. He was aroused, aching with wanting her, wanting to kiss her senseless, to take her now, but he wasn't going to do any such thing. If they made love, he wanted to take a long time to give her all the pleasure and loving he could. He wanted to make her happy, leave her with the kind of memories she wanted. Do everything in his power to excite her and give her a night she could remember. He'd had his own cold, lonely nights, losses and hurts. Without even trying, he knew she would give him all the pleasure, memories, hot sex and excitement he craved.

He wrapped his arms around her and held her close to kiss her passionately. In minutes, he shifted, trailing kisses across her cheek, his tongue tracing the curve of her ear, his breath hot on her skin as he whispered, "I want to excite you as much as I possibly can, darlin'. I want to kiss and caress every beautiful inch of you and feel you moving and responding to my touch."

"Mike," she gasped, turning to kiss him.

He pulled her up tightly against him, holding her close, his tongue stroking hers while he slipped one hand down her back, unfastening her zipper and stroking her bare skin. He tangled his fingers in her hair and kissed her while she clung to him, moaning softly and kissing him in return. He wanted her with a need that felt like desperation. He wanted to spend the night with her in his arms. He'd tried to do the right thing. He'd tried to do the smart thing and walk away, but he couldn't and clearly she didn't want to, either.

She moaned softly, thrusting her hips against him, her hands playing over him as she opened the buttons

of his shirt and tugged its shirttails out of his trousers.
Desire swept over him and he leaned away slightly so he
could pull the thin spaghetti straps of her blue dress off
her shoulders. He slipped his arm around her and drew
her close to kiss her again. As they kissed, he pushed
her dress away and let it fall. It dropped in a puff and a
whisper around her feet. When she stepped out of it, she
left behind her shoes, as well.

The diamond pendant lay between the rise of her
breasts. Mike touched it lightly, his fingers brushing her
warm skin. "Do you always keep this on?"

"Yes, I do," she said.

He leaned back, placing his hands on her hips as he
looked at her. She hadn't worn a bra beneath her dress
and he cupped her bare breasts with his calloused hands.
She wore only lacy bikini panties. "You're beautiful, darlin'. You take my breath away."

"Just kiss me, Mike," she whispered, clinging to him
and leaning closer, her nipples brushing his chest. He
cupped her breasts again, holding her. She was soft, filling his hands, so warm. He kissed first one breast and
then the other, tracing each rosy peak with his tongue.
"Ah, Vivian, you're beautiful and perfect. So soft, so gorgeous," he whispered.

She had her eyes closed, her head thrown back as she
ran one hand through his hair and ran her other hand
over his shoulder beneath his shirt. "I want this, Mike.
I want you to kiss and hold me the rest of the night and
drive away my hurt."

"Ah, Vivian. You shouldn't hurt and you shouldn't be
lonely. You're too beautiful." He kissed her and she clung
to him. He was aroused, his hard shaft between them,
pressing into her. "Oh, baby, you should have a man's

arms around you every night of your life. You were made to pleasure a man and take him to paradise." His gaze roamed over her. "I want you," he whispered hoarsely. "I want to kiss and touch you. We'll give each other tonight."

"I'm not protected. I'm not on the pill."

"I've got a condom." They looked into each other's eyes and he saw the desire he felt mirrored in her expression. He drew her to him to hold her naked body against his.

Wrapping her arms around his neck, Vivian stood on tiptoe to kiss him. "I want you, too," she said. "I want to kiss and touch you, to have it all for tonight."

The way she looked at him, the emotion he saw in her eyes, the need that reflected his own, all combined to take away the last of his control. In that moment, he wished he really could take away all her hurt. While he couldn't do that, he knew he could give her pleasure and he set about doing just that. He knew he was breaking all his rules and promises to himself. He wasn't avoiding trouble. Instead, he was running into heartache and regret with open arms. But he could no more stop and resist her now than he could quit his job and walk away. He wanted her more than he had ever desired any other woman. He might be tearing up his life for a long time to come, but wanted Vivian this night. He wanted to hold and love her, give and take the excitement and pleasure of one night with her. This was the time and the opportunity and he wasn't going to back away from the most desirable woman he had ever known. He only hoped he could survive the consequences of tonight.

Vivian tingled from head-to-toe. Desire was hot, pulsing, an aching need, but she wanted this night to last, to make love for hours. There had been so many empty nights and now Mike was holding her, kissing her and making excitement race through her.

She pushed away his shirt, letting it fall while she unfastened his belt. She looked up and was caught in his hungry gaze. His slow perusal roamed over her body, and she trembled with eagerness, feeling as if he had drawn his fingers over her.

He took off his trousers and yanked away his socks and boots. He had on briefs that she peeled down to free him and then held and caressed his manhood that was hot and hard, ready for her. He held her hips lightly with his hands as she stroked him.

For a moment he let her take him in her mouth to run her tongue slowly over him, and then he pulled her up to trail kisses along her throat and down to her breasts, kissing first one and then the other, his tongue circling taut peaks, hot and wet, exciting her more.

Moaning softly with pleasure, she closed her eyes while he showered kisses on her and caressed her, feathery strokes that made her sigh softly.

Touching him, she explored his marvelous physique, discovering his body that was muscular and in peak shape. She tangled her fingers in the sprinkling of crisp, curly black hair across his chest. His chest was rock hard, all muscle, broad and warm as she trailed her hands over him.

With a low sound deep in his throat, he whispered in her ear. "I want you, Vivian. I want to make love to you all the rest of this night."

"That's what I want, too. To kiss and touch and discover each other. I want to excite you and pleasure you every way you want."

"Ah, darlin'," he said, showering kisses on her breasts as he cupped them in his big hands. "You excite me just by letting me look at you. You'll never know how much I want you, more than you can possibly imagine. I've dreamed about you, fantasized about you, longed for you. I don't want to let you go until this night is over and the sun is high in the sky. And only then, because I know I'll have to. I can't keep you and hold you forever, but for tonight, I don't want to take my hands off you. Or my mouth," he whispered, kissing away her answer.

His kiss was possessive, demanding, and she returned his kiss passionately and clung to him. They stood in each other's arms and she ran her hands over his shoulders and nape while one leg rose up to pull him even closer. His deep moan thrilled her, because it meant she had excited him as he had her. Knowing that, she burned with need, wanting his hands and mouth and body all over hers.

As she started to put her foot down, he caught her leg, holding it and sliding his hand up along her calf, over her knee, going higher till he touched her intimately and she gasped as his fingers rubbed and caressed her.

Her breath was coming in short bursts when he finally picked her up. "A bed?"

She pointed behind her and pulled his head down to kiss him, needing the contact as he carried her through the condo to set her on her feet beside her bed. He yanked back the covers and placed her on the bed, coming down beside her to pull her into his arms and continue kissing her.

He was hard muscle, warm against her, and she ran her hand over his marvelous body. Minutes later, he moved to her feet, holding her foot and watching her, while he trailed his tongue across her ankle and along her leg. His fingers caressed her leg, sliding slowly, so lightly up her leg and the back of her thigh, barely touching her.

He showered kisses on her leg, rolling her over on her stomach to caress the back of her thighs and run his tongue over her. She moaned softly and in minutes turned over again as his hands drifted to the inside of her thighs while he leaned down to kiss her, his tongue touching hers. She wrapped her arms around his neck, holding him, kissing him in return until he moved back, letting his tongue slide down her front, circling each nipple and then moving lower, his mouth joining his hands where they played between her thighs.

Crying out, she arched, raising her hips, giving him more access to her while he stroked her intimately, gently at first then with more pressure, his fingers and tongue taking her near the pinnacle. But she didn't want the pleasure to end.

With a cry she sat up and pushed him back on the bed, moving over him to stroke his manhood, to tease and pleasure him as he had her. She ran her tongue, hot and wet, over him in long, slow strokes until he reached down to lift her back on the bed where he could move between her legs.

She held his hips. "Love me, now, Mike. I want you inside me. I want your hardness, your body and mouth on me."

"Not yet, darlin'," he whispered, kissing her throat while his fingers toyed intimately with her and then he moved down to kiss her, his tongue stroking where his fingers just been, making her cry out and spread her legs for him to have total access.

He knelt between her legs, leaning down, his tongue going over her as much as his fingers while she writhed with desire. Her hands drifted over him to grasp his shoulders to draw him to her. "Mike, come here," she whispered.

He kissed her as he moved up until he stretched out beside her, his hands still toying with her, exciting her, and her hands seeking out and holding his thick rod.

"I can't wait any longer," she cried as she straddled him.

"Yes, you can. You wanted me to make love to you for a long time tonight. You told me that, so that's what we'll do." He rolled her over so he was on top, laving her nipples as his roaming fingers found a home in her most intimate place. "Let's make this last. This is good, Vivian, so good."

But she couldn't withstand any more of the tender onslaught. She gripped his shoulders, arching her back and thrusting her hips against him. "Mike, I want you now. I need you inside me. I want to love you and I want you to make love to me."

He stepped off the bed to get his billfold and took out a packet. In minutes, he knelt between her legs as he put on the condom and lowered himself, easing into her. She gasped, raising her hips for him while she wrapped her long legs around him.

He moved slowly, his hard rod teasing her and heightening her desire with each thrust. She wanted him desperately, wanted more each time he entered her and withdrew, and she moved with his rhythm, arching her back and locking her legs more tightly around him.

"Mike, I want you," she whispered, running her hands over him. Her eyes were squeezed shut, her whole world was focused on moving with him, on the sensations rocking her. He withdrew slowly and she felt bereft, empty, until he plunged deeply into her and then pumped hard and fast. She kept pace with him as need drove her, until she reached the point of no return. When her release burst over her, she cried out and shuddered. Yet she moved with him, faster than ever, ecstasy streaking through her with each thrust of her hips, her climax shattering, fulfilling needs and dreams. She cried out, turning her head to kiss his shoulder while he pumped frantically and then his climax came.

They slowed, both gasping for breath. She held him tightly as rapture enveloped her, a happiness that she hadn't felt in a long time. She kissed his jaw, and he turned his head, moving on his side and keeping her with him. She kissed him lightly, showering kisses over his ear. "You sexy man," she whispered.

He smiled while he toyed with long locks of her hair. "Darlin', you absolutely hands-down win the prize for being the most sexy possible. I don't think I can move again."

"Mike, this is such a special time in my life. Tonight is filled with fun, laughter, red hot sex, dancing, partying, being together, wild pleasure—a heap of fabulous things that all add up to happiness. Tonight was the happiest night I've had in so long."

"Ah, Vivian, this is just a tough time. We all have that. You'll move on and times will be good again."

"You're an optimist, too."

He shifted slightly to look at her. "What's this 'too' business? What else am I?"

"Definitely, you're thoroughly an al—"

"—pha male," he finished for her. "Well, let me tell you, sweetie, you better keep hiring alpha males to run this ranch."

She twisted to look more closely at him. "You're not here to stay? Forever?"

He smiled at her. "Let's not let life intrude. Think about the past hour instead of the future. I could spend the rest of the night thinking about the past hour," he said, rolling over on his back and placing his hand behind his head, to prop his head up slightly.

She shifted and rested her chin on her palm to look down at him.

"You're serious. You're not keeping this job forever."

"Darlin'. I must not have carried you out of this world tonight. You're back worrying about the ranch."

She stared at him a moment and knew her suspicions were correct that he would quit and move on after he had fulfilled what he felt he needed to for Thane. She should be so much more cautious or he would give her another terrible heartbreak on top of losing Thane. She stopped all thoughts of his job or the ranch and instead thought about his kisses and his hands moving on her. She nuzzled his neck. "You're right," she said softly. "The last hour has been wonderful. Definitely. And I will think about it over and over because every moment was fabulous, sensuous and exciting."

"That's better. That's good to hear as a matter of fact. That makes me think we might have an encore. In a few more minutes, of course."

He turned on his side and they gazed at each other. She smiled and he touched the raised corner of her lips lightly with his index finger. "You're beautiful, Vivian. Absolutely, totally beautiful."

She loved hearing the compliment and gave him one in return. "Mike, tonight was wonderful. The dinner, the dancing, the loving, the company were everything

I wanted, everything I dreamed about and longed for. You're too sexy for words."

"Good, darlin'. I want you happy." He ran his hand over her shoulder, down her back and over her bottom. "You have the softest, smoothest skin in the entire US of A."

They looked at each other and both smiled. She ran her finger along his jaw, feeling the short bristly stubble. "A sexy man, so rugged, so handsome. You know, you could be a model."

He laughed. "I don't think so, but you can keep thinking that. Now in reality, you are the model type. Maybe a few more delightful curves on you than some, thank goodness." His smile vanished. "It was good, Vivian. A really good night. You're a wonderful woman."

She laughed and rose up slightly to brush his cheek with a kiss. "I suppose you're my knight in shining armor."

"Oh, no. I'm just a Texas cowboy." He pulled her into the crook of his arm, tightly pressed against his side. "This is paradise," he said, and she felt the vibration in his chest when he talked.

"We should talk about you moving in to the main house. You should come check out the suite and make arrangements for help to bring over your things." She halted his reply with her finger on his lips. "I know, you don't have much."

"Vivian, I think we should stick to just talking about tonight, making love, your fabulous body, the past hour, what fun it was to dance tonight, and keep all that other stuff out of the bedroom. We'll have a whole lot more fun and we won't get into anything serious, disturbing or worrisome. Do you agree?"

She laughed. "Tell me that again."

"You heard me and you know what I said."

"I surely do. We can leave off my fabulous body because you have the fab body, dear sir," she said, squeezing a bicep. "Oh, my. That makes my heart go pitter-patter."

"Let me feel and see," he said, placing his hand lightly on her breast. She laughed and rolled over to look at him.

"By the way, I have a fabulous shower and tub," she said, pointing past him to her en suite.

"Let's try them out," he said, stepping off the bed and leaning over to scoop her up in his arms.

"Oh, my. See, I told you that you have fabulous muscles."

"You're a featherweight. Did you know that I haven't even seen your condo? Not only that, this place has all glass walls and we're naked. Are we on display for the world?"

"No, we're not. They can't see in. We can see out."

He peered out the window. "If I'm not mistaken, there's a balcony all around this place."

"That's correct. A rather large balcony with a swimming pool."

He continued to the bathroom.

"Here's the light switch," she said, reaching out to the wall and flipping it on.

He looked around a large room with palm trees in pots, a chaise lounge in deep red and purple throw rugs on a marble floor. Along with the recessed lighting she had also switched on music at a control panel and a soft tune emanated from hidden speakers. He carried her over to the raised tub; set high on three steps. It was a large marble bath with gold fixtures. He had a feeling they were real gold.

She punched more buttons and water splashed into the tub. "At this point, I suggest you put me down and I'll check on the water."

"How about turning that off and let's try the shower."

"Sure," she said and pointed to a large glassed-in shower at the other side of the bathroom.

They showered together and in minutes he picked her up, stepped out of the spray and let her slide down on his hard manhood while he kissed her. She wrapped her legs around him, moving with him, holding him tightly while his thrusts came hard and fast until they climaxed together. She cried out in ecstasy, holding him tightly, tilting his head up to kiss him. She slid down the length of his body and finally put her feet on the floor. She looked up to see him smile at her as he ran his fingers through her hair, pushing it back from her face.

"You're marvelous, Vivian. Hot, sexy. Let's try that shower again."

"This time let's make it back to the bed."

He laughed as they showered together and then dried each other. He picked her up again to carry her to bed, stretching out and holding her close against him.

"I want you in my arms tonight."

"I'm not arguing with that," she said, snuggling against him. She was happy and he was right when he said she shouldn't think beyond the present hour, but it was hard not to. The night had been fabulous, a temporary fix for loneliness and losing Thane, and it would help for a long time. The hot sex they'd shared would drive away some of her demons, be a lasting memory she could pull out that wouldn't hold so much sadness and longing.

She and Mike weren't in love with each other. But she had a feeling if he came around as much in the coming months as he had been since he started working for her, she could fall in love with him. He'd told her not to think of the future, but it was impossible not to.

She looked at him and wondered if he was asleep or just lying there holding her.

She didn't want to fall in love with him because he would never ever return it. He would never get past that damn stubborn view of her fortune. She didn't even think it was a woman boss that bothered him. It was a woman-billionaire boss. He had been a total gentleman with Marta at the gallery and he hadn't displayed any dismay when he reported to Vivian on the ranch. He hadn't even cared this time when she picked up the tab at the club. It was her inheritance that he couldn't deal with. That and some miguided loyalty to Thane who was gone and would never be part of her life. Thane wanted Mike to take his place. She was beginning to suspect Thane hoped she and Mike would fall in love. Thane loved the ranch and probably thought once Mike was here, he would stay. She was sure he wouldn't. Also, Thane must not have known how strongly Mike felt about a very wealthy woman. How could someone object to money? She rose up to look at him.

"What?" he asked without opening his eyes.

"I thought you were asleep."

"Just about."

"You haven't even opened your eyes."

He opened them to look at her. "What are you worrying about?"

"Are you an incredibly light sleeper or were you just lying there with your eyes closed?"

"A little of both. Probably the military life and being in places where you could get killed if you didn't wake up easily." He held out his arms and she scooted down against him.

"Mmm, I like this. This is good," he said quietly, running his hand over her breast.

She inhaled. "I don't think you're going back to sleep."

He turned on his side. "I don't think so either," he said in a husky voice. He pulled her closer to kiss her. She slipped one arm around him to hold him close as she shut her eyes and kissed him in return.

It was over two hours later when she lay in the dark trying once again to go to sleep. He was an incredibly light sleeper and if he woke up again, she suspected they would make love once more. Her body ached in places she had forgotten even existed.

What would happen when they returned to the ranch? She guessed life would go right back to like it had been before even if he was just down the hall and no one else was in that wing. Would he treat this night as if it had never happened?

Six

Mike turned to her, placing his palm against her cheek. "What's worrying you, Vivian? Is it Thane?"

"Thane?" she asked in surprise. "Not at all. Thane's gone, Mike, and he's never coming back to me. I keep saying it—he would want me to go on with my life. I know that for certain."

"You're right about that," Mike said, caressing her cheek and then playing with a long lock of her hair. "He would want you to, just as you would want him to if something had happened to you. So what is it?"

"I just don't understand your attitude about my inheritance."

There was a long moment of silence.

"If I didn't have that kind of income and inheritance, you would date me after tonight, wouldn't you?" she asked.

"I probably would, but there's no way to think about you without your inheritance because it exists and it isn't going away. I can't deal with that, Vivian. Maybe it was because of growing up without much, but there's no way I can go out with a woman who has inherited millions from her husband and is heir to a man worth billions. I was raised to feel that a man who relies on a woman for money isn't really a man. Before my aunt divorced my uncle, she offered to give dad money to pay when my youngest brother was born. I can still remember that fight and my dad wouldn't take a penny. It might not have been smart, but that's just the way I am."

She sat up and pulled the sheet up beneath her arms. "I have never known anyone who objected to money."

"I don't object to money. I'd be happy to have a bunch, but not from the woman I love. I'd feel like a kept man. I'd feel like I couldn't be myself, argue about anything. You'll never understand, because you were born into that and you've lived with it all your life. It's your family and your family money. It has belonged to you since the day you were born." He tunneled his fingers through his hair and blew out a breath. "You may not be able to understand how I feel but my feelings are real. My dad had strong feelings about it and taught his sons that the man should pay, the man should have the money. Also, his brother married a wealthy woman, and they fought over everything and she was snippy when she would come to our house. She would leave my mom in tears about what a dump we lived in. It was home and we liked it. They finally divorced, but she caused some hard feelings and bad times. As a kid there were times I've gone hungry rather than have some woman who wasn't related, buy my dinner. The year dad died was bad and we did go to bed hungry. I had a teacher who would try to buy my lunch and I just couldn't let her do it. That's just how I was brought up. So, no, we can't date. I don't want to fall in love with a woman worth billions. What could I ever buy for you that would thrill you, surprise you? Impossible."

"Can you hear yourself and what you're saying?"

"Damn well can and it makes sense to me. I told you to avoid thinking about life back at the ranch and about tomorrow, to just stick with tonight." He pulled her down on his chest. "Darlin', don't you ever get sleepy?"

She sat up again and poked his chest lightly with her finger. "You're an alpha male who can't let a woman pay your way. You're archaic—from another century."

"Hell yes, I'm old-fashioned. I can't deal with a woman who is a billionaire when I make a very measly salary in comparison."

"Are you through?"

"Absolutely."

"Life is more than money in the bank."

"It sure as hell isn't when you're starving."

"Don't give me that. You may have had a tough child-hood, but you've done well. Not like my dad, no. But you've done well and you're a damn good rancher."

"Dammit, Vivian. I'm tired of hearing about that. I am what I am. Let's just go from there and I'll do what alpha males do. Come here." He pulled her into his arms and kissed her.

She opened her mouth to object and pushed against his chest, her anger rising, but he tightened his arm around her while his mouth covered her protest and his tongue went deep. Despite his plundering lips, his touch was gentle. He caressed her breast, so lightly, a feather touch that made her tremble, and all her anger disappeared. She moaned in response, wanting his caresses, wanting him as she held his wrist and kept his hand on her breast. She wanted his loving, his hot, passionate kisses that were possessive this time, his sexy tongue stroking hers, touching the corners of her mouth, teasing and tormenting and making her crave him desperately.

She wrapped her arms around his neck and rubbed her bare breasts against his chest, shifting and straddling him as they both sat in bed and continued to kiss. The conflicting emotions of anger and desire drove her to want to kiss him until he wouldn't be able to walk away so easily. If he just wasn't so stubborn, they could have something good together.

She stopped thinking because she was lost in his fiery kiss. Suddenly he rolled her over and he was on top, moving over her and looking down at her. Gone was the anger she'd heard in his voice. His green eyes were dark with lust. He looked at her as if she were the most desirable woman he had ever encountered. Her heart thudded as she looked up at him and felt as if he wanted her more than anyone else on earth.

His hands caressed her breasts lightly, slowly while he shifted, moving down so he could kiss her breasts. His lovemaking was possessive and erotic, driving her wild. "Mike, love me," she whispered, kissing his throat, stroking his manhood rising up to run her tongue over him.

He turned her, pulling her up to kiss her again—another kiss that melted her.

He entered her then withdrew, teasing, making her want him beyond anything she'd felt earlier. Finally, he eased into her and let go of his iron control and then pumped wildly, each thrust going deeper inside her. She cried out with her climax. And then still driven, she had the second climax with his, gasping and holding him as they both reached ecstasy.

It seemed hours before her heartbeat and her breathing were normal. She clung to him, holding him tightly, wondering if she had made a huge mistake tonight. She didn't want to fall in love with him and she feared making love to him tonight had just brought her closer to him, made him more important to her.

She needed to go back to the ranch and not see Mike for a while unless she had to for business. Too late for that, she realized. He was moving into her house, on her floor, down the hall from her suite.

He pulled her close against him. "That was fantastic, darlin'. That's one place we don't have an argument in the world. You're incredibly sexy."

She held him tightly in silence, wondering how much he had captured her heart tonight. She wondered if he would quit working at the ranch when the three months he had promised Thane were up. She knew he wouldn't go and leave her in the lurch. He'd stay till she hired someone and he trained the person. Suddenly, she was certain that that was exactly what he would do and probably what he had planned all along. The more she thought about it, the more certain she was that she was right.

Thane was gone. Slade would soon be gone and then Mike would eventually leave, as well. There would be absolutely nothing to hold her at the ranch. Thane's dad didn't like the ranch. His grandfather was no longer living. And she and Thane had no children, no heirs. Thane always said he was the only one in his family now who wanted to be a rancher.

Why would she stay on the ranch? She shook her head. The Tumbling T would be filled with memories that would hurt too much.

Mike turned, shifting to look at her. "This has been

a special night, Vivian. Come here," he said, pulling her against his side with his arm around her. "Try to get some sleep. We've been awake the entire night and it's getting so late that we'll see the sun come up soon. Stop worrying about my attitude. You and I aren't in love. We've had a wonderful time together and that was a gift for me and I hope one for you. I promise you, Vivian, your life will be happy. You'll never miss me being in it."

She snuggled against him, holding him tightly, seizing the moment and temporarily letting go of all her worries. For the next hour, she wasn't going to think about tomorrow or telling him goodbye or anything else except his marvelous body, the feel of his arms around her and this night of loving that had been hot, sexy and joyous. The more she thought about his lovemaking, his hands and mouth and hard muscular body, the more aroused she was until she shifted slightly and ran her tongue along his ear. She heard and felt his deep breath as his arm tightened around her and he caressed her breast.

It took no time to arouse him. After putting on a condom, he lifted her on top of him and eased slowly inside her, filling her. She moaned, relishing his hard rod.

He thrust into her, going faster, until she was wild with passion, riding him as her climax burst with hot pleasure that set her body ablaze. He continued and she could feel another climax coming. This time they moved together and she cried out as rapture spilled over her.

She showered kisses on his throat, his ear, his mouth, holding him and then sliding off him to lie beside him again. He turned on his side, pulling her close and brushing strands of hair away from her face.

"It's good, Vivian. So very good together."

When their breathing returned to normal, he picked

her up and carried her to the en suite where he ran hot water into the big tub and sank down, holding her on his lap. She wiggled her bottom and he chuckled. "You haven't had enough yet?"

She twisted to caress and kiss him. "You adorable, sexy man. I still want you to make love to me, but let's sit here and talk a few minutes then dry off and get back in a bed."

"That's a plan because this is a fine moment right now." He ran his hands over her, covering her breasts and belly, sliding down her legs and up her back. "Every inch of you is sexy, sleek, soft and beautiful and I want to touch you everywhere, to excite you again."

She leaned back against him while he wrapped both arms around her waist to hold her. "Now relax and tell me about your life. Tell me things I don't know. Tell me things you want in life," she said.

"I want you and I want to make love to you for several more hours. As for what I want in life—I can't think past this night. This is fabulous, Vivian."

After a few minutes, he stood and stepped out of the tub and helped her up, grabbing a towel to dry her off while she ran another towel over his exciting, masculine body.

"I think the sun has come up, Mike. We haven't slept at all. It's Saturday."

"So it is."

Tingling, wanting to kiss him, she turned and looked up at him. "I have an appointment at eleven o'clock to take some frames to be repaired."

"Call them and postpone it. Tell them something urgent has come up. And that's the truth," he said, rubbing his thick rod against her thigh while he nibbled her ear.

She turned her head to kiss him as she wound her arm around his neck. "I bet you have to get back, too."

"Not so, darlin'. I'll send a text when I get time," he said, nuzzling her neck. "I want to stay right here in your plush, ritzy condo on top of the world, at least our corner of it, and make love all day long."

"That is so decadent."

"You wanted to have a life again. You wanted laughter, sex and fun. Here it is, just waiting for you."

She laughed. "You're wicked, Mike Moretti. And you are the most fun I've had in a long time. When you put it that way—" She held out both hands. "On one hand, I can get my picture frames fixed. On the other, I can have raging, blazing sex with you." She twisted to look into his eyes. "I do believe you win out."

"That makes me feel really important. And sexy. I beat the picture frame repair."

"Mike, you do better than that," she said, brushing a light kiss on his mouth.

His smile vanished and desire filled his expression. "I want you as if we haven't made love ever. I want you now, Vivian." He picked her up to carry her back to bed, holding her close as he kissed her.

The sun was low in the western sky when she sat up cross-legged in bed, pulled the sheet beneath her arms and poked his shoulder with her finger. "Listen to me. From the first few minutes we came here after leaving the club last night, we have either been in bed or in the shower or in my tub. It is almost night again. We haven't eaten and my stomach is protesting. This is super-decadent. I haven't had clothes on since yesterday."

"I find that an absolutely terrific argument to continue what we've been doing. Is there any way to get food up here to you besides dropping a basket on a rope over the balcony?"

"Of course, although it hasn't come up before. I'm not here a lot and when I am, I've planned ahead more than I did this time. I thought we'd be up and out of here by nine this morning. I didn't realize how lusty and sex-starved you were."

"I see several choices here—we dress and I take you out to eat. The drawback to that one is for about two hours we will have to wear clothes. I won't be able to touch you where and when I want to touch you. I won't be able to kiss you, bathe with you or do fun things with you. Eating with you is way down that list.

"Another choice is to call in and have something delivered. That means clothes for about an hour while we wait for the delivery and going down to get the stuff. Much better choice to my way of thinking.

"Or, send me out. There are hotels around us. For a little extra, I'll bet I can get an adequate meal in a jiffy and get back here."

"Remember, you don't have a car."

"That doesn't matter. There are probably two hotels on this block and I'm fast."

"I'll bet you are when you think there's a naked lady waiting in your bed," she said, smiling at him and he smiled in return.

"I vote for choice three," he said after feigning serious contemplation. "Now I can come up with a fourth choice, but I don't think you'll want it. Just eat tomorrow. To get to stay naked and in bed with you, I can go that route easily."

"That's because of your ranger training. You could

go until Tuesday if you had to. But for me that choice is out. I haven't had any ranger training and I'm hungry for some real food."

"Darlin', why didn't you stock the fridge up here?"

"I didn't think we'd be here long."

"That is an amazing lack of foresight. Okay, choice number three it is. Send me out. I'm efficient, fast and you get a little bonus or two if I do this."

She leaned closer. "So what is this wonderful bonus? Am I going to be interested?"

"I think so. I will give you a wonderful, relaxing massage before we have sex."

She laughed. "You don't know one thing about giving a massage."

He grinned. "You have no idea what I all know. Try me and see. I promise you won't be disappointed."

"Just go get us something to eat. I'm not particular about what it is. I just want food."

"Breakfast, lunch or dinner kind of food?"

"I better have a steak so I can keep up my strength. I need it with you. I haven't been working out every day for the past few years the way you have."

"You are in absolutely perfect shape, sweetie. You couldn't be in any better shape."

She smiled at him. "Thank you." She held the sheet as she stepped out of bed. "Now, you get going before I faint from hunger."

"For such a dainty little thing, you have such a big appetite."

"I've been busy," she teased.

"Well, rest up, darlin', you'll be busy when I get back with the steaks."

"I hope that's a promise," she said in a sultry voice, flirting with him and having fun doing it.

He wrapped his arms around her and kissed her—a long, steamy kiss. When he finally stopped, she opened her eyes to find him gazing at her. "That was definitely a promise," he said in a husky voice. "I'm going to set a speed record for getting you a steak and getting back here."

She nodded. She wanted him and if he had wanted to go back to bed right now, she wouldn't have protested. Her night of reckless lovemaking had spilled into another day and she couldn't be happier. She'd relish it right up until they had to leave.

The following Thursday, Mike came for dinner and while Francie got the meal ready with Henry's help, Vivian greeted Mike at the door.

Vivian had spent an hour dressing and changing before she was satisfied with a short-sleeved red linen blouse and slacks with high-heeled sandals. When Mike walked in the door, he gave her his hat and followed her into the study. As he walked toward her, her breathing quickened. He looked more handsome than ever. He wore a white dress shirt under his tan jacket and dark brown slacks with brown boots. His black hair was slightly windblown over his forehead.

"Do you want the house tour now or after dinner?" she asked him.

"Definitely now. I'd hate to get lost in this place."

"It's not that big."

"Would you like a drink before we start the tour?"

"Oh, yeah. That would be nice." He crossed the room to her. "We're being mighty formal when you think about the last time we were together. And let me tell you now—you look beautiful."

She felt her cheeks grow warm. "Thank you for the compliment. As for your greeting—you surely didn't expect me to throw myself into your arms, did you?"

"I might have hoped. This isn't a bad substitute," he said, wrapping his arms around her and leaning forward to brush his lips on hers.

She couldn't protest. Her heartbeat quickened, even faster than when she'd first seen him come in the door looking so handsome and strong and sexy, reminding her of being naked in his arms.

When he released her, she looked up at him and felt dazed. "Wow. You'll make me forget dinner and Francie has cooked all afternoon."

"I'm not going to hurt her feelings, but I'll tell you, Vivian, I could ditch the best dinner on earth for your kisses."

"That's very flattering, Mike. Am I going to be able to let you move into my house? We can't stay in bed together. We aren't moving into the same bedroom."

"I'll work on that one. I'd like to see these rooms we're talking about. Beer first, though."

"I'll do that, but right now, let's cover the big news of the day. I imagine you already know it because he said he was going to talk to you next. Slade came by with his resignation."

"I know. He told me. I'm glad for him, putting any feelings I have aside. His back bothers him and he shouldn't be doing what he does. He said he gave you a two-week notice."

"He did. I told him he doesn't have to wait two weeks. We all will miss him, but you're right. His family is in south Texas and they want him with them and he wants to go. I think he'll go a little sooner than two weeks."

"I told him we'd help him any way we can," Mike said and she nodded.

"I told him we'd have a party. He said it's not necessary, but we will. Maybe next Tuesday night if the guys are okay with it. You see what night might be best. We'll have a barbeque if it's good weather. Also, congratulations, Mike. You'll officially become foreman when he leaves and your salary will go up."

"Thank you," he said, smiling at her.

"Now I'll see about our drinks and the tour. I'll be right back." She left and in less than a minute she was back, followed by Henry who had a tray with a cold, open beer, a bowl of pretzels and a glass of iced tea. He held out the glass to Vivian and went to Mike.

"Would you like a cold beer?"

"Oh, would I ever. Thanks, Henry. I'd set the pretzels close by, too."

When they were alone, he sipped his beer, lowered the bottle and looked at her. "Now, I think you were going to show me around before dinner."

"Then we'll get to it. The third floor has suites where Henry and Millie live, and Francie lives on that floor, too. Heather and Waldo also live on the third floor. In short, we stay off the third floor. I have a suite on the second floor. That's where you'll be. They don't come on the second floor. We don't go to the third floor. Now, in the basement is a wine cellar, a storage area and another library for the kind of papers and stuff that would look junky in the main library." She stopped when she heard him chuckle. "Why are you laughing?"

"You live in what's half museum and half hotel. Holy saints, where is an ordinary room?"

"You're standing in one and there are plenty of ordinary rooms," she said, thinking his smile and laughter were irresistible. She could detect a faint scent of aftershave and when she looked at his broad shoulders, all she could think about was last weekend and how those shoulders felt beneath her hands when they were both naked.

He looked around. "It's difficult to think of this as Thane's home. He was practical and sort of a minimalist."

"That was his military persona. Otherwise, you're wrong there. He lived all over the place here. In the gym with an indoor pool. In the ballroom. Even in the indoor tennis court down in the basement."

He waved her off. "Show me where I'll sleep and come in and go out, and where you sleep and where I'll eat. That's enough of a tour for me."

"I'm beginning to wonder about you," she said.

"And what are you wondering?"

"You sound as if you live under a bridge." She shook her head at him then continued the tour. "You know where the garage is. You can come in the back like you did tonight. We'll go up these stairs. There's a back staircase, too and separate elevators to the second and third floors. The elevator's handy when they move furniture, times like that, but I never take it." She walked with Mike up the sweeping spiral staircase in the front hall and she stopped in the center of a wide second-floor hallway. "To the right is my suite," she said, pointing. "To the left will be your suite. Let's go look. We'll be the only ones living on this floor."

"I can't wait," he said, sipping his beer. "Are you sure

this house wasn't your idea? This doesn't look like something Thane would have built."

"The house I grew up in is a two-story frame and brick house with five bedrooms, six bathrooms, a three-car garage, a great room, a family room, a dining room and a kitchen. Nothing like this. I think Thane had ideas we would fill it with people and kids but that isn't ever going to happen now."

They walked down the hall to double doors that were open. She stepped inside and he followed her into what would be his suite, starting with a living area with floor-to-ceiling windows and glass doors that slid open on to a wide balcony.

"It's beautiful," he said. His voice had changed and he set his beer on a table as he turned to her. "Now that we're alone, it's time for what's really important," he said, slipping his arms around her waist and leaning down to kiss her.

She couldn't say no. Her heart missed beats as she wound her arms around his neck, stood on tiptoe and kissed him in return. She moaned softly, pleased to be back in his arms.

"Tell the staff to go home soon. I don't care if I ever eat. I want you, Vivian. I want you in my arms."

She clung to him, kissing him, knowing she was going to have giant regrets, yet she couldn't stop. All week she had dreamed about him, about his kisses, about his arms around her, holding her tightly. She ran her hands over him as they kissed.

"Which room do we sleep in tonight? In here? In yours?"

"Mike, we're going to get hurt."

"I can't say we won't. But that doesn't stop me from wanting you."

They kissed and conversation ended temporarily. Finally, she raised her head. "I didn't ask you to move into my bedroom."

"Okay, we can move—"

"No, we're not moving in here."

"Fine. You and I know how to walk down a hall. That's what we'll do. You can't tell me you don't want this," he said, his mouth covering any answer she might have had.

She knew this was folly and she was headed straight for heartbreak. He would never change and all too soon he would leave the Tumbling T and tell her goodbye, but she couldn't resist when he was kissing her senseless and she couldn't deny that she wanted him to. She didn't want dinner and she doubted if he did, but they'd have to go eat and then come back upstairs where they could be alone.

"Mike, let's go sit downstairs and make some semblance of having dinner and spending the evening together without going to bed."

She wasn't sure if her words were getting through to him. He seemed intent on running his fingers along her cheek, his eyes never leaving her. "So soft," he whispered. Then he looked up at her. "All right. We'll go downstairs for a while. How soon will the house empty out of the other residents?"

"About half an hour after dinner," she said. "So we might as well go ahead and eat something."

He nodded. "This takes great restraint. I've thought about you all day long and wanted you in my arms. I dream about you at night."

"Mike, asking you to move here wasn't an invitation to move into my bed."

He caught her chin with his hand, bent his knees so he was on her level and could look directly into her eyes. "You don't want to make love tonight?"

"You know I do and I can't resist you, but that isn't smart and that is not why I wanted you to move in here."

"I'll do what you want. I'll sleep in my bed and leave you alone to sleep in yours if that's what you want. But the least you can do is let me kiss you and squeeze you and—"

She backed up. "You're not paying attention. We should avoid all that physical stuff if we want to avoid a boatload of hurt. You've seen where you sleep and you know where I sleep. We'll have lots of time after dinner. Right now while Francie is getting dinner on and Henry is underfoot, let's go back downstairs and sit and talk until we're called to dinner."

"Fine, Vivian. I'll act as if I have little interest in you or your luscious, sexy body."

She threw up her hands. "I give up."

He moved closer to talk softly in her ear. "You, my darlin', love sex, love making love and you are as eager as I am when the opportunity arises. During dinner, it won't hurt for you to go ahead and think about kisses afterward."

"Mike, you are shameless," she said, but she tingled and wanted to be in his arms, and she couldn't stop thinking about kissing him later. She wanted more from him while at the same time she knew that wasn't going to happen and she should treat their affair as lightly as he was because she hadn't wanted to fall in love with him. That would mean rushing straight into more hurt and another broken heart. He didn't want anything from her except sex and she was already getting a heartache over him. Had she already fallen in love with him? She hoped not.

As they left the suite, she asked about his day.

"I have some news—Leon turned in his resignation, so he is out of your life for good. He's got a job on a horse ranch in southwest Texas. Everyone wished him well. His last day is next week. I doubt if he'll come say goodbye, but if he does and you want me around, just call. I have an idea that this may end Clint's information source on where you are, but that's a guess on my part."

"I'm glad he has a good job offer and he'll be gone soon. It's wonderful news. I think your moving in here will take care of my neighbor, too."

"Your problems are solved," he said.

"No, they're not," she said. "But Leon leaving and you moving in take care of two big ones that I needed help to handle."

He stood looking at her and she tilted her head. "What?"

"You look beautiful, Vivian," he said solemnly.

"Thank you," she answered, wondering what was bothering him because he looked worried. "We should go down for dinner."

"You're right." He walked downstairs beside her without taking her arm, which she found unusual. Was he thinking about Thane? She didn't know Mike well enough to guess what made him so somber all of a sudden so she decided just to ask.

"What's wrong, Mike?"

He turned to meet her questioning gaze. "You are an observant one, aren't you? Actually, I was thinking about us. I don't want to hurt you ever, Vivian."

She smiled and patted his hand. "I don't want to hurt

you, either. Maybe we both should use a little more restraint and caution. After all, you may disappear out of my life when your three months are over. If I'm not careful, you could say goodbye and go, taking my heart with you. I can't go through that after losing Thane."

"We're not that serious, Vivian."

"You're not. And I'm not yet. Besides, you're never going to change, Mike."

"Don't tell me again that I'm an alpha male. I know that's how you see me."

"They don't change to beta males or whatever the other kind is—the ones who don't have to run the show and be top dog."

He leaned close to whisper, "We're fun in bed."

She pushed him away. "You have a one-track mind."

When they got downstairs, Henry told them their dinner would be served out on the patio where they could enjoy the warm spring evening. Mike held her chair out and then sat facing her. Gone was his solemn expression, replaced by a cheerful smile and a positive attitude as he talked about the ranch.

Mike ate heartily, clearly enjoying his meal. As he cut into his meat, he smiled at Vivian. "You're right. Francie can cook. This meat is delicious—our own and so tender I can cut it with my fork. The veggies are from the ranch, too, aren't they? The greenhouses help, but this is asparagus season and steamed asparagus from the garden can't be beat."

"I agree, Mike. Francie is a great cook. She's widowed but she dates Merrick, one of the cowhands who work for you. I expect them to marry one day and I hope I don't lose her."

After a few minutes, Vivian sipped her water and

placed the glass on the table while she looked at Mike. "You told me about your family, Mike. A little bit about them. Where are they now?"

"In Amarillo, Texas. Mom didn't finish a high school education and she had four boys. We're all scattered now but we take care of Mom. We've bought her a house, have someone to clean for her, someone to take care of the yard. She has lots of friends and has a church group. She's happy and she's seems to be doing okay."

"That's good."

"She took care of us. Now we take care of her. It's a simple equation, but a lot of people don't get it."

Vivian and Mike both passed on dessert and moved inside to the family room to get out of Francie's way while she cleaned up the patio table.

"My things are in the pickup," Mike told her after a while. "Maybe I should take them in now."

"Go get your stuff moved so you and I can kiss."

"Now you have my full attention and cooperation."

It was fun having him around. But she admitted the truth to herself. She was falling in love with him and she knew he would not return it. He was not in love with her and he never would be unless her family lost their fortune.

"Stubborn, stubborn man," she whispered, hurting because Mike was so many great things, so capable, kind, brave, funny—but so old-fashioned. That always came up, each time she was with him. She knew he was well-fixed for himself and cared for his mother financially. Other than that, she didn't know how much money he had, but it wasn't an issue for her. She sighed. How could she have fallen in love with someone so difficult?

Tonight, was she going to be in his bed? Or Mike in

hers? She knew the answer. It was just another link in the chain that would bind her heart to him. He would never fall in love with her. All he could see was her financial worth, which to him translated to power. And that went against everything he was—something he made her aware of every time they were together.

She got up to see if she could help Francie finish so the woman could retire for the night. Francie was still putting things away and Vivian began to help in spite of her protests.

"You'll be through and then you can go. Thanks for dinner. It was delicious as always."

"Thank you."

After a few minutes, they finished and Francie told her good-night, leaving for her suite on the third floor.

Vivian walked upstairs to see how Mike was doing and met Mike at the top of the stairs. "I was just coming to see how you are doing."

"Henry helped and we're finished moving me in."

"You do travel light. That didn't take any time at all."

"No, darlin', and that gives me a lot more time for you. Henry has gone to make some outdoor rounds and then he'll go home, which I suppose means the third floor. In the meantime, let's go try out my new digs. I'll bet you've never spent the night there."

"Henry takes care of locking up the house and setting the alarms every night. But just in case of an emergency, I'll show you how to do it. I can do it from up here," she said. "See that little box?" She started to turn to point, but his arm wrapped around her waist.

"There is only one thing I can see, and that is you. I've waited for this moment for almost a week now. I want you, Vivian. You look sexy and beautiful tonight. You just take my breath away when I look at you."

She gazed into his eyes that had darkened as they always did when he was aroused. The look he gave her made her heart beat faster. She wanted his kisses and wanted his arms around her, holding her against his heart. She wanted to hold him and try to avoid the knowledge that she couldn't hold him long. He would always leave her and someday he wouldn't return and she was going to have another big heartache. She knew all that, but she was determined to grab all the happiness she could...for as long as she could.

He kissed her, his tongue touching hers, ending her worries, making her forget everything except Mike and his lovemaking.

While he still kissed her, he picked her up to carry her to his bedroom. There was only a sheet on the bed, but she didn't care as he stood her on her feet again.

He wound his fingers in her hair. "I haven't slept for thinking about you, for wanting you," he said gruffly, looking into her eyes.

"Vivian, I want to kiss and make love to you all night long," he whispered while his hands moved over her. He peeled away her red blouse, tossing it aside as she unfastened the buttons of his cotton shirt. Soon all their clothing was gone and he picked her up to kiss her. She wrapped her long legs around him, holding him tightly as he moved to the bed and laid her down. He left her only long enough to sheath himself in a condom and then returned to her. Lifting her astride him, he filled her with his manhood.

He caressed her breasts while she moved on him, his thumbs circling her nipples as he thrust into her. She set the pace, riding him faster, her hair flying across her shoulders. Her need built, and he thrust deeper, harder and faster until finally she cried out with her climax, moving wildly on him. After he shuddered with his own release, she collapsed on him.

He stroked her gently, his fingers combing through her hair and continuing lower over her back, down over the curve of her bottom, playing lightly along the back of her thigh.

"That was rushed," he said, his voice husky. "Next time will be slow for you. I want to pleasure you for hours, to excite you, make you reach the most climaxes ever. I want my hands and my mouth all over you and I want you to touch and kiss me," he said, raising his head to kiss her shoulder.

She slid down beside him and he pulled her close into his embrace. "You're quiet, Vivian."

"I want you in my arms, Mike. At least for tonight. I'm not going to be in your bed every night and you're not going to be in mine."

"Shh. Stop worrying. This is just the first night. You can sleep in your room tomorrow night and I'll go back to the guesthouse if you want."

"No, just sleep in here without me."

"Fine. But tonight we're together and I want to hold you and to make love to you. You are so sexy, darlin'. You have no idea what you do to me," he whispered. "Stay here with me now. I want another night with you."

"How can I resist you, Mike?" She kissed him passionately, rolling on top of him, and in minutes she felt his arousal again.

They made love once more and afterward, she fell asleep in his arms.

* * *

The next four nights she didn't see Mike at all. He ate with the men and he didn't come up to her house while she was downstairs. She missed him. The farewell party for Slade was going to be Thursday night and he would leave Friday for south Texas.

On Tuesday at about six, she heard a pickup and glanced out the window to see Mike heading toward the house. He had on working clothes, a cotton shirt, jeans, his gray hat and his boots, and he looked fantastic to her. She hurried to meet him.

"Hello," she said, opening the back door.

"Damn, I've missed you," he said, wrapping his arms around her and kissing her.

For a couple of seconds, she didn't know whether to tell him to slow down or to kiss him back. His lips took away her decision. Wrapping her arms around his neck, she clung to him and kissed him in return. The only thought she had left was how much she wanted him.

Finally, he leaned away, his gaze roaming over her. "You do look good enough to eat. Or something even more fun. Damn, I've missed you," he said again.

"I've missed you. What brings you here?"

"The party for Slade. What can I do for you? Do you want Henry and me to cook? I can barbeque."

"Fine. If you're half as good as Henry, we'll have a wonderful dinner."

"I'll get ribs and steaks—how's that?"

"Excellent." She gave him a brief rundown of the other party plans. "I think we're getting things lined up. How's it going on the ranch?"

"I'm trying to help Slade get ready to move when

his sons come up and I'm busy trying to do my job, too. That's why you haven't seen me."

"I thought maybe you decided to stay in the guesthouse."

"No, I'm staying here. See, this place is so big you don't know who's here and who's not. I'm in my suite, but not until about ten or eleven at night. Want me to call you and you can come over tonight?" he asked with laughter in his voice.

"Thank you, but I'll pass at that hour. I may be sound asleep."

"I'll promise to get you back to sleep."

Laughing, she shook her head.

"I'll get back with you, darlin'. For now, I just wanted to see about the party. We're going to have a crowd. People in the next six counties know him and like him and want to say goodbye."

"I'm sure of that. Thane certainly loved him." She felt the sadness then. "It seems like he should be here, Mike."

He hugged her. "It seems like that to me as well, too, and often—but not because of the ranch. I didn't know him here."

"Out-of-the-blue it just hits me that Thane's gone and he'll never be back. Sometimes it takes my breath away. Other times I can cope with it."

"It'll get easier with time, I guess."

"It already has a little. Part of that is because of you. You're full of life and you've filled a void." Turning to Mike to fill that void meant taking big risks that she would be hurt even more because Mike would never really fill the void. She didn't expect anything lasting with Mike. He was helping her get over Thane, but in doing so she was going to fall in love with him and be hurt again.

He gave her another hug and stepped away. "I have to go back, darlin'. Afraid I won't see you tonight unless you want me to just tiptoe in and slip into bed with you."

She smiled at him. "You might try and see what happens."

"Then I just might be back earlier this evening."

Seven

The party drew even more people than they had expected. But they had enough food because Henry and Mike had planned for hundreds. After all, Slade had worked at the Tumbling T for sixty years, first for Thane's grandfather and then Thane. He'd been just eighteen when he'd started working for the Warners.

It was three in the morning when the last guest finally left and Vivian lay in bed in Mike's arms.

"The party was a success, darlin'."

"Thanks for all you did. Slade and his family had a good time and that idea of presenting him with a stuffed Longhorn head to mount on the wall—that was a masterful touch, Mike. His little grandson's eyes were enormous. They loved those big horns. The best part was that bull died of old age so it wasn't killed for its horns."

"Those horns will give the old man some memories and he can tell his friends some of the cattle stories."

"Another nice thing—neither Leon nor Clint Woodson was there."

"I noticed. I wondered about Woodson and I'm glad he stayed away. I guess you got your message across."

"I think you did. They think I'm your woman."

"At this point in life, I'd say they're right," he said, nuzzling her ear and sending chills down her spine.

She rolled over on top of him, looking down at him. Before she could say or do anything, he reached out and straddled her face in his hands.

"C'mere, my woman," he said, pulling her closer so he could kiss her.

She held him tightly, closing her eyes and kissing him in return.

It was daylight when they stopped.

They'd made love all night long, which was a good thing, she later reasoned, because all the next week his first as the official Tumbling T foreman—she didn't see any sign of Mike. But she had a new worry looming in her life.

She had missed a period.

She didn't think she could possibly be pregnant because she and Thane had tried so many times and she hadn't gotten pregnant. Besides, she and Mike had always used protection. She couldn't imagine that was it, but to eliminate the possibility, she got a test kit.

It was the next day when she used it. She followed the directions then waited the allotted minutes. They seemed to be more like years as she anticipated the results. When the timer dinged, she looked down at the stick—unable to believe what she was seeing.

She laid it aside and immediately called her doctor to make an appointment to go to Dallas tomorrow.

She was pregnant with Mike's baby.

Stunned, she first felt a huge rush of joy. She was going to have a baby.

"Oh, Thane," she whispered. "Why couldn't it have been yours? A baby we both would have loved." A baby that might have kept him from going into the service.

Instead, she was going to have Mike's baby. She stiffened and sat up, blinking and turning cold. Mike was an alpha male through and through, and he would have all the coinciding typical attitudes toward an unexpected pregnancy and a baby. A baby born to an unwed mother. A baby born to a widowed mom. Mike would absolutely insist on marriage and it wouldn't make an iota of difference to him that love wasn't in his equation.

She didn't want to marry when he didn't love her. She loved him and he could be so much fun, but marriage needed love on both sides. Love was the stuff that got couples through when things were rough. Mike wasn't in this affair for love and her wealth might cause problems.

She put her head in her hands, trying to think of how to deal with him. She couldn't come up with any happy solution. Nor did she have anyone she could trust for advice—she wasn't that close to anyone. No one except Millie. She worked with Millie and they had a good relationship. Millie would be infinitely better than her mother that thought made her shake her head and laugh sarcastically. Her mother would be aghast and want to marry her off to the first possible candidate who would fit her mother's qualifications—good job, old money, right contacts, right country clubs. No, there was no hope there. She couldn't bear to be locked into a marriage without love on Mike's part. She'd marry him in a second if she believed he loved her, but she didn't think he would change and fall in love. If they married, he would worry about her inheritance for the rest of his life—unless she gave it to charity and lived on his income. If he didn't like it today, she felt certain he wouldn't like it tomorrow or the next year or the year after that. She'd give that fortune to charity if Mike would really love her, but she didn't think he was falling in love at all.

When and how was she going to tell him? She groaned and locked her fingers together. She didn't want to tell him because from that moment on, he would try to get her to marry him, probably until she gave in and did so. She'd better get her plans made because he would be taking charge as soon as she made the announcement.

That night she ate early and shut herself in her room. She didn't want to encounter Mike until she had an agenda for herself and was ready to deal with him.

In fact, she didn't see him for the next week and she no longer was making an effort to avoid him. She didn't need to because he didn't come home early enough for them to see each other. She wondered if they were growing apart. Then she realized he had a lot more to do with Slade gone and after a time things would settle into a routine.

Late in the afternoon she was in her studio when she glanced outside, looking at the landscaped yard that took lots of money to maintain and keep watered. Maybe she should sell the ranch and move back to Dallas and then work out with Mike how they would deal with both of them having their child in their lives.

Tears started and she wiped her eyes. Crying wouldn't be good for her or for her baby. She heard a light knock on her open door and turned to see Henry.

"Come in, Henry."

He walked into the studio and strolled around, looking at the paintings she had lined up against the wall and on her easel. "You're a good artist, Vivian."

She set aside her brush, wiped her hands and sat in a nearby chair. "Sit down, Henry. I know you didn't come up here to look at my art. What's up?"

Sitting in a maroon leather chair, he turned to face her. "Millie will tell you our news today, too, but I wanted to talk to you myself. We're expecting our first child."

"Congratulations! That's wonderful. I'm sure you're both happy."

"Yes, we are," he said, grinning. "Millie feels good and the doc said everything is fine. I know you want your bodyguard nearby, so if this isn't going to work, we'll do something else, but we'd like to move out of this house into a house here on the ranch. We'll be happy still living here on the ranch, but we want our own house and our own yard."

She nodded. "I can understand that. Maybe we can get you an assistant who would stay in the house at night. What do you think?"

"I think that would be a good solution. In fact, I have a friend who I'd recommend for the job."

"Well, that was easy," she said smiling. She wished she could solve her problems as quickly.

Henry stood and walked toward the door, turning to face her. "I'll talk to my friend if you'd like and tell him if he is interested to call you."

"Thank you. That'd be good. And tell Millie to come in here when she's finished working on those expense sheets for me." She gave him a sincere grin. "I'm so happy for both of you. That's wonderful news."

"We think so," he said with a big smile and she felt a wistful pang, knowing Mike was not going to be so happy with her news. She had no idea how or when she would tell him.

She didn't see Millie for another hour until she had put away her paints and was getting ready to go to the kitchen and eat an early dinner.

Millie knocked on the open door and came inside with papers in her hand. She was a willowy blonde and her pregnancy definitely didn't show.

"Millie, please close the door," Vivian said, standing and crossing the room. "Henry told me your news and I'm so happy for you. Congratulations," she said and hugged Millie lightly.

Millie smiled. "Thank you. We're so excited. We've wanted to have a baby and I had about given up and—surprise, we're going to have one! We're both thrilled. Henry is kind of silly about it, he's so excited."

"Sit down, please. That's wonderful. Be thankful you have Henry."

She laughed. "I've very thankful I have Henry." She glanced down at the papers in her hand, almost as if she just remembered them. "Here are your expense reports," she said, holding them out.

Vivian scanned them then put them on the table. "How are you feeling?"

"I feel great. I have a doctor in Dallas I like and when I'm in my last month, we'll probably move to the city. But we'll be back after the baby is born and my mom is coming to stay with us for a week."

"That's something you'll never hear me say. My mom would never come. She'd send someone. Partly because she can't imagine anyone taking care of a newborn unaided. I don't know what she thinks women do all over the world. Not everyone can hire a nurse or nanny," she said and they both laughed.

"Millie, I want to talk to you. We've been friends now for the past three years. I haven't told anyone this and I'm going to have to figure out how to deal with it, but… I'm pregnant."

Millie squealed and hugged Vivian. "Congratulations, yourself!

"Well, you're the only one who knows and you may tell Henry, but the dad doesn't know, so tell Henry to keep my news quiet."

"I won't tell another soul." She placed a hand over her heart as if swearing an oath. "Would you like one of my baby books? I have a bunch and I've already read a couple that I thought were good."

"Thanks, I would love to look at them." Vivian looked away a moment. "I hate to tell someone else first before I tell the father, but I don't think it's going to work out so well when I tell him."

"He doesn't like children?"

"Oh, no, that's not it. He doesn't like my money."

"Oh," she repeated.

I'm trying to get in mind what I want to do. I haven't known this long myself."

"Well, I hope you work it out and I'm sorry, because this should be the happiest time. Maybe your money will be more welcome now that there's a baby to spend it on. Henry would be turning cartwheels if I had a lot."

Vivian looked down at her diamond pendant. "Thane and I tried to have a baby. If only it had worked out then, but it didn't," she said. "Ah, well. Bring the baby books when it's convenient. If I'm not here, you can just put them on my desk in the study. No one ever goes in there except to clean. Thane and I were the only ones who used that room."

"I will. I hope you work things out. I'm glad we're having babies at the same time. Our kids can be friends."

Vivian smiled and nodded, going to open the door to see Millie out. She sighed and turned away. She had a lot of decisions to make. It was May now and Slade was gone. If she left the ranch, she would have to put it up for sale and that would hurt a lot of people, but there seemed little point in her staying. Eventually, she would have to leave it and get closer to a private school in Dallas, probably choosing the private schools she attended. The biggest decision she faced right now was when she would tell Mike. But she needed to have a plan in place before he started trying to take charge. For the ranch, Thane had picked one of the best foremen to run the business from what Thane and Slade had said about Mike. As far as meddling in her life, that was a whole different story.

She decided to forego dinner and stay in her suite, working on her life plan. By nightfall, she wasn't any closer to an agenda and later she lay in bed in the dark, thinking about what she wanted to do. She placed her hand on her stomach. Her baby and Mike's. Tears came and she wiped them away. This should be one of the happiest times in her life and here she was, crying. She had to stop thinking about that and just make plans. If nothing else, she'd move back to Dallas, buy a house, get a nursery ready and hire a nanny.

She thought about Millie's mother coming and smiled. Her mother had immediately turned each of her own children over to nannies. Vivian wanted some help, but she wasn't giving up taking care of her precious little baby that she had wanted so badly when Thane was alive.

She would ask Mike if he would mind if they named a boy Thane. She would like that and maybe Mike would, too. Hopefully, it would be one thing they could agree on. She might as well break the news to him soon and let him start adjusting. Was the fight just beginning or could they work it out peacefully? Mike had his moments when he surprised her and was incredibly kind and considerate—like the night when she felt so despondent telling him good-night and he had turned around to look at her and then came back to hold her and kiss away her tears.

She didn't expect that kind of reaction this time, but she could always hope. There was just no way to accurately guess his reaction to learning he was about to be a dad.

Mike worked until late every day and he got up early in the morning to eat and get to work. Slade had made everything look so damned easy. Or had a lot of things happened after Slade left and it was just pure coincidence that he seemed to have way more to do than Slade had?

It was Thursday and Mike hadn't seen Vivian in days and he missed her. He wanted to take her out the soonest possible weekend he felt he could get away. They needed a night to themselves. He needed a night with her. What he wanted was a weekend with her where they could get away from the ranch and its problems and just enjoy each other's company and spend hours making love.

He made a mental note to find her tonight and ask her to spend the weekend with him.

He had three guys who were great cowboys. He'd be

able to fall back on any one of them if something came up and he was away from the ranch or unable to work for any reason. Slade had told him to find three and Mike had taken his advice. It was a good feeling knowing these men were there. It was also a good feeling knowing Leon was gone. He hadn't worked but a short time with the man, so losing Leon wasn't a blow as far as Mike was concerned and he didn't have to worry about Leon and Vivian. He didn't have to worry about Clint and Vivian either and that was good. The neighboring rancher hadn't been around in a while.

Thinking of Vivian made him yearn to hear the sound of her voice. He tried calling her but the phone rang unanswered until her voice mail came on. It had been like that for days. He ended up not leaving a message when he got another call. He took it and got caught up in discussing some missing cattle. He turned his pickup around and headed in the opposite direction and forgot about talking to Vivian.

It was evening when he got back to the house. He had seen lights on in her suite when he had driven up, so he walked upstairs and knocked. She opened the door.

She was in cutoffs and a blue T-shirt but to him she looked beautiful. "Hi, stranger," he said.

"Hi. You're working late now and a lot more."

"I sure am. I didn't realize how much Slade did. He made it look easy. I don't have the knack for making it look easy or be easy. Can I come in for a minute?"

"Sure," she said, stepping back. He walked in to stand close to her.

"You look wonderful."

"Thank you, Mike. We haven't seen each other much."

"No, and I want to change that. Let me take you to

Dallas tomorrow night. Some place fun or even just to your condo. I want to get away from the ranch and the problems here. We can go to dinner and then you pick it—dancing, a show. What would you like to do? Anything sounds good to me."

"That would be fine. Let's go to dinner at the club in downtown Dallas. It's quiet and has a piano player and excellent food by a super chef. We can stay in my condo again."

"Oh, baby, you have a date. I can't wait to go."

"Are you sorry you have Slade's job?"

"Not at all. It's just that a lot has happened this past week. It'll settle down. On top of other problems, we need rain and a lot of it. I'm sure we'll eventually get it. Vivian, do you know where your phone is?"

"Yes. It's in the other room on my desk."

"For a couple days now I haven't been able to get you when I call."

"I'll pay more attention. I was probably wrapped up in painting or something and didn't even hear it. I didn't think you would call me when you're working."

"Well, I have and I'd like to get you when I call. Is anything wrong?"

"Wrong? No," she said and smiled at him.

"You seem preoccupied," he said, feeling an invisible wall between them that he didn't expect. He couldn't figure out why he felt that way when he never had before with her. He wanted to take her in his arms, kiss her for the next hour and make love to her all night, but he had a feeling if he tried to hug her, she would stop him. They stood looking at each other and his suspicions grew that something was wrong, but he didn't know what and she obviously wasn't going to tell him.

He closed the gap between them, seeing her eyes widen and a flush make her cheeks pink. He wrapped his arms around her, leaned over her and kissed her. For a moment she didn't respond, didn't do anything, but then her arms went around his neck and her lips yielded to his.

When she kissed him in return, she was as passionate and sexy as ever. Shaking, he wanted her with all his being. He tightened one arm around her while he ran his other hand over her, tugging her shirt out of her shorts and slipping beneath it to caress her breast.

His heart pounded and he regretted that he had waited this long to come see her. He stepped back a moment and, watching her, yanked her T-shirt over her head to toss it away. Her bra was gone swiftly and then he unfastened her shorts and let them fall around her ankles and she stepped out of them.

He looked at her, his gaze drifting slowly over her as if he had to memorize every inch. He finally looked into her eyes again and saw longing and desire in her gaze. Wrapping his arms around her, he kissed her hard again.

"I've missed you, called you a dozen damn times, wanted to see you, but every night I got in too late to bother you," he whispered as he showered kisses on her, leaning down to run his tongue over her nipple, his hands sliding over her. "You feel wonderful. I want to spend the weekend in bed with you." He leaned back as she opened her eyes to look at him.

"I'll take you out first and feed you," he said, "and we can dance a few dances if you want. I need you, Vivian."

She looked up at him. "I don't think you really need me. You can be so wonderful, Mike."

He focused more intently on her. "I'm waiting for the other half of that sentence," he said, feeling anxious, more certain than ever that something was wrong between them. He thought of all the unanswered phone calls. "Vivian—"

She slipped her hand to his nape and brought his head down to kiss him. One touch was all it took. He picked her up to carry her to bed and he forgot his worries.

The next day, Mike tried to slip out of bed without waking her, but she opened her eyes and turned to him. He came back to take her into his arms and kiss her and it was a little more than an hour later that he got out of bed again.

"This time I'm going. I need to go to work, but I don't want to leave you. I'll see you tonight about seven. I'll make the reservations—"

She smiled. "I will. I'm the club member." Her gaze ran over him and she rolled over to get closer to him and run her hand across his chest. "You are one sexy man."

"I'm glad you think so." He kissed her. "Oh, hell, I can be late to work once." He threw himself onto the bed.

Minutes later, after some serious kissing, she pushed him away.

"Go on. We'll kiss tonight."

He looked into her gorgeous blue eyes. "Vivian, you're beautiful."

"Thank you. You need to move, Mike." She scooted across the bed and bent to grab her T-shirt from the floor, glancing over her shoulder at him.

He straightened his clothes and crossed the room. "If I walk down the hall to my suite, am I going to encounter anyone?"

"No, usually they clean this floor on Tuesdays."

"Usually. That leaves a loophole. See you tonight." He

left, hurrying down the hall and already thinking about the evening. He intended to ask her about the missed phone calls. She needed to take his calls or tell him why she hadn't answered and whether it had been deliberate because she hadn't wanted to talk to him. But why would that be? When they had made love, it was as if everything was fine between them and the uneasy feeling he'd had for a few minutes had vanished into the night and never returned. But not taking his calls was odd. He had a feeling there was something he was missing. If so, surely he would find out what it was tonight.

Vivian finished dressing almost an hour before she expected to see Mike. He had called three times today. First he called to check on the reservations, the second time just to talk to her and the third time to tell her he would try to be on time. If she hadn't been facing the evening that she knew was ahead, she would have laughed at his last call, but she couldn't. She had the feeling that tonight would change their relationship forever and she didn't think that the change would be good.

She was going to tell him about the baby.

At seven o'clock she checked herself again in front of a full-length mirror and turned first one way and then another. She looked at herself and ran her hand over her flat stomach. She wore a slim, sleeveless, figure-clinging black dinner dress that ended at her knees. It had a deep V-neckline and the diamond pendant was perfect with it. She did not look pregnant at all, but then it was so early.

Her phone buzzed and she answered to hear Mike's greeting. Her pulse sped up at the sound of his voice and she wondered how long she would continue to have such an intense reaction to just seeing him or hearing him speak.

"Hi. I'm downstairs and I'm ready. Shall I come up or do you want to come down?"

"I'll be right down. I'm ready."

"Wow, you really are a wonderful woman—beautiful and on time," he teased. "See you in the hall."

He was gone before she could say goodbye. "If you only knew. You're not going to feel that way about me later tonight. And I won't feel the same about you, either," she said.

She glanced at a picture of her with Thane on their wedding day. A sharp pain stabbed her. She had been so happy at that moment when that picture was taken. The future looked golden, perfect with Thane in it.

She picked up the picture. "How I wish I could have given this news of a baby to you. You would have been the happiest man on the planet. Well, maybe you and Henry would have been. It didn't work out that way. I love you. I miss you so much." She thought of the man waiting downstairs for her. "In so many ways, he's a good guy. But I guess I don't have to tell you that."

She replaced the picture, gathered her things and left her suite. Mike stood at the bottom of the stairs and watched her as she walked down. As usual, at the sight of him, her heart beat faster. She wanted to laugh and dance and go to her condo and make love later. She didn't know at what point tonight she would break the news to him. Or should she wait until the next weekend? It wouldn't change anything, she rationalized. She sighed, knowing in her heart she should tell him tonight so they could both get on with the changes in their lives.

"Hi, handsome cowboy," she said, looking at him.

"You know, taking you out for a fun night and a good dinner and going to your condo afterward seemed a great idea at the time. But right at this moment, looking at you as you came down the stairs, I want to carry you right back upstairs and take that sexy black dress off you and kiss you all over, put my hands all over you and make love to you the rest of the night."

Dropping the little purse she carried, she wrapped her arms around his neck. She stood on the second step that put her on his level and she could look directly into his eyes. "I won't argue with that one," she said, wanting him with all her being and wondering if this would be the last time they would make love. She had a feeling he wasn't going to take her news well at all.

His eyes narrowed. "Do you really mean that? I can call and cancel our reservations. I don't want you to get a bad name with your club."

"I won't. This is kind of fun, being on your level."

"I don't care where you stand, you're irresistible," he said, nuzzling her neck and then kissing her.

After a moment, she placed her hand against him and leaned back slightly. "Call the club. I can go get you a beer or a drink or whatever you want."

"I want you. Put some steaks out to thaw. By breakfast, they may be ready to cook."

"I've already put steaks out. I had a feeling we might not ever get out of the house when the time arrived."

"I promise you, I will take you out, just not tonight."

"I think this is better." She dropped a light kiss on his mouth. "I'll go get our drinks and you call the club and cancel the reservations."

"Sounds like a plan," he said.

She went to the kitchen and got a beer and a glass of

water for herself and carried them to the family room. It was her favorite room because it was informal, a colorful, cheerful space that she enjoyed.

He caught up with her to take the drinks from her hands and set them on a game table. He shed his charcoal sports jacket and turned to reach for her. "Come here, Vivian. I just can't wait."

"Mike, you're going to have to wait a little. I want to talk first. We have something to talk about."

He looked intently at her.

"Okay, we'll talk," he said. "But first I'll have that beer. This sound serious."

"It is serious," she said, knowing there was no going back now as she looked into his curious green eyes.

Mike took a swallow of his beer. He wondered if she had decided to sell the ranch. He couldn't figure out why she stayed now. If she did sell it, he wouldn't care. All along, he'd planned to leave when his three months were up, but that had been before they had slept together. Since that time, he did some rethinking on that and decided he would stay where he was, at least as long as Vivian was in his life. Continuing their affair sounded good to him.

He took another pull on the beer bottle then set it down and looked at her. "What do we need to discuss?"

"I don't know any way to say it except just to come right out and say it. I was shocked and you're going to be shocked, too."

He figured he knew what she was about to say and said it for her. "You're going to sell the ranch and move back to Dallas."

To his surprise, she shook her head. "No, not at this

time. I may do that in the not-too-distant future, though. No, I have something else to tell you. Mike, I'm pregnant."

Her words hit him like a lightning bolt. He felt stunned, paralyzed, as if the breath had been knocked out of him. He stared at her and repeated the words, as if doing so would help him process them. "You're pregnant."

"Yes, I am. I bought a pregnancy test kit and then I went to see a doctor. I'm definitely pregnant."

Once more he felt as if he were back in a minefield in Afghanistan. He stood, picked up his beer and walked to the window, just to move around and take a moment to think. She waited in silence and he was thankful for the moment to try to wrap his thoughts around her news. Finally, he turned around to face her.

"I don't know how shocked you were, but this is not anything I anticipated. I'm going to be a dad. Vivian. That is something I absolutely never expected."

She sat in a wing chair and sipped her water, waiting quietly, saying nothing, giving him the time he needed to work through the announcement.

"I thought you said you'd had trouble getting pregnant. And we used a condom, always."

"Right and right. Thane and I wanted a baby, but it just never happened." She set down her glass and looked up at him. "Mike, I'm financially taken care of. I don't need anything, so you're really off the hook, so to speak."

He took a long drink of beer, more to give himself some time to absorb the news of his change in status than for thirst. He had gotten Vivian pregnant and he was going to be a dad. That had seemed impossible with the protection they had used and the fact that she and

Thane had wanted and tried for a baby but she'd never gotten pregnant.

"If you had told me to guess what you were going to tell me, we would have been here until the sun was high tomorrow and I still wouldn't have come up with the correct answer. Pregnancy is the last possibility I thought might happen."

"I agree. I felt just as shocked as you must feel because Thane and I wanted a baby so badly. When everything physically checked out as normal, the doctor said I might have been too uptight about it and if I could just relax I might get pregnant. I must have been relaxed with you."

He couldn't begin to label the emotions that were running through him. All he could do was state the obvious. "Wow. This is a big one. Our lives will change forever."

"That's right. Other than you and Millie and Henry and my doctor, no one knows. I would just as soon keep it that way for a little while until we sort out how we'll deal with the future."

"I agree with that one. I want to be able to answer questions." Then her words finally found their way into his brain. "Millie and Henry? You've told them?"

"I guess Henry hasn't said anything to you yet. Millie is pregnant and not much farther along than I am. I told them I hadn't told you yet. They're not going to say anything about it."

He looked at her. She had turned her head away and was sitting quietly again, giving him more time to think. A baby… Financially, she wouldn't ever need anything from him, but there was more to raising a baby than money. He thought of his own family, his mother.

He knew what he had to do. Just as he had been raised to believe the man should have the money and be the provider, he also had been raised to believe in shouldering his responsibilities and that if possible, children should have their mother and dad. His mother and dad had instilled strong beliefs in their kids and he didn't see any choice about it.

He went to her side and squatted down next to her, resting his hands on her forearms. "Vivian, I want to know my baby. I want to watch my child grow up. It seems to me, there's an obvious solution. Vivian, will you marry me?"

Eight

Vivian stood up and took a step back as she shook her head. "That's a knee-jerk reaction and no, I will not marry you. Your mom raised four kids by herself. I am financially very well-fixed and I can hire all the help I need and build the kind of house I want and do what I want."

This wasn't the reaction to his proposal that Mike was hoping for. He closed the distance between them. "Are you thinking about this baby at all?"

"Definitely," she replied. "You're doing exactly what I expected you to do. I knew you'd propose to me tonight."

"And that's so terrible? You don't want a dad for your baby?"

"You're our baby's dad, but I don't want to marry you. You're proposing to me only because I'm pregnant."

"Well, hell yes, I am."

"When I marry again, I want the man who proposes to me to love me. Really love me," she said softly.

He stared at her a moment. "Vivian—"

"Don't say you love me when you don't. You have never declared your love."

"And you haven't said you love me. That doesn't mean we can't fall in love."

"Mike," she said quietly, "when we fall in love and then you ask me if I'll marry you, I'll say yes."

"You're being ridiculous about this," he said, trying to hang on to his temper.

"No, I'm not. Now I'm the old-fashioned one who wants to get married because a guy is in love with me. You're not. If we fall in love later, we can talk about marrying then. Life is tough. Marriages don't work well where there's no love. Love can get you through a lot."

He ran a hand through his hair and blew out a breath, his patience fraying. "I live down the hall from you. We're living in the same damn house and we're in the same damn bed a lot of nights. That's mighty close to being married. If we get married and live the same way we do now, we can raise our baby, fall in love, have more kids, live like normal parents—"

She held up a palm, interrupting his argument. "Are you going to be happy married to me with all my money?"

He stared at her and it was difficult to get his breath. Her logic was skewed as far as he was concerned, but she was right. Her damn money was a problem. He didn't like it now and he wouldn't like it tomorrow and he hadn't liked it since he first drove up to the ranch to see about working for her.

"No, I won't be happy if you want an honest answer. That is an old-fashioned view. I'm trying to get beyond it and be happy about it like some other guys would be. I can adjust, I think, to having a very wealthy wife. I want my baby in my life. I want you in my life. I—"

She closed the space between them to put her finger on his lips. "Shh. Don't you say you love me, because you don't."

Anger blazed in his expression and they stared at each other. Suddenly, he wrapped his arms around her, drew her against him and kissed her hard and passionately, leaning over her until she wrapped her arms around him and kissed him in return. His kiss was demanding, thorough, sexy, his lips challenging her to do what his words could not. Forget everything else but the passion between them.

As he held her, his mouth hard on hers, Vivian's anger boiled because she loved him and she knew she did. She had fallen in love while he hadn't and that hurt. He wanted sex. She wanted love and sex. She kissed him, feeling as if she really kissed him goodbye. They would never have the same relationship they'd had before tonight and the news of the baby.

His hand slipped beneath the deep vee of her dress and his fingers stroked her breast through her lacy bra. Desire burned away her anger and she wanted him. She stopped thinking about the future and being pregnant. Instead, she thought about the here and now. Right now, she wanted Mike to make love to her. She wanted to lose herself in hot sex and stop fighting and quit worrying about tomorrow and next month and nine months from now.

He must have wanted the same thing because he picked her up and carried her to a downstairs bedroom. He shoved the door closed and in minutes they were both naked. He picked her up to place her on the bed and then he moved over her, between her legs, coming down to enter her in one smooth motion.

Crying out in passion, she wrapped her legs around him and arched against him. While he thrust into her, she ran her hands over his back and his butt, tugging him against her as she thrashed beneath him. Finally, she arched her back and let her climax burst through her. Almost at the same time, he shuddered with his own release.

Minutes later they were still gasping for breath. He kept her with him as he rolled over and held her. "Vivian, marry me. It'll be good and we'll fall in love."

His voice was deep in the quiet room and she hurt. She was tempted to say yes, but all she had to do was think about what it would be like if she married Mike. They would go through the motions and everyone would congratulate them, but they wouldn't have that wonderful happiness that two people in love had.

She cupped his jaw with her hand so he would pay attention to her. "Mike, I've been married to a man I loved with all my heart. I know how good it can be. I know how exciting it can be. I would be miserable if we married now. You wouldn't be happy. In bed and having sex—yes, you'd like that and so would I, but there's a lot of living beyond that and love is important."

He stroked her hair and held her close. "You're probably right about love, Vivian. I think I'm probably right, too. I think we'd fall in love if you'd give us a chance."

"I'm going back to Dallas for a while to think about what I want to do. I want some time and some space."

"This is why you haven't taken my calls."

She wouldn't lie to him. "Yes, it is."

"I should have known there was something."

"You've been busy and you have a new job."

He hesitated a second, his eyes skirting from hers. "Do you know which one of the guys Lewis Owens is?"

"Yes, I do. Thane liked Lewis and said he worked hard."

He looked back at her. "I want him next in line after me. If I'm gone, I'm turning things over to Lewis."

"When your three months are up that you promised Thane, you'll be gone, won't you?" He'd already been there more than a month so he had less than two months left now.

"I promise I won't leave you in the lurch."

She felt the loss times two. Mike would be gone from her life and from the ranch.

Before he left, there was something she had to ask him. "I want to ask you—if we have a little boy, will it be all right with you to name him Thane?"

"That's fine with me."

"You know I don't even know your full name."

"Michael Cassano Moretti. A little Italian influence there, I think. Don't hang those on a little baby, but then you won't be using any of my names. I'm sure if it's a boy you'll name him Thane Warner—right?" he asked.

"I don't know, Mike. We have time to think about names."

He sat up on the side of the bed. "I'll go shower and cook those steaks if you want."

"I can probably find something Francie left that would be a lot easier to just heat and eat "

"I'd like that. I'll probably be hungry later. I'm not right now." He left to go into the adjoining bathroom.

As soon as he closed the door, she got out of bed and gathered her clothes to take them to her room and shower.

When she went downstairs later, there was no sign of Mike. In the kitchen she found a note in neat handwriting: *I need to think things over. I will talk to you tomorrow.*

She wondered if he would talk to her tomorrow or if that was just putting off saying goodbye. She decided to pack her things that she wanted for the next week and go to Dallas to stay in her condo. She could get away from Mike, from hurtful memories, from ranch responsibilities. She'd leave a note for Francie and give her the week off. Mike ate his meals with the men anyway.

Tears fell. She would miss Mike. She had done what she knew she shouldn't—she had fallen in love with him and it hurt to decline his proposal, but she didn't want to marry him when he wasn't in love and he still couldn't cope with her inheritance at all.

Why was he so wonderful in so many other ways, but not in that way? So old-fashioned and unyielding. He wanted to marry her anyway, but she couldn't see how marriage without love on his part would ever work out.

If they married without his love, it would be like tonight—he would just leave as he had done now. She couldn't see him anymore because there wasn't any future in it. They couldn't continue this relationship. She wasn't going to just be there for sex and no love.

She sank into a chair, put her head in her hands and cried. She missed Mike already. If only he felt differently...

Her hand rested on her middle as if cradling the baby that grew there. "Michael Thane Warner," she whispered aloud. "Thane Michael Warner." She didn't care if she had a boy or a girl. She just wanted a healthy baby. "I love both of you," she said. Thane was gone but he'd never had a choice. But Mike did. He'd made his choice. He wasn't in love and he had let her go.

Tomorrow, she was leaving the ranch and she didn't think she would ever come back to live there.

Mike showered and dressed for work, hoping he could keep his mind on what he was doing long enough to be useful. He was going to be a dad. Vivian was carrying his baby. What a muddle he had made of things. She wanted love. She should get a little more practical and think about having a dad around for their baby. He expected her to sell the ranch. There was nothing to hold her here. He had planned to leave. The worst would be putting the ranch on the market and having Clint Woodson buy it. Mike shook his head. He wasn't going to worry over that one. He had enough to think about.

Since Vivian was financially covered, the dynamics were different than they would have been otherwise. She didn't need Mike to help support their baby. She didn't need him at all. She was independent in every way.

He would just have to let her go and they would have to work out some kind of schedule where they could each spend time with their child. This was something he had never expected to have happen in his life. He dreaded going home and telling his mother. She would never understand why he and Vivian weren't married.

As soon as he was dressed for the day, he went downstairs. Vivian was nowhere around, not that he expected to see her. He thought about the unanswered phone calls. She had been avoiding him. He'd had a slight nagging feeling that something was wrong, but he'd shrugged it off. Now he knew he had been right to feel that way.

In a couple of months, his life would be changing

again. He had planned to leave when the three months were up anyway. This wasn't the place for him to work. He had always felt there was no future for him with Vivian. Not when she had "billion-dollar heiress" attached to her résumé.

"Damn," he said softly as he moved around the kitchen, pouring orange juice, getting black coffee, making toast. If he stayed, they might fall in love. If he left, they for sure wouldn't. Falling in love would be best for their child, but could he live with her with all that money? Some men would think he was ridiculous and out of touch with this century, but he just wasn't wired to accept his wife having one of the biggest fortunes in the state.

Would Vivian be happy staying on the ranch? During the baby and toddler years, it would probably be better if he stayed on the ranch with her if she did. He still wanted to leave, but he couldn't walk away now. He needed to be here for Vivian and for his child. Then a thought struck him and he shook his head. Vivian might prefer that he get out of her life. She could date other men, meet someone else and get married.

That thought hurt. He didn't like to think of her out with any other man. He definitely didn't like to think about her marrying someone else and another man raising his child.

Mike swore again softly, raking his fingers through his hair and standing. His appetite was gone. He threw away the toast, put the dishes in the dishwasher and finally got his hat and left the house. He wouldn't come back until late. That was one thing he could lose himself in—hard, physical labor—and he welcomed it so he could stop thinking about Vivian.

He thought about moving back to the guesthouse.

There was no point in it. He could stay right where he was in the main house and never see Vivian if she didn't want to see him or if he didn't want to see her. All suites on the second floor had outside exits. He would stay in the main house. He would do something to acknowledge Lewis taking more responsibility. If Lewis would accept moving up, Mike could let him move into the foreman's house and get it done over the way Lewis wanted.

And if Mike changed his mind about staying on the ranch, there was always the guesthouse that he could move back into.

He couldn't stop being amazed at the fact that he was going to be a dad. How long would it take for the shock to wear off? He wondered if Vivian would cooperate. She had sounded hurt, angry and matter-of-fact about the situation. Part of her easy acceptance was the security of the money, he was sure. That would take a number of worries away. And it really left him free because she didn't want any monetary help from him and she didn't want to marry him. He could turn his back and walk away and she would merely say goodbye.

They weren't in love and that was another big factor. If they had been in love, the simple and instant solution would have been to get married.

That wasn't the case and it was one more reason for him to leave the Tumbling T Ranch. Although, he thought Vivian might be gone before he was.

He had a feeling that he and Vivian had spent their last night together. He didn't expect to see much of her from now on, though eventually, she would have to sit down with him and talk about their future and their baby.

He left the house and jumped into his pickup, hoping

a day of work could take his mind off Vivian and the baby. He'd much prefer worrying about the ranch and a bunch of cattle.

It took all morning for Vivian to pack, and in the early afternoon, Henry carried her things to the limo. There were no calls from Mike and she knew they were over. They wouldn't ever keep that date to go to the club to dinner and go dancing. She missed him already and she hurt because she loved him. For the second time in her life she had fallen in love and it had come to a disastrous end. This time, though, it wasn't fate that had taken her man; it was her fortune.

"Stubborn, stubborn old-fashioned man," she whispered. And he wouldn't change. It was ingrained in him.

She glanced around the suite, making sure one last time that she had everything then went downstairs. She wanted off the ranch, away from the memories with Mike. She had clung to the ranch and the memories she'd had there with Thane because they had been wonderful and a comfort. The memories of the happy times there with Mike just made her long for him and wish things were different when they never would be.

She hoped she could move back to the city, pick up her city life and her friends again and find someone to enjoy going out with, to have a casual, happy relationship with.

Henry approached her, insisting on carrying out the small tote bag she held. She was so grateful for him. He and Millie would be staying in one of Vivian's family's condos as long as she was in Dallas. It was close by and she could get him on his cell phone any time she needed him.

She was just about to leave when Millie appeared. "I put the baby books in the desk drawer in the library."

"Thank you. I already have them packed and in the car. Henry won't let me carry anything."

Millie laughed. "I'm sure he won't. I'm rather enjoying getting waited on hand and foot. Henry and I will be moving into the Dallas condo this afternoon so we'll be nearby. I'm getting things together now."

"I hope this isn't a big upheaval."

"Actually, we'll both be happy to be in Dallas. Henry isn't a cowboy and I love the city, so it will be a nice change."

"I'm glad." She gave Millie a few final instructions about her artwork then felt compelled to fill her in on her personal situation. "I've told Mike about the baby. He was shocked and he's probably still in shock, which I can understand."

Millie's expression sobered. "I hope you two can work things out. Henry says Mike is a really good guy like Thane was."

"Yes, he is. He asked me to marry him, but he's not in love and I don't think it would really work out."

"You don't think you would fall in love with each other?"

"I don't know, but for now that doesn't seem the thing to do."

"I hope you can work it out. I'm just so excited about us having babies around the same time."

Millie was due in December and Vivian in February. Their babies would grow up together. That was one thing Vivian could look forward to.

Millie said goodbye, going upstairs to get more things packed, and Vivian decided she needed one last look around the house before she got in the limo. She had put one of the baby books in her purse to read on the drive to Dallas. She really didn't know much about babies, but she was going to learn. She suspected she would learn very quickly.

She turned around as Mike came down the hall from the back.

"What are you doing here?" she asked.

"I heard you were ready to leave soon, so I thought I'd come say goodbye."

"Henry is loading the limo and it's waiting for me now."

"That's good." Mike walked up to her and touched her hand, rubbing it lightly with his fingers. She had the usual tingles that she got when she first saw him. That hadn't changed at all. And the sizzle increased when he held her hand firmly in his. She wanted his arms around her, his mouth on hers. She wanted to be with him, to have him hold and love her and tell her that he loved her, but that wasn't going to happen.

Saying goodbye now was going to be rough. In some ways, she wished he hadn't come back to say goodbye. She had been doing all right about leaving, but now it wasn't going to be easy to smile through telling him goodbye, knowing that it might be absolute.

Henry came in. "Hi, Mike. I didn't mean to interrupt anything." He turned to Vivian. "We have the car packed. Ben is ready to drive. Is there anything else?"

She shook her head.

"Then I think you should be ready to go in a couple of minutes."

"I'm in no hurry, Henry."

"Sure," he said and disappeared down the hall.

She turned back to Mike. "I guess this is goodbye for now."

He still ran his finger back and forth on her hand. "You'll be at your condo?"

"Yes, and you know my phone number." There was a moment of silence between them as their gazes locked, and Vivian felt the pain so sharply. She didn't want to think about how final in so many ways this goodbye would be.

He took her arm lightly. "Come here," he said and they walked into the library and he closed the door. He turned to look at her and his eyes looked dark and stormy. He slipped his arms around her waist and drew her to him to kiss her, his mouth covering hers and his tongue stroking hers.

She wanted his lovemaking. She wanted his strong body against hers and his strong arms around her while they kissed. She wanted his love. She wanted him in her life.

She knew that wasn't going to happen, but his body was hard and he was aroused, ready to love. She trembled and clung to him, kissing him with all the passion and need she could pour into their kiss.

She wanted to hold him, to hear words of love, to stay on the ranch with him. Instead, there were just the sounds of their heavy breathing as she shifted against him.

Finally, she leaned away a fraction. She wanted to say, "I love you," but she wasn't going to when he didn't love her. "I'd better get going."

Neither could she say goodbye. Because of their baby, they had locked their lives together for the next twenty years or more, but this was goodbye to their nights of loving, goodbye to the hot sex and the fun, goodbye to the intimacy. Goodbye to spending time with him. She had to stop thinking about it or she would burst in to tears and she was not going to do that when she was with him. He had made his choice and was doing what he wanted to do. She just had to let him go.

Mike spoke in to the silence, erasing the need for her to utter the dreaded word. "Okay, Vivian. We'll talk. I'll call you and we can go out like we started to do."

"Sure, Mike," she said, knowing he wouldn't call and they wouldn't go out. This was goodbye.

He gave her a long look and then turned and left without looking back. She heard his boots as he went down the hall. She walked out, but he had already gone out of sight. She ran back into the library and closed the door, letting the tears fall.

When she got her emotions under control, she wiped her eyes and walked to the window to look out, knowing Mike had left and he probably wouldn't give a lot of thought to the past.

When would losing Mike stop hurting? Every place they had been together would stir memories and cause her pain if she was there again. How long would it be before it stopped aching to remember being with Mike? Was it going to hurt like this each time they had to get together after their baby was born?

The pain racked her, and she couldn't help wondering: Did he even hurt at all or wish things were different?

Nine

A week later as evening approached, Mike climbed into his pickup and turned to drive home. Home. He shook his head. He was beginning to think of the suite where he lived in the main house as his home. In reality, it was a temporary place that he really should move out of. He had moved in for Vivian, to help get rid of Clint. He must have succeeded because he hadn't heard a thing from her about Clint. Actually, he hadn't heard anything from her at all. Not since she'd left the ranch.

He missed her. The big house was empty without her. He worked late and he ate dinner with the men so that by the time he got to his suite he was pretty much ready for bed. Even then, he was still unable to sleep, even when he was exhausted.

He missed Vivian badly. He thought with extra work, hard work, he would drive away the loneliness and longing for her. Every time he reached for his phone to call her, he thought about the fortune she had, her net worth, her feelings about money and his views that she definitely found antiquated, and he decided against the call.

He couldn't change and she couldn't, either. He also didn't think she was in love with him. And he wasn't with her.

If you're not in love, why do you miss her so badly? asked an inner voice.

Because they'd had something good between them and they'd had fun together. He'd been in the military and she had been widowed, and when they met, both of them were ready for friends, a social life, a real life and getting out again, so they just clicked.

That answer had to suffice. Because he wasn't in love.

But when another week rolled past, Mike was still having a hard time forgetting her. He strolled through the mansion library, glancing at the books, but nothing grabbed his interest. And no one was around to talk to. Aside from Henry and Millie, the staff was still there, but he never saw them. They attended to the household chores when he was out on the ranch, except for Francie who didn't need to come down to cook for him at all.

And everywhere he looked he thought of Vivian.

He left the library and wandered up to his suite, telling himself he had other things to think about and some decisions to make. He thought about turning in his resignation. But if he got a job far away from Dallas or the Tumbling T, the places where Vivian would be, it would be more difficult working out how to get their baby back-and-forth.

If Vivian put the ranch on the market and Clint bought it, Mike wasn't staying and he didn't think a lot of the guys would stay. But if she sold the ranch, she wouldn't have much say about who bought it and she couldn't refuse to sell to Clint.

Mike swore and walked out on to his balcony. There was a starry sky overhead and a bright moon lighting the night. He missed her and he wanted her. Did that mean he was in love with her? He no longer knew the answer to that question. All he knew was that he couldn't deal with her fortune and he didn't want to.

He looked at the date on his watch. Mid-June. He had hoped as time passed that he would miss Vivian less, but he missed her more now than ever.

How had she come to be so important to him?

A couple of days ago he hadn't been able to resist the temptation and he'd called her to see how she was and to just hear her voice.

She'd said she felt fine, with no morning sickness. Her voice sounded guarded and they'd talked only briefly when she said she had to go. Since then he'd tried to call her a couple other times, but she never answered so he stopped trying.

How were they going to work out sharing a baby? He would have to see Vivian when he would pick up their baby, unless she hired someone to be there for that. The more he thought about it, the more certain he was that that was exactly what she'd do. And, most likely, she would marry again. That thought brought him up short and he cut it off. Another man with Vivian. Another man raising his child. Mike swore quietly. The image was too upsetting to contemplate.

He thought about going to bed, but he had slept with Vivian enough that he missed her being with him. He pulled out his phone to call her then stared at it as he thought about all the reasons that was a bad move. She lived in Dallas now in that ritzy penthouse apartment. She might even be dating.

As he held the phone it buzzed with a new text. He dared to hope it would be Vivian. To his surprise it was from his army buddy Noah Grant.

Will be out of Rangers next month. Need to get together. Jake still over there. See you when I get home. Hope you like your job. How's Thane's wife? Lunch or dinner? I'll let you know when I'll be in area.

Mike smiled as he typed in a reply. In July, Noah would be home. Then Jake would be back last. If only Thane had made it and he had come home to the Tumbling T. Instead, Thane's wife was going to have Mike's baby. Not what Thane had intended when he'd sent Mike to the ranch. And she was leaving the ranch. Again, not what Thane had intended. Mike shook his head. Things hadn't gone well and he felt responsible for them being so far off course. There were some pluses, though: Slade got to retire. Clint Woodson had stopped bothering Vivian; Lewis Owens was getting a well-deserved promotion; and the ranch was doing well. He'd be sorry to see it go, but luckily Thane would never know if Vivian were to leave the ranch and put it up for sale.

It was too bad that Mike couldn't afford to buy the ranch. When it went on the market, it would be out of his price range. The bad thing was if Clint Woodson were to buy it. If only there was a way to let certain people know and maybe do it when Clint was out of town. Mike shrugged. That would be up to Vivian. It wouldn't be his responsibility.

He should never have come to work on the ranch. He almost didn't, but he felt honor bound to keep his promise to Thane. Maybe that was why Thane had given him the money. He knew Mike could never have come home and gone to work at another ranch with the gift that Thane had given him.

If Thane only knew how everything had turned out, he wouldn't be so happy that he'd sent Mike to the Tumbling T Ranch.

Mike was glad he was going home soon to see his family. He was not looking forward to telling his mom about his baby, however. She wasn't going to be happy with him because she loved babies and this one would really not be with them a lot of the time. He dreaded telling her. He dreaded telling his brothers, too, but he knew they'd understand his feelings about Vivian and her future inheritance, her multi-millionaire status now. They'd all been raised to take charge, take responsibility.

He decided right then and there to move out of the big house and back into the guesthouse. At least Sandy would come see him there. He had one month to go to keep his promise to Thane and then he was going to turn in his resignation and look elsewhere for a ranch job. Now, he had more experience as a foreman so that would be good.

He moved his things that evening out to the guesthouse, opening it up to let it air out after being closed up. There was no one living on the second floor in the main house now. At least some were still on the third floor. He was glad Thane couldn't know what was happening to his beloved ranch.

Mike changed clothes and went for a run, trying to keep busy, to wear himself down so he'd get a few hours of sleep. He jogged six miles and finally went back to

move a few more of his things to the guesthouse. He went
through the house until he found a small framed picture
of Vivian. He wanted her picture in the guesthouse. He
knew that wasn't the way to forget her or to get over her
and maybe it was just because evening was setting in and
he missed her more than ever. He carried the picture upstairs to get his own things.

As he gathered his boots and hats he had left behind,
he glanced at his bed and remembered her there, smiling
at him. Emotions racked him, pain and desire. He missed
her so much and he wanted her. He wanted her laughter,
her fun, her hot lovemaking, her gorgeous body. She was
the mother of his baby. He was throwing all that away
because of a bunch of money. Her money—no matter
how much she had—was not more important than their
love, being a family and raising and loving their baby. He
needed to really think things through. Life changes. He
had grown up with certain ideas about life, but maybe he
needed to rethink and adapt before he lost what was the
most important thing in his life—Vivian's love. Was he
giving too much importance to her wealth? It hurt like
hell to lose her. For the first time in his life, he wondered
if he had fallen in love.

With each passing day, Vivian missed Mike more.
She longed to see him, to feel his arms around her. She
was going to have to sell the ranch, move to Dallas permanently. She would ask Thane's family if they wanted
the ranch, but she didn't think any of them would, certainly not his father. She'd have to sell it. She thought of
her studio there that she loved so much, the quiet days
of painting. She had been happy there, but a baby would

change everything and it wasn't going to work out for her to stay at the ranch.

She couldn't bear to think about selling the ranch because she knew Clint Woodson would immediately grab it up. She had to think about any way to avoid that happening. Even her neighbors had asked her not to let Clint buy it.

Thoughts of the ranch led to thoughts of her handsome foreman. She still mourned the loss of Thane and now she had added the pain of losing Mike. Would she have been better off if Thane hadn't hired him? She placed her hand on her flat stomach and thought about the precious baby she was going to have and knew her answer. She didn't have any regrets about Thane hiring Mike. His baby was growing inside her, and joy filled her every time she thought about it. A baby to love and cherish and watch grow up. Tears stung her eyes. If only Mike wanted this baby the way she did. If only he missed her the way she yearned for him.

He must miss her some, she realized, because he still called her even though she wasn't taking his calls.

She thought about what his old fashioned narrow-mindedness was causing them both to give up, what he had to gain from his actions, what he must really feel. Why would he keep calling her if he wasn't interested in her? Maybe she ought to talk to Mike one more time. He had tried to call several times but she hadn't answered because she was avoiding the pain she had felt after talking to him. She knew it wasn't about business because if it was business, he would just call Henry and tell him to tell her.

Maybe she should go to the ranch and have a talk with Mike and see if he still felt the same about her money now that they had been apart awhile. She sat mulling over whether to go back to the ranch or not. Was she just fooling herself and trying to find an excuse to see Mike? She better decide because she suspected that soon he would be gone. Should she call him and tell him she wanted to come see him or just go?

While she thought about it, her phone rang.

She answered and heard Mike's voice. "I'm about a block away. Is it convenient to come see you now?"

Startled, she glanced in the mirror. "Yes, you can come see me. I'll call downstairs and give them your name so you can come up."

"I'll see you in a few minutes."

Curious and wondering about what he wanted, she raced into the bedroom to yank off her T-shirt and cutoffs. She pulled on a red cotton sleeveless blouse and matching red linen slacks and sandals. She ran a brush through her hair and was picking up the room when she heard the bell that indicated someone was coming up in the elevator. She went to the entryway and waited to see him.

It seemed to take forever before the elevator doors opened and he stood before her.

He looked so incredibly handsome in his black Stetson, black boots, his charcoal jacket, white shirt and crisp jeans. Her heart thudded and it was an effort to resist reaching out to hug and kiss him.

"This is a surprise," she said instead.

"I've tried to call you."

"I know. I should have taken your calls. Come in."

He carried a small white box in his hands and she wondered why he was in Dallas.

"I've been thinking about us," he said, stopping only

a few feet into her condo and turning to face her. "You look gorgeous."

"You look rather good yourself. I might have looked a little bit better if you'd told me you were coming."

"You look wonderful. I brought you a present because I've missed you," he said, holding out the white box. It was tied with a white satin bow.

Her heart pounded and she stared at him in surprise. She took the box from his hands. "I've missed you, too, Mike," she said, gazing into his green eyes and wanting to toss aside the box and throw herself into his arms.

"I hope you like it," he said, glancing at the present in her hands that she had forgotten about—mainly because she was envisioning kissing him. He obviously wanted her to open it, so she untied the bow and opened the box to stare at a gold ring with a dazzling huge diamond surrounded by sparkling smaller ones. She looked up at him in question. "This is beautiful," she whispered. "But—"

He tossed his hat and jacket away and stepped close to take the ring and hold her hand. "Vivian Warner, I love you with all my heart and I want to marry you. Will you marry me?"

Tears filled her eyes. "You've never said you love me," she whispered while her heart pounded.

"I didn't know I did until you left and I hurt without you. I think about you, miss you and want you every minute. All the joy has gone out of my life and off the ranch." He took her other hand in his. "Vivian, I love you. Will you marry me?"

She watched him put the ring on her finger, unable to believe that this was happening, that he was here saying these things she'd longed to hear. "It's beautiful."

"You're beautiful and I need you. I love you with all

my heart and I just didn't realize or recognize what I felt until you were gone."

She looked at the ring on her finger, but she was still holding her breath.

"Mike, what about the money?"

"Oh, hell, it's money. It's pieces of paper. I figured there must be some way to work this out. I can live on mine and you can live on yours or whatever you want to do. As you said, it's a pile of money, but it's not as important as love and people. You're the woman I love and you're carrying our baby whom we'll love, and we'll have more babies. So maybe I have been a little too hardheaded and obtuse and—"

She threw her arms around his neck and kissed him, her heart thumping wildly with joy. She leaned back laughing. "Oh, yes, my love, my handsome cowboy, I love you and I will marry you."

He gave a whoop and twirled her around. Then he kissed her, his lips never leaving hers until he'd carried her to her bedroom. He stood her on her feet and as if by magic their clothes disappeared. All she was aware of was Mike in her arms, his lips on hers and he loved her.

"Mike, I'm so happy. I love you with all my heart. You're wonderful. You're not an alpha male right now."

"Ha, that's what you think, darlin'. But I'm not when it comes to pleasing my woman. I want to make you happy. I love you so much. I can't tell you how awful it's been without you at the ranch."

The reminder pulled her up. "The ranch. Mike, I was getting ready to sell it."

"And I was getting ready to quit. Well, we'll both have to change our plans and—" He stopped and shrugged.

"Except I've already promised Lewis Owens the foreman job. Now what the hell am I going to do?"

She giggled. "Make love to the owner."

"Vivian," he said as she nuzzled his neck, trailing kisses to his ear. "Get serious."

She looked up at him. "I know exactly what you're going to do. Just a minute, Mike." She slipped out of his arms and disappeared into the closet. She came back with the torn, wrinkled brown paper that had been in the packet Thane had given Mike to give to her.

Mike raised his eyebrows. "What?"

"Look on the back of this paper that was wrapped around my diamond pendant. It's Thane's handwriting. Read it."

She handed the paper to Mike and he read aloud: "Vivian, I love you. Love Mike. He will take care of you and the ranch. T."

She placed her hand over his. "I know what we'll do. We'll marry. We'll have a small wedding, just our families and closest friends and the ranch people."

"Yeah, that's a small wedding—about three hundred."

She smiled. "That's okay. And after we marry, we'll put the ranch in both our names and you'll be the owner like Thane was. Lewis will be our foreman, the way Slade was, and he'll work for you just like he's doing now. And I'll be a mama for our baby and our babies. Plus I'll be an artist and your wife." She looked at him, knowing all her love shone in her eyes for him to see. "What do you think?"

He gazed at her solemnly and looked at the note in his hand. "I think Thane had a premonition he wouldn't make it home. He covered his bases. The money he gave me was enough that I'd be obliged to stay the three months. He knew that. By then he knew I'd be hooked. I think he wanted us to fall in love if he didn't make it home because I'd take care of you and take care of the ranch. And when you cry over Thane, I won't be jealous because I'll cry with you. I loved him, too. He was the best friend possible and I'm sure he was a good husband to you."

"Like you will be."

"For as long as I live." He pulled her to him, wrapping her in his strong arms. "I didn't do so well catching on that I was in love, but it's the first time I've ever been in love. And the last." He kissed her.

It wasn't the most passionate kiss Mike had ever given her, nor the longest, but it was the best because it came with a declaration of his love.

When he broke the kiss, he asked a favor. "One of our fellow rangers, Noah Grant, is getting out of the service next month. I'd like to wait to have the wedding so we can include him. He was important to Thane, and to me."

"Of course, we can include him."

"I'll have to meet your family and you'll have to meet mine—soon, if we want to have the wedding next month and get on with life."

"I think so," she said dreamily, holding her hand up to twist it and admire her ring. She looked at him. "I want to hear the 'I love you' part again."

He took her hand in his and gazed into her eyes. "My darlin' Vivian, I love you with all my heart. I love you now and forever."

"That is so wonderful," she said, smiling at him. "And I love you, Mike Moretti, with all my heart. Mike, I'm so happy. I've loved you for a long time."

"Well, you didn't tell me."

"I would think not, when I didn't hear any words of love from you."

"Well, darlin', all that's about to change. Now that I realize what love is, I'll be telling you every day of my life."

"Oh, I'm so glad. I love you, my old-fashioned alpha male who stopped being one long enough to win my heart and find love."

He shrugged. "I don't have an alpha male bone left in my body. Well, maybe one."

She giggled and hugged him. "You've made me so happy. If Thane couldn't come home, this is what he would have wanted."

"I think you're right, Vivian. He was looking out for you, that ranch and maybe me. We have to name the first boy Thane."

"I agree," she said, holding Mike tightly while she kissed him and felt showered with love and blessings and fulfillment.

* * * * *

*If you loved this Texas-set romance from
USA TODAY bestselling author Sara Orwig,
pick up these other titles!*

*The Texan's Contract Marriage
One Texas Night...
Her Texan to Tame
The Texan's Forbidden Fiancée
Expecting the Rancher's Child*

Available now from Mills & Boon Desire!

MILLS & BOON®

Desire™

PASSIONATE AND DRAMATIC LOVE STORIES

A sneak peek at next month's titles...

In stores from 16th October 2017:

- **The Christmas Baby Bonus** – Yvonne Lindsay *and* **Little Secrets: His Pregnant Secretary** – Joanne Rock

- **Best Man Under the Mistletoe** – Jules Bennett *and* **Baby in the Making** – Elizabeth Bevarly

- **Snowed in with a Billionaire** – Karen Booth *and* **His Secret Son** – Brenda Jackson

Just can't wait?
Buy our books online before they hit the shops!
www.millsandboon.co.uk

Also available as eBooks.